BLEEDING EMPIRE

C L RAVEN

Copyright © 2018 C L Raven

Cover by David V G Davies

ISBN 13:-978-1986089555

ISBN- 198608955X

Set in Garamond

Other books by C L Raven:

Novels

Soul Asylum
Silent Dawn

Historical horror novels

The Malignant Dead
The Devil's Servants

Short story collections

Romance Is Dead Trilogy:
Gunning Down Romance
Bad Romance
Romance is Dead

Disenchanted
Deadly Reflections
Romance is Dead trilogy

iv

For our D&D/RPG group, Disaster Class: Amy, Jordan, Helen and especially our long suffering DM/GM Tom (also known as God/Igor). Because if we tried to end the world, it would end up something like this.

CHAPTER 1

"Are you ready to end the world?"

Ash sprinkled smoky kisses over the desolate city. Scarlet electricity pulsed through the clouds' open veins. Thunder pounded like a desperate heart as night swept down on funereal wings to steal the light, and with it, all hope of redemption.

The ash swirled, the city shaking as Death picked up the glass globe and traced her black nail across its smooth surface, tiny fractures chasing her fingertip. A smile danced on her violet lips then she hurled the globe to the crypt's floor. The glass shattered; the city exploding from its spherical prison as Hell arrived on Earth.

***

The sky cracked like a torn open ribcage, its beating heart ripped out and sacrificed to the god of death. Its blood seeped over the clouds. Ashes fell like burning tears.

Five figures materialised in Lemures city centre beneath a metal sculpture of a hand holding the world. One tripped. A fissure crawled over the centre of the globe. A Victorian streetlight exploded, glass raining onto Friday night revellers. One man glanced up as shards landed in his pint glass then he continued staggering and drinking.

"Well that was anti-climactic." Morgan put her hands on her hips, her purple lips twisted in a scowl.

"Told you we should've gone with the horses," Marsden said, pulling his electric guitar from his back to his chest.

"The horses are clichéd, Mars. Every Apocalypse opens with them. It's the equivalent of starting a horror film with a busty blonde getting slaughtered, her boobs jiggling like grapefruits in a sack as she face plants in her own blood. Or fun-loving friends setting out on the trip of a lifetime, only to break down by a cannibals' tea party. We're doing this *our* way."

"Your way's just won Least Dramatic Entrance at the Nobody Cares Awards. Maybe you should've put up posters."

Aeron, Morgan's twin brother, slapped Marsden across the head. "*You're* not in charge, Fight Club."

"I should be."

"Tradition states *Death* is the lead Horseman. So suck it up, buttercup."

"Funny how you're willing to discard every tradition except that one."

"Are we going to begin the Apocalypse bickering? Is that what you want our legacy to be? The Squabblingmen of the Apocalypse?"

"I'm just saying, people see the horses galloping across the world, they know it's the Apocalypse. It creates an atmosphere of dread. Now they think a streetlight's broken. They'll blame the council, not us."

"What do you want us to do, Mars? Hit replay? We'll look *really* professional, won't we? 'Sorry mortals, can we do that again, please? You weren't watching'."

"They won't know we've redone it, seeing as they didn't notice the first arrival."

"Our fathers will. What would we say when they ask why we're back in Purgatory after five minutes? 'We forgot our keys'?"

"Forgot to make an effort more like."

Aeron twisted Marsden's ear. "This is our big moment. *Don't* ruin it with your negative attitude." He frowned. "We should've put an ad in the papers: 'The Horsemen of the Apocalypse: Coming to end a world near you'."

Marsden rubbed his ear, glaring. "Why not write a musical and take it to the West End?"

"Do you realise how hard it is getting a production into theatres?"

"Give me a globe and I'll redo my entrance. I had three planned and *none* of them involved blowing a streetlight and Mac tripping over."

"Sorry," Mac mumbled.

Aeron glowered at Marsden. "You touch my globe and I'll scythe your pretty face in half."

Marsden folded his arms, his jaw clenching. Uneasy silence settled like scattered petals.

"I liked the thunder," Mac stuttered. "That was biblical."

"Nobody asked you, Pizza Butt," Demi snapped. "When we want your opinion, we'll give you a suggestions box. And put a mask on. Your face is upsetting me. I'd lose my appetite if I had one. I swear to *Sassy!* magazine you're uglier up here. Let's be honest, it's not a face a mother could love, or even daddy Pestilence for that matter. I'm surprised you weren't drowned at birth."

Mac sighed and pulled his hood over his patchy fair hair and scabbed scalp. Blood dripped from his nose, spattering on his shoe.

"You can't drown diseases," Morgan said. "That's not how you eradicate them. He does look worse here though. It's the lighting. You can see him in all his pestilent glory."

Mac's shoulders slumped and he turned his disease-riddled face away from Morgan's grimace.

"Where are we?" Demi looked around, her lip curling at the Christmas decorations hanging above them like festive gibbet cages. "It looks like somewhere hope comes to die."

"Gallows Street, Lemures," Marsden replied.

"Never heard of it. It sounds made-up." She scanned the street. "Dear god, humans are ugly. I'm glad we're killing them off. Why were they allowed to breed? Are they an experiment gone horribly wrong?"

A woman wearing L plates and a veil ran towards them. Marsden gripped the neck of his guitar. The woman ducked behind the sculpture. Retching and splattering filled the silence. Regurgitated alcohol and stomach acid perfumed the air.

Demi's face contorted. "That's a stink I could've done without. Oi, go home and choke on it in your bed, Pukahontas."

Marsden chuckled and disappeared behind the statue. Gurgling replaced the retching then the bride-to-be was slung upside down across the sculpture's palm. A crimson necklace parted her throat and dripped down her face, staining her veil. Marsden reappeared, wiping his plectrum on his jeans. Blood trickled down the sculpture's wrist. Mac stepped away.

Aeron licked his thumb then wiped Marsden's face. He slapped Aeron's hand away.

"Well Mars has smashed the champagne bottle against the good ship Apocalypse," Morgan said. "This is going to be the best Apocalypse ever. And what a way to celebrate our thirtieth. It will be the party to end all parties and we'll save people from horrific hangovers."

"You did fuck all for my thirtieth," Marsden said.

"I'm sorry the end of the world got in the way of buying you a thirtieth balloon. We've all got problems, Mars. Deal with it." Morgan clapped. "Aer and I will check us into our hotel, you lot start your Kill-o-metres."

"Make sure it's a five star hotel, with a health spa," Demi said.

"Sorry Dems, Travel Inn had their winter sale. They don't give refunds on saver rooms."

Marsden laughed. "I'm sorry, but the Horsemen of the Apocalypse staying in a *Travel Inn*? That won't inspire a graphic novel or strike fear into the hearts of men."

Demi smiled. "Thank you, Marsden."

"We should be in a castle, or a mausoleum."

"I'm not staying in a mausoleum like some kind of *corpse*!"

"Good point. We'd lose you amongst the skeletons."

Aeron laughed. Morgan produced a small whip from her pocket and slapped Marsden and Demi's hands with it.

"Is this the Apocalypse or a school trip? Don't make me send letters of complaint home to your fathers. Get out there and start ending the world, before we're arrested for murder most fabulous. We're not having the shame of being the first Horsemen to spend their first night on Earth in a prison cell."

"Because Travel Inn is *far* more glamorous," Demi bitched.

Marsden slung his guitar onto his back and walked away, stuffing his hands into his jeans pockets. "Text me the address. I'm going to start a war."

***

On Hangman's Rise, Marsden stood on a silver Volkswagen Golf's roof, beneath a dying streetlight. The alarm wailed like a banshee foretelling death, but no-one listened. He caressed his black guitar. A snake formed the neck, its ruby eyes glinting. His blood streaked the guitar's skull body, his suffering enhancing its beauty. He strummed the blood stained strings. People crept forwards until a crowd surrounded his rusted stage.

He played their pain to them, resurrecting desires they hid from society's judging eyes. He knew their inner turmoil better than their intimate journals. His fingers moved faster, his plectrum plucking their nerves. Two groups of guys on a night out traded insults across the road. A fight erupted between neighbours over an ancient misdemeanour involving a broken lawnmower and a missing gnome. Two play-fighting friends kissed; the passion they harboured too powerful to control. A couple began a war of words; lethal bullets that gunned down their marriage in the dismal street beneath the ash raining from the sky.

Raw emotions bled into the night, infecting the crowd. The groups clashed in violent unity in the middle of the road. The couple spat fatally wounding words. The neighbours wrestled, the attacker delivering one final blow to his opponent's swollen face, his grazed knuckles tarnished with his neighbour's blood. The lovers shed their inhibitions, their clothes torn beneath them; bloodied scratches souvenirs on their backs as they surrendered to ecstasy.

The song died.

The married couple withdrew from each other, singed by the betrayal they couldn't erase. The attacker hugged his lifeless neighbour, his tears washing away the damage he'd inflicted. The lovers shared one last lingering kiss, holding each other a moment too long before self-consciously dressing in their ripped clothes. The warring groups separated, dragging their injured friends to safety. The crowd trudged away, their gazes lost and empty. A man tossed a crumpled five pound note at Marsden's feet.

The victim died in the gutter.

"Busking on a Golf. This is exactly how Revelations depicted your arrival." A twenty-eight-year-old man stood in the shadows, wearing grey jeans, a black military jacket and a black jumper, which sported a motif of an angel tied to a grave. Stubble kissed his cheeks and head. A silver band choker burdened his neck.

"Drew!" Marsden's chest constricted, his heart pounding like it was trying to break free. He pocketed the fiver. "If you want bloodshed and violence, I can re-string my guitar with angels' vocal chords."

Drew smiled. "Sorry, I need them for my harp."

Marsden leapt off the car into Drew's embrace, wincing as their bodies scorched with a vicious hiss. Pleasure fused with the pain. The stench of their burning flesh mixed with Drew's fruity deodorant. They separated, their skin healing.

"Shit. Forgot how much that hurt." Marsden fought to conceal his smile as he rubbed his chest, extinguishing the writhing flame. He was surprised he'd missed that burn. He wanted to hug Drew until their skin melted, their bones ignited and all that remained were their ashes and broken vows.

"I still can't tell if I'm allergic to you or you're allergic to me," Drew said.

"It's you – you're too good for me."

"I nearly filed a missing persons' report for you."

"Purgatory's out of the police's jurisdiction and mobile phone companies are yet to build towers there." Marsden pushed his guitar around his back and blew on his bruised fingertips. "I didn't think you'd want anything to do with me."

"I convinced myself I didn't. And yet…moths and flames." Drew nudged the fight victim with the toe of his combat boot. "It's begun."

"There was nothing else pencilled in for today."

"I had to cancel my halo polishing class. D'you know how hard that class is to get on? There's a two year waiting list."

"They teach you to…polish your halo? Wow. I hope they supply the tissue."

Drew laughed. "That's a sin. Are the others here?"

"I tried leaving them behind, but Death's as inescapable as a nuclear blast and Demi can travel through drainpipes. I don't think much of your welcoming party. I expected banners, balloons, maybe a bouncy castle. Nothing too extravagant."

"Budget cuts. I could stretch to one party popper and a fairy cake. But no candle. I thought your arrival would be more…noticeable: thundering hooves, bloodshed, damnation, worldwide news bulletins interrupting *Singing Sensation* final."

"I wanted that. I was outvoted. We broke a streetlight."

"Epic. So more 'notice in the personal ads' than 'headline-grabbing'."

"Budget cuts. And incompetent leaders. If I was in charge, we would've trampled Earth, not snuck in the back door like we're dodging a train fare."

"Suppose I should be grateful you're not in charge."

"The world deserves to be destroyed by me, not accidentally trodden on by them. It's what people want. It's what they make films about. The ultimate destruction of the human race should be a fiery bloodbath; people dying in wretched agony where they stand. Like the dinosaurs."

"Now I'm definitely grateful you're not in charge. The bruised sky's pretty. It looks like your horses stampeded over it. And the ash is a nice touch." He held his hand out. Embers landed in his palm and ignited. Lightning flashed. "It's like humanity's already dead and the angels are scattering their ashes." He blew them away.

"Nice foreshadowing." Marsden folded his arms. "Why are you here?"

"Welcoming party. And damage control."

"You can't stop it."

"I can stop *you*." They stared at each other. "Or change your playlist."

"I don't take requests."

"I didn't think you were the karaoke type." Drew grinned and poked Marsden's shoulder, his fingertip burning on Marsden's biker jacket.

Marsden snorted. "You haven't heard my Gloria Gaynor."

Drew laughed. "Now I'm afraid. And petrified. Give them a chance of salvation."

"The world is ending, Drew. Salvation won't keep them alive. What's the point in me giving them hope for a happy ever after when I know it ends with all the cast dead?"

"Your sunny outlook is your most endearing quality. Once a day, promise you'll play something upbeat."

Marsden wiped ash off Drew's forehead, leaving a charcoal smear and a line of blistered skin. "Put it in my suggestions box."

"You don't retrieve voicemails; you'll never empty your suggestions box."

"People thrive on misery. That's why executions were popular."

"The world can't exist on pain alone."

***

Demi sauntered through Salvation. Stained glass windows betrayed the club's former life as a church. DJ decks stood in the altar's place. People danced where couples had exchanged their vows and coffins were laid to rest.

The bell tower housed stripper poles on different levels. A man and woman stumbled out of the confessional, adjusting their clothes. Another couple barged in. The woman's dress hit the floor as the curtain closed. God's name was shouted, but in pleasure, not penitence. Music thrashed a heartbeat against Demi's hollow chest. She climbed the stairs to the upper gallery, her tight blueberry dress shimmering under the pulsating lights.

She stepped onto a raised platform and danced. Girls whispered, then glimpsed themselves in reflective surfaces and looked away, their bodies feeling two sizes too big.

"She looks like a skeleton," one girl murmured to her friend.

"At least I wasn't made with self-raising flour," Demi retorted. "The only place I want to see muffins is in a bakery."

The girl fled.

"Bitch!" Her friend tugged Demi's limp brown hair.

Demi backhanded her, laughing as the girl's arse hit the floor with a thud. "Some Romanian child was paid adequately to provide me with these extensions. She'd be devastated you used her hair as a tug toy."

Demi's gaze locked with a man auditioning for the Dad Dancing Championships. *Is that thing human or a pork pie with legs? If I cut him open, will he bleed blood or gravy?* She looked away, hoping he didn't mistake her look of disgust for lust. His beer and kebab aroma wafted over before he did.

"Hey sexy, how about you come back to mine and dance for me in private?"

Demi shuddered. "Hey Teletubby, how about you dip your Tinky Winky in acid? And take a bath. I didn't realise Old Spice was made from stale curry. I wouldn't touch you if I had cancer and shagging you was the cure."

His mates jeered as she strolled to a group of girls dancing provocatively near four men. One girl twerked. Demi pushed into the centre of their circle and swayed her protruding hips, the lights casting shadows under her sharp cheekbones. "It's supposed to look sensuous, not like jelly on a pogo stick. And your arse nearly wiped out Russia."

Another Demi Ceres burn victim. I should write a book of my putdowns. Demi peered at the throng below. Despite Mac's hood concealing his face, she spotted him lurking in the corner – disgusting things were eye-catching. She gestured to a man loitering on the opposite side of the club. Mac slunk through the dancers, vanishing from sight.

***

Mac grabbed the man Demi had spied and bundled him through the fire exit into the dank alley. Stale urine, tobacco and the sickly sweet smell of marijuana assaulted Mac's nostrils. Empty beer bottles rolled into the wall. A used condom floated in a puddle. Mac nodded at Marsden, who perched on a black wheelie bin like a human vulture.

The man stumbled but saved himself. "What are you doing?"

"Putting you out of business," Mac mumbled.

"Fuck off." He flicked out a knife.

Mac retreated, raising his hands. *I should've joined Mars's combat lessons.*

Marsden jumped down. "A new corporation has moved into Lemures and we're closing you down."

"Thanks." Mac's tentative smile displayed broken, blackened teeth set in bleeding gums.

Mac disappeared into the club. The DJ's beat muffled the first punch as the door shut. He shoved his gloved hands into his hoody's pockets. If Mars was in a bad mood, the man might die slowly. Mac waited ten minutes before slipping out the fire exit. The man was sprawled on the wet ground, a gaping wound in his throat, his bloodied knife lying beside him. A horseshoe with a sword through it had been carved into his forehead.

Mac ransacked his pockets, taking cash and sachets of pills before returning inside.

A man approached. "Where's Vinny? I saw you with him."

Mac stepped back. "He's taken early retirement. What can I get you?"

"Two pills."

Mac relinquished the pills, taking the cash with a handshake before disappearing into the crowd.

***

Broken glass crunched beneath Morgan and Aeron's boots as they stepped onto Hangman's Rise, their black PVC outfits almost as identical as they were. Both twins were tall and slim with black hair. Aeron's was short, whereas Morgan's was longer, her plaits piled on her head like a nest of snakes. They stopped by a man in the gutter, his battered face swollen into a Halloween mask. A horseshoe with a sword had been painted on a silver Golf's bonnet in blood.

"Do you want the honours?" Aeron asked.

"It'll be my pleasure."

Morgan crouched and produced a glass globe from the man's pocket – the soul for the twenty first century. Hourglasses were as outdated as Victorian death shots. She rolled it around her fingers, the glass chinking against her Gothic rings. She shook it, ash spiralling around the tiny graveyard imprisoned in the glass. When it settled, a new headstone grew.

Wings beat the air. Morgan rose and offered her arm to the raven. She squeezed the globe until it shrank to a marble then slipped it into a black pouch around the raven's neck.

"Corpse," the raven cawed and took flight; a stark contrast to the crimson clouds covering the sky like a blood soaked bandage.

Aeron squatted, fingering a broken guitar string. "We should warn Mars about littering. People will think we're amateurs." He pocketed the string.

An ambulance raced past, its blue lights turning their pale skin into a sickly death hue. They meandered through streets until the beat from Salvation throbbed through them. Weaving around the brown stone church, they slipped into the alley, where a man lay framed by his own blood. The UV light illuminating the alley exposed skulls beneath the twins' faces.

"My turn." Aeron freed a soul globe from the corpse's coat pocket and tossed it in the air. He caught it, watching ash rest on a new grave.

CHAPTER 2

Rain and ash battered the window of room 13 in Travel Inn. Morgan slapped a smiley face sticker on the cream wall then pivoted. Aeron stood beside the TV, trying to decide which daytime show was the least suicide-inducing. He switched it off. He didn't want his death certificate to read: *'Died watching Paternity Tests: Live!'*

"Three to Mars, none to you." Morgan eyed Mac and Demi. "Loser does a forfeit. Something so embarrassing, your glow of shame will make the Northern Lights resemble fairy lights."

"Snog Pus-sy Galore?" Demi smirked, pointing to Mac. She lounged on the double bed like a depressed stick insect.

"One of Mars's was mine," Mac protested, slouching in a white plastic chair by the chipboard desk. He wiped his nose in his sleeve then played with the complementary milk pots. "He completed the move."

"This job's like being in sales," Morgan said. "You get the commission when you close the deal. Mars got your monthly bonus and gift vouchers."

"Ooh I can have that manicure I promised myself." Marsden examined his chipped black nails as he leaned against a terracotta wall, one foot resting on it, his guitar propped against his leg.

Morgan's eyes narrowed. Marsden radiated insubordination like a furious sunbeam. She'd have to quash whatever rebellion he was planning.

"Mine's a long term plan, like trust funds," Demi replied, filing her nails. "Mars snaps a string and–" she clicked her fingers, "someone dies. That's not *work*. Besides, you two have blank columns."

"We're the clean-up crew. Leaders start the wars but it's their foot soldiers that die in battle." Morgan drew a fancy table around the scoreboard. "Let's spread death like it's going out of fashion. No-one ended the world sitting in Travel Inn."

Demi scowled. "I can't influence people here. I need to be in a five-star hotel. People idolise and imitate the rich. Once I'm in magazines, watch my tally rise."

"Nobody Digest is advertising for a cover model," Marsden said.

"You won't be laughing when I'm on the cover of *Catwalk* and living in The Bohemian."

"Is that a feeding clinic?"

"The fanciest hotel in Lemures."

"That's like getting the best room in a leper colony."

"Fiver says you fail," Aeron told her.

Demi smirked. "By tonight, I'll be relaxing in a hot tub while you losers are fighting over who gets the bed."

"Aer and I are top of the food chain," Morgan said. "We get the bed."

"What does that make me?" Mac grouched.

Demi smiled. "Pond scum."

"Why *are* we in one room?" Marsden asked. "It implies trust issues."

"Why do you need your own room if you've got nothing to hide?" Aeron countered.

"What if Mars and I wanted privacy?" Demi asked.

"I have no problems killing you with an audience," Marsden replied.

"Right, get out there and earn your smiley stickers," Morgan said.

She and Aeron left, their PVC coats billowing around their ankles as they stepped outside.

"Demi's right," Aeron said. "Why should they have all the fun? We're on holiday, we should collect souvenirs."

"They'd confiscate ours at customs."

A child shrank against the wall as they passed. They jumped onto their skeleton motorbike and sped away, the stone-fronted Travel Inn fading into the background. Morgan mused about their lack of helmets, but they were immortal and wanted to set a bad example to impressionable youths.

The bike purred along The Boulevard. On the moss-stained road sign, someone had added 'of Broken Dreams' in black pen. The bike struck an empty bottle, sending it skidding into the kerb. A crisp packet skittered along the pavement. People laden with bags ambled through the streets; others hurried past, frustrated at slow walkers. Morgan pulled a death globe from her pocket and threw it at the car overtaking them. It smashed on the door. The car swerved, hit a bollard and flipped over.

"Boom."

The car felled shoppers before resting on its side amongst broken glass and shattered lives. Witnesses screamed a siren song, luring onlookers to the scene. Aeron flicked out the bike's scythe kickstand.

"Someone phone an ambulance!" a man ordered, filming the carnage on his phone like everyone else.

The car toppled onto its wheels, glass fragments sprinkling the ground.

Morgan and Aeron approached the car and removed soul globes from the dead people's pockets. They shook them, new headstones rising from the blackened ground within each one.

"Three in the car, four outside." Aeron counted the bodies. "It's like getting all your Christmas presents from one shop. The others need to up their games."

"I hope not. I want those gift vouchers."

Morgan stepped over a trapped pushchair and collected the final globe. They shrunk them to marbles then returned to the bike, where the raven perched on the skull. Morgan slipped the marbles into his neck pouch and he flew away, his wings beating the funeral march.

Sirens sang the victims' misery as the clouds shed tears on a world that had stopped crying.

***

Demi gazed at The Bohemian. With its cylindrical porch and stone pillars, it looked more like an empty carousel than a hotel entrance. The roof was V shaped, with a balcony above the entrance. Tinted arched windows obscured the sins of the rich.

She sauntered through the doors, her grape stiletto boots ringing on the cream marble floor. To her left, a marble staircase curved out of sight. Skirting the large reception desk, she entered the bar to her right. Laminate flooring shone under harsh spotlights. Chrome barstools lined the frosted glass bar. She perched on a stool and adopted her best forlorn expression, making a show of checking her watch. Orphans in charity campaigns looked happier.

"What's a pretty young thing like you doing all alone?"

Demi eyed the man beside her. A cheese grater to the face might've improved his looks. His nose was redder than Rudolf's, the lights reflecting off his head could start a fire and his belt was in serious danger of snapping and taking out someone's eye.

"I've been stood up."

The barman handed her a Flirtini cocktail.

"I'd never stand you up. Unless you like it standing up." He winked.

Ugh, I'd vomit if I had anything to throw up. "I'm supposed to stay here tonight, but the room's in his name." *Too blatant.* She might as well have a sign 'warning: con artist at work'. "I blew my wages on this dress and lingerie." She lifted the hem of her skirt an inch, teasing him with what pleasures may await underneath.

"I have a room." He smiled, fondling her knee. "Be a shame to waste your new lingerie."

He must've registered 8.9 on the Stupidity Scale. And his ego's bigger than his stomach. Like hell a ten like me would be interested in a bargain basement Marshmallow Man. Her stomach contorted. She rubbed his thigh, her other hand slipping into his pocket and relieving him of his key card. "If I wanted to bang a fat guy with alcohol issues, I'd hump Father Christmas. At least he gives presents when I pull his cracker." She downed her drink then left the hotel, kissing the key card triumphantly.

"Careful. Fingerprint sweat may have calories."

Demi turned, smiling at Marsden. "Are you following me?"

"I was going to busk in the park and ruin a family fun day, but watching you spit venom is more entertaining."

"Jealous?"

"I dream of a sweaty businessman with whisky breath offering to show me the size of his wallet."

"Go wrap your guitar strings around your throat, Fraggle Cock."

"Now *that* sounds more entertaining than talking to you. I could stick my plectrums in my eyes – ramp up the fun factor."

She stroked his jaw. "Can you do me a teeny favour?"

"End your miserable existence?" He pulled his guitar in front of him. "You hum it, I'll play it."

She gripped his jacket collar. "Play a song for Baldylocks. He's a sleaze who thinks a woman alone in a bar is fair game to be groped."

"You heard the Terror Twins. You're losing. If you don't want a forfeit, you kill him."

"You killed for Doctor Spot." She pouted. "Or do you only perform for boys? A little horsey told me you've added songs to your repertoire that *aren't* on your playlist; at the request of an angelic dreamboat."

Marsden raised his eyebrows. "Dreamboat? Did you teleport from the nineties?"

She touched his chest. His heart fluttered. "Help me and I won't tell the Death Squad you're a traitor."

He hit her hand away. "I'm not a fucking traitor!"

Her lips twisted into a smirk. "Guilty conscience?"

"I hope you fall down a drain and drown in stale chip fat."

Marsden shoved open the tinted glass hotel door and marched through the foyer. Demi trotted after him, admiring his arse in his jeans.

"Room 61."

He ran upstairs to the sixth floor and strode along the blue carpeted corridor. The sleaze stood outside his door, hunting through his pockets.

Demi held the card between two fingers. "It must've fallen into my bag." He grabbed for it. "Ah ah, no snatching." She opened the door then pushed him in. Marsden followed and closed the door.

"What's this?" the man demanded.

"The end of your life. Enjoy it. It's a once-in-a-lifetime experience." She nodded at Marsden.

Marsden plucked a slow song called 'Breathless'.

The man dropped to his knees, clutching his chest, a cranberry blush spreading through his face. "Help...me."

Demi smiled. "Do I look like an emergency helpline?"

He gasped and lunged for her.

She leapt backwards, her nose wrinkling. "This dress is dry clean only, Sweaty Betty. I don't want your hands greasing it up. It's not a napkin." His fingers dug into the carpet. "Mars, hurry up. His wheezing's spoiling my good mood."

"You can't demand a favour then suck the fun out of it." Marsden broke his G string. The man's head slumped, drool escaping his open mouth. "I could've dragged that out for ten minutes."

"Men always overestimate how long they can last." Demi unzipped her dress and let it fall to the floor, revealing navy satin lingerie.

Marsden watched her dress fall then glanced up. "You've dropped something."

Demi lay on the bed, propping herself on her elbows. "I'm expressing my gratitude."

"Text me an appropriate emoticon."

She ran her fingers up her thigh. "I'll tell the twins about who makes your heart gallop."

"*Blackmail's* your seduction technique? Did you read that on a dating website?"

She rose and sashayed towards him, trapping him against the door. "I know you want me."

"The only way I want you is headfirst in a wood chipper."

"Mars, we're amongst mortals now. Sex isn't about *liking* the person. It's about satisfying your needs." She kissed him, his lips tasting of Red Bull. "And right now, I need you to make me scream."

He pushed her away. "Kiss me again and the only thing I'll put in your mouth is a bullet."

He opened the door and escaped. She swore and kicked the dead man on her way to the mini bar. The door opened.

"Changed your mind, hotstuff?"

Aeron picked up the broken guitar string. "No smiley sticker for you."

"Mars owed me." She poured herself champagne.

Aeron produced the soul globe. "Seems you were halfway to inducing the heart attack yourself."

"A thank you present to Mars."

He laughed. "I guess he exchanged you for store credit."

Her expression darkened and she held out her hand. "You owe me a fiver."

Aeron pulled a five pound note from his pocket and slapped it into her palm. It bounced onto the floor. "Buy yourself some charisma. The only way to win Mars's heart is to give him someone else's. Preferably still beating."

"Move that eyesore. If I wanted to step over him every time I fetch a drink, I'd turn him into a rug."

Aeron dragged the man to the bathroom. "You have a few days until he smells. There's a mattress for you at Travel Inn."

CHAPTER 3

Haunting music filtered through Gallows Street. Stressed, weary parents dragged screaming children on their present-buying mission. Christmas lights hung above shops like executed fairies. The music grew louder, agonised lyrics plucked from a broken heart.

Marsden straddled his blood red Ferrari V4 motorbike, in front of the sculptured hand squeezing the world. Two centuries ago, an execution stage marked the spot. Marsden pulled the shoppers' puppet strings, making them dance to his tune. 'Where Angels Burn' would force even the happiest person to reach for the suicidal blade and fill their bathtub with ruby regret.

The wrapping paper vendor wiped his eye as footprints ruined the sheets arranged on the ground.

A pavement preacher on the corner thrust yellow leaflets at people. "Lucifer's coming! Confess your sins and God will forgive you!"

A leaflet fluttered to Marsden's feet, twitching in its death throes. *How to get to Heaven.* "Is there a postcode for my SatNav?" He called, pocketing the leaflet. "I'll go when Travel Inn have their summer sale."

He switched to playing 'Aftermath', strumming the shoppers' hidden wounds raw. They wore misery on their faces like the latest makeup range from the Mourning Glory Colour Collection.

Marsden smelled Drew's deodorant before he saw him. He looked good enough to eat in charcoal jeans, a black and grey marbled t-shirt with a silhouette of a winged demon motif and a slate military jacket.

"You didn't get your fashion sense from Jesus."

"Jeans hadn't been invented two thousand years ago." Drew hugged a grey checked blanket and a dog coat. "Christmas is a happy time. These people look like they'd have more fun in a torture chamber."

"Christmas shopping turns men into monsters. And torture chambers provide hours of fun."

Drew crossed to a homeless man and draped the blanket over him then fastened the coat around his shivering dog. He gave them food then jogged back and slid onto the bike. Marsden imagined Drew's arms slipping around his waist and glanced over his shoulder. Drew gripped his thighs, his knuckles white.

The preacher pointed at Marsden. "You'll burn in Hell!"

"I'll wear sun cream!"

"Don't antagonise him, he'll never leave us alone," Drew chastised.

"I'll kill him."

"Murder isn't the go-to option for every situation."

"You don't want fanatics like him being the voice of your cause."

"Doesn't mean I want him hung up like a stocking, his intestines spilling out like gruesome candy canes."

"I like that image. Mac can fill him with little gifts to give to the coroner."

The man approached.

Drew groaned. "Great. I'll have to flash him. If his soul's not pure, he'll go blind."

"You don't go blind from seeing it, only from playing with it. Did your father not have this chat with you?"

Drew laughed. "I meant flashing my soul. You have a dirty mind." He locked gazes with the man and touched his choker, muttering in an ancient language. His eyes glowed silver. Shadow wings spread across the ground.

Marsden's eyes burned, the veins bursting and spilling their blood over the whites of his eyes and down his cheeks. He winced, covering his ears, his eyes feeling as though they were about to explode.

The man retreated, leaflets slipping from his grasp. Wind snatched them. He fell to his knees, screaming and clawing his eyes. "The devil will come for your soul!"

Marsden wiped the blood off his eyes with the heels of his hands. "I'll kill the lights, pretend I'm out. Drew, next time you do that, warn me so I can buy earplugs. Fucking stings."

"Shit," Drew said. "I just blinded a man on a busy shopping street. I'm supposed to be discreet! I might as well change my Friendzone employment status to 'one of Heaven's angels and pub landlord'. I'll get arrested. D'you know what they'd do to me in jail?"

"Tell them your arse is mine, bitch."

"I don't recall seeing your name stamped on my arse cheeks." Drew dismounted, crouched beside the shrieking preacher and kissed his eyelids. The man fell silent, tears seeping from his ruined eyes. "Great. That's three in the past two months."

"You've blinded *three* people?"

"I can't tell if they're pure until I've flashed them. By then they've lost their sight and I've gained another disciplinary hearing." Drew slumped back on the bike. "You owe me. Play a Christmas song."

"And steal custom from the busker on Asylum Row? Besides, you should be grateful."

"That you're the biggest cause of depression since Justin Bieber started making records?"

"I'm reminding them Christmas isn't about sinking into debt to buy presents that people will flog on eBay. Or buying enough food for one day that would feed the starving for a month. They're remembering everything they've lost so they'll stop taking things for granted. When it comes to guilt tripping, I kick religion's arse."

"Christmas has the highest number of suicides, apart from New Year and the latest Apple product selling out."

Marsden laughed and reached behind to slap Drew's thigh, wincing when his hand scorched. "Does sir have any requests?"

"'All I Want for Christmas is You'?"

Their gazes met in Marsden's wing mirror. Drew's silver eyes made Marsden's look a darker shade of black. Marsden shifted as his body responded, his breath catching in his throat. He longed for Drew's words to be real. But they never would be.

"Mariah Carey? Haven't they suffered enough?"

Drew smiled mischievously. Marsden's jaw tightened. He inflicted his angry agony on the guitar. A fight erupted near the wrapping paper vendor, who tumbled into a pile of shiny paper and festive bows. In Saucy Secrets, two women argued over the last diamante thong, which proved unsuitable for tug o' war.

Marsden grinned at Drew. "That G string snapped quicker than mine does."

"Please say it's not a 'pull my cracker' one."

"I wanted my bells to jingle all the way."

Drew burst out laughing. "I'll never get that image out of my head."

Marsden winked. "Think how much fun I'll have as the Big Day dawns. Those last minute shoppers prepared to kill each other for the Christmas top toy."

"Did you find the Bad Mood Bear in your cereal packet?"

"Skeletor knows about you."

"Shit. How much?"

"She's more Mystery Inc. than MI5. But a fallen angel's hard to hide."

Drew glared. "I haven't fallen."

"You're not here on holiday."

"What did Skeletor say?"

"She tried blackmailing me into having sex with her."

Drew watched the shoppers. "Did it work?"

"If I wanted to shag a bag of bones with a toxic personality, I'd dig up Henry VIII."

"So you're taking it out on mortals."

Marsden shrugged. "I can't kill her; it says so on page 4 of the *Horseman's Handbook.*"

Marsden reached the final rousing chorus. A man barged into a woman, spilling her shopping. Her screaming fit punctuated the air as she pummelled him with an oversized cuddly panda.

The E string snapped.

"I should stop buying budget strings."

The man thrust a wooden sword into her stomach. She collapsed, blood blossoming on her clothes and dripping onto her bulging bags.

"Fuck's sake, Mars, it's Christmas."

"Christmas isn't an elixir that protects them from death."

Drew ran to her and tried staunching the flow, his hands soon drenched with her blood. Marsden looked away from Drew's stricken face. Drew's pain was the only one he didn't crave.

"He's stealing my presents!" She fought Drew off.

"Believe it or not, Barbie's Princess Castle isn't on my Christmas list," Drew retorted.

A woman snatched the castle and fled. The pavement preacher edged closer, his discarded leaflets falling from people's hands, becoming stained with their footprints. Bloodied scratches and raw burns replaced his eyes.

"The end is coming!"

Marsden smiled. "It's already here."

***

Mac shuffled down Funeral Way, rubbish blowing around him. He pulled his hood over his eyes and stuffed his gloved hands into his pockets, his shoulders hunched.

Footsteps echoed through the gloom. He turned, pushing his hood down as a man approached. The man stared at the lesions, his silver choker glinting when captured by a car's sweeping headlights.

"You ok?"

A coughing fit attacked Mac and he doubled over, tar-like substance spilling from his mouth.

The man touched Mac's head. His fingers burned. "Oh god! You're—" The man stumbled backwards, gagging and praying.

Mac grabbed him. Black mist rushed into the man's nose, ears and mouth. The man retched, pushing Mac's face away and bursting his pimples. The victim's hand scorched and blistered. He screamed, his skin melting from his bones. Pus-filled lesions erupted over his spasming body. He coughed, spraying putrid liquid then lay still, his eyes wide with suffering. His choker burned and blackened, dropping to the wet ground.

"Sorry."

Mac sniffled and dabbed his mouth, nudging the man with his boot. His legs flopped as he lay like a discarded scarecrow. Wind battered the alley. Wings flapped and light blinded Mac. Blood trickled from his eyes. An agonised scream deafened him. Black shadowy wings stained the alley wall. Pulling his hood up, he slunk towards the mouth of the alley. Morgan blocked it, silhouetted against the gloomy sky.

"A present? It's not even Christmas." She batted her lashes as she approached the spot where the angel died and scooped up a globe. She smashed it, retrieving a silver ring from the shards and slipping it on her finger.

"I hate Christmas." He wiped his eyes with his hoody sleeve.

"Nobody wants your ulcerated tongue licking their envelopes."

"Can't I infect the water supply? I wouldn't have to watch them...expire."

"It's character-building. I'll let you off, seeing as you've started your tally and you get bonus points for killing an angel, but next time, give gifts they can share with their loved ones." She smiled. "Spread some festive cheer. Tell them there's no refund."

Mac slouched away. People avoided eye contact, shielding their children as they passed. He entered a needle exchange and queued, shifting impatiently. People stepped away. He folded his arms, shivering. The woman in front fled when Mac coughed. A gorgeous man with a silver choker manned the table, his badge identifying him as Drew. Mac pouted. Even mortals were less revolting than him.

"I need needles," Mac wheezed.

"I'm not giving you needles so you can infect people. Pestilence."

Mac snatched the box and ran. The door opened, pounding feet pursuing him.

"Drop them or I'll inject you with penicillin!"

A dagger brushed Mac's calf and clattered to the floor. Swearing, Mac scuttled over a wall into another alley, waiting until the footsteps faded and a curse echoed around the streets. He sat in a makeshift cardboard shelter and rolled up his sleeve. Removing a rubber tube from his pocket, he tied it around his arm, slapping the vein until it rose. He emptied the needles from their packets and inserted the first one into his vein, easing the plunger out. Black mist floated in the syringe, blood globules roaming inside like a twisted lava lamp.

When he'd filled half the needles, he replaced their stoppers and released the tube. He lay back, closing his eyes as exhaustion and nausea suffocated him.

Scuffling feet disturbed him. He opened his eyes as a teenager snatched a syringe.

"It's not Heroin."

"What is it?"

"My own recipe. Consider that a free sample."

The teenager ran, concealing the needle in his pocket.
"Pity you can't afford the cure."

CHAPTER 4

Nervous chatter resonated through the school hall as people removed their coats and grabbed refreshments. Demi sat on an uncomfortable plastic chair in the corner, inching away from anyone brushing past. A woman with a clipboard and measuring tape stood at the front. Demi could hang her with that tape. Make her death ironic. Demi scanned the peeling lemon walls, wishing the chair stacks along the far end would topple and crush everyone. A board on one wall displayed the Reception classes' Father Christmas paintings. They clearly had no idea about perspective. Had they even *seen* another person? Their efforts should be scrumpled in a bin, not decorating the wall.

"Welcome back, slimmers! I can't believe this is the same group I met four months ago! You're half the women you used to be." The woman beamed over her blancmange glasses. Demi mimed sticking her fingers down her throat. Any more sugary, she'd be detrimental to diabetics. "I have new recipe cards, with calories listed for each meal." She gestured to the precarious pile of binders on the table.

"They need to lay *off* the recipes," Demi muttered.

"Who's first?"

"Me." Demi marched to the front.

"You clearly don't need Diet Divas." The woman smiled, her words coated with envy icing.

"I led Winners Are Thinner before I moved here. It helps me resist temptation." Demi kicked off her

30

strawberry stiletto boots and climbed on the scales, bellowing her weight to the group. "I've lost *six* pounds!" She hopped off, applauding herself and enjoying watching their positive expressions collapse like a badly cooked pie.

"We'd love to hear your success story."

"I stopped eating fatty foods and started exercising. The weight fell off."

"I've tried," one woman grumbled. "Nothing happens."

"Probably because you returned to your gluttonous ways. I've dieted every day for ten years. It's no good blaming food – you didn't morph into Marshmallow Man after some terrible dream."

"This is an *encouragement* group," the leader stressed.

"Maybe you should *encourage* them to follow my example."

She took her seat while the group guiltily shoved their refreshments in the bin and queued. The two pound loss which was a great achievement last week, now etched disappointment into their faces and they slouched back to their seats.

"I've lost four pounds!" one woman cheered. The group clapped.

"Good girl, get yourself a cake," Demi replied.

"There's nothing wrong with the occasional treat."

"You look like you've had hourly treats. You have more spare tyres than a garage."

"I'd like you to leave," the leader said. "I won't have you upsetting these women. They've worked hard to get where they are."

"Shovelling chocolate éclairs in their mouths must be exhausting."

"You're undermining *everything* they've done."

Demi grabbed her oversized plum bag and strode for the door. "Doctors should stop dishing out antidepressants and start prescribing Battenburgs."

The door closed behind her. She laughed and skipped down the street. The others got kicks from taking lives but her method was more satisfying. She didn't take lives – she broke them.

She spotted two slim women in their early twenties admiring an aubergine dress in a shop window.

She sidled over, smiling spitefully. "Stunning."

"I want it for my graduation," one woman answered, her gloved fingers stroking the glass.

"Just because you *could* wear it, doesn't mean you *should*. No offence, but it'd look better on the mannequin. Don't despair – they're bound to do *something* in your size. Try maternity wear."

"You bitch!" The woman turned to slap her.

Demi caught her wrist. "I'd hate for you to spend your wages on that gorgeous dress only to look like a sugar plump fairy."

"At least I don't look like a twig."

"That'll sting when I'm patrolling the catwalk, getting paid millions to wear clothes that'll cost more than your house. At least my BMI is lower than my IQ. Never mind. Plus Size models are becoming popular. You should send your head shot in." Her smile twisted. "They won't want the rest of you."

She adjusted her hair in the reflection from the woman's tears then entered the shop. Moments later, she emerged wearing the dress. She twirled, the mullet skirt floating around her.

"Maybe *I'll* wear it to your graduation." She strutted away, laughing.

The alleyway beside the shop led to a deserted shopping street. Our Lady of Sorrows church across the road sported a banner advertising bEat It, a group for people suffering with eating disorders. Demi trotted across the road and pushed open the ancient wooden door. She sat in a pew, reaching down her collar to rip off the tags. She shivered, rubbing her arms.

"Welcome to bEat It," a woman at the front said. "I see new faces. Would you like to introduce yourselves?"

Demi walked down the aisle, her stilettos ringing off the stone floor like the dying chimes of a church bell.

"I'm Demi and I'm here because my boyfriend thinks I have an eating disorder."

"Hello Demi," the group chorused.

"I eat healthily and enjoy exercise, like the Government advises. Waistlines are increasing – two thirds of this country are now overweight – so people who were considered slender a few years ago, are branded 'anorexic'. I'm sick of being told to 'eat a sandwich' because I don't have stretch marks. People want *me* to gain weight so *they* don't have to make the effort to lose it. I'm a constant reminder of their failure, their laziness, and instead of changing their lives to make themselves feel better, it's easier to take it out on me."

Half the room clapped, the other half stared. They probably thought she was the new Messiah and were in awe of her beauty and power. She returned to her seat, smiling at the potential tallies.

She nudged the teenage girl beside her. "That outfit looks great."

The girl tugged her sleeves over her hands. "Thanks. My friend says it shows my bones. She reckons I'll end up in hospital, being force-fed through a tube."

Demi studied the girl's protruding collarbones. In a few weeks, she'd raise her tally. "She's jealous. Take vitamins to get nutrients. Vitamins don't have calories."

During the break she mingled, spreading her 'winners are thinner' mantra then escaped before the meeting reconvened. Footsteps stalked her. She turned and saw Marsden, hands in his pockets, his guitar on his back. His black pirate jacket looked so good on him, Demi wanted to tear it from his body, followed by his grey ripped jeans and black skull t-shirt.

"Is this *really* your strategy?"

"The others aren't fun."

"Poisoning crops and killing half a country through starvation and suffering doesn't sound fun? Your father obviously didn't hype it up. People imagine us riding across the world, leaving a trail of terror and death. Not sitting in self-help groups, telling people chewing gum makes them fat. You're a disgrace to your heritage."

Demi linked her arm through his. "I'm like you, babe – seeing my work close up gives me that warm, tingly feeling most people get from receiving a teddy bear on Valentine's Day. I might even start my own slimming group." She smirked. "Don't act like you care about them. You take their lives with one pluck of a string, or sit back and watch them kill each other. Did you download a conscience from iTunes?"

"Amazon. On a thirty day free trial. Go torment people in Ethiopia and Rwanda – those who'll appreciate your 'moment on the lips, lifetime on the hips' motto."

"One moment on *my* lips, you'll want to spend a lifetime on my hips." She spun towards him, hooking her fingers into his jeans pockets to pull him closer. She couldn't resist squeezing his arse. She had to succumb to *one* temptation.

A gorgeous man wearing a silver choker stopped halfway across the road and stared at them. Marsden pushed Demi against a wall, blocking her view. Her heart pounded as his lips were millimetres from hers. The church door banged shut.

"Give them the kiss of death."

"Look what that did to my father." She leaned forwards to kiss him.

Marsden stepped back. "The last time you kissed me, I had to send terrorists on a shooting spree in Paris to cleanse my soul."

"That's what unresolved sexual tension does for you. Makes you *explode*."

"Do you know how many die from eating disorders in the first ten years? *Ten* per cent. Even if you targeted a rally with a thousand sufferers, you'll only gather a hundred souls. I take that many lives in *one* gig." He clicked his bruised fingers.

"So? You can only take a quarter of the world. We might as well enjoy it before we destroy it. You're like all men, rushing to the finish line and not savouring the journey. The destination is a bonus after a *long*, pleasurable trip." She stroked his dark, spiked hair, her tongue gliding over her lips.

They walked to where her black motorbike lurked in an alley.

"Your chariot awaits." Marsden bowed then walked backwards. "Don't fuck up my Apocalypse."

"*Your* Apocalypse?" She laughed. "You're not the only Horseman in town."

CHAPTER 5

Streetlights flickered like a dying heart thrumming its final beat. Tarmac was slick with the sky's fallen tears as the phantom bike devoured the road. Aeron gripped Morgan's shoulder with one hand, his other hand brandishing a soul globe. Wind buffeted their faces, stealing their breath.

"We should do something creative," Aeron mused. "Street art is popular."

"So are kebabs on a Friday night."

"Squashed kebabs won't create headlines."

"We could make it festive. People are probably sick of the same Christmas decorations on Gallows Street year after year. Plus we'll be saving the council a job and compensating them for smashing their streetlight."

"Until they cut the bodies down."

"Then we'll be keeping those in the death trade in business. They'll be grateful getting work this time of year."

"Technically, as we create the death trade, does that make us their bosses?"

"Bosses?" Morgan snorted. "We're their gods."

They parked their bike and patrolled Gallows Street, watching shoppers carrying their January debt in coloured bags. Morgan eyed a bare tree imprisoned by benches made from black chain links. They didn't look comfortable but what would that matter if they won design awards?

She tapped Aeron's shoulder. "What's the most popular symbol of Christmas?"

"A fat man sitting children on his knee and bribing them with gifts?" He frowned. "Suddenly, that doesn't sound so wholesome."

"Ooh we should dress Mac up. He could infect them, and the beard will hide his pestilent face. 'Here, tiny human, have a dolly. And some smallpox'."

"See, it's ideas like that that prove we're the perfect pair to lead the Apocalypse. Mars would massacre everyone in the grotto and Demi would send them home in tears. They have no finesse. No eye for detail. No friggin' *class*." He smiled up at the tree. "Are you thinking what I'm thinking?"

"Let's make this the season of Death."

***

Morgan and Aeron dumped their spoils at the base of the tree. No wonder people moaned about Christmas shopping. Morgan would have more fun pulling out her teeth and juggling with them. She'd been forced to headbutt a woman reaching for the last bag of tree chocolates. Well, maybe not 'forced', but the woman looked like a complainer and Morgan didn't have time to complete an incident report. They had a tree to decorate. Bureaucracy would run much smoother if people indulged in the occasional headbutt.

Aeron rifled through the bags. "Tinsel, check. Baubles, check. Lights, check. Chocolates, check. All we need are angels."

Morgan nodded towards carollers dressed in festive jumpers and Santa hats outside a sports shop, Sporting Heroes. "Check."

"I love it when you think festive."

They sidled over to the carollers, slipping amongst them and singing the wrong words to the joyous songs.

"Away in a manger, using shepherds as sleds, the little Lord Jesus cut off Mary's head."

A man stood near them, shaking a tinsel-adorned coin bucket.

"Allow me." Aeron relieved him of the bucket then dropped ten globes into it. "I'm making a large donation. There's nothing more priceless than life."

He shook the bucket. Pained expressions crossed the carollers' faces. Some clutched their hearts. Aeron stepped back then chucked the contents of the bucket over the carollers with an exaggerated flourish, like a clown tossing glitter. Gasps of pain replaced the singing as the globes shattered on the floor and coins rained over the carollers. They collapsed until Morgan was the only one left singing. She finished the song with jazz hands. The raven landed on the upturned bucket as they gathered the carollers' soul globes.

"Corpse!"

Aeron filled the raven's pouch with the marbles then the twins grabbed the carollers. Aeron dropped a globe and they vanished, reappearing in the tree. They took their time decorating it. Morgan tied black tinsel around her head. Aeron draped a bauble over each ear.

"How cute and Christmassy do we look?" He flicked a bauble.

"We need pics for our scrapbook."

They posed together in their tree as Aeron took a selfie. "Say Christmas!"

"Christmas!" They chorused.

"We could make a postcard for Dad. He'd love it!"

Half an hour later, they swung out of the tree. Aeron took photos from every angle as Morgan circled it. They were true creative geniuses.

"Have you ever seen something so beautiful?" Aeron asked.

"I now understand why people love Christmas. Look how pretty the lights are!"

The carollers hung from tinsel nooses. Fairy lights fastened their bodies to the bare branches, twinkling like little stars. Baubles hung from their ears, fingers and some branches. Chocolates dangled from spindly twigs. The conductor sat at the top of the tree, wearing a halo of fairy lights. More lights hung from his outstretched arms to create wings. They reflected in his empty eyes.

"Gotta have an angel on top of the tree," Aeron remarked.

"What's Christmas without tradition?"

They burst into song. "Oh Christmas tree, oh Christmas tree, your corpses hang so prettily."

A lady walked past and stared at the twins as they took another selfie. Morgan grinned and pointed to the tree. The lady looked up. And screamed.

"Well that's not polite." Morgan frowned. "How would you like it if we came round your house and screamed at your decorations?"

Aeron made a flicking motion with his fingers. "Begone, puny mortal. Your uneducated palette clearly doesn't appreciate modern street art."

The woman ran off screaming and pointing to the tree.

"She must be impressed; she's telling everyone." Morgan high-fived Aeron. "Is that a police officer she's talking to? Why is she fetching him and not a news crew?"

"We'd better make like Santa's trousers and split." Aeron grabbed her arm and broke a globe. They vanished, leaving the carollers hanging from their Christmas gallows like human candy canes.

***

Mac slunk in the twins' wake, pulling his hoody further over his face to block out shoppers' disgusted stares. Gallows Street was alive with people. Identical

Christmas songs spilled from every busy shop. As they drew closer to a crowd, sirens silenced the songs.

The twins forced their way through the crowd. People stood aside then looked confused as they failed to see who they'd moved for. Mac scuttled through the gaps, wishing he had the gift of invisibility. Infecting people would be easier if he didn't have to endure their horrified expressions. He sighed. Why couldn't he be as pretty as bird flu bacteria?

Police tape bound benches surrounding a tree. Amongst the branches, people twirled from tinsel nooses. Lights bathed them in a macabre Christmassy glow, turning their swollen faces into grotesque death masks. Aeron snatched chocolates off the lower branches and passed one to Morgan.

"Chocolate?" He offered one to Mac. Mac shook his head. Aeron shrugged. "Suit yourself."

"Why have they cordoned off our masterpiece? They're spoiling the ambience of the piece. Police tape doesn't fill you with that warm, magical feeling. They could've used present tape." Morgan bit a chocolate elf's head off. "Are they claiming credit for our work?"

"Nah, I think it's like when they have those ropes in museums and tourist attractions to stop peasants sullying stuff with their sweaty mitts." Aeron stuffed a chocolate snowman in his mouth.

"What do you think, Mac? It's our gift to Lemures."

"Very…festive." He kept his voice low. It was bad enough people saw him as an abomination. He didn't want them thinking he talked to himself too.

Aeron slapped his thigh. "I *knew* there was something we'd forgotten – bells."

"Balls." Morgan scowled. "They could've tinkled as they twinkled. Sadly, we can't stand here admiring our art all day. We have children to entertain."

They pushed back through the crowd, Mac keeping close. As soon as the twins were inside Midas shopping centre, people turned to stare.

"I don't think it's a good idea to just reappear," Mac said. "People aren't used to it."

"They'll think they imagined it," Aeron said. "Never underestimate people's ability to lie to themselves: 'I didn't see people appearing out of thin air', 'I can afford that diamond-encrusted coffee dispenser'. 'My significant other would never butcher me in my sleep'." He stopped outside an electrical shop. "Morg, we've made the news! Check us out being headline heroes!" Every TV in the window showed their tree. "Why have they pixelated the angels' faces? They're denying them their fame! And ruining our art. Would they pixelate Mona Lisa?"

He photographed the display.

"Mona Lisa wasn't murdered and hung from a tree," Mac mumbled.

"*Murdered?*" Aeron gaped. "They weren't *murdered*. They expired."

"I thought you smashed their globes?"

"That's not *murder*. That's our *job*. You're making us sound like Jack the Ripper. I'm hurt you think that way of us."

Mac looked at his feet. "Sorry."

"Just teasing. You need feelings for them to get hurt."

Morgan led the way to a large log cabin in the middle of the shopping centre. Fake snow covered the ground and roof. Plastic reindeer guarded a sleigh burdened with presents. The twins pretended to ice skate down the path and disappeared into the cabin. Mac loitered by the fence, trying not to look like a criminal. The security guard watched him, keeping one hand on his walkie-talkie. Mac looked away.

A hand touched his shoulder then he found himself in a storeroom. Aeron had an unconscious Father

Christmas slung over his shoulder like a gruesome sack of presents.

"Time to switch," Morgan said. "And be quick. You don't want security catching you with your jingle bells shaking free."

The twins turned around while Mac changed into the Santa outfit. Morgan tied the man up with left over tinsel then slapped a bow on his forehead.

"I don't think this is a good idea," Mac said, the long sleeves covering his hands. He hitched the trousers up then tied tinsel around his waist to stop them falling down. Accidentally exposing himself to children would ruin the innocent grotto for everyone.

"It's a great idea," Aeron replied. "We're tying the Apocalypse to Christmas, and with the hood and beard, you can barely be seen. I mean, nobody will know you're not him." He smiled.

"The beard itches."

"Success requires suffering."

Morgan gripped his shoulder and crushed a globe. They appeared in the grotto. Two model elves stood by Santa's throne. A sack of presents sat to the side.

"Can you stop doing that? I get travel sick."

Morgan rolled her eyes. "Stop whining. It's time to greet your adoring public." She opened the door. "Welcome children! Step this way. Father Christmas is ready to empty his sack."

Aeron snorted. "Morg! PG talk only. Think of the children."

A little girl entered the grotto. "Who are you?"

"Santa's elves."

"You don't look like elves."

"We're cool elves." Morgan pulled an elf's hat off the model and put it on. "Jingle, jingle."

Aeron donned the other hat. "Sit on Santa's knee and tell him what you want for Christmas. I bet I can guess. Is it…" he touched his temples. "The total annihilation of mankind?"

"I want Barbie's Buckingham Palace."

"How will that aid the Apocalypse?"

The little girl climbed onto Mac's lap. Morgan and Aeron knelt either side of the throne and posed with their thumbs up as her mother took a photo. "I want Cinderella Barbie, a pink pony, a princess dress."

"How about a scythe and an outfit like mine?" Morgan gestured to her clothes.

"Does it come in pink?"

Morgan's mouth dropped open. Mac almost laughed. The girl counted on her fingers her list of presents. Mac reached into the sack and pulled out a present with pink paper.

"Here you go little girl. I'll see you on Christmas Eve. Be good now."

"He'll know if you're not," Aeron said. "He watches you while you sleep." He smiled. The girl stared. He winked.

"Say thank you to Father Christmas." The mother ushered her out.

"Ooh what did you give her?" Morgan asked Mac.

"I don't know, they're already wrapped."

"Not *those* presents, Mistletoad, *your* presents. The ones that can't be bought in shops."

"Oh. I forgot." He lowered his gaze. "Sorry. I was panicking about getting caught."

"Don't forget again or we'll roast your chestnuts on an open fire."

A boy entered the grotto. As soon as he sat on Mac's lap, he bawled.

"I don't blame you, kid," Aeron said. "It's not a place I'd like to sit either. You don't know what you'll catch."

The twins grinned for the camera by the sobbing boy. Aeron also took a photo. Mac discreetly coughed into the sack then handed the boy a present. The boy trotted out, clutching it. The purple specks coating it were prettier than the plain blue wrapping paper.

"They'll all get the gift of diphtheria," Mac said.

"You could've hidden twelve diseases in there," Aeron said. "Y'know, to fit with the twelve days of Christmas."

The twins burst into song. "On the first day of Christmas, Santa gave to me, a stocking filled with Hep B!"

"I gave them diphtheria, not Hep B," Mac mumbled.

Morgan glared. "Do you want to ruin our song with accuracy? Diphtheria doesn't rhyme with anything."

After twenty more children, even the twins were losing their enthusiasm.

"I swear to Krampus, if I hear one more wailing child, I'll tie them up in the sack and bury them in the forest," Morgan muttered. "Why don't they come with off buttons? They're killing my Christmas spirit."

"Can I stop now?" Mac asked. "I think some of them peed on me. I'm…damp."

Morgan grimaced.

"Have you emptied your sack?" Aeron asked.

"Almost."

"Almost is not a satisfying conclusion."

Another boy entered. "You're not Santa."

"Oops, busted," Aeron whispered. "You may have to kill him, stop him telling his friends."

"Yes I am," Mac answered.

"You're not fat."

"Being obese is bad for your health," Morgan said. "Father Christmas went to a fitness boot camp and stopped gorging on mince pies. He was considered high risk from heart disease and diabetes. And he was setting a bad example to children."

"How can you deliver to every house on Christmas Eve?"

"It's not *every* house. Naughty children don't get presents." Morgan nudged the boy. "Naughty children

44

who interrogate Father Christmas get a visit from his horrible brother, Krampus. Krampus eats naughty children."

"I think he just spanks them," Aeron said.

"Are you sure? I thought he dragged them to Hell and ate them."

The boy burst into tears.

"See what you did?" Mac asked.

"He was trying to blow your cover," Morgan said.

"There *is* no cover. Santa isn't real!"

The boy cried harder. "Santa isn't *real?*"

"Cold, Mac," Aeron said. "I understand you're bored, but there's no need to be cruel."

Mac shoved a present into the boy's hands. "Merry Christmas!"

CHAPTER 6

The Razor and the Rosary sign creaked beneath the wind's attack. Faded paint revealed split wood. Jagged letters scribed the pub's name. Rosary beads strangled the bloody razor blade. The beads gave false hope; there was no salvation here, only suffering.

The front of the stone pub was short, with a slanted roof. The back part was taller, slanting the opposite way. Rusty Victorian gas lamps guarded the cracked car park. Only one worked. The pub shared Desolation Row with the prostitutes under the railway bridge, and Honest Dave's, an abandoned used car garage. Dave was serving time for selling stolen cars.

Marsden entered and sat on a slashed barstool, slinging his guitar around his back. Black beams supported the ceiling and the flaking crimson walls. It hadn't changed much since it opened in 1605. Except they no longer hanged people outside. The bar and furniture were made from battered mahogany, each scar telling a story, where happily ever after withered and died.

Marsden's heart raced each time he glimpsed Drew, who wore a grey t-shirt under a black waistcoat. A black trilby covered his short hair. Charcoal jeans clung to him in teasing places. He bent to fetch Smirnoff Ice from the fridge, the slate waistband of his trunks escaping his jeans. Marsden's breath caught. Each day Drew looked more beautiful. Each day being around him was harder. Pleasure and pain were a bewitching, damning combination.

Drew served two young women then approached Marsden. The women's gazes stalked him. "What's your poison?"

"You. But you're also my antidote."

"Ooh, multi-talented. I should charge extra." Drew lined up five shot glasses on the bar and filled them with gin, rum, brandy, whisky and port. He emptied each glass into a pint glass and topped it up with Guinness and champagne. He dropped a black straw and a cocktail umbrella in the glass then slid it towards Marsden, smiling.

"What the hell is that?" Marsden picked up the pink umbrella.

"My customers aren't the cocktail types, despite my best efforts to make this place look less like a crack den. My cocktail skills are gathering dust."

"I'm not the cocktail type either."

"True, but I don't have a skull for you to drink the blood of your enemies from. Plus as my best friend, you have to humour me."

"Give me a Screaming Orgasm then."

Marsden saw Drew's heartbeat through his t-shirt and imagined it beat faster at his words. Drew licked his lips. Marsden's chest constricted, his temperature soaring as he pictured running his tongue over Drew's lips. He dug his nails into the bar, shifting on his seat.

"I wish I could," Drew murmured. He cleared his throat. "But I'm out of Bailey's. You'll have to settle for Hangman's Blood." He tapped the glass, his pewter crown ring chinking musically. The ring was decorated with skulls and black jewels.

"Does it contain real blood?" Marsden sniffed it then sucked on the straw.

"Knew there was something I forgot." Drew pretended to slice his palm and made a fist over the glass. "Bleeding into drinks is the easiest way to convert people. If it's good enough for vampires…"

Marsden chuckled. "Vampires kill people *then* turn them."

"Heaven doesn't accept post mortem conversion. You have to try before you die. What's up? If your face looked any glummer, the government could use it on depression posters."

"Would you prefer I was smiling like a walking toothpaste advert?"

"I don't take pleasure in the destruction of mankind. Judging by your gloomy face, neither do you."

"I've dreamt of this moment my whole life. Not *once* did I imagine it involving Travel Inn, smiley face achievement stickers and picking on fat people."

Drew's amused smile sparked Marsden's dead heart to life. He couldn't help returning it; Drew's smile was a puppet master pulling his lips' strings until they mirrored his own.

"That's not what Revelations predicted either. Are you narked because someone got the sticker you wanted?"

Marsden leaned over and flicked Drew's trilby, his fingers brushing Drew's stubble. Miniscule flames erupted. Drew smothered them with his hat. Marsden sat back, the barstool's shorter leg nearly pitching him off. He created a mini whirlpool in his drink with the umbrella.

"Don't you have skull print umbrellas?" He tossed it at Drew. "I look like I'm in a bloody romcom."

"Any minute now, your sexy lead will walk through the door then stalk you in a non-creepy way."

My sexy lead is standing right in front of me. The words were desperate to escape his lips, but he couldn't say them. They would decimate what he had, even if what he had wasn't truly what he wanted.

The door opened, wind rushing in to nip people's exposed flesh.

"*Four* sexy leads? Hollywood's finally changed its formula," Drew said. "Scrap that. Two."

Marsden looked over his shoulder and groaned, slumping so his forehead hit the bar. "Fucktastic."

Mac slunk to a corner table and sat with his hood over his eyes and his hands up his sleeves.

"They're not what I expected. Mind you, neither were you."

"Am I better or worse?"

"Much better." Drew grinned. "Which is worse." His smile died, his gaze dulling. "War's portrayed as an armour-clad warrior, his glowing eyes matching his horse's, like creatures born from Hell's fiery pits."

"You've met my father then."

"Thankfully, no. I can guess who Halloween Barbie is, though Famine's always depicted as obese. I met Pestilence at the shelter – he stole a box of needles. I chased him and nearly put a dagger in his leg but he's surprisingly fast for someone who looks like a leaf could kill him."

"Diseases have to be fast to be successful."

"Who are the twins?"

"The bane of my existence. Death's better at reaping than reproduction. They're a job share."

"How can a skeleton have sex? I've seen pictures online of digitally drawn skeletons performing the Kama Sutra, but it's not physically possible."

"Why were you viewing skeleton porn?"

"I wasn't! I stumbled across it."

"That's what they all say. 'Your Honour, I swear my credit card details entered themselves!' How much praying did you have to do to absolve that sin?"

"I had to lead a scout meeting. I'll never look at skeleton porn again." Drew winked. "Gives a new meaning to jumping someone's bones."

Marsden snorted, spraying his drink across the bar. Drew jumped back then swatted Marsden's head. "These jeans are clean."

"Death didn't have sex. It was bone marrow DNA."

"It's weird. They're identical, but clearly female and male. And their faces are like skull holograms." Drew shuddered.

"If you think that's weird, you should have a conversation with them. Not many people can see their skulls. Or them, if they choose not to be seen."

"Angel Vision lets me see people's true selves."

"What do I look like in Angel Vision?"

"I haven't used it on you. Do I need to arrange stables for your horses?"

"Health and safety forbade them. Plus there's nowhere to park them. Hence the bike."

Drew laughed. "Motorbikemen of the Apocalypse doesn't exactly strike fear into the heart."

"We don't have the budget to rebrand a millennia-old franchise."

Morgan and Aeron flanked Marsden, putting their arms around him. Demi draped herself over the bar like a squashed maiden fly.

Morgan smiled at Drew. "You must be the one tempting him to fall. Or is it the other way around?"

"Mars *is* mouth-watering," Aeron agreed. "Like chocolate. I bet he melts in your mouth."

"And is bad for your hips."

"I wouldn't know. Human meat isn't something we serve here," Drew replied. "Problems with suppliers."

"Mars, we wondered why you insisted out of all the cities in the world, Lemures was *the* place to start our campaign. And why your scouting mission took months," Aeron said. "Guessing it's not Lemures's supermarket loyalty card scheme."

Marsden glared. "Lemures is a shithole and nobody would notice its descent into Hell until the devil spit roasted their souls. You try travelling the world without a horse or teleporting. Teleporting doesn't involve traffic jams and trying to get your sword through customs."

Demi laughed. "Your 'sword' is hardly a weapon of mass seduction." She smiled at Drew. "Fancy joining me for a night of passion you'll never forget?"

"I've got enough bad memories on my conscience."

"He's learned his lesson about skeleton porn," Marsden said.

Demi slipped Drew a business card and stroked his arm, leaving a trail of blistered skin. Drew winced, yanking his arm away.

"Is he allergic to us?" She grabbed Drew's hand.

Drew swore as his skin bubbled. Marsden sprang up and pinned Demi to the bar. His stool crashed to the floor. He held a bowl of peanuts over her head. Demi laughed and released Drew, who cradled his hand, his face contorting.

"I know I'm hot but I didn't realise our flames of passion would be real." Demi blew Drew a kiss.

"Let her go." Morgan warned in a low voice.

Marsden pressed Demi into the bar then stood back and thumped the peanuts down. "It's a two-way allergy. Touch him again and you'll catch fire. I wonder what flaming Twiglet smells like."

"Don't get attached to parasites, Mars," Demi muttered. "They eat you from the inside, suck your blood then you have to crap them out before repairing the damage they've done."

Marsden's eyes darkened. "Fuck off, all of you. You're giving me herpes."

Demi, Morgan and Aeron moved to Mac's table.

"I'd better go." Marsden sighed. "Heads of Department meeting." He glanced at Drew's hand. "You ok?"

"Your burns are worse. What's their poison?"

"Penicillin for Germ Bag, Elixir for the Terror Twins and cyanide with a double shot of rat poison for Skeletor. Sprinkled with broken glass and shattered dreams. Don't bother with a glass, a funnel will do. Or give her your soup of the day."

Marsden joined the group and strummed his guitar, the atmosphere changing as he conquered customers' emotions.

"Why are we here?" Demi wrinkled her nose, nudging a chair with her toe. Foam spilled through a tear in the seat. "There are sewers less disgusting."

"Go live there then," Marsden snapped. "Though if you died, the rats would starve."

"We're here because someone's incapable of answering his phone." Morgan eyed Marsden.

"Wonderful. I need a Tetanus jab because Rock God's making googly eyes at Touch-me-Not." Demi laid her coat on the chair and slumped into it. "Is this *vinyl*?"

"*Fish* make googly eyes," Marsden retorted. "I'm writing new songs."

Morgan smirked. "Sorry we interrupted your music career with something as trivial as ending the world. Anyway, history's greatest plots took place in pubs. The Gunpowder Plot for instance."

"That was a roaring success. How did you find me?"

"Death is always just around the corner, lovely boy. Remember that."

"Morg and I had a productive day – we hung carollers from a tree," Aeron said. "And decorated it."

"How does that aid the Apocalypse?" Marsden asked.

"Ten people died. And we linked it with Christmas."

"You just distracted the media from our cause. You should've killed the pope. You could've made him into a tree and electrocuted him with fairy lights if you wanted to link it to Christmas."

Aeron and Morgan exchanged glances then inflicted identical glowers on Marsden.

"Well excuse us for having fun," Morgan said. "We also had Mac imitate Father Christmas and infect children in a grotto."

"That's more like it."

"All you ever do is criticise. This is why you're not in charge. Leaders should *inspire* their team. Remember our hand puppet show, *The Nativity*, which explored the theme of how your negativity spoils things?"

"How can I forget those three hours of my life I'll never get back?"

"It would've been four but we had to cut some songs 'cos the dance routines were tricky with the hand puppets."

"I'm ramping up my campaign," Demi contributed. "I've infiltrated slimming groups, eating disorder groups, gyms. I've set up my own group – Winners are Thinner. My motto is 'Dying to be skinny'. I even spent an afternoon in McFry's."

"Did you have your nose against the glass, drooling?" Marsden grinned.

"I did when you were in the shower." She winked.

He shuddered. He needed to invest in a better shower curtain. And door locks.

"What happened in McFry's?" Morgan asked.

"Ugh. It was like being inside a pig farm, with their faces in their polystyrene troughs, snorting, squealing and chewing. There's enough grease to coat the oceans. Just being there blocked my pores. Nevertheless, I made teenagers leave without finishing their slop. Right now they'll be standing naked before their mirrors, disgusted with their bodies."

"How the fuck does ruining people's self-esteem aid the Apocalypse?" Marsden asked.

"Their self-loathing will lead to suicide. Suicide is fashionable among teenagers. How does sitting in here, lusting after Los Angeles aid the Apocalypse?"

"I'm keeping the enemy close. You're just getting kicked out of slimming clubs."

"You can say it – I'm a genius." She flipped her hair back, smiling smugly.

"You're a waste of oxygen," Mac muttered.

"What have *you* done, Hazmat?" She stretched a bony finger to jab him then withdrew it, grimacing.

"Killed an angel, infected children with diphtheria and made a virus. I'm hoping doctors name it after me. The Maciesitis virus."

"The most disgusting virus mankind has ever known. Please tell me people won't start looking like you. The world can't cope with that much ugly. God will incinerate it before we've had our shot at glory."

"*You* killed an angel?" Marsden seethed. "You cried when you shot someone in *Resident Evil*."

"He asked if I was alright and...I breathed into him. It was horrible." Mac picked a scab on his hand. "When I close my eyes, I see his terror. Should I ask Drew to apologise?"

"Never apologise on the battlefield." Marsden looked at the twins. "Remind me why we've brought these two?"

"Don't sulk Mars, there are plenty of angels left." Morgan nodded towards Drew. "We'll tour Heaven in an open top Jeep, like humans hunting game. I could do with some new gloves."

"I don't need to kill angels. I have a gig tonight. I'll take every soul here."

Demi scowled. "I work my tiny tush off to corrupt people and all *he* does is pluck strings and they're his for the taking."

"If I plucked *your* strings, you'd be mine for the taking." He played a sexy song.

The couple on the neighbouring table kissed. Demi grabbed Marsden's jacket collar and kissed him. His chair crashed over and he banged his head on the uneven wooden floor. Drew's combat boots stopped by his head. A tray banged the table.

Demi straddled him like a bony praying mantis about to eat her prey. "Ooh your weapon's ready to make me scream." She rocked her hips.

Drew strode back to the bar.

"The only weapon I want to put in you is my sword." Marsden glared at her. "Damn right I'll make you scream."

Demi rose, rolling her eyes. Marsden scrambled up and thumped his chair down. Glowering, he downed his drink then played a new song, plucking the rage from his soul. The mood in the pub darkened.

"When we're done riding each other, can we brainstorm?" Morgan asked. "The end of the world takes a *little* more planning than a cinema trip."

Behind the bar, a glass smashed. Raised voices disturbed the peace. "This is bullshit," Marsden said. "I don't need to be here. I have enough strategies."

"How many?" Aeron asked.

"Nine. Five of them include contingency plans for when you cockwaffles balls it up. Though I've underestimated your incompetency."

Morgan rose and stood behind Marsden's chair. "How do you propose to end the world without us?"

"I'll kill you all and take the world for myself."

Morgan leaned over him and put her fingers to the guitar strings. Her new angel wing ring blinded him. She played a chord. Marsden jerked as pain shot through his heart.

Mac coughed. "Are we done? I've got waiting rooms to sit in."

Morgan ruffled Marsden's black hair and returned to her seat. More glasses smashed. "Mars, you're working with Demi." Behind them, a fight broke out. "She'll attend your gigs, being seen by influential people."

"I don't want people knowing I know her. Some stains never wash off." He switched to strumming. A man crashed onto a table, breaking it. "I'd rather shag Mac and get genital warts."

A man smashed his opponent's face into the bar.

"Mac will provide refreshments," Morgan said. "Aer and I will clean up accidents."

The fighting men barged into Demi. She stood, picked up a chair and smashed it on their heads. "Don't touch me you vile vermin! Don't you know who I am?"

"Mars. Enough." Drew sprang over the bar, separating the men. One swung a punch at him. He deflected it, punched the man in the face then dragged him out.

Marsden stopped playing. The other man returned to his seat.

"Thanks for that slice of entertainment." Aeron smiled. "After tonight, find somewhere new to gig. Keep starting fights here and–" he jerked his thumb towards Drew, "Someone will get hurt."

CHAPTER 7

The crowd in the Razor and the Rosary were blank canvases, waiting for Marsden's guitar to fill them with emotion, like actors waiting for the cue to smile. As the sky smouldered from the night's midnight kiss, more people gathered to be seduced by his demons.

"It's nice you've finally invited us to a gig," Demi said as they loitered by the bar. Mac fingered the bar snacks. Drew removed the bowls, dumped the snacks in the bin, dropped a lit match in it then carried the bin out. "Fancy giving me a private performance in your dressing room?"

"I'll rewrite Green Day's 'Ha Ha You're Dead'."

"That's not team spirited," Morgan chastised.

"We should do those–" Aeron began.

"Team building exercises," he and Morgan said simultaneously then high-fived each other.

"Army obstacle course," Morgan suggested.

"Paintballing."

"We'll bond over Demi's death. I'll play it, you guys and Mac can don matching feather boas and be my backing singers," Marsden said.

Drew approached and slapped his back. It sizzled. "You'll knock 'em dead, Mars."

"Fingers crossed." Aeron crossed his fingers.

"Music's not a recognised defence." Marsden's thumb traced graffiti scratched into the bar. Drunken, meaningless words stained with beer and cigarette ash. His black sword ring stabbed his knuckle. Voices bulleted his ears until their words became static on a broken signal.

Drew laughed. "Pretty boy like you would be traded for cigarettes. Tell them your arse is mine, bitch."

Aeron clapped. "Places! Where you see people, you'll soon see body bags."

Drew looked pleadingly at Marsden then headed for the stage.

Mac moved amongst the crowd, Morgan stalking him like a stylish shadow.

Sasha, Drew's redheaded barmaid entered the pub and waved to Marsden as she slipped behind the bar.

Drew bounded onto the stage at the far end of the pub. 'Stage' was an ambitious word for the pallets nailed together, painted black and covered with charred floorboards stolen from an arsonist's house.

"He has more talent in his pinky finger than the whole of *Singing Sensation* and will pluck your heart strings with every song."

Drew flashed him a disarming smile that would convince Satan to surrender. Marsden smiled. His heart wasn't bulletproof.

That was the problem.

"Marsden Slaughter."

Demi wolf-whistled from her barstool. Thunderous applause accompanied Marsden on stage like execution drums beating the rhythm of a man's dying heartbeat. They wouldn't applaud if they knew the tragedy he could inflict upon them.

Marsden caressed his guitar's snake neck then played 'Bleeding Wounds'. Halfway through, he stole a glance at the crowd. Some wiped their eyes but ghosts of smiles remained. That wouldn't satisfy his soul.

Not tonight.

Mac lurked amongst the crowd, spreading germs and distributing drugs like flyers. Demi tried convincing someone peanuts would lead to obesity and a lifetime of boils. Morgan and Aeron were lost in the shadows.

By the song's final chorus, half the room was saturated in misery. Marsden played 'Six String Heart' followed by 'Suicide Sanctuary' and watched the rest of them yield to their agony. One man slunk towards the toilets. Marsden's E string snapped.

When the set ended, Marsden hopped off stage and headed to the bar, dodging a broken barstool. Drew had his drink ready, a bright blue umbrella clinging to the rim. Marsden sniffed the peach drink before taking a sip.

"Kiss Me."

Marsden choked, spraying the drink. Fireflies ignited his stomach with pleasurable tingles. His eyes watered, his heart pounding. *He grabbed Drew's t-shirt and yanked him into a bruising kiss.*

Drew laughed. "I'm buying you a bib. Your cocktail is called Kiss Me." He mopped up the spilled drink.

Marsden's heart sank, the fireflies in his stomach withering and dying. Every time he thought there was a chance Drew reciprocated his feelings, Drew said or did something that proved otherwise. He couldn't live like this any longer. But he couldn't walk away.

He masked his hurt behind a smile. "I'd prefer the blood of my enemies."

"Sorry, I drained the last one yesterday. If I'd known you were doing the sad set, I would've bought shares in Kleenex."

Marsden coughed and wiped his eyes. "Misery's fashionable." He replaced the broken string with one from his pocket.

"If someone slips on their tears, you're responsible. I don't have a caution sign."

"Lie on the floor in the pose. People will get the idea." He drummed his nails on the bar then played an upbeat rock song. "What tears?"

Dancing patrons smiled, their sorrow banished beneath his fingertips.

Drew grinned. "You're a god."

"Is that blasphemy?" Demi said, slinking up behind Marsden like a tapeworm trying to devour his intestines. "How about you and I go upstairs and you can show me Heaven?" Drew escaped to serve someone. Demi rolled her eyes. "If you flirt any harder, you're going to have to wear a health warning. While there's a church full of boy scouts to take Prudas Priest's place, *you're* irreplaceable." She prodded Marsden's arm with a Fuscia Fusion nail. "I'll never get the stench of cooked flesh out of my hair. There's no cream for naughty bits with holy burns."

He glowered. "There's no cream for charred Horsemen either."

"All this sexual tension's so...stifling. I'm going to spread my 'Thin is In' message."

"Get yourself crucified. You'll be a martyr and frighten crows."

She flipped him off and walked away. Aeron emerged from the toilets and winked.

Drew returned and grabbed three Santa's Butt ales for his customer. "Play something happier."

"I don't do Disney."

"What's that noise?" Drew cupped his ear as he walked backwards. "Disney's heart breaking."

Marsden cackled and plucked a new song, the hypnotic rhythm enrapturing those listening.

Drew returned and leaned on the bar. His t-shirt sleeve rode up, revealing a toned bicep. Marsden bit his tongue, wishing his fingers were skimming along Drew's pale skin. "No sexy songs. This is a bar, not a brothel. The condom machines in the toilets are broken."

"Like angels know what condoms are. Lust's the easiest way to lure people to the dark side."

"And the hardest to save them from."

"Worried you can't control your sinful urges?" Marsden smiled.

Drew's gaze blazed. Marsden's heart raced, his breath shackled behind his ribcage's prison bars. He wanted something to prove Drew felt the same. A certain smile. A wink. A touch. Words that weren't ambiguous.

"Angels weren't designed to have sinful urges."

There was the sign. But not the one he wanted. Marsden dropped his plectrum, smacking his face on the bar as he retrieved it. He swore, his cheekbone smarting.

Drew laughed. "Don't dent my bar with your face. I'm not insured for Acts of Horsemen."

Marsden barely heard him as his good intentions died, his stomach twisting, his pleasure turning to ash. Suddenly, he didn't want to be around Drew. He wanted to be home, butchering the souls in Purgatory until the pain went away. He wanted to hate him. But he couldn't. The crowd would suffer his torment.

Applause stalked him onto the stage. He started with his metal track, 'Dying Souls'. The crowd responded passionately, air guitaring and head banging, devil horns thrust high. Mac started a one-man mosh pit, touching people with his lesions. Marsden moved into 'Darkest Desires'. A couple in the corner embraced in fierce lust, tearing each other's clothes and kissing as though the world would end.

Maybe it would tonight.

Demi leapt on stage and danced raunchily around Marsden, capturing a photographer's attention. Marsden sensed the blackness in the crowd's minds, yearning to surrender their control to him. He obliged, playing 'Violent Delights'.

Primal tension smothered the atmosphere. He strummed their anger, frustration and anguish then blasted it at them through the amp. A dying light flickered shadows over them, pulsing to their hearts. Mac jostled a man, who fell, his blood seeping across the floor to join in unholy matrimony with spilled beer. A woman trampled him. One man whacked another with a chair, splintering it on his back. A woman smashed a bottle on the bar then shredded her friend's face with it. She slashed Drew as he marched her out. When he returned, he hopped onto the bar, surveying the carnage, a scarlet wound weeping down his arm. His black waistcoat was undone, his t-shirt stained with blood. Mac used the chaos to breathe black mist over people.

Marsden attacked the guitar until his fingertips split, his blood streaking the guitar's neck. His right hand scraped the strings, the plectrum slippery in his bloodied grip as he unleashed their darkness upon them.

The song ended.

The music died.

The fight was over.

Dazed people staggered out. Mac and Sasha helped the trampled man up. The couple rose, lipstick smearing their passion over their faces. They straightened their clothing and filed out.

Drew rang the bell. "Time, ladies and gentlemen!"

Nobody stayed for last drinks.

Mac approached the stage, staring at Marsden's feet. "I'm doing a pub crawl. See if I can raise my tally. Wanna come?"

"I'll come," Demi said. "Nobody here was interested in my anti-fat lecture."

"Nobody ever is," Marsden retorted.

"Jesus, just shag me already."

"He'd prefer to shag me," Mac reminded her.

"Even zombies find you repulsive."

They left.

Drew jumped off the bar to talk to stragglers. Only one stuck around to hear his words. Marsden held a chord down and touched the plectrum to the strings. Drew's gaze met his. Marsden lowered the plectrum. The man left, smiling.

Morgan stood by the stage, hands on hips. "What the *fuck* was that?"

"A gig."

She arched an eyebrow. "You promised to take *every* soul! You took *one*, Mars. That was more disappointing than discovering Bigfoot is a man in a monkey suit."

"My music will haunt them. There's plenty of time for them to die, or murder their friends and family, increasing the death count. If I killed everyone, the police would be suspicious."

"Horsemen have Diplomatic Immunity. Your familial line has been slaughtering people for centuries and you're worried some poxy police force will slap handcuffs on you? You're War, not some spotty teen on his second strike."

"If they close this place down, I lose my link to Drew. He isn't the only angel on Earth. I need to find the others. Infiltrating the enemy is a classic military move."

"It's not his 'enemy' you want to infiltrate. You promised a bloodbath. You gave us a bloody nose. *Cows* kill more people than you did tonight." She strode towards Aeron, who waited by the door. They stormed out.

Marsden slung his guitar around his back and sprang off the stage, leaving bloody fingerprints on everything he touched. No matter what did, somebody was mad at him. Drew thumped a chair down, breathing hard. His eyes were the colour of a mortuary slab.

"You're staining my furniture. Come on."

Marsden trailed him to the toilets.

Drew noticed feet protruding under a cubicle door and rapped on the door. "This isn't a hotel."

Drew slapped the feet. They flopped over. He shoulder barged the door then dragged the man out by his ankles. A bloodied necklace decorated his throat, a mirror shard clenched in his fist. His eyes stared into a world Marsden knew intimately. Drew knelt by the man, whispered something then looked up.

"Don't look at me like that. It's bad enough the twins are pissed at me. I don't need it from you too. D'you have any idea what it's like being bollocked in stereo? I was supposed to kill everyone here. I *wanted* to kill everyone."

"Clearly your version of happy doesn't mirror mine."

"Mine involves blood, yours involves salvation."

Drew rose and opened the door. "Sash! Phone the police. We have a suicide." He returned to Marsden and grabbed a first aid kid from under the sink.

"You know who I am. What I do."

"How will I regain my promotion if you keep stealing my customers?"

"I don't want you to get promoted."

"I don't want *you* to succeed but I don't sabotage you."

"Why do you let me play here?"

Drew wiped the blood off Marsden's fingers before cleaning his own arm, the wound already healed. "Father won't let me bar you. And it gives me a legitimate reason to see you."

"I'm sorry about your angel."

"Sorry he's dead or that you didn't kill him?"

He should've been the first to kill an angel. Not Mac. His father would be furious. "I'll play an upbeat set next time, but you'll never see my name in a cabaret act, prancing around in sequins and smiles."

"If I'd known you'd play the sexy set, I would've bought shares in Kleenex."

Drew stood so close, Marsden could feel his body heat and smell the faint scent of strawberry shower gel mixed with Drew's sweat. He fought the urge to slam Drew into the wall and kiss the sweat from his skin. His breathing quickened, his heart pounding. Drew's silver choker glinted under the unforgiving lights. Marsden wanted to rip it from his throat and cast it into Hell's hottest inferno.

Marsden curled his trembling hands into fists and bit his lip until he tasted blood. His body was on fire.

"Stop punishing them because you can't banish whatever demon plagues you."

"Demi's a bitch, but she's not a demon."

Drew's fingers brushed Marsden's fist, sending a jolt through him. Marsden spread his fingers but Drew only touched his fingertips then withdrew. The tips stung, the cloying stench tickling Marsden's nostrils.

"I don't know why I'm healing you. It'd be better if you couldn't play for a couple of days."

"Because you're good."

"Some days I wish I wasn't."

Drew returned to the bar. Marsden watched his fingertips bubble then heal, as though Drew's touch never existed. Some wounds should never heal. He pivoted and punched the mirror. A fractured spider web crawled across the glass, ruby droplets caught in its trap.

Marsden helped Drew clean up then slipped out the back when the emergency services arrived. He stood in the shadows watching blue lights streak the sky like a strobe light display in Hell's disco. Sirens foretold a death but no-one was listening. They'd heard it too many times.

CHAPTER 8

"Guess who's got a modelling job?" Demi strode into the Travel Inn room and twirled, opening her oatmeal trench coat. Mac glowered from the chair while Morgan made coffee.

Aeron leaned against the bathroom doorframe. "My money's on Mac for posters warning against meth use."

Marsden sat on the orange settee, polishing his guitar. "Are you modelling the Ugly Collection from Hideous Inc.? Or the Skeleton Collection for Halloween? No, clothing for stick insects."

"You should do stand-up comedy instead of music." She pouted over her shoulder. "A modelling agency saw the photo of me dancing at your gig and invited me in for head shots."

"Please say they'll cut off your head, mount it on a plaque and put it in the Tate Modern. I want it when the exhibition's over. I need somewhere to store my keys."

A skull key pot would come in handy, Aeron mused. He and Morgan were always losing their bike keys.

"Having a model girlfriend will boost your profile."

"*Women's* profiles are raised by dating celebrities."

"People love hell-raising couples. Look at Bonnie and Clyde."

"Fred and Rose West aren't national heroes."

"They weren't young and beautiful. Oh, I forgot, you're hungry for Saint Stubbles. Dating *him* will kill your career. Rock gods can't be gay."

He tripped her.

"Don't make me bang your heads together," Aeron said. "Twiggy can corrupt people globally if she's in magazines."

"Gracing the cover of *Bricklayer's Monthly* won't inspire the masses." Marsden grinned. "Unless she gets her builder's crack out."

"Kiss my crack." She smirked. "I'll remind you of this moment when you're busking for loose change while I have A-list celebrities eating out of my hand."

"I hope you'll feed them cyanide."

"We're not here to be celebrities, we're here to end the world," Morgan interrupted, juggling three globes. One dropped, shattering against the desk. A muffled scream from the next room killed the conversation. Morgan vanished. Seconds later, she returned, trotted to the wall and slapped a smiley face sticker under her name. "Naked on the toilet. That's an embarrassing way to go."

"We should become celebrities," Aeron told her. "Make death fashionable."

"We'll start an ad campaign."

"'Live fast, die young'."

"'Death lasts longer than relationships'."

"We could design t-shirts!" Aeron's eyes lit up.

"Banners."

"Beermats! The inebriated always do stupid things. Their deaths could be the one thing that *doesn't* end up on ViewYou the morning after."

"Cost price merchandise is the in thing," Morgan said. "We'll design business cards!"

"Tell people we're in the death business."

"You *are* the death business," Mac grouched.

"Just prettier and younger than our predecessor."

"We're the sexy update for today's beauty-obsessed society," Morgan added. "Like turning a well-known fancy dress costume into a raunchy dress for women."

"My brain hurts," Demi said. "I'm going shopping for my photoshoot."

"It's probably a porn operation," Marsden remarked. "Wear your heels and a smile, save yourself money."

"I'll blow that shot up for you." She knelt up on the bed and placed her hands behind her head, adopting a sultry expression.

"There goes my appetite." He made a flying motion with his hand. She blew him a kiss and skipped out.

"Have the police figured out who made the gallows tree?" Mac asked, picking a scab behind his ear.

"Nope," Aeron replied. "I think we'll get away with it. Though credit would be nice."

"It won't end the world," Marsden muttered.

"It's done, Mars. Let it go. Mac, how's your homemade virus? The death tally is as poor as the turnout for a nuclear bomb survivors' reunion."

"Their immune systems react differently. Five people from the gig suffered boil outbreaks."

"Boils will excite the religious," Marsden said. "Pity they're not fatal."

"We need global panic," Aeron said. "Bigger than bird flu and a more successful mortality rate than that overhyped swine flu."

"They were mine!" Mac protested.

"Chemistry clearly isn't your strong point. We want hospitals closing, people panic-buying vaccines, makeshift morgues in school halls."

"People wearing those masks that were popular in China," Morgan said.

"We want them wearing gas masks."

"Hazmat suits!"

"I'd like a return of plague masks," Marsden said, tuning his guitar. "And plague epidemics. Killing sixty people a year in Madagascar isn't enough. We need the sixty thousand that London's 1665 plague wiped out. People dying where they stand."

Mac rubbed his face. "I'm *one* man."

Aeron smiled. "A *Horse*man. Now saddle up and spread it quicker than an STI at a Playboy party."

"Start with measles," Marsden said. "It'll instigate another debate on the vaccine's dangers then you can infect children who weren't inoculated."

Mac pulled his hood over his eyes and slouched out of the room.

"The place just got healthier." Morgan smiled. "Better disinfect where he sat. Or fumigate the room. And Mars, stop giving orders. You're not in charge."

"I should be. Why are we still here? This is suspicious. They probably think we're a terrorist cell."

"We're saving our money for the gift shop."

Morgan and Aeron flanked Marsden on the settee and put their arms around him. "Am I about to get the sex chat?"

"If your father had given you this chat, we wouldn't have to," Morgan replied. "He taught you about using your sword, not your gun."

"I know about kidnapping women and forcing them to marry you. He told me when I was ten and I'd asked how he met my mother."

"Tell us about your relationship with Drew," Aeron said.

Marsden stiffened. "There isn't one."

"You stare at him with the longing lust of a lover," Morgan said.

"You want to kiss him," Aeron added.

"Touch him."

"Make sweet love to him."

"Drew and Marsden sitting in a tree, touching each other inappropriately," they sang.

"But you can't." Morgan nudged his shoulder. "It's forbidden."

"You're Romeo and Juliet," Aeron said. "Only..."

"Male."

"Immortal."

"Alive."

"Leave me alone," Marsden said. "I haven't had enough Red Bull to tune into your frequency. I gig at his pub."

"It can't be good for business," Aeron said.

"He's trying to earn his father's forgiveness so he can return to Heaven. Corrupted souls are worth more."

"You can't have him," Morgan said. "You know what'll happen if you do."

"I'll be lectured?"

"Burnt."

"Sizzled," Aeron chipped in.

"Scorched beyond recognition," Morgan continued. "He'll lose his job."

"His status."

"His life."

Marsden stood. "Isn't killing angels part of the plan?"

Morgan smiled like a hungry snake. "Oh don't worry, the fortune cookies of life already know his fate."

"Am I allowed to know?"

"And ruin the surprise ending? I know you can resist any torture your father inflicts on you, but Daddy War never tried loosening your tongue with a hunky angel."

"This is absurd. The destroyer of mankind and a disgraced angel who thinks the parasites are worth saving? Not even Hollywood could make that match convincing. My interest in him is purely strategic."

"Good." Aeron stood and slammed his hand into Marsden's crotch then squeezed. Perhaps it wasn't the most dignified way to discipline him, but it was effective.

Marsden swore and doubled over, gripping Aeron's arms.

"Now we've sorted that misunderstanding, you can find somewhere new to hang out." He released him.

Marsden dropped to his knees, screwing his eyes shut.

"Glad we had this chat," Morgan said. "We don't spend as much time with you as we should. You're more competent than the others; we forget you need guidance." Marsden rolled onto his side, curling up. Morgan rolled her eyes. "Stop acting like it's the worst pain in the world. You've never experienced childbirth."

"Neither have you." His voice was hoarse as he forced himself to his feet.

"I'm disappointed in you. Of all the team we had to have this talk with, I never thought it'd be you. You're so...soulless."

"Cold," Aeron supplied.

"My money was on Aeron. He's such a romantic."

Marsden snorted. "I melted at his tender touch."

Morgan swept his legs away. He hit the floor on his back, smacking his head. She crouched and waved a globe under his nose.

"Step out of line again and the next time Aeron touches your little warrior, will be the last time it rises." She rose, pocketing the globe. "All this talking's made me thirsty. Anyone for cocktails?"

"I'd kill for a Slippery Nipple and a chocolate chip cookie," Aeron answered. "Seeing as we're ending the world, it would seem cold not to toast its demise."

CHAPTER 9

Footsteps echoed in the sepulchral street. Orange streetlights gave the area a fake fiery glow, as though Hell claimed the world. Demi stopped by a faded road sign – Nemesis Avenue – and turned around. Deserted pavement greeted her. Shadows whispered nefarious tales of monsters, mayhem and murder. She wished she'd brought her bike but the modelling studio wasn't far from The Bohemian and she needed the exercise. One more inch round her calves and a starving orphan would mistake them for chicken drumsticks and start snacking on them.

Wrapping her coat around her, she walked on, every nerve tingling. An empty bottle clinked against the gutter. Music throbbed to a deafening bass a few streets over then faded, like a heart that could no longer beat. Wind ran its fingers through her hair and tugged her clothes like an impatient lover.

Footsteps.

She whirled around. A man stood behind her clutching a McFry's bag. Grease stained the brown paper. She shuddered. He looked like the product from an illicit encounter between an egg and a sausage roll.

"You were at The Razor gig," he said. "I should call the fire brigade because you're seriously hot."

Why is it always the creepy perverts who find me attractive? Am I giving off a silent alarm only they can hear? "Did you get that off CheesyChatUpLines.com?"

He stepped forwards. Demi stepped back into a wall bordering an alley.

"Why are you alone on a night like this?"

"I didn't realise Tuesdays were chaperone night. There's never a boogeyman around when you want one."

His breathing quickened. Sweat glistened on his face. "It'll be more fun if we walk together. I'll protect you."

"Hmm, poison my oxygen inhaling your grease or take my chances with perverts? How *is* a lady to choose?" She tapped her lips.

He stepped closer, trapping her against the wall. "Where are you going, all dressed up?"

"Your funeral."

"Stop being a tease. I saw you dancing like a slut. I know you want it."

Demi kneed him in the stomach then spun out of the way and kicked him in the back of the knees. As his legs buckled, she rammed her heel into his arse, enjoying the grunt as he hit the pavement and dropped his bag.

"It's *you* who needs protecting. From *me*. I have the right to walk down the street without being harassed. But since you've tried to take that right away, I'm going to return the favour." She checked her stilettos for damage. "These shoes cost some poor woman one hundred pounds. She'll be devastated if you've broken them." She booted him in the stomach. "I want to hear you screaming my name. But it won't be from pleasure. It'll be for mercy."

"There's no need to be a bitch. Crazy dyke."

"Oh my *god*. Your ego's bigger than your tighty whities. You seriously think the only reasons I'm not interested are because I'm crazy, or gay? How's this for a startling revelation, Sleazeburger? You're as desirable as regurgitated ratatouille and I don't find raping tendencies attractive in a man."

He tried to rise so she gripped his collar and placed her lips on his. He whimpered as black electricity flowed from him into her, his body shrinking two inches while her bones became slightly less visible. He struggled, trying to push her away.

"What's wrong? Thought you wanted to kiss me."

She released him and he scrabbled into the dark alley. She grabbed his bag, the whiff of processed meat turning her stomach. Once they were safe from witnesses, she knocked him onto his back.

"Listen up, Burger Ming, there's only one reason I'm in this cesspit of a city, and it's not to get raped by the Pilsbury Dough Boy."

She produced a set of balances from her bag and pressed the top of them. A spike shot out from the base. She rammed it into his chest. He screamed, blood spreading across his t-shirt like a ketchup stain from a burst packet. Instead of measuring bowls, her balances had spiked balls. Demi took one of the balls and stretched the chain, revealing razor wire. She wrapped it around his right wrist and secured the ball to a drainpipe. She did the same with the other chain, tying his left wrist to a wheelie bin.

"Please, let me go."

"You wanted to be alone with me. Think of me as a genie, granting your wishes." She perched on his stomach like a spider on an upturned bowl.

"I won't say anything, I promise."

"You won't tell people you planned to rape me? How noble of you to spare my dignity. Don't worry, your secret's safe – dead men can only communicate through a medium." His eyes widened. "What have we here?" She opened his paper bag. "I'm impressed they bother packaging this crap. It'd be a shame for you to waste money on slop because you failed to assault me, especially when starving children would kill for this fine fare."

"I didn't try to assault you!"

"Had I been a mortal woman, you would've dragged me down this alley and raped me as your burger grew as cold and soggy as your cocktail sausage. It's the only way it'll get any fun time. Unfortunately for you, I'm the third

Horseman of the Apocalypse and the only stiff here tonight will be your bloated corpse. Now open wide and say 'burger'."

She forced his mouth open and rammed the burger in. He spluttered and tried rolling away. The wire gnawed his wrists, blood trickling down his skin.

"Wanna make things...saucy?" She tore the ketchup packet and squeezed the ketchup into his mouth. "I know you want it – why else would you have bought it? After all, there's no difference between eating for enjoyment and being force-fed against your will."

She grimaced as her finger punctured the meat. He choked, saliva dribbling down his chin with the ketchup. She took a photo on her phone.

"Looks like you bit off more than you can chew. I'll post this inspiring pic at my slimming club. It could be my logo. 'What goes in the mouth soon heads south'. The twins can have it for their scrapbook page 'Eating Out'." Her face contorted as a slimy piece of lettuce made a bid for freedom. "You must eat your greens." She gingerly picked it up between her thumb and fingernail and dropped it into his mouth. "Would you like fries with that?"

She fished fries out of the box and pushed them in. Tears glistened in his eyes. He coughed, mushed meat spraying out.

"Eww! This isn't a meal for two!" Retching, she shovelled more fries in. "They could've supplied a fork. If my skin absorbs this and I get fat, I'll dig up your corpse and feed it through the mincer. They could turn you into sausages – they're filled with disgusting remains."

His face reddened as he gurgled.

"Fancy washing this glorious meal down with the house wine?" She tipped his cup over his face.

Ice cubes hit him in the eye. He gasped as he drowned in cola.

"This isn't what I'd have chosen for a last meal, but you seem to be enjoying it. I never realised eating out could be fun!" Demi wedged the remaining fries into his mouth. He flailed. "Be glad you didn't ask them to jumbosize you. Your pleasure would last all night." Demi removed her nail file from her pocket and filed her nails. "This is the most disgusting thing I've ever seen and I saw my father sitting in a bathtub eating his weight in chocolate éclairs." She straightened her fingers, examining her nails. "Hurry up, I've got a modelling shoot."

Tears streaked his face.

"Crying will make it harder to breathe. You're like all bullies – gaining pleasure from other people's pain and humiliation but react badly when someone returns the favour. You planned to do vile things to me and I would've lived with those memories my entire life, and been branded a slut, a liar and a tease because I've dared to wear an outfit that doesn't completely cover my skin. If you can't walk down the street without raping someone, you're the problem. If I'd begged you to stop, you would've ignored me, so I'm ignoring you. Karma's a bitch. And so am I. I just work quicker." She pinched his nose shut. "Didn't your mother teach you not to chew with your mouth open?"

He thrashed, fear staining his bulging eyes, his face a fetching shade of Tomato Tranquillity. He lay still, food tumbling from his parted lips. Ketchup streaked his chin. Demi filed the nails on her other hand then checked his pulse.

"Cheer up, your family could sue McFry's. They might name a burger after you: the McPervert."

She rose, collected her balances and sauntered out of the alley. Morgan blocked the mouth.

"I'd love to chat but I have places to go, lives to ruin." Demi smiled.

"I'm glad you're working. You get a sparkly smiley for that death. You've got something on you."

Demi scowled at the cola stains on her coat. "I'll send his family the cleaning bill. Compensation for the distress I've suffered."

She reached the modelling agency and stopped to study photos of beautiful people in the window.

"You might be pretty, but you'd never inspire genocide."

She pushed open the door and entered, smiling at the receptionist. "Sorry I'm late. My self-defence class overran."

"Not a problem, take a seat."

Demi sat, scrutinising the two women in the waiting area. She bit her lip, insults vying for pole position. Should she attack their appalling fashion sense, their carbon copy hairstyles or their looks? This was a modelling agency. Looks would hurt the most.

She nudged the girl beside her. "I *love* your outfit. Really enhances your orange skin tone. Oompa-Loompa is the exact shade I want for my living room." She pulled her phone out and snapped a photo of the girl. "Now I can colour match."

The girl burst into tears and fled.

Demi smiled at the woman sitting opposite. "I like how they feature mature women. After all, older women buy clothes too."

She glared. "I'm twenty seven."

"I'm so *sorry*! You have the haggard look of an overworked mother whose kids are now in school so she has time for a second shot at stardom. Your confidence is *inspiring*. Did your husband buy you a modelling shoot for your birthday? One of those discount specials on those voucher sites?"

"*Excuse* me?"

"Demi Ceres," a man called.

She patted the woman's hand. "Word of advice – lose the granny cardi. It accentuates your wrinkles. Wrinkles are only cute on dogs."

Demi followed the man into a studio. She stood before the camera and removed her coat, revealing a figure-hugging black wet look dress with a plunging neckline. Fishnet stockings complemented her outfit. She flicked her hair.

The photographer smiled. "Beautiful. Have you done much modelling?"

"First time."

"You're a natural. I've photographed hundreds of women. I can tell star quality."

She rolled her eyes at his overcooked lines. Who did he think she was? A naïve teenager? A desperate, attention seeking housewife? "My father said I was born to take over the world."

CHAPTER 10

Drew dismounted his black and chrome Harley Davidson and entered Salvation. The stained glass saints had been replaced by stained glass alcohol brands. The organ's pipes were now bubble tubes. Drew headed to the office in the vestry and knocked on the door. A blonde woman in her thirties opened it. He almost laughed at her white skirt suit and bun hair style. All she needed to complete her stereotypical secretary look was an affair with the boss.

"Is Michael in?"

"Do you have an appointment?" She cast a disdainful look at his ripped grey jeans, slate military jacket and black t-shirt with a motif of a skeleton on horseback.

"I don't need an appointment to see my brother."

He followed her in and waited while she knocked on another door. She opened it, announced Drew then returned to her desk, tucking her silver choker beneath her collar.

Drew entered the office. A mahogany desk dominated the room, a leather executive chair behind it. A bag of golf clubs which cost more than his pub, rested against a large chrome and glass bookcase. Tropical plants shaded the white walls. A black leather settee sat against one wall. The blue carpet felt soft under his combat boots. The walls boasted framed photos of Michael posing with VIPs who frequented his club.

Drew slumped into the small chair opposite the desk.

Michael's slicked back black hair and expensive Italian suit belonged in a 1930s gangster film. A gold choker adorned his neck. Gold balances sat on the desk in front of him and a gold sword decorated the wall behind the desk.

Michael smirked. "To what do I owe this pleasure? Have you run out of souls to save?"

"The Horsemen are here."

"That's no way to greet your brother."

"If I wanted a social chat, I'd write on your Friendzone page. We need to stop the Horsemen."

Michael leaned forwards, clasping his hands. "How do you propose we do that?"

"If I knew, I wouldn't be here. Google wasn't helpful."

"I see time on Earth hasn't cured your sharp tongue. Father should send you downstairs. While we're on the subject of your bad behaviour, could you stop blinding people? We can't maintain a low profile if you're flashing your halo to all and sundry."

"Nobody will believe them." Drew ran his hand over his head. "Can I have angels to slow the Horsemen 'til reinforcements arrive?"

"You can have three."

Drew raised his eyebrows. "There are *five* Horsemen."

"I could've spared four, but Pestilence killed Joshua. I didn't think he was capable. One angel for Pestilence, one for Famine and one to help you with Warquest, or whatever he calls himself."

"Marsden."

"Cute. They've given themselves human names. Unfortunately you can't do anything about Death – it's part of life."

"They have a world to destroy and you're giving me *three* angels? What the hell are you doing with the others? Making them mine for gold?"

Michael raised an eyebrow. "Lemures isn't the only city in the world. Angels are needed elsewhere."

"Give me the angel out there. You don't need a secretary. I need a warrior."

"Harriett's not trained for warfare."

"I'm not deploying her to Afghanistan. She could join Famine's slimming group then sabotage her methods."

"When will you learn? This is not a democracy. Harriett stays with me."

"Ordering alcohol is *far* more important than stopping the Apocalypse. Or is your plan to get everyone so drunk they don't notice the world ending?"

Michael's eye twitched. "I'll send Mark, John and Jael to your shithole later."

"What about Eden?"

"He's in prison."

"*What?*"

"You're both being made an example of. Father couldn't send him down here with you to reform your mini rebellion, so kept him upstairs. Teach the others the price of disobedience."

"Are you aware Pestilence deals in your club?"

"I'm keeping my enemies close. Isn't that why you let Warquest gig at your pub?"

"I'm following orders."

"So you *do* know how to obey? Or do you only listen to orders you like? The order states you can't *ban* Warquest. It mentions nothing about *befriending* him."

Drew glared. "Are your orders to corrupt people's souls through debauchery? I'm getting close so I can learn what they're planning. The Horseman of War won't divulge battle secrets to the enemy."

"Be careful you don't get so close you forget which side you're on."

"I could say the same for you. I thought you worked for Father, not the fallen."

Michael picked up his gold pen. "See yourself out."

Drew stood. "Enjoy your comfortable office. It'll be no good to you when we're dead."

***

"There are growing fears of a new drug that's hit the streets." The newsreader's voice was as solemn as his beige tie. *"Three people have died after injecting the latest party drug, Red Mist, which is being distributed in Lemures's clubs and rave scenes. Sixteen year old Gareth Farley suffered lesions over his face and body after injecting the drug in Salvation nightclub. He died two hours later in hospital. A post mortem is scheduled for the morning."*

"Good work." Aeron added three marks below Mac's name on a serviette in Grease Lightning, Lemures's American 1950s style diner. "Low on death count, but every new venture has teething problems."

"I wanted them to name it after me," Mac grouched.

"No-one knows who you are," Morgan pointed out.

Grease Lightning was the only circular building on Witches Walk. Four hundred years ago, the street witnessed witch trials, where witches had to crawl continuously. If they stopped, they were drowned. If they passed, they were burned at the stake.

The Horsemen sat in a booth shaped like a Cadillac's back seat. The fin sides contained brake lights and flashing indicators. Headlights shone on the walls and ceiling.

"If they named it after you, people would expect a McFry's Surprise with every needle," Morgan said. "'Mac' doesn't inspire terror."

"We'd inspire terror," Aeron said.

"We should name a drug after ourselves."

"Aergan."

"Moron."

They laughed and high-fived each other.

"McPus has a certain ring to it," Morgan said. "McPlague."

"The Deluxe McDeath," Aeron suggested.

"With added Syphilis Sauce."

"Ooh spicy. Why's it so popular, Mac? Do they see flying music notes? Does everyone become more attractive? Does it give them wings?"

"They feel spaced out, feverish then become riddled with disease," Mac replied. "The disease depends on their immune system – plague, smallpox, flu, TB."

"No wonder it's so popular with the kids!"

"Fun in a tube." Morgan grinned. "That'll top this year's Christmas list. Goodbye Harry Potter, hello putrid sores. It doesn't sound like a party drug, unless wakes count as parties."

Mac scratched a lesion on his arm. "Now it's newsworthy, clubbers will try it."

"You need a catchy slogan." Aeron drew on his serviette.

"Sick is sick," Morgan suggested.

"A jab is fab."

"I manufacture and distribute it. You want a slogan, hire a PR guy," Mac said.

"Mars could write a jingle. Best-selling products need a memorable jingle," Aeron said.

"Is their pus contagious?" Morgan asked.

Mac shrugged. "Mine is and the drug is all me."

"You're like a sperm donor."

"Only more disgusting." Aeron grimaced. "You give birth to pus not placenta."

"Humans give to birth to babies, not placenta."

"No-one would want to kiss his 'babies' heads during an election campaign."

"Should I sell more tonight?" Mac interrupted.

"Try a different city. The cops might be hunting you now a teenager's died."

"Two men died earlier this week. They didn't make the news."

"They weren't sweet sixteen with everything to live for."

"He injected my drug – I doubt he had much to live for." Mac spun the gear knob salt shaker.

Aeron studied the menu as the news story moved to whoever was voted off *Celebrity Dirty Washing*. He went to the dashboard counter and returned with two cocktails.

"A 'Sloe Comfortable Screw Against The Wall' for you, m'lady and a 'Blow Job' for me." He set them down.

"They have umbrellas, how cute." Morgan took a sip. "Mmm, sensuous."

Aeron tried his cocktail. "Meh. I've had better Blow Jobs." Mac looked at him. "This cocktail bar we visited in Hawaii did amazing Blow Jobs. Their Corpse Reviver was to die for. Their Screaming Orgasm was so creamy and heavenly."

"Everything tastes like charcoal mixed with catarrh to me." Mac sighed.

Morgan pulled a face. "Way to kill the sunny atmosphere, Catarrh Hero."

"I'm going to cook up another Mac special for the weekend."

"Use a different needle exchange centre," Aeron said. "Saint Celibate's conscience will insist he does his angelic duty and toss your pimply arse in jail."

"I'll wipe out the prison population, be hailed a hero."

"How public spirited of you."

"The drugs trade is rife inside. I'll be King of the Wing."

"You're becoming quite the entrepreneur," Morgan remarked. She waved. "Waiter! Another Sloe Comfortable Screw Against The Wall please. The last one left me satisfied and wanting more."

"It's time I had a Screaming Orgasm," Aeron said. "I've held out long enough."

Mac trudged out, shoulders hunched, his grey hood covering his face.

"Do mortals have to put up with miserable colleagues?" Aeron asked. "It's depressing."

"I think it's what happens to mortals. Utter misery 'til they die."

"Maybe it's being surrounded by psychopaths." Marsden slid into a car seat beside Aeron, facing the diner.

"What brings you to our table?" Aeron asked.

"Can't I sit with my favourite colleagues without being interrogated?"

Aeron squeezed him, kissing his head. "That's so sweet."

"Not really," Morgan answered. "He wants to see Demi strung up like tinsel and not even Mac likes Mac."

"I want to see Demi's *insides* strung up like tinsel. Or wrapped around her like she's a Christmas tree," Marsden said.

"Can we get you a drink?" Aeron asked. "You should try a Kick in the Balls."

Marsden played with the menu. "I'm off fluids."

"Ohhhh, are you pissing fire?"

"Razor blades wrapped in barbed wire."

"Sorry about that, but without discipline, people run amok. If it's any consolation, you're quite a...handful." He winked.

Marsden stared at him.

"Now you've stopped sulking, you can return to your job," Morgan said. "Do some karaoke."

"I've been dying to show off my 'Barbie Girl' rendition."

"We do a great version," Aeron enthused. "Morg goes really deep on the male's part."

Marsden laughed. "I'm going to ruin people's late night shopping and Christmas parties in Misery."

"While you're there, look for somewhere to live," Morgan said. "We're starting to resemble a terrorist cell, without the religion and blowing ourselves up."

"Make Demi go."

"She needs to be seen by the right people."

"Lemures isn't exactly fashion capital of the world."

"The origami paper decider chose *you*." Aeron pointed at him.

"Mac can spread his poison anywhere. He'll fit in with the homeless. You two are transient."

"I'm sensing resistance," Morgan said. "What does *this* city have that other cities don't?" She rubbed her chin. "I'm guessing it's not the cocktails."

"The dinosaur museum?" Aeron suggested.

"I've been here longer than any of you. I shouldn't be the one who leaves," Marsden said. "I'm happy to find somewhere else to live, but it'll be here. Where I can keep an eye on you."

Morgan raised her eyebrows. "It's cute the way you think you're in charge. And extremely irritating. You're *not* in charge, Sir Stabalot and you never will be. You should see someone about your inability to accept things. You may have military training and strategies, but that makes you a good advisor. *Not* a leader."

"How does a smiley face achievement chart make you two good leaders?"

"It boosts morale. Gives everyone something to strive for. You're like your daddy – a firm believer in the stick over the carrot."

"You won't like where I'll stick your carrot."

Morgan made a shooing gesture. "Go kill someone, cheer yourself up. You're curdling our cocktails."

Marsden stood. "Fine. Forget ruining Christmas parties in Misery, I'll create a scene so beautiful, it can go on the front of your scrapbook."

"Sorry, that spot's taken by our glorious tree," Aeron said.

"By the time I'm done, everyone will know we're here."

CHAPTER 11

Marsden's bike sped through Lemures, weaving between cars and swerving away at the last moment. Its hungry engine growled as Marsden prowled the streets, desire for slaughter igniting his veins. Lights and music emerged from the night sky, as if Hell had opened its gates, enticing people to its Carnival of the Damned.

Marsden killed the engine and flicked out the sword kickstand. He yanked off his black and red helmet. A silhouetted rearing horse and a rider brandishing a sword decorated it. Raising his hood, he marched towards Winter Wonderland, his guitar burdening his back, yearning to unleash its music on the crowd. His fingertips itched and burned as he leaned on the outdoor ice rink.

A blood soaked scene tantalised his mind: *riding through the park, his sword experiencing its first taste of mortal blood. Screams of joy turning to screams of terror. Winter Wonderland becoming a battlefield, the white scenery now red.*

Three seventeen year old girls skated past him repeatedly, giggling. The blonde fell, shrieking like she'd fallen into a wood chipper, her skirt riding up to display thighs the colour of bruises. Marsden laughed.

Her friends helped her up, whispering and shooting glances his way.

"Sorry to destroy your Twilight fantasy, but I'm not a brooding, romantic hero of teenage fiction, troubled by a bloody past but ready to leap to your rescue, fangs showing, crotch bulging. Don't teenage girls date guys who

88

are centuries old and anaemic?" He lowered his voice. "I'd rather kill you than save you."

"You play the guitar?" the brunette asked.

"No, I carry it to impress people."

"Play us a song."

Two hundred people infested Necropolis Park. Perfect for a slaughter party. They could RSVP at the wake.

He played the raw, upbeat 'Walking Wounded', hypnotising them with his husky voice. Two teenage groups spilled onto the rink, trading insults and shoves, poisoned words inflicting deeper wounds than the physical blows.

Marsden played 'Fire and Ice', a song of scorching rage and cold hatred. People flocked around the rink, their phones immortalising the mayhem. Security guards rushed to break it up, but vanished in the throng. Three teenagers fell, toppling a toddler. She bawled as her mother pulled her free. Her father administered justice to the nearest boy, his blade piercing the boy's head. Blood snaked down his temple, slipping across the ice.

Two teenagers knocked the father down, kicking him until he surrendered his life. His wife screamed for help.

Nobody listened.

By the strong man game, a couple's past misdeeds returned to haunt them. The woman slapped her boyfriend across the face. He battered her head with the hammer until her spurting blood proved his superiority. The bell chimed his victory.

Marsden moved towards the ribcage-shaped Helter Skelter, the slide a tongue spiralling around the bones. The girls followed him into its shadow. Two fathers argued from the top of the slide, insisting it was their child's turn. Marsden played 'Death Rites'. One father plummeted, landing at Marsden's feet like a broken marionette. The victor's child used the slide, stepping over the man's body on his way back up.

On the Dodgems, two people ganged up against the person guarding the ride, crushing his legs between their cars. He fell to the floor when one reversed. They barged him into a wall until his screams died.

Two women crashed into the huge Christmas tree that guarded proceedings. Branches shook as they grappled amongst the lights and baubles, their venomous shrieks smothering the overplayed Christmas songs.

During 'Broken Lives', families bickered over Christmas, the kids and whose turn it was to put the bins out. Children fought each other when it emerged one was getting an iPad for Christmas whilst the others had to settle for toys. Marsden switched to the chilling yet sensuous 'Bleeding Scars'.

"I saw him first." The redhead elbowed her friends.

"He's looking at me." The blonde smiled at Marsden.

"He's looking at your breasts. They're more attractive than your face."

"I was imagining what you'd look like dismembered," he muttered. "But sure, convince yourself a thirty year old man fancies you."

"You're jealous I get more attention from guys."

"Because you shove your tits in their faces." The redhead cupped her breasts, pushing them out whilst mimicking a whiny voice. "'Pay me attention so I feel loved'. You're pathetic."

"Least I'm not a virgin."

"Oh, of all the things I could be, you think being a virgin is worse? More guys have scored in your vagina than in the basketball ring in school. At this rate, you'll be getting a positive pregnancy test with your A Levels."

Why did people waste their lives on soaps when real life was more entertaining? When some of the cast wouldn't walk away when the credits finish rolling? The brunette grabbed Marsden's arm. He pushed her away. She yanked his head down for a kiss. He swung his guitar into her face. She hit the ground, her life seeping into the mud.

The redhead knocked the blonde over and straddled her. "I'm sick of you bragging about your conquests. I'm sick of you *constantly* admiring your reflection. And I'm sick of being the only person who can see what a shallow, selfish *bitch* you are!" With each sentence, she slammed the shrieking blonde's head against the ground. "I'm sick to *death* of hearing about your boring life on repeat. At least now there'll be two minutes where your voice isn't piercing my ears like a smashed fire alarm!"

The redhead yanked off her shoe and beat her friend's face with it. The heel punctured the blonde's eyeball, tearing it out of her face. She screamed, weeping scarlet tears. The redhead cleaned her shoe on her friend's skirt then sat back, breathing hard as the blonde's blood pooled around her head like a crimson halo. The redhead staggered away, wiping her hands on her jeans.

Every guitar string snapped, the crowd surrendering to the chaos and darkness rotting them inside.

"It's time to make your empire bleed."

Marsden stalked the redhead through the fighting crowd to the cuddly toy stall.

"Excuse me."

She turned, smiling. He reached up, plucked a teddy off a hook and offered it to her. As she took it, he lifted her by the waist and impaled her head on the hook. She thrashed, blood spilling from her mouth. The teddy dropped to the floor, its face splattered with crimson rain. She dangled like a twisted Halloween prop among the cute prizes.

Marsden ran to the rink, grabbed a spare skate and vaulted over the side. He pulled an injured man to his feet, slitting his throat with the skate's blade. Marsden tossed him aside and stalked a woman, the skate dripping a bloody trail. She crawled away, pleading. He grabbed her legs, flipped her onto her back and plunged the blade into her throat, almost severing her head from her body. She choked on the ruby necklace adorning her neck.

A young man edged towards the exit. Marsden shadowed him and rammed the tip of the skate's blade up through his chin. The man collapsed, his blood creating a marble effect on the ice. Marsden dipped his fingers in it and drew a large horseshoe with a sword through it.

A woman hanged from the Christmas tree like an ornamental angel, twinkling fairy lights forming a festive noose.

"Help…me."

Marsden tugged her legs until she stopped struggling.

A man plunged from the top of the Ferris wheel, his head shattering on a cart before he landed in a heap of twisted limbs beside the cuddly toy stall.

"I saw what you did." A man pointed at Marsden. "The police are coming."

Marsden punched him, sending him stumbling backwards onto a carousel horse. He swiped an unopened toffee apple from the ground and planted it in the man's eye like a flag of victory.

Injured or dead people lay amongst dropped burger wrappers and empty paper cups, their lives discarded like the half-eaten food squashed underfoot. A man groaned and slumped over the candyfloss machine, his blood seeping into the pink sugar. Marsden turned the heat up then held the man's head in the bowl. The caramelised sugar wrapped around his face, burning his skin and forming a gruesome mask. The candyfloss smothered his screams. Marsden released him and surveyed the carnage, his demons finally silent.

"Someone's been busy," Morgan remarked, a sickly green carousel horse carrying her to Marsden. She jumped off, her coat billowing. The raven flew from the horse's head onto Morgan's shoulder.

"Who'd have thought Winter Wonderland could be fun? I thought it was for kids."

Aeron slid down the Helter Skelter with a young woman. "I thought you were turning to the dark side." He fished her globe out of her handbag, shook it then shrunk it. "It's amazing parents will kill each other because their child was robbed of a turn on the slide. Parenting here is so different from Purgatory."

"I'll never understand humans."

"You don't have to understand them, sweetums." Morgan wiped blood from Marsden's face. "You just have to kill them."

"I hope Santa's updating his naughty or nice list." Aeron took a globe off a child. "I saw you kick your friend to death because he took your toffee apple. At least his daddy dealt out old-school justice to you. I miss those vigilante days. People are too busy playing video games or watching TV to hang someone from a tree." He grabbed the candyfloss man and ripped a chunk of the pink sugar from his face with his teeth. "Weird. I bet that's what clouds taste like."

"This will certainly make the headlines," Morgan said. "You've created a legacy of tragedy that will forever haunt this magical place."

Marsden shrugged. "My advent calendar suggested it."

Morgan plucked a globe from the toffee apple victim's pocket. She shook it then pushed the marble into the raven's pouch. She yanked the toffee apple out, took a bite then offered it to the raven, who pecked it.

Marsden re-strung his guitar as he traipsed out of Necropolis Park. Santa tumbled out of his toppled sleigh, his candy canes snapping beneath him. Marsden swooped to snatch a cane. Santa groaned. Marsden snapped the cane and stabbed it into his neck.

"Drew's right – Christmas *is* the season of death."

CHAPTER 12

"Headlines this morning: tragedy at Winter Wonderland; new drug, Red Mist claims two more lives; another celebrity is named in the child abuse scandal; and we find out who washed their last load in Celebrity Dirty Washing."

Marsden stopped playing his guitar and leaned over from the foot of the bed to turn up the TV in Travel Inn. "Ooh *Celebrity Dirty Washing*. The most exciting programme since *Paint Drying: Live!*"

"Scenes of devastation have left Lemures in mourning after last night's tragic events at Winter Wonderland in Necropolis Park," the newsreader announced in a voice grim enough for funerals, natural disasters and wedding speeches. *"What started as a dream turned into a nightmare as fights erupted in this family-friendly event. Police were saddened and horrified by the scene that greeted them after receiving emergency calls from distressed witnesses."*

"Show a genius at work."

Film flashed up of a deserted Wonderland; the ground covered in scattered litter, the rides silent and still. Crime scene tape fluttered in the breeze. Body bags awaited collection. Blood-stained ice skates lay abandoned near the rink. The camera zoomed in on the blood splattered teddy.

"Nice cinematography – rams the devastation home. This footage will feature in Cannes."

"It's not clear what started these senseless acts of violence."

"The second Horseman of the Apocalypse."

"A fight broke out between two teenage gangs and spilled onto the rink." The female reporter moved amongst the horses on the carousel, her face as brightly painted as the ride. *"Most suffered minor injuries, but fifteen year old Darren Whittaker died at the scene from a head injury."* His smiling picture flashed up. She recited the roll call of the dead and how they met their grisly end in the 'Fairground of Horror'. *"Police worked through the night identifying bodies. The youngest victim was just eight years old."*

It cut to shots of witnesses recounting the event, some looking more delighted than distressed.

"Our correspondent at the hospital has this to say—"

"I've gained two pounds!" Demi rushed from the bathroom in contusion-coloured lingerie, clutching her scales.

"Did you forget to put your organs in when you put your skin suit on? If you get wet, you'll go see-through."

"Look at those figures!" She thrust the scales under his nose. "It says 'fat cow'."

"You need to buy nicer scales, Skeletor." Marsden pushed them away. "How did you get in here? I put the plugs in the sink and bath. Shouldn't you be in The Bohemian ruining rich people's self-esteem and convincing them water has calories?"

Demi flung the scales down, stood on them and pinched her body. "What did I do wrong?"

"How much does spite weigh?" He put his guitar down.

"I bet it was sucking the life out of that creep in the alleyway."

"You did *what* to a creep in an alleyway? I thought you were a lady."

"This isn't funny!" She slapped his arm. "How can I lead the masses if I'm as fat as them? The kiss of death is exactly how my father got so fat."

He grabbed her wrist. "Oh my god! I can only get my hand around your wrist one and a half times! You porker!"

He smacked her arse as she lunged for him. "Look at the flubber fly!" She rained blows on him as he protected his head and laughed. "Did I squeeze a boob or a fat pocket?"

"I'm a *whale*!"

"Don't lie on a beach – they'll never float you back into the ocean."

"Two. Whole. *Pounds*!"

Marsden released her and pulled out his phone. "Is that *Paparazzi* magazine? I have breaking news. Demi Ceres has gained two pounds!...I can get a lingerie shot...it looks like someone's put the Pilsbury Dough Boy in the Stripper Chic Collection. Actually, it's hard to see the sexy lingerie – her arse has swallowed most of it...what do you mean you don't know her?...you print celebrities nobody's heard of all the time."

Demi snatched the phone. When she saw there was nobody on the other end, she hurled it at him. It bounced off his forehead.

"Ow!"

"How much do you weigh?"

"I don't know. I don't have body image issues."

"You should. You have more scars than a determined self-harmer. They ruin a perfect body."

"Ouch."

"Get on the scales, Scarface." She tried pulling him off the bed.

"I'm a *guy*, Bone Jangles. You can't compare your weight to mine. I have muscles – they weigh more than fat. Ask Mac. You can compete to see who's wasted away more. I bet it's him. He's been taking his own blood. Donate a pint then weigh again."

Demi flopped onto the bed, her arm draped over her forehead. Her ribs protruded like skeletal mouth of a basking shark. "My modelling career is *over*."

"Don't get upset; you never had a modelling career." Marsden stabbed his plectrum between Demi's toes. She yelled and kicked his back. "I've made top billing on the news and all you're doing is moaning. You're like a storm cloud pissing on my sunshine."

"You played the guitar. Big wow. Ten year olds can do that."

"I killed people with an ice skate, a toffee apple and candyfloss. And I killed Santa."

"I force-fed a man his burger and watched him choke to death. He took longer to die than any of *your* victims. For the Horseman of War, you're pretty merciful in your executions."

"Don't take your weight gain out on me, Captain Flabulous. If this was about enjoying ourselves, I would've made medieval tortures seem like a massage. It's about decimating the population. We don't have time to sight-see."

Demi rubbed his back with her foot. "Speaking of fun – sex burns calories." She rose onto all fours, wriggling her arse and looking more like a skeleton in a scare attraction than an erotic tease. "Spank me. I've been a *very* bad girl."

"I didn't want you before, I certainly don't want you now you're fat."

"Cock womble!" She thumped his arm.

He pushed her down. "I'm going to celebrate making headline news."

"No-one cares."

"At least I've achieved something. All you've done is gain weight."

She kicked his thigh then buried her face in the pillow. The chains on his black trousers jingled as he sang Queen's 'Fat Bottomed Girls' and danced out of the room.

***

Maybe someone spiked her water. It could be her new shampoo. What if coconut and almonds were filled with calories? Demi dressed in designer exercise clothes and stomped out, nearly colliding with the Ooze. Why did he have to be as disgusting on the outside as he was on the inside?

"Watch where you're going, Spotted Dick. I can't afford to fumigate my clothes."

"I made the news again."

"Let me guess – someone saw you and now believes aliens are real. Please say Area 51 is going to strap you to a table and probe you? Donating your body to medical science would be a kindness."

"My drug is killing people."

"Drugs kill people every day. They don't make statues of the manufacturers." She turned around. "Wear a gas mask when talking to me in future. Your breath stinks like a mouldy armpit and I keep getting distracted by pus-filled pimples on your face. I can't decide whether they should be squeezed or your whole face acid dipped."

Mac's shoulders slumped and he trudged into Travel Inn. The receptionist's smile froze. He pulled his hood further over his face, coughed into his hand then wiped it over the door handle.

Demi shuddered and left. "Note to self – wear rubber gloves. Or melt his hands off."

She parked her bike outside the gym and marched inside, the two pounds burdening her skinny frame. She headed to the treadmills. A woman laboured on the treadmill beside her, her reddened skin glistening like a glazed doughnut.

"I gained two pounds," Demi moaned. "I'm not leaving 'til I've worked them off."

"I kept buying clothes in the size I used to be, convinced I'd slim into them. I'm now two sizes bigger again. My husband says I look great but I feel too unattractive to be intimate with him. He'll find someone else if I keep gaining weight."

Demi discreetly rolled her eyes. Did she look like a therapist who cared about people's feelings? "Overshare!

If he leaves you over anything, it'll be your moaning," she murmured. "Can I offer advice?" The woman nodded. "Buy control underwear. It'll stop you wobbling when you run."

The woman glanced down before increasing the treadmill's speed. Demi kept pace. Through the window in front of her, she watched people entering and leaving the gym. Humans were hideous. It was a miracle they found someone desperate enough to mate with them.

After half an hour, she switched to the elliptical. A gym instructor loitered nearby. She beckoned him over.

"Could you show me how to use this?" She tuned out while he explained it in language befitting idiots. "You must work out loads."

"Perks of working here – free gym membership."

"That *is* an advantage. Now you've hit thirty, the weight will pile on."

"I'm twenty one."

"Sorry, you look older. It's the blossoming beer gut." She patted his stomach.

"Just because I don't have a six pack doesn't mean I have a beer gut."

"It's ok, some people have design flaws. God invented plastic surgery to correct his mistakes."

"Nobody's perfect."

"With that attitude you never will be. I'm sorry if I've offended you – I don't want you to be one of those people who are slim until their twenties are over then they settle down and their waists expand quicker than a pop-up lifeboat. Will your girlfriend still love you when Mr Muscle melts into Mr Blobby?"

"I don't have a girlfriend."

"If you took more care over your appearance, you would. We could go back to mine and I'll give you a *personal* workout. Half an hour of sex burns over 140 calories. More if it's energetic and we moan a lot."

"You probably don't date 'fat' guys." He stormed off.

Demi sighed and climbed onto the elliptical. She *knew* those two pounds would ruin her life. Without them, he would've slung her over his shoulder, marched her into the first aid room and ridden her like a champion. She scowled. If *she* couldn't stay slim, how would she convince the world skinny was worth dying for?

CHAPTER 13

Frost infected the ground, creating patterns resembling diseases under a microscope. Mac stuffed his hands into his hoody pockets and shuffled along Desolation Row, his shoulders hunched. He passed the Razor and the Rosary, convinced the angel's gaze stalked him. A carrier bag floated towards him; a plastic ghost forced to wander the earth for eternity. Rubbish skipped around his feet, like faeries luring him into the perpetual dance. A plastic bottle rolled into the gutter as he walked under the railway bridge.

"Like what you see?" A woman stopped in front of him and spread her burgundy PVC jacket. He eyed her tight black miniskirt and purple cami vest. Goose pimples covered her skin.

He nodded.

She led him into an alley behind Honest Dave's. Toxic black clouds suffocated the moonlight, turning the alley into a hellacious passageway. Stale urine, decaying vegetables and desperation tormented Mac's nostrils. He kicked a half empty beer can. Bins vomited their rotting insides over the ground.

The prostitute smiled, twirling a strand of her afro around her finger. "What do you want?"

"Full sex."

"Fifty."

"Without the glove."

"Seventy. You clean?"

He had more STIs than every clinic in Lemures. Some the Government weren't aware existed yet.

Mac pushed her against the wall and raised her skirt, discovering she wasn't wearing knickers. She moaned, gripping his shoulders as he pushed into her. *Hepatitis? HIV? Syphilis? What STI should you give someone you've just met?*

"Oh god!"

"You don't have to fake it."

"Believe me babes, I'm not faking."

She probably uses the same script for every man.

She cried out as he thrust into her one last time before withdrawing. Pink specs glowed over the top of her legs from his gift of chlamydia. He fastened his trousers and pulled a handful of notes from his pocket. He handed over seventy pounds, avoiding eye contact.

Mac scuttled onto Desolation Row, feeling better now he'd cleared some disease from his system.

"Bit of business?" one girl asked.

She followed him up the railway bridge, the steps clanging. Dark tracks resembling a stitched wound disappeared into the night. The bridge swayed in the wind.

The girl rubbed her arms.

"How much for a blow job?"

"Twenty without a glove, fifteen with."

"Without."

Mac leaned against the side as she took him in her mouth. He tried not to stare at her diminished septum, so studied her dirty blonde hair. *Chlamydia? No. If they both had it, they'd suspect me. Herpes? Gonorrhoea throat infections are difficult to treat, so she could infect plenty of men whilst thinking she had tonsillitis.*

As he came, he infected her with gonorrhoea, watching the red spheres disappear into her mouth. He zipped up his trousers before pulling a twenty from his pocket and stuffing it into her hand. He trotted down the steps, leaving her on the bridge.

He headed to town and shuffled along Gallows Street, nodding at Marsden who busked to late night shoppers. Four girls fought near him.

"Good night?" Mac asked.

"No-one's died."

"What are they fighting over?"

"Me."

"Girls never fight over me. It's so unfair. I'm great in bed. Everyone says so. You're not interested yet they'd kill each other to spend the night with you." Marsden motioned to his guitar, without missing a chord. "They'd fight over you anyway. You're a babe."

"That sounds wrong coming from your blistered lips."

"Musicians don't have to be hot. I'd put your looks to better use."

Marsden laughed. "I'm not giving you my face. I have more important things to do than sleep around. Like destroying the world. People should cower in terror when they see me. Even when their blood is seeping from their bodies, they have this look of disbelief that this face is capable of cruelty." He scowled. "What've you been up to? Spreading influenza on buses? Giving E. coli to kids with their school meals? Have you started the measles outbreak?"

"I'm spreading STIs."

"I'm surprised they don't report you to Public Health the minute they clap eyes on you."

"I use prostitutes. And I keep my hood up. My..."

"Weapon of Mass Infection?"

"Isn't that noticeable."

Marsden sniggered. "That's not something most blokes admit to."

Mac's cheeks burned. "I mean, it doesn't look diseased. I'm nearly broke though."

"Try clubs. Some people will shag anyone so they don't go home alone."

"You could be my wing man."

"You mean your honey trap." Marsden pulled a twenty from his pocket. "Buy yourself someone pretty. And give them something fatal. The world won't end with genital warts."

"Cheers, Mars. You're not as bad as the rest of them."

"Vlad the Impaler isn't as bad as the rest of them."

Mac headed down Curry Lane, passing several curry, kebab and chip shops then ducked down a side alley.

"Alright darling?" a guy asked.

Mac stopped. "Any girls here?"

"Girls are that way." He nodded towards Desolation Row.

Infecting rent boys meant spreading STIs among even more men. "Blow job. Without the glove." The words felt wrong being spoken to a guy.

"Twenty five."

Mac raised his eyebrows. "Inflation's higher this end of the city is it?"

"I'm the vintage French wine compared to the supermarket value range lurking under the bridge."

Mac trailed the guy behind a wheelie bin and undid his trousers. He gripped the bin and closed his eyes, pretending he was with a woman. He gasped as he came, almost forgetting to give the rent boy his surprise present of herpes. The little spiked balls would cling to the base of the guy's nerve cells, planning their attack. Mac tossed cash at him and scurried off, zipping up his trousers.

He headed for Salvation and slipped through the back entrance, palming drugs to regulars and tucking their cash into his back pocket.

A guy stopped him. "Got any Red Mist?"

"Thirty quid." Mac eyed the man's silver choker, recognition tingling his brain like a cold sore.

"*Thirty?*"

"I've got other customers, so if you're not buying, move along. I don't allow window shopping. This isn't that kind of high street." He'd practised that line so his voice wouldn't shake when he said it. Mars said drug dealers were confident, so he had to play the part.

"My mates want some. Give me all your stash."

"Three hundred."

Grumbling, the guy slapped the money into Mac's hand. Mac removed his syringes from a hidden pocket inside his hoody and relinquished them.

Mac weaved through the crowd, waiting for people to move so he could reach the bar. Some clubbers took a while to notice him and longer to move aside, but he finally got to an empty seat. He ordered cider then sat playing with the glass.

"Gonna buy me a drink?" a girl asked.

Her black crop top was so low cut and short, her boobs and belly bulged out either end. As she sat, her skirt rode up, displaying lilac lace knickers. Her face was almost attractive under the makeup and blue lighting.

"I've not seen you before." She edged closer so their knees touched.

"Just moved here."

"Which part?"

"I'm in a hotel until my sales business takes off."

She leaned towards him. "What do you sell?"

"Dreams and nightmares."

She giggled. "Fancy purging your…sins in the confessional? You can give me a wet dream."

He trailed her through the dancers. The curtain was closed, but Mac saw two pairs of feet in the gap. The girl pushed him against the confessional and kissed him. The confessional rocked then fell silent. When the couple left, the girl dragged Mac in and reached under her skirt to pull her knickers off. She rummaged in her handbag and handed him a condom.

"Can we…not use one?" he asked. "I'm allergic."

"Gotta play safe, babes."

He kissed her breast, one hand slipping between her thighs. "If I wear one, I'll swell up then it will be too painful to perform."

"Just for tonight."

He grinned as he thrust into her. She shrieked, panted and shouted the wrong name.

"What's wrong with your skin?" Her nails clawed under his hoody as she forced his face into her breasts, nearly suffocating him.

"I got burnt rescuing my baby sister from a house fire."

"A hero!"

He groaned as he came, infecting her with syphilis. Her legs were decorated with what looked like little worms.

"That was amazing!"

Mac smiled, his warty fingers fondling her breast while she squirmed and grabbed what Morgan called his 'Centre of Disease Control'.

"You wanna come back to mine and make me scream again?"

"This will be a night you'll never forget."

***

"Did you get it all?" Drew emerged from the alley and ushered the angel, Mark, behind a wheelie bin.

"Three hundred pounds! No wonder the drugs trade is popular."

"I'll get you more money."

"How?"

"I'll mug Michael on his way home."

"I'm committing a crime."

"You're saving lives."

"This doesn't feel like we're stopping an Apocalypse. All I'm doing is buying drugs, which allows him to indulge in carnal acts with prostitutes." Mark relinquished the needles.

"Pestilence's drugs kill people; his STIs don't."

"I'm funding fornication! In nine months' time, Pestilence's disease-riddled offspring will turn this world into a horror film."

"In nine months' time, this world won't exist."

Drew rolled up his sleeves and injected the Red Mist into his vein, tossing each empty needle into a tub by his feet. He gasped as the diseases invaded his blood, burning through his insides as though his blood had turned to lava. He doubled over, his body fighting to eject the poison. "You're battling the greater of two evils. I'll persuade the ladies to visit the clinic or by next week, half of Lemures will feature on Government sexual health adverts."

"Shouldn't we…kill the Horsemen?"

"We can't kill them; they belong to Father. Or they used to." Drew leaned against the wall, grimacing as his body battled the disease. He switched to injecting his other arm.

"Better they die than Father's creations. Look what War did to the Winter Wonderland."

Drew's jaw clenched as he fought the nausea rising inside him. "We don't know that was him. John lost him."

"I thought you were following him?"

"I trailed him to the diner, where he met with the Deaths. He left and they delayed me. They're suspicious of my involvement with him. They may be psychotic, but they're not stupid. Fuck, this stuff is nasty." The veins on his arms turned black, red dots glowing as the drug surged through him. His fists clenched. Steam rose from his skin. He cried out, gripping the wall. Scarlet tears trickled from his eyes.

Mark kissed Drew's forehead. Drew's fingers released their hold on the wall as Mark's healing kiss cooled his veins.

Mark released him. "You could easily kill War. Spike his cocktail."

"I doubt arsenic works on Horsemen."

"You're best friends with the enemy. He won't suspect you. Play on his desire for glory – convince him he'd end the world quicker without the others scuppering his plans then once they're dead, kill him. His quest to end the world could help us save it."

Drew crept to the mouth of the alley and peered out. He waved Mark forwards. "Meet me here tomorrow night. I'll get you more money. If Pestilence succeeds, he could wipe out half the world in months."

"It feels unnecessary when all we have to do is kill the Horsemen."

CHAPTER 14

Aeron entered Travel Inn and slapped a heart-shaped Post-It note on the bathroom mirror. *Meet me at the children's play park on Tabes Lane D x*

He jogged out to his bike and sped towards the park. Everything was silent. Maybe the nightmares had gone to sleep. The playground was still, like a scene from a post-Apocalyptic film where the dust was disturbed by a child's long-forgotten doll.

Morgan swung on the aerial slide, her coat swirling around her as she landed. "Race you to the top." She tripped him and scurried up the slide. Cursing, Aeron clambered up the netting.

Marsden hopped over the railings and approached the graffiti-tagged apparatus, smiling.

"Boom!" Aeron slid down the fireman's pole, almost landing on him. "Get my note?"

"You." His smile died.

"Who did you think wrote it? I signed it 'D', as in Death."

Marsden folded his arms. "What do you want? And why the cryptic message? You could've texted."

"Ohhhh, you thought 'D' meant *'Drew'*! Did you think he was luring you for a secret lover's tryst? So you could hold hands on the swings like loved-up teenagers? Slide down his fireman's pole?" He grabbed the pole and ground his hips up and down it. Marsden glared, taking deep breaths as though he was plotting an inventive use for the see-saw and Aeron's soul globe. "Hate to break it to you, but Drew won't open his pearly gates unless you swear your love before God. If you like it, then you'll have to put a ring on it." Aeron turned, waggling his ring finger and twerking against the pole, enjoying Marsden's fury. "And you can't do that because you know what happens to wars when love muscles its way on to the battlefield. They end."

"Howdy stranger." Morgan leaned off the rope and chain bridge. "Wanna play?"

Aeron nudged Marsden's back, so he picked up the rope and climbed the wooden slats to the platform. Aeron jumped on the monkey bars and swung to another platform, imagining he was escaping a shark lurking in the bark.

"Are you going to beat me up and steal my lunch money?" Marsden crawled through a chain tunnel, cursing when it snared his guitar.

Morgan freed him and pulled him up. "Why would we do that? We're buddies."

"This feels like an ambush. Where are the others?"

"You called an Apocalypse meeting *here*?" Demi's indignant voice pierced the darkness before Aeron saw her. "I'm in my best heels! I can't be seen hanging around play parks like some druggie teenager!"

"You can leave, but we'll have the town meeting without you." Morgan manoeuvred across planks suspended by chains. "Any vote that goes against you, stands." She reached the other side then retraced her steps.

"I vote we tie her to a pole and leave her in a field, scaring crows," Marsden said.

Muttering, Demi kicked off her silver and diamante strappy stilettos and tiptoed towards the park. Mac snuck up behind her and slung her over his shoulder.

"Put me down you walking bag of rabies!"

"I'm stopping your feet getting muddy."

"By giving me *scurvy*?"

He dumped her on the slide and sat in the tyre swing. Marsden perched on the edge of a wooden bridge, his arms hooked through the chain sides. Aeron stood behind him, while Morgan sat on the bridge's post.

Aeron squinted at Mac. "What happened to your face? Seems someone tried to smash it like an Easter egg. I hope you spilled your syphilitic sweeties."

Mac rubbed his black eye. An upside down crown imprint was stamped on his cheekbone. "I was mugged. I sold all my Red Mist last night, so I was gonna use the profits to infect more prostitutes. I lost three hundred pounds!"

"A Horseman of the Apocalypse being mugged by a petty street thief, that's not humiliating at all," Marsden scoffed. "Did you get a look at him?"

"No, he wore a hood and a scarf around his face. He smelled nice though. Like he'd been bathing in strawberries."

Marsden chuckled.

"The town meeting is in order," Morgan announced. "Does anyone have issues they'd like to discuss?"

"Why drag us out here? It's cold, wet and smells of children," Demi retorted. "I'm sure I'm sitting in a puddle. If this *isn't* rainwater, someone will die."

"Travel Inn has ears, Skinny Latte."

"I have an issue," Marsden said. "Why am I the only one inciting the Apocalypse outside Lemures? We can't bring the world to its knees from *one city*. This isn't Hollywood."

"I've visited three cities – Misery, Moirai and Parcae," Mac said.

"Glad *someone's* prepared to travel."

"Some of us don't have puppets, we have to do the dirty work ourselves," Demi retorted.

"You've killed *one* man! I killed a hundred in Libya this morning!"

"How?"

"Three suicide bombers."

"*You* didn't kill them, lunatics did."

"I don't think you understand the concept of war. I also had three vans mowing down pedestrians in Nice, Barcelona and London. Fifty dead, ninety eight injured."

"Thanks for your contribution, Mars, but this isn't a pissing contest," Aeron said. "Morgan and I have regular deaths to contend with too. Humans don't stop dying 'cos the world is ending. And FYI, we started bushfires in Australia. Ruined a school camping trip. It wasn't just their marshmallows roasting on the fire. We found great bunyip costumes. Chased those brats right into the flames."

He and Morgan laughed and high fived each other. Marsden facepalmed.

"I'm the only one who seems to remember we're here to end the world. We're so far off target it's embarrassing. I've scrapped *six* plans because you wankensteins aren't sticking to your strategies. Do you even *have* strategies or are you relying on fortune cookies and a Magic 8 ball for guidance?"

"One more word and I'll break open your fortune cookies. And *no-one* bad mouths the Magic 8 ball. It told us the bunyip costumes were a great idea." Morgan cleared her throat. "Mac, you've been spreading festive joy like a secret Santa."

"Prostitutes are expensive! I'm spending all my drug money on them."

"Spoken like a rock star." Morgan devil-horned him.

"STIs won't kill them," Marsden said. "Why not strangle them during sex? Create a panic that a serial killer is hunting."

Mac picked at his hoody cuff. "I couldn't watch the life die in their eyes."

"This is the end of the world! They're *supposed* to die. Why not visit Congo and spread the plague? Visit food processing plants and contaminate the produce. You and String Bean could team up. Swim in reservoirs. Without fresh water, people will succumb to disease and death quicker. You don't just lack confidence, you lack imagination too. Give me a sample of every disease you have. I'll annihilate this world within a *month*."

"I've got a modelling shoot," Demi interrupted.

"Are they shots for undertakers? Government adverts warning of the dangers of anorexia? Accompanied by creepy music and a close up of you being zipped up in a body bag?" Marsden crossed his fingers.

"A catalogue shoot, actually."

"Catalogues won't end the fucking world!"

"I need to explode onto the scene. If you stop wasting your time on shoppers and get a record deal, we can be seen in the right hangouts. Your songs can affect everyone who listens to the radio."

"You want to ride my coattails?"

"That's not your only tail I want to ride." She blew him a kiss.

"Demi's right," Aeron said. "Forget that pub gig and busking, put your stuff on ViewYou. Entrance people into killing themselves or each other over the Internet. That's the latest craze." He sighed. "People just aren't in to Yo-Yos anymore. Instead of decimating the world using Mac's talents, do it with your own."

"I don't want to be famous for my music; I want to be remembered by the bodies I leave behind. Like my Winter Wonderland massacre."

"We can't live on past glories," Demi retorted. "If you don't want to be famous for your music, put your guitar away and get your sword out."

"My guitar is my invisibility cloak. I can make an entire crowd maul each other and no-one suspects me. I walk around with my sword, I'll be gunned down by the police before I've plunged it through someone's heart."

"Don't worry, you'll survive." Aeron squeezed Marsden's shoulder. "It might sting a bit though."

"Mars suggested spreading E. coli in schools," Mac said. "And measles."

"Kids get ill easily," Marsden said. "Their parents can't afford to take time off work so force their kids into school then they spread it to others, who then infect *their* families, who pass it on to their colleagues."

"You're a germ-spreading genius!" Aeron kissed Marsden's head. "Mac, whip up a batch of E. coli and deliver it to every school in the county. Something else too – E. coli won't generate many deaths."

"Hospital superbug?" Marsden suggested.

"You're *full* of good ideas tonight. But you don't give the orders. In future, run them past us."

"He's not giving *me* ideas," Demi moaned.

"I've told you *three times* to release locusts on crops," Marsden said. "For fuck's sake, Bonio, you're Famine's daughter. Cause some fucking famine! Instead of guilt-tripping people to stop eating, destroy crops so they *can't* eat."

"I meant ideas on making it big. I have no interest in agriculture."

Marsden gripped his head and took several deep breaths. Aeron massaged his shoulders. "Date a footballer."

"Their stupid plastic girlfriends are always in the papers! They're obsessed with surgery so I can make them feel shit about themselves then teenage girls will copy me. Where do footballers hang out?"

"Brothels."

"McScabies, if you see a footballer next time you're humping hookers, blackmail him in to dating me."

"What do I get out of it?" Mac grumbled.

"I don't push your face against an electric sander."

"At least girls *want* to screw me. You can't convince *one* guy to screw you."

She glowered. "I preferred you when you sulked in the corner and smelled bad."

"Aw look at them, all grown up and getting on," Aeron remarked.

"Makes me realise what good guardians we are," Morgan replied. "We should reward them with a picnic. Isn't that what families do? Play frisbee, kick sand over other families' picnics then throw their kids in the sea?"

"No wonder picnics are so popular! We could make jelly moulds!"

"I can't think of anything more dreadful," Demi groaned. "No…sticking hot pokers in my eyes actually comes second."

"You can't have a picnic with pretend food," Marsden said. "You'd better stay behind. You'd make the breadsticks look fat."

Morgan raised her hand. They fell silent, listening to squeaks of the restless swings, the groan of the trees and hum of distant traffic. Voices filtered through the night then a group of teenagers approached, accompanied by the sickly sweet smell of marijuana, cigarettes and cheap cider.

"Get out of our playground, paedos," one of the boys said.

"Isn't it past your bedtime?" Aeron called. "Go home, have some cocoa and cookies and ask your parents to read you a bedtime story."

"Fuck off," another boy answered. "This is our playground."

"Don't see your names on it," Morgan said.

"Over there, on the platform."

She crossed the bridge and crouched on the platform. "Colour me jiggered, there they are. You misspelled 'cock'."

Aeron grinned. "Ask the council to rename it after you: Wankers Planet."

The teenagers drew closer.

"What did you say?"

"Sorry, was that offensive? We can change the name. Tosser Park."

"You wanna say that to our faces?"

"If you insist, though it'd be easier if I shouted it, so everyone can enjoy it." Aeron swung off the bridge, landing like a superhero in front of them. "Tosser. Park."

Tense guitar music filled the night. The teenagers shifted as Marsden plucked their nerves and pulled their strings. Morgan zipped down the aerial slide, landing by Aeron. The teenagers moved closer, fists clenching.

"Is this an action film? Are we waiting for the rescue team to save us while you tell us your dastardly plan? It's always the women who have to step up." Demi marched over and smacked a girl in the face with her stiletto. She spun and headbutted a boy. "Gotta burn off my two pounds."

Every time the teenagers turned to leave, Marsden played an angrier song, forcing their deep-seated fury to the surface as petty jealousy and bitter resentment erupted amongst the group. Demi stepped back as a girl was pushed towards her.

"You dare get blood on this dress. I worked hard to smuggle it past security." She kicked the girl in the knee then rammed her elbow into her face.

"Isn't the objective to make them fight each other?" Mac asked Demi. "Like ancient death matches?"

"Even I tire of unleashing my hatred on humans through quick-witted putdowns. Some days you just have to smack someone in the face with a shoe."

She drove the girl headfirst into the fireman's pole, which vibrated with each dull thunk. The girl slithered down, her face a bloodied pulp. Morgan crouched over her, removed her globe from her pocket and rolled it over the back of her hand.

The raven landed on the bridge. "Corpse."

Morgan slipped the marble into his pouch. He hopped onto her shoulder while the playground became an amphitheatre, the bark stained with spilled blood.

Morgan swung around the pole, kicking a boy into the bark. She released the pole then smashed her heel into his face. She ran at the aerial slide, grabbed it then swung, kicking a girl over.

A boy swung a punch at Aeron, who ducked and swept his legs away. The boy scrambled up and tackled him. Aeron hit the floor, flicking the boy over his head towards the tyre swing like a video game hero. Mac slid off it and stepped aside. Aeron twisted the tyre swing to its tightest point, leapt in it then kicked three boys as he twirled. The nausea was worth it.

Marsden jumped off the bridge, pushing his guitar round his back. One of the boys grabbed a swing and hurled it at him.

Marsden jumped and landed on the swing. He swung towards the kid then sprang off, kicking him. He pulled his guitar off and beat the teenager to death with it. Another boy leapt onto his back. He slammed the boy into the apparatus's wooden wall then pivoted and punched the teenager in the face. As the teenager lunged for him, Marsden slit his throat with his plectrum.

Aeron removed a globe from his pocket and tossed it in the air. He caught it, squeezing it until it shattered.

"That was a fun, team building exercise." Morgan grinned. "We should hang out more. Next time, Mac, *all* members must participate."

Marsden wiped blood from his eyes and picked up his guitar. Morgan and Aeron collected the teenagers' globes, watching new headstones rise amongst the ashes.

CHAPTER 15

The Razor and the Rosary's sign swung like a gibbet cage warning others against entering its decaying lair. Three cars were spaced out in the decrepit car park, as though being in adjoining spaces would invite murder. Glass from one car's back window sprinkled the ground like forgotten wedding confetti. A dying bush ensnared a discarded car stereo. Marsden parked away from the sink hole threatening to swallow unwary cars.

Marsden pushed open the oak door that bore scars from its turbulent past and made his way to the bar. He leaned on it, his black thumbnail instinctively finding the carved graffiti. Rain lashed the windows, driven against the glass by the mournful wind.

"It's a good day to die."

Sasha beamed at him, tucking her auburn hair behind her ear. "Hey handsome. What can I get you?"

"Drew around?"

"Night off."

"Helping the homeless is he?"

"Not tonight." She fetched a beer and prised the top off.

"Boy Scout sing-a-long?"

"Nope." She slid the beer to him.

"Knitting Hats for Hedgehogs is on Wednesdays, so it must be..." he clicked his fingers, "clean the collection coins Friday."

She laughed "I'll tell him you said that. If you're lonely, I'm happy to entertain you."

"Another time. Can I go up?"

"Don't come crying to me when you're forced to participate with Coin Cleaning Friday."

Marsden took the beer, darted behind the bar and up the creaking wooden stairs to Drew's flat. His fingers tingled as he entered the narrow crimson hall, tripping over a stack of books and falling into the doorframe. He crept into the deep blue living room and vaulted over the back of the black settee, landing beside Drew.

"Mars! Shit!" Drew switched off the TV.

Marsden cackled. "You watching porn? I can come back."

He snorted. "My social life isn't so tragic I resort to porn for company."

"Your social life is tragic. You waste it on no-hopers, the underbelly and me." Marsden snatched the remote. Drew grabbed it, his arm brushing Marsden's. They swore and pulled away. Marsden switched on the TV. *EsSex Life* flashed up. "Ugh! This is *worse*! Porn is more believable with stronger characterisation and doesn't try to pass itself off as reality."

"How can I help people if I don't understand them?"

"Drew, these are the dregs of society, not a cross-cut of the population. They think flashing their boobs or dicks is a form of greeting."

"They need my help more than anyone."

"The best help you can give them is a trip to the vets to get them neutered; stop the human race devolving."

"They can't devolve if they're wiped out."

"I'm doing mankind a favour! Never considered myself a Samaritan before."

"You don't even know what a Samaritan is."

"They work in call centres and prevent suicides."

Drew stole the remote. His knuckles were grazed and bruised. "Taking the night off the Apocalypse?"

"I wanted to spend time with someone I don't want to throw into a meat grinder."

"Hallmark need you to write their Valentine's cards."

"Damn right they do. They've forgotten St Valentine was beaten and beheaded."

Drew laughed and shook his head. "What've you been up to?"

"Hanging with the H-Team."

"Have fun?"

"I'd rather be covered in fire ants. I'm suing Demi for sexual harassment in the workplace. Although killing teenagers using playground equipment caused unexpected fun."

Drew frowned. "How does that help the Apocalypse?"

"It doesn't. I think the twins wanted to practise their martial arts, Demi wanted to shed the weight she's gained and I…like killing people. Mac didn't join in. I wish we'd left him at home."

Drew chewed the side of his finger.

"I did what you said – I let Mac touch me. Through several layers of clothing, and I use his proper name."

"Think how he feels, being found repulsive by everyone."

"You've never seen him naked."

"How would you feel if nobody wanted to touch you or be around you?"

"I'd welcome it. I'm sick of being pawed by Bone Jangles and the Terror Twins." He eyed Drew. "Mac was mugged of his prostitute fund."

"Lemures is a dangerous place."

"He said his attacker smelled of strawberries. I gather you didn't cut your knuckles thumping a bible. His cheek has a crown imprint."

Drew studied his legs. "I feel bad, but I couldn't risk him infecting more prostitutes. Some STIs kill people. The others ruin lives. Some guy could catch one from Mac's prostitutes, pass it onto his pregnant wife then her innocent baby gets born with defects. Babies shouldn't suffer for their fathers' sins."

"The world's ending, Drew. There will be no more babies."

"I suppose you have to report me."

"He should've taken my self-defence class." He smiled. "You're not as angelic as your halo likes to pretend."

Marsden stood, ducked out of his guitar strap and removed his jacket. The sword tattoo on his right bicep peeked out from his black t-shirt sleeve. He rested the guitar against the armchair and drained half his beer.

"You're *not* surgically attached to that thing?" Drew nodded at the guitar.

"You're a fine one to talk. D'you take your halo off to wash?" He dropped onto the settee.

"It's the only thing I wear in the shower."

Pleasurable pressure burned in Marsden's groin. He brought his knees up and turned so they rested against the arm. He tugged his jeans away from his crotch, his pulse quickening. His imagination teased him with water caressing Drew's naked body, his hands touching every part of him Marsden wanted to touch.

He forced it out of his head, hating being so out of control, yet addicted to the way he felt when around Drew. He pointed to the TV. "Enlighten me on the gene pool dregs' shenanigans. Are they communicating in words yet?"

"Gemma's discovered her boyfriend, Lee's been shagging Carly. She found their sex tape. And Tabitha—"

"That's a cat's name."

"Tabitha and Mercedes had an intense discussion on why ladies in period dramas never wear nice lingerie."

Marsden made his fingers into a gun and pointed them under his chin. "Boom!" His head flopped back over the settee and his arms dropped to his sides.

"I'm not cleaning up your brain matter."

"You're supposed to help those in need. I need a new sanity."

"You've never seen the programme, yet you're bitching about it."

"I've never had my gonads pulverised with a spiked bat, but I know I wouldn't enjoy it. Can I vote for someone to be thrown into a piranha tank?"

Drew gave him a smile and a sideways glance that made his chest constrict. Every second of the programme that passed, he was torn between clawing out his eyes, or sticking skewers in his ears. He fidgeted and clenched his fists. Drew fast forwarded the adverts as Marsden screwed his eyes shut and curled his toes.

"I can't take anymore!" Marsden snatched up his guitar and played a furious song. His E string snapped. "Die, you worthless wastes of lives!"

Drew hit him with a cushion. "You can't hurt people in TV Land, numbnuts."

"I can end the world, but I can't end this programme." Marsden's shoulders slumped. "My powers are useless."

Drew laughed as Marsden restrung his guitar and put it back against the armchair. *EsSex Life* finished, so Drew switched channels.

"What's next? *Prostitute Boulevard?*" The theme tune to *Celebrity Dirty Washing* started. "You've *got* to be kidding me! What is *wrong* with you?"

"It's eviction night."

Marsden stared at him. "Please don't tell me you vote."

Drew snorted. "Don't be daft."

"Why did God trap such poor taste in…this package?" Marsden waved towards Drew. "It's like finding out your Easter egg is filled with ashes."

"*Your* creator filled your perfect shell with a bloodthirsty sociopath with serial killer tendencies. You got the better deal out of our relationship."

Marsden's heart raced. He licked his dry lips. Images of them together plagued his mind, the feel of Drew's skin against his, the taste of his lips, his skin tingling where Drew touched it, Drew's pleasure-filled moans as he tortured him with his tongue. Marsden escaped to the bathroom.

Minutes later, he left and leaned against the hall wall. Drew was engrossed in the programme, chewing the side of his finger.

"Did you get lost?"

"I tried slitting my wrists, but apparently I can't die that way." Marsden returned to the settee.

"Can you die?"

"Do you think the others would still be alive if we could? Have I missed anything vital?"

"Some glamour model has gone in to have lingerie washed."

"Washing her knickers where the public can't see them wouldn't be entertaining."

"Her ex-boyfriend, Justin, works there. He was in some boyband a few years ago."

"I understand why the Apocalypse is scheduled for now. All the advances in the world and mankind chooses to watch nobodies wash their underwear."

"Ssh, I want to hear what she says."

"It won't be a speech that will define a generation."

"It's research."

"They probably *were* researched on in some laboratory. But the government cut their funding and they had to release the unfinished projects into the wild." Marsden shook his head. "I hope she dies of rabies. I should text Mac. Is she going to spend the entire episode with her boobs out? I'm tempted to draw on them. Or pop them with a pin. How is this entertainment? Nobody's died."

"She'll be in the papers tomorrow: 'Busty blonde puts former boyband member in a spin'. 'Candy gets her twin tubs out'."

"You should write these headlines. Who'd call their kid Candy? She was destined for the stripper life. I'm going to puke. She looks like an anaconda devouring an antelope." Marsden imitated the wet kissing sounds coming from the TV.

Drew looked pained. "Not even I can save her."

"Good, let me kill her."

The episode finally ended.

"I can't believe you made me watch that. Didn't know you were a sadist."

Drew poked his tongue out. "It's revenge for the broken furniture from your gig. Be grateful – I could make you volunteer at the orphanage."

"I'll just kill the orphans. Save them the pain of never finding a home."

"Everyone has an Achilles' heel. I'll find yours and torture it 'til you surrender."

Marsden snorted. "You haven't seen my father's parenting style. I'm unbreakable."

Drew flipped open his phone, dialled a number and listened. Marsden snatched it off him.

"Congratulations! You voted for 'Justin' to be put through the wringer. Tune in at ten p.m. to see who's done their last load."

He hung up and flung the phone into Drew's lap. "They got to you."

"Ow!" Drew laughed.

"Like you felt that."

"I'm an angel, not an eunuch."

"If angels aren't designed to have sinful urges, why give you working parts?"

"Just because we're not designed to have them, doesn't mean I– we don't."

Marsden bit his lip, his body temperature soaring. "You said you didn't vote. I thought angels couldn't lie."

"He took her out the back and loaded her drum. That behaviour's unacceptable."

Marsden burst out laughing. "I can't believe you said that."

"I can't believe they *did* that! Yes she threw herself at him but he should've been a gentleman and preserved her dignity."

"She *has* no dignity. She probably can't even spell it."

"You could hear her pantomime porno shrieks over the machines! My innocence is more soiled than her knickers."

Marsden roared with laughter. "I hope his detergent didn't spill out."

Drew tried smothering his laughter and failed. "Fancy a game of *Resident Evil 5?*" Drew rose and switched the PS3 on, tossing a controller to Marsden. "I have a sudden urge to kill people."

Marsden smiled wickedly. "I knew I'd lure you to the dark side."

CHAPTER 16

"Meet me under the bridge on Desolation Row." Marsden hung up.

Mac pocketed his phone then sloped out of Travel Inn and mounted his white bike. He kept to the speed limit – he'd seen what happened to bikers who fell off. His face couldn't take being mangled. Demi would definitely make him play ducking apples in acid. Or insist on duct taping his face together.

He stopped under the rusting railway bridge. Prostitutes patrolled past fading graffiti and a dried blood stain. Headlight shrapnel scattered beneath the stain like a shrine. A pink stiletto lay in the gutter, shrouded in mould and bugs. Black knickers entangled in tights were strewn over the pavement. Rain's deafening roar and the prostitutes' clipping heels disturbed the night. Mac stared at the tunnel's mouth, a curtain of rain sealing him inside the brick tomb.

A train passed overhead, shaking the bridge, the rails clattering beneath its wheels before it vanished with a mournful wail. A black car glided up and a prostitute climbed in. The car drove away, stopping beside filthy public toilets. A lone headlight illuminated the bridge, sending shadows scurrying to safety. The red bike roared as it drew alongside Mac. Marsden raised his visor.

"Why the secrecy?" Mac asked.

"We're going to start a war."

Marsden slammed down his visor and sped off. Mac followed, torn between keeping to the speed limit and

126

keeping Marsden in sight. They left Lemures behind, riding through deserted roads until Marsden pulled into a bus layby outside a council estate in Thanatos.

Ugly, neglected tower blocks rose out of the night like markers for the dead. The dark hid their flaws, but enhanced their menacing appearance. Half the street sign was painted over, the other half missing. Marsden dismounted and removed his helmet, messing his hair with his fingers.

Mac pulled off his helmet and raised his hood. He wished he could wear the helmet permanently, that way people could fantasise about his face, rather than deal with his grotesque reality. "Why here and why me?"

"This is where hope comes to die. It's the territory of the Tower Hill Gang. Over there." Marsden pointed across the road, "is home to the Sunny Vale Crew. They avoid each other's turf, because there's enough business to share and they have a 'respect' thing going. Businesses need competition. You're going to steal their drugs, cut it with pestilence and become the dealer for both estates, so they become addicted to the diseases that will kill them. I'll murder a crew member from each side and start a turf war."

"Is there not enough work for you in Afghanistan?"

"I've got political saboteurs working out there for me."

"Why are you bothering with estates no-one outside of Thanatos knows exist? How will this aid the Apocalypse?"

"Civil unrest topples governments. It creates conflict between the police and the people they've sworn to protect. In America, I have white cops shooting unarmed black teenagers. The rage that's stirring up is apocalyptic." He smiled. "Not all wars are fought with soldiers."

He pulled his skull print bandana over his nose and mouth and strode towards the Tower Hill estate, looking like a formidable warrior. Mac slouched after him, hands in his pockets, feeling like a pretender to the throne. If only there was a red button to end the world. Annihilating people from the comfort of a chair seemed less barbaric than killing them face to face.

Mac scuttled to catch up. The tower blocks loomed like petrified giants, glowering over the estate and devouring anyone who entered their broken mouths. "The twins were looking for you."

"Did the diner run out of cocktails?"

"Where were you?"

"Here, doing surveillance."

"Where do you go every night?"

"We can't end the world by destroying one country, and I can't meet my saboteurs in Travel Inn. We should be in the four corners of the world, leaving trails of destruction, misery and mass graves behind as we collide in the centre for the world's final act, leaving all the players dead and the audience rotting in their seats."

Mac fidgeted with his hoody's toggles. "I get travel sick."

Of the four street lamps standing like sentries around the courtyard, two had broken lamps, one flickered and the other's wires dangled like ripped out intestines. Graffiti marked them. Four grey tower blocks formed a square, joined by stone bridges covered in tags, the most popular being THG. Boards covered some windows, other windows were smashed. Weeds struggled to grow through the courtyard's cracks. A charred bin stood in the centre, like a modern art version of a city centre's statue; not celebrating someone's life but desecrating people's hope. A burnt car lurked near a playground's remains. Marsden swore as a needle shattered beneath his boot.

"I've probably caught HIV. D'you have antidotes floating around inside you?"

"You'll die from everything else before you find it. I'm the most lethal pic 'n' mix going."

"I won't touch your coconut mushrooms. Nature always provides antidotes."

"I wasn't made from nature." Mac shrugged. "Death is a good antidote."

"They need you as the face of the NHS."

"My face will never be used as a positive message."

Marsden ducked through a boarded up doorway. The dank corridor smelled of stale urine, marijuana, tobacco and sweat. Used condoms covered in dust, gravel and chewing gum told a story not found in erotic novels. A positive pregnancy test lay against a fractured wall. Stagnant water and decay poisoned the air. Damp crawled up the walls.

"I don't think this is a good idea," Mac stuttered. "It's not safe."

"Mac, *they* are mortals. *You* are the first Horseman of the Apocalypse. They're more scared of you than you are of them."

"I think that's spiders."

They crept up a stairway, broken vinyl tiles cracking under their feet. More graffiti covered grubby paint. A sodden sock dangled off a step. On level one, Marsden opened the broken red door. He peered into the dark corridor then slipped inside and entered the first door on his right.

"Drugs are through there." Marsden pointed to the far room.

Mac crept through the living room, removing his knife from his pocket. He eased it behind the lock and ripped it out of the door. Clothes, coins, broken furniture and games consoles littered the small bedroom. A Spiderman lunchbox containing cocaine, heroin and ecstasy sat on the unmade bed. He collected it and returned to the living room, admiring the state-of-the-art home cinema system. It beat Travel Inn's TV.

Marsden dragged a man out from another bedroom and kicked the back of his knees, forcing him down. "Your business is under new management."

He clubbed the man then kicked him in the face before grabbing his vest and punching him repeatedly. Mac looked away, trying to muffle the sounds of fists on flesh, cracking bones and pained moans. He glanced back. Marsden stamped on the man's ribs. They snapped. Marsden drew his dagger from his belt sheath.

Mac licked his cracked lips. "What are you gonna do?"

"Carve our initials into a tree to prove our everlasting love. What do you think I'm going to do?"

Marsden slit the man's throat and carved SVC into his forehead.

"Uh, you've got blood on your face," Mac said.

Marsden wiped it with his bandana.

They fled the tower block and didn't stop running until they reached their bikes. Mac doubled over, coughing phlegm up. He spat. The ground sizzled. He wiped his mouth then checked behind him. A man darted into the tower block they'd just left, a flash of silver glinting around his neck. Mac stored the drugs under his seat, tossed the lunchbox over a fence then wheeled his bike across the road after Marsden.

"Where are the drug headquarters?" Mac hid his bike behind a skip.

"Youth centre. Kids act as runners in exchange for video games. It's the perfect business plan. If they're arrested, they won't serve time. If they're old enough for juvenile detention, their younger siblings replace them."

"I could profit from this established operation."

Marsden saluted Mac with the dagger, before running into the shadowy estate.

Mac broke into the youth centre, finding drugs in an Xbox in a games cupboard and bags of pills stuffed inside

Barbies' heads. He carried them out and stashed them under his seat.

"What the fuck you doing?"

Mac whirled around. A tall, spotty man in his late twenties glared at him. If 'thug' had a picture in the dictionary, this man's photo would adorn it. His head looked as though it had been bashed down to merge with his shoulders.

"Get off my turf."

Mac raised his hands. "I don't want to hurt you."

"I'll hurt *you* if you don't fuck off."

"I'm a…Horseman."

"You're a dead man."

He moved to headbutt Mac. Mac sidestepped, removed his glove and pressed his hand against the man's forehead. Red roses blossomed on the man's skin. He coughed, blood spilling down his chin as he gasped and clawed his throat. Mac grabbed his arm. His skin blackened and rotted.

"I didn't want to do that. Sorry. If it's any consolation, you'll die in one day, not three."

Mac dumped the man in the skip and covered him with broken tiles and an old pink bath before heading for the flats. He sidestepped crusted vomit spilling off the steps leading to a gangway and headed through a short tunnel, emerging on a balcony. Disembodied shouts echoed around the block. A man stormed towards Mac, a woman flinging bulging bin bags at his back, boxers and jogging bottoms spilling over the balcony.

"You think I want you after you've been shoving your dick into that Chantelle slapper?" The woman fastened her fluffy robe over her baggy t-shirt and Freger Value knickers. "You show your face here again, I'll cut your balls off! She can have them for her Christmas tree!"

"I'm taking the kids to my mother's this weekend!"

"You're not taking my fucking kids!"

Mac coughed into his hand then bumped into the man, muttering 'sorry' as he brushed the man's fingers, passing on surprise gifts of pneumonia and septicaemia. Septicaemia's deadly potential was still largely unknown. The man would likely die without knowing he had it.

Mac climbed to another level. A suicide cage was welded to the banisters, a wilting bunch of flowers tied to it, the card now meaningless smudges. Mac peeked over the balcony to make sure no-one stole his bike or investigated the skip. The estate was unnervingly quiet. No teenage gangs terrorised older residents. No babies screamed, no exhausted parents yelled at each other. It was as though they had already died but hadn't realised it yet. Mac opened someone's letterbox and coughed, watching strings of Anthrax float into the hallway with the junk mail. Nobody would suspect the flu-like symptoms were Anthrax. It wasn't something people expected through their letterbox. Marsden beckoned from a higher balcony. Mac weaved his way through balconies and stairwells until he joined him.

"There're more drugs in here."

Mac grimaced at the dead body sprawled in the living room. Not even the man's mother would recognise his pulverised face. His throat was cut, his eyes open. THG was scrawled on the wall in dripping blood. Mac hadn't really expected the Apocalypse would be this…bloody. He trailed Marsden into the bedroom and stole the drugs in the underwear drawer.

"Why do you have to be so vicious?"

"Gangs don't smother each other with pillows. Once the corpses are discovered, war will hit the estates. We don't want to be among the bodies on the battlefield."

CHAPTER 17

"You're a *genius*!" Demi kissed Marsden.

He pushed her away, wiping his mouth. "I hope you haven't been sucking the life out of more perverts. I don't want to get fat by proxy."

"What's caused this celebration?" Morgan asked, playing *Golden Axe 3* on a PS3. They'd stolen it from a gamer who'd died during an online game, surrounded by empty pizza boxes, energy drink cans and an unholy stench indicating an aversion to personal hygiene. Nobody would notice he'd gone – smelly people weren't missed – and it seemed a shame to let a good console gather dust. "Let me guess – Marsden's discovered a wonder drug that lets you unzip your fat suit and step out of it slim, trim and hot to the brim." Tyris Flare ran across the screen, somersaulted and stabbed an armoured knight. "Eat steel and die, jackass in a can!"

"I *wish*! Mars says I should go on *Celebrity Dirty Washing*. Instant exposure." Demi checked her reflection in the mirror. "Why the change of heart? You abhorred my fame campaign."

"A good leader adapts his strategies to fit the crisis."

Morgan laughed humourlessly. "You're not in charge, Bloody Mary."

"I should be."

Morgan eyed Marsden. Him being nice to Demi wasn't ringing alarm bells, it was sounding air raid sirens. "I'd have thought your TV listing contained serial killer documentaries and public executions. I'm surprised one of your precious 'strategies' includes watching has-been celebrities doing laundry. Washing knickers doesn't spark genocide."

"Really? It made me want to go out and slaughter everyone. It was on in the shop window when I was busking. Papers and trashy celeb magazines love it. It's in the news more than we are. Z-list celebs feature, so they won't know Starving Marvin's an imposter. The last model stripped off before having loud sex with her ex out the back. She was all over the Internet like arterial spray."

"Ugh that's tackier than gold teeth." Demi turned away from the mirror, wrinkling her nose.

"Your best weapon is your quick wit."

"You're being *nice* to me?" She touched her chest, gaping like a shocked skeleton. "It really *is* the end of the world. My tiny, diet pill heart just gave a post mortem twitch."

Morgan frowned. "Maybe Mars caught something when he let Mac touch him. That's *my* dragon, Dick Turdpin!" She hammered the buttons. "I'm gonna carve you like a Sunday roast."

"Press left, right, left then square and x simultaneously," Marsden said.

She obeyed. Tyris's sword spun across the screen. "While you're in a sunshiney mood, have you found somewhere to live?"

"I've been too busy starting gang wars to visit estate agents. I also have no money."

"Have you considered prostitution? Twenty quid per blow job, knock out ten an hour, you'll make your deposit in one night." Morgan swore as Tyris was torched by fire breathing men in the desert. "I'll kick your arse so hard I'll wear you as slippers!"

Demi put her fingers in her mouth and retched. "I'm not kissing you if you've been sucking off sweaty men."

Marsden grinned. "Suddenly prostitution sounds like a marvellous idea! I'll stock up on mouthwash."

"I'm going to select outfits for the laundrette. The next time you see me, I'll be on TV." She blew him a kiss and skipped out.

Morgan flung the controller as Tyris was beaten to death by busty warrioresses with flails. She switched it off. "Congratulations on the gang war. I collected your gifts. You pounded them into Picassos. Mac's offering took a while to die. Aeron heard his moans echoing through the bathtub. He finished him off out of mercy, but really I know he was eyeing up the green glittery smiley face sticker and didn't want Mac to have it. Also, I don't think inserting broken bathroom tiles into the victim so he resembles a hedgehog can be classed as a mercy killing. It comes more under art. Maybe we'll get innocent casualties gatecrashing our death party."

Marsden cleaned dried blood off his guitar. "I'll get the town involved. Like a street party without bunting and pretending to like the queen."

"Intriguing. Are you going to share your dastardly plan?"

"I'd have to kill you to preserve the secret."

"I'd kill you like that, pretty boy." She clicked her fingers.

"Then you'd be left with Bone Ranger and McScabies."

"There's more fun in a funeral. At least funerals have cake. Demi's would consist of skinny water and vitamins. Health and safety would ban food at Mac's."

"I'm going to give my condolences to the grieving. Play them moving songs."

He pushed his guitar around to his back and walked out.

Morgan stalked him and hopped onto his bike. She tapped his shoulders. "Drive, James! And don't spare the horses."

He raced towards the estates and parked in the next street. They walked towards Tower Hill, where a crowd gathered around crime scene tape. Some held candles, others held knives. Teddy bears blocked the entrance.

"I feel overdressed." Morgan gestured to her black PVC outfit – trousers and a bandage style top exposing some of her flesh below her long coat. The residents wore a uniform of hoodies and tracksuit bottoms.

Marsden snuck up behind a lone police officer and slit his throat with his plectrum. The officer gurgled as he drowned in his blood.

Morgan played keepy-uppy with the officer's globe. "Are we about to play real-life *Streets of Rage*?"

Marsden winked. "Let's start a riot."

***

"Riots have broken out at the Sunny Vale and Tower Hill estates in Thanatos, following the deaths of two rival gang members," the news reporter announced. Morgan and Aeron clinked their Death in the Afternoon cocktails in celebration as they watched the footage from a nearby pub, The Hangman's Noose. *"Police have declared the estates a no-go area. Public Health are investigating following the discovery of a man believed to have died from the plague."*

"That was fast," Aeron commented.

"That's what she said." Morgan winked.

"Gotta love technology. In the olden days it'd take weeks to start a riot. Now we can flash mob one." Aeron photographed the cocktails for their scrapbook. On the way out, he photographed the pub sign, as a record of where they'd drunk these cocktails. It would be nice looking back on photos of places they'd visited. Soon these places would no longer exist. They'd be the only ones left to remember them.

They returned to the estates, where Marsden and his guitar kept the crowds entertained from a wall topped with barbed wire. Riot vans lined the street, blue lights flashing like damned disco balls as people hurled stones, bottles and petrol bombs at officers sheltering behind their shields. Incoherent shouts drowned among the violent cacophony.

"Torching your estate is a great way of getting your message across," Aeron remarked. "Never mind you'll have nowhere to live."

Morgan smiled. "These wanker blossoms can barely function past the ability to grunt and scratch themselves."

"How's it going, Mars?"

"People from neighbouring towns are getting involved."

"Community spirit is so refreshing in these selfish times. You've united them in a way no Neighbourhood Watch scheme can."

Marsden played a faster chorus, shouts increasing as more people spilled onto the streets. He ducked a flying stone.

"It's fantastic they're defending guys who lured their kids into the drugs trade," Morgan remarked. "I guess kids have to earn money somehow since they can't go down mines anymore."

"A mother who confronted the gang was killed here a fortnight ago. They didn't know she was dead 'til someone complained to the council about what she thought was a burst sewage pipe. They found the mother's body stuffed in a wheely bin." Marsden batted a petrol bomb with the guitar. It smashed on the floor, inches from a man. "Shit. I missed." He jumped off the wall.

Another petrol bomb shattered a car window. The alarm wailed, outraged. Flames licked the paintwork, the car's blackened skeleton emerging from its fiery shroud. The three Horsemen retreated as the car exploded, spitting flaming debris over the rioters. Morgan's coat sleeve ignited. She touched the flame. It writhed and died, her coat unharmed. Residents beat the police back. Sirens shrieked about the tragedy, the crews watching helplessly from the barricade.

Aeron smiled. "I have a craving for barbecue ribs."

He ran to the scorched people on the roadside and ransacked the burning man's pockets. He fished his globe out, balanced it on the back of his hand then rolled it up his arm, across his shoulders and down the other arm, catching it. The new headstone rose from the small graveyard scene before Aeron shrank it and rolled it around his fingers. Morgan fetched a globe from a woman whose blistered face was a striking contrast to her white eyes.

"Who are you?" she gasped.

"Death."

"You don't look like Death."

"The catalogue said models may vary."

"I don't want to die."

"Tell that to the idiot who torched the car. And the morons who've blocked the emergency services. Nice neighbours. I hope they're on your Christmas card list."

"I have kids."

"Oh! My mistake! Let me exchange your globe for someone who's single and childless. Nobody grieves for them." Morgan held the globe out. "If it's any consolation, your death might cause outrage and they'll riot in your honour." She spun the globe on her fingertip. The woman scratched the pavement before lying still, eyes and mouth open. The raven landed on Morgan's shoulder so she dropped the marble into his pouch.

"Corpse!"

"Only two bodies?" Aeron asked. "We've had more on a Black Friday shopping spree."

"Mars can orchestrate beatings."

"Not sure we'll need him. People love a good riot."

"Gives them a chance to get new trainers."

"And a toaster."

"Life would be terrible without toast in the morning," Morgan mused. "I feel this riot lacks something."

"Bunting?"

"Sponsorship endorsement?"

"'The Sunny Hill riots, brought to you by Moisturiser for Men'," Aeron suggested.

"A hashtag. #amrioting."

"When are they going to start looting? I want new car mats."

"You don't have a car."

"You can't leave a looting party empty-handed. It's bad etiquette."

"Got it!" Morgan clapped twice. "Mars! Play something anarchisty. The one thing *guaranteed* to escalate this is police brutality. It's time we gave riots a bad name."

CHAPTER 18

Marsden crept towards a police officer, pulling a discarded guitar string from his pocket. He slipped it around the officer's throat, burying the wire into his flesh until it tasted blood. The officer struggled before slumping to the floor, his life seeping down the storm drain.

"Officer down!"

A policeman ran over. He radioed for assistance and checked his colleague's pulse. "Did you see anything?"

"Four kids from the estate. There's another cop over there." He pointed to where the first officer's body lay.

"I need to take your statement."

As soon as the officer turned his back, Marsden ran to where Aeron and Morgan watched the restless crowd.

"I can taste the tension," Morgan remarked. "I imagine it's the same excitement people get when a play's about to start. Except when the curtain rises, the cast will die."

"You're bleeding," Aeron commented.

Marsden examined the bloodied slashes in his fingers. "Battle scars."

"They're the sexiest kind."

Officers ran to their fallen colleagues then glowered at the crowd as the bodies were covered. Blood bloomed through the white sheets – Rorshach pictures showing a twisted mind.

Marsden immersed himself in the crowd, playing 'Brutal Lives' and spreading the news two officers were dead. A cheer erupted, along with chants of 'death to pigs'.

A man swung his fist at an officer. The officer struck him across the head with his baton then pushed him to the floor with his shield and stamped on him.

Several people filmed on their phones.

"Hey!" a woman lunged at him. "Police brutality!"

He snapped her arm with his baton. She screamed.

"This looks fun!" Morgan said. "I don't know why people demonise it."

The crowd surged towards the officers. Marsden retreated to a recycling bank. Grabbing an armful of bottles, he hurried to a car with its petrol tank door open and a siphon hanging out like a shed snake skin. He siphoned petrol into the bottles then spat, wishing he *had* bought mouthwash. He ransacked a clothing bank, ripping t-shirts into strips and stuffing them into the bottles.

"I gather you're *not* on a recycling drive."

Marsden reeled around, scooping up the bottles. "Do you often ignore police warnings about no-go areas?"

"When there's nothing on TV." Drew put his hands in his jeans pockets. His face, hands and white t-shirt with a skull and cross bones motif, were stained with grime and blood. He'd never looked more beautiful. "Petrol bombs aren't mentioned in Revelations."

"Neither are angelic bartenders. Fancy a Molotov cocktail? It's on the house."

"I'm not the cocktail kind."

"No wonder your customers won't buy them. Is that your blood?"

"No. I guess that's not yours." Drew gestured to Marsden's hands. "Is this your doing?"

"Mac helped and the Terror Twins are doing crowd control. It'd be nice to have a big event named after me."

"The Apocalypse not big enough?"

"I'll have to share the credit."

"Unless you kill your colleagues."

"I've plotted that so much I could write a book on it: *A Thousand and One Ways to Kill a Horseman.* I'm even planning a sequel."

"Why are you doing this?"

"Jesus told me to."

Drew folded his arms. "Jesus doesn't endorse riots. No, wait, there was that incident in the temple with the bankers…still, he wasn't chucking petrol bombs. Just tables."

"Maybe it was Ballerina Barbie."

A smile twitched on Drew's lips. "I know for a *fact* Ballerina Barbie isn't a twisted riot starter. *Hula* Barbie on the other hand…"

Marsden laughed. "I was supposed to come here earlier. Instead I spent the evening with you. I've been lecturing the H-Team about not playing their parts but I'm just as guilty. As much as I enjoy pulling people's strings, it's not in my job description."

"What is?"

"War."

Drew looked away. "You're starting a *war? Here?*"

"Until my passport comes."

"There are good people here."

"War exposes people's true natures. Look around, Drew. If you think they're good, show them your soul. How many will still be able to see the destruction they've caused?"

"Just because their souls aren't pure, doesn't mean they don't deserve redemption." Drew scanned the angry mob, the smouldering cars, the ambulances and fire engines being pelted with stones and bottles. "*You* made this happen."

"I lit the match. They torched their buildings with it. In war, there *are* no good and bad guys. There's just death. Death doesn't take sides." He moved to pass Drew, who grabbed his arm. They flinched. "Careful. I might've spilled petrol on me. I could go up in flames. I'd never live it down."

"Leave them alone. They'll come to their senses." His imploring gaze almost pierced Marsden's armour.

"Stop trying to save them. There's a *reason* I didn't start this in Lemures. Why I'm trying to get the H-Team to live elsewhere. Stop following me. You'll get hurt."

Drew looked at his armful of petrol bombs. "No."

Marsden's stomach squirmed with longing. All he could think of was dropping his bombs and kissing Drew like they'd die tomorrow. He wanted to rip Drew's filthy t-shirt off him and kiss the blood from his lips, his petrol scented hands exploring Drew's warm body. Drew's stricken gaze watched the crowd then rested on Marsden. His desire wasn't reflected.

"Don't die for them. They won't die for you."

He turned his back on Drew, distributing bottles to rioters the way people gave marathon runners water. He sprang onto a wall, surveying the carnage.

Police beat back marauding rioters. Bottles smashed against a riot van. The crowd cheered as the van burned, the 'POLICE' decal vanishing beneath the fire's furious tongue. The mob surged, trapping officers against the flames. The stench of blistering skin poisoned the air, screams smothered by the crowd's celebrations.

Firemen drove up the street. As they jumped out, the mob pelted them with missiles. Shrapnel rained off their helmets, some pieces drawing blood. They scrambled into their engine and reversed to safety. Paramedics ran through a gauntlet of stones to injured people. Drew ran into the mob surrounding the paramedics.

"No!" Marsden leapt off the wall and knocked people aside.

A man punched Drew and he vanished beneath merciless feet. A woman tried tearing the choker from Drew's neck then shrieked, cradling her scalding hand as silver light glowed. Others yelled and shielded their faces.

Blood streamed from their charred eyes. Shadow wings spread over them.

"Shit!"

He sprang onto a car, plucking a ballad. The crowd stood still, weapons slipping from their grasp, blood and tears streaking their faces from eyes that could no longer see. Drew staggered up, blood trickling down his face. He didn't look at Marsden as he helped paramedics rescue the injured.

"What the hell are you doing?" Morgan waded through the zombiefied crowd towards him. "Restart the riot by the time I count to five, or I'm throwing you in the nearest crocodile pond!"

When the ambulance pulled away and Drew sheltered down an alley, Marsden switched to a violent song. The riot resumed as though it had never stopped. Some people swung their weapons blindly, others dropped to their knees, weeping, screaming and clawing at their scorched eyes. The officers' cries were silenced as they succumbed to the fire ravaging their bodies; burning effigies celebrating the death of humanity.

***

Every TV report and newspaper broadcasted the riot, despairing at the depths to which humanity had sunk whilst relishing their inflated ratings. Shop owners lamented their looted shops, the local minister prayed for their souls and residents vented their fury at dead police officers.

"This is our biggest success yet!" Aeron grinned, clapping Marsden on the back as they sat in a booth in Grease Lightning. "Cocktails all round!" He summoned the waiter. "An Apocalypse Now for me, Happily Ever After for my twin, Love Potion for Mac, Look Better Naked for Demi and Screaming Orgasm for Marsden. He deserves it."

He picked up the next black question card of Cards Against Humanity and read out the question about how the world ends.

Morgan cackled as she slapped her answer card down. "I got this, you lot might as well quit now."

Marsden thumped his down. "I don't think so. This round's mine."

Demi slid hers across to Aeron. "I've got shit cards."

Aeron gathered everyone's answer cards. He sighed. "Mac, stop putting nice ones in. That's not in the spirit of the game."

"He's not in the spirit of the Apocalypse," Marsden said.

Two mothers with toddlers chatted about last night's episode of *The Killer Next Door*. A man stood by the jukebox, selecting random songs so a disjointed melody haunted the diner. Demi stared at a couple until they became so uncomfortable they left without finishing their burgers and fries. A three year old boy ran up and down the diner screeching. Demi stuck her foot out. He tripped, smacking his face on the floor, his screeches turning to agonised wailing. His mother sighed and got up.

"Put him on a lead," Demi told her. "Wild animals shouldn't roam free. That's why they tranquilise loose ones on motorways."

"He's not a wild animal!"

"Then he should stop acting like one or I'll phone the zoo. I'm tempted to buy peanuts and make him do tricks."

Marsden laughed. "You're such a bitch."

The mother glared, picked her son up and stormed out.

Demi smiled. "I should trip children more often. It's done wonders for my mood."

Aeron rose and turned the TV up.

"Police urge the public to avoid Sunny Vale and Tower Hill estates and the surrounding area as looting and rioting continues. Other riots have broken out across the country with civilians and the

police clashing violently. The Prime Minister has condemned the rioters' actions, calling it a 'disgrace'."

The report cut to scenes of Gallows Street. People marched through it, some emerging from shops with TVs, games consoles and toasters.

Morgan nudged Aeron. "See? People can't cope without toast for breakfast."

"Many shops suffered arson attacks and looting in the aftermath of what has become known as the Sunny Hill Riots."

"They stole my name!" Aeron objected. "Who do I sue for this?"

"The Nobody Gives a Shit Department?" Marsden asked.

"I don't think they'd give a shit."

"One man is leading a crew of residents in cleaning up the area and returning stolen goods. He was also seen risking his life to help the injured."

There was a distant shot of the hero, his white t-shirt torn and blood stained, his silver choker glowing.

The waiter brought their cocktails over.

"A toast," Aeron declared.

"To war," Marsden said.

"To pestilence," Mac mumbled.

"To famine," Demi said.

"To death!" Aeron and Morgan chorused.

They clinked glasses.

"To the end of the world!"

CHAPTER 19

Rain pattered the window of room 13, like gnarled fingers of damned souls scratching their way out of Hell. Shadows swept over the room. Blinds danced in the draught from the window.

Aeron scrawled *Operation Bible Class* in fancy calligraphy on an A1 drawing pad on an easel. He clicked the lid on the pen and faced the bed, where Marsden sat like a grumpy gargoyle. Morgan stood by the pad, her mini cat 'o' nine tails dangling from her fingers. Demi lounged on the settee below the window like an upturned giraffe. Mac slumped on the chair between the bed and the settee.

"If you're sitting this close to me, you should be in a bubble." Demi glared at Mac. "Better yet – a body bag. No, a gas chamber. And FYI, wearing a plum coloured hoody makes you look like a giant tumour that's just been removed from someone's gut. They should incinerate you with the medical waste."

Mac inched his chair closer to the bed.

Aeron cleared his throat. "Can anyone tell me what Operation Bible Class is?"

"If I'd known this was a lesson, I would've worn a schoolgirl outfit," Demi said.

"Thanks for that," Marsden replied. "I now have to scrub my mind with bleach."

"When you see me in it you'll be *dying* to bend me over the desk."

"Yeah, so I can chop your head off."

"It'll *blow* your head off." She winked.

"I'd blow my own head off. With a rocket launcher."

"Shoot yourselves on your own time." Aeron scowled. They were supposed to be the feared Horsemen, whose names made the world tremble and fall to its knees. Bickering and name-calling dented their terror-inducing legend. Like discovering Vlad the Impaler collected Beanie Babies. "What is Operation Bible Class?"

Morgan tapped her palm with her whip. Marsden sighed and raised his hand.

"Not you."

Marsden lowered his hand and raised his middle finger.

"Demi? Mac?" Morgan asked. "Now's your chance to prove you were paying attention during our shadow puppet theatre's production of The End is Nigh and There Will Be No Dessert."

"Who could forget that shambolic display of shitness?" Marsden said.

"It got rave reviews."

"I have to prepare for my visit to the laundrette later," Demi said.

"Handing over a bag of dirty washing doesn't need rehearsal."

"Operation Bible Class." Aeron underlined each word as he said them, "is the next stage of our glorious quest. Marsden, come out the front and explain it to the class."

"Why not do a PowerPoint presentation?"

"My laptop crashed."

Marsden rose. "Can I draw on it?"

"You do not have control of the pen."

Marsden stared at him. "How the *hell* are you in charge?"

"Luck of breeding. Get on with it." Aeron narrowed his eyes. He'd like Marsden more if he wasn't constantly trying to be in charge. If he wasn't so beautiful, he'd maim him for his disrespect. Maybe he could take a toe…

"Operation Bible Class is the fifth seal," Marsden said.

"What was the first seal?" Demi asked. "I feel like I've gone to the cinema to watch *Scream 5* when I missed the others."

"We're the first four seals."

"The arrival of the four Horsemen is one event, therefore one seal."

"Four Horsemen, four seals."

"There are five of us."

"The Bible didn't account for Death's biology failure, Slim Fast. Take it up with management."

"Time of the month is it, Bitchtits?"

He glared. "It'll be the time of your death in a minute."

"Can you *please* stop threatening to kill everyone?" Aeron pleaded. "It's bad for morale and undermines all those trust exercises we did."

"When do we get our horses?" Demi asked.

"Health and safety forbade them."

"Thank god. Nobody would take me seriously if they saw Pavlova. They'd think he's part of the pet obesity sweeping the country."

Marsden slapped the pad. "The fifth seal is the most fun – slaughter of the martyrs. There's one who harasses me when I busk. I could carve flaps into him so he resembles an advent calendar. But instead of lifting the flaps to find chocolate, people will find organs."

"I like how you've tied it in with Christmas." Morgan smiled. "Makes me warm and tingly in my Christmas stockings."

Demi yawned. "This doesn't involve me. Can I go?"

"No." Morgan twirled the whip around her head threateningly. "This is a team exercise. Like lynching. Non-participants will be forced to conduct the rest of the Apocalypse in this." She reached under the bed then held up a giant cockroach suit.

"For fuck's sake," Marsden muttered.

"Make HazMac wear it," Demi said. "Hopefully pest control will spray him in the face with chemicals."

"I have feelings," Mac mumbled, tightening his hoody around his face.

"They're probably diseased too." Demi twisted around and sat up. "Mindless slaughter isn't my thing. Blood stains, and the sound of screaming..."

"Is the best sound in the world," Marsden finished.

"For *you*. It gives me headaches. Some of us aren't psychopaths."

"Don't start on me because you have to work. I haven't said anything horrible to you the whole hour we've been here."

"You threatened to cut my head off!"

"It's the quickest form of execution! If done right."

Morgan lashed Marsden and Demi's thighs, the sound satisfying on Marsden's PVC trousers. "No talking in class! Mac. Plans on how you'll complete your assignment?"

Mac shrugged. "I could poison holy water fonts so baptised babies fall ill. Contaminate holy books with flesh-eating diseases. Spread STIs amongst the flock."

"Are you making us write essays on this?" Marsden asked. "I don't know enough synonyms for 'blood', 'decapitation' or 'screaming in abject agony'."

"We'll accept interpretive dance," Aeron told him. "Demi. Would you like to share your ideas with the class?"

Morgan shook the cockroach suit at her. "You'll look adorable in this. You could adorn catwalks as Cockroach Cutie. But people may stamp on you."

"I'll tell cults fasting is the only way they'll hear God's voice. Con celebrities into participating. They're always chasing the next diet fad."

Marsden cupped his hands to his mouth. "Booooorrrriiiiiiing."

She threw her shoe at him. It hit Mac's head, bursting a boil. "That has to be steam cleaned." Mac rubbed his head as pus seeped down his cheek. "We can't all slice and dice them. Some of us have different talents."

"You have *no* talents. Instead of fasting, you could imprison martyrs in gibbet cages lining the street and leave them to starve to death. Nothing spreads messages like corpses in a cage."

"Where will I get gibbets and cages? They don't sell them on Amazon. Besides, some do-gooder will free them. This isn't medieval times. Public torture died when underwear was invented."

"Star pupil," Aeron said. "What are your plans?"

"Bloodbath. Have them screaming in torturous despair as they ask God why he's forsaken them. Crucifixions. What better way to slaughter martyrs than emulating the king of martyrs? I'll arrange suicide bombings at churches worldwide."

Aeron fanned himself. "I'm getting hot and bothered."

"He waves his sword around and everyone fawns over him," Demi muttered. "Why is his idea better than mine?"

"Didn't you hear me?" Marsden asked. "*Blood. Bath.* So some cults starve themselves to death? Nobody cares. People get mindlessly butchered, everyone will notice. They'll be outraged, sickened. Delighted they lived through a headline event. People *love* crucifixion because it's rare. It'll be remembered."

"There'll be no-one left to remember anything."

"They won't remember fasting. It's as entertaining as a sponsored silence in a monastery."

"I fucking hate you. Glory stealer."

"You want to be remembered, put martyrs in gibbets."

"I like that idea," Aeron said. "We could call it Operation Birds of Pray."

"Where do cults hang out?" Demi asked. "If they're not on the first page of Google, I'm not bothering."

"We've already found them. Don't say we never do anything nice for our team. We've divided the list so you can target different areas and we won't tag team them by accident or leave anyone out." Morgan handed out tablet computers.

"Does anyone else have ideas worth noting?" Aeron asked, his pen hovering over the pad. "Marsden's look lonely up here."

"Plagues of boils and disease are biblical," Mac said. "They'll believe the Apocalypse is coming."

"The Apocalypse *is* coming. Didn't you get the memo? We're not here because our health spa coupons were expiring."

"It'll cause panic amongst the religious community. I'll give them leprosy."

"Spread the plague," Marsden told him. "Target a country with strong religious beliefs and they'll believe their sins caused it."

Aeron exchanged a glance with Morgan and she lashed Marsden's arse with the whip.

"What the fuck?" He spun around and pinned her to the wall.

Aeron yanked him away. "You're. Not. In. Charge. Don't give orders without running them past us."

He released Marsden, who straightened his grey grunge print t-shirt and glowered like a psychopath.

"The religious always bleat on about the end of the world." Demi snorted. "No-one believes them. Look what happened with the Rapture. What a poor turn-out *that* was."

"Maybe someone forgot to flash mob it," Morgan said.

"Boils, fasting and bloodbath is a sure sign the end of the world is nigh," Mac mumbled.

"We're only missing locusts and frogs," Marsden said.

"I see where Mac is going with this," Aeron said. "It's going on the pad." He wrote it down. "We need the religious to spread the word."

"Create a Chatter account. There's a fake God on there."

"We could set up a real account, pretending to be a fake account so everyone will think we're comic geniuses and not nutcases. No-one will believe we're *actually* the Horsemen. Gold star for you!"

He grabbed Marsden and kissed him.

"Get off! Why does everyone molest me?"

"I ran out of gold stars."

"You've could've drawn one on my hand."

"If I do it now, it looks like an afterthought. You got a reward, stop whining."

"I can't stick that on my progress chart to take home to my parents."

"Can I go?" Demi asked. "Imagine if photographers snapped me here? I'd never live it down."

"Tell people you were banging a politician. You'll make headlines while people speculate about his identity."

"Can *I* tongue you?"

"No."

"You let The Terminator do it."

"Being boss has privileges," Aeron said. "Molesting you lot is one of them."

Morgan tapped the board with her whip. "Now you can go."

Demi trotted out.

"I'll hang out at church services," Mac said.

"We admire your dedication to the cause," Morgan said. "Get out there and spread some boils!"

She and Aeron inched back as Mac shuffled past. He sighed.

"Nothing personal," Aeron said. "You're riddled with diseases."

"You can't catch them."

"True, but you're...disgusting. Sorry."

Mac slouched out of the room.

"Aw I hate seeing that pimply face look so dejected," Morgan said. "But his face is a bringer of nightmares. It's a shame. He's a nice guy when you get below the pus. He'd make a lovely husband."

"To who?" Aeron asked. "The Swamp Beast?"

"Bride of Frankenstein."

Aeron smiled at Marsden. "So then, star pupil, this slaughter of the martyrs has to be big. Biblical proportions. We want Heaven to hear them scream."

CHAPTER 20

Marsden knocked on Drew's door. His heart thrashed against his chest. This didn't seem like a good idea anymore.

Drew opened it. "You never knock."

"I wasn't sure I'd be welcome."

"Forgiving people comes with the halo. Besides, Jesus hung out with unsavoury types." Drew stepped aside. Marsden went into the living room and stood by the settee. Drew fetched two Red Bulls from the fridge and handed him one. "I get it, Mars. You're doing your job. It's not a holiday where you can absorb the culture and send postcards to your parents."

"The Royal Mail doesn't deliver to Purgatory."

Drew sat on the settee. Marsden removed his guitar and jacket then joined him.

"The Winter Wonderland was you, wasn't it?"

"Yes." He listened to the clock, which was barely audible over his heart. "The more I repress the urge to kill, the worse the outcome when I surrender." He turned to face Drew. "Why do you like me? I'm a fucking Horseman. The *worst* Horseman. I want to destroy the world you're trying to save."

"I don't see War the Horseman, I see Mars, my best friend. I don't get why *you* like *me*. I watch shit TV, hang out with undesirables and I'm as exciting as colonic irrigation."

Marsden laughed. "Isn't it obvious?"

"Not to me."

155

"Then you're the only one who doesn't know."

Now. This was the moment. Marsden curled his trembling hands into fists. He knew his voice would shake and he desperately didn't want to speak the words he longed to say. Some words lasted forever, like an epitaph carved into a headstone. Weathered, beaten and barely legible, but always there, always wounding.

"Do you get a kick out of being friends with an angel?"

"I hate angels."

"Being a force for good is such a hateful quality."

Marsden pictured slamming Drew against a wall and kissing him so hard his lips bruised. Or so softly they barely felt it, their bodies never feeling close enough. Drew's gaze was intense, as though he could see inside Marsden's head. He *wanted* him to see the thoughts that plagued him. To feel the sensations tormenting his body.

He pushed Drew backwards on the settee, ripped his t-shirt from him and ran his tongue up his body while Drew arched beneath him. He tugged off his own t-shirt before kissing him, their tongues as entwined as their bodies, each touch bringing more pleasure than the last.

Marsden rested his elbows on his knees, gripping his head. Each breath felt laboured. He always fought these images, because when they invaded his mind, he didn't want them to leave. He'd rather live with the fantasy of them together than deal with the painful reality of Drew's rejection. It would be embedded in his brain, playing on repeat like a siren song of suffering.

Drew clicked his fingers in Marsden's face. "I lost you. Are you planning your next attack? Let me guess – poisoning baby food? Crucifixion?"

"Poisoning baby food is Demi's domain." His voice was strained. "Wouldn't want to step on her toes. She thinks babies are chubby. People cooing over them encourages their gluttonous ways."

"Has she poisoned baby food?"

"She boasted about putting laxative into one 'exceptionally fat' baby's food. And his mother's, for letting him 'blimpify'."

He closed his eyes. *Sweat glistened on Drew's chest, his breathing heavy. Marsden's lips glided over it, its salty taste lingering in his mouth, slipping down his throat. Drew's heart pounded against him.*

He dug his nails into his head, clenching his jaw. Drew was so close. His heartbeat too loud. His scent overpowering.

He had to leave. Before he surrendered to the desire devouring him.

"What's wrong? It's not guilt over the deaths – you don't suffer that." Drew chewed the side of his finger. "Are you…using me?"

"What?"

"Infiltrating the enemy to destroy them from inside their camp is a classic military move. I've often wondered if that's why you're friends with me. I didn't want to ask because I couldn't bear the answer."

"No! I've told the twins that's my strategy, and when I first arrived, that was my intention, but I swear on the Apocalypse I'd never betray you like that."

"Then why risk everything by befriending me? When the end comes, one of us will die. Most probably me."

Marsden met Drew's gaze. "I'm in love with you."

Drew's hands shook. Marsden tugged his hair, pulling his head down to his knees, cursing. He could never erase those words. They were out there, poisoning their friendship. He'd ruined everything to ease his torment.

Marsden stood, grabbed his guitar by its neck and flung it across the room. It smashed into the bookcase. He kicked the table over, spilling Drew's Red Bull.

Drew hugged his knees. "I paid ten quid for that table in the charity shop. They don't give refunds. And I haven't touched my Red Bull yet."

Marsden sat, playing with his fingers.

"You have no problems admitting you slaughtered a park full of people, yet admitting you love me is apparently torture."

"I've killed hundreds of men. I've only loved one. And he's a fucking angel. Not only are you out of bounds, you don't feel the same."

"I'm in love with you too."

"What?" Blood surged in his ears.

Drew moved closer. "I think about what it would be like to kiss you. To touch you without getting third degree burns."

"If I don't go, there'll be a friggin' inferno on the settee, both of us charred beyond recognition, only identifiable by our dental records."

"What a steamy image." Drew fanned himself. "You should write for Mills and Boon. You'll arouse thousands of housewives with your sensual descriptions."

"How can an angel be gay? The Bible wants you put to death."

"The Bible condemns left-handed people more than homosexuals. And it's not like I can commit any debauchery with you. You'll burn my body, Lucifer will burn my soul. But just because I can't do anything about it, doesn't mean I don't feel it."

Drew plucked his jeans cuffs. Silence suffocated the room. Unspoken words dangled between them, like a hanging man on the stage they pretended wasn't there.

"What are we going to do?"

Marsden shrugged. "The Terror Twins gave me the 'stay away from Drew' chat. Complete with graphic demonstration of what fate lies in store for my gonads if I disobey."

"They *know*?"

"They know everything. They can teleport and turn invisible to humans. They're like bloody Father Christmas only instead of giving presents, they take lives. They kept a close eye on us because you're the enemy."

"We can't even *touch* each other, let alone do anything else."

"Having feelings for you jeopardises everything. I've known the H-Team my entire life and I couldn't care less if they died. Well, I'd miss the twins. I'd like them a lot more if they weren't in charge. I can't believe you feel the same. I *enjoy* killing people. I'm everything you hate. Everything you dedicate your life to stopping."

"Nobody's perfect. Yes, you commit mass murder with the same regularity people do their Tesco shop, but that's your job. I hate that, not you."

"I hate your job too."

"I know running a bar isn't everyone's ideal choice of employment, but that's harsh."

Marsden laughed and slapped Drew's leg, hissing at the burn. "Your *real* job, numbnuts." He fingered his studded choker.

Drew touched his halo. "It's who I am."

Marsden rolled up his t-shirt sleeve and touched his sword tattoo. "This is who *I* am."

"Have you considered *not* being a Horseman?"

"I can't stop being a Horseman any more than you can stop being an angel. As a kid, I'd dream of riding across the world with my fellow Horsemen, leaving a trail of destruction in my wake."

"Is it how you imagined?"

"No." Marsden laughed bitterly. "I'd listen to my father recounting his Apocalypse and I'd burn with desire for the day I became a Horseman. There wasn't a day I didn't think about it, prepare for it. Have you ever lain awake at night, *terrified* you'd never get the one thing you wanted? I would've given my life to be a Horseman. I never imagined I'd be saddled with incompetent clowns and cockroach costumes. We're not galloping across the world, destroying everything in our path. We're living in Travel Inn, hanging out at diners while Pestilence shags prostitutes, Famine launches a modelling career, War falls for a fucking angel and Death…fuck knows how they spend their time. Playing Hopscotch with people's globes, probably." Marsden dug his nail into a scar on his knee, visible through the rip in his jeans. "I was born a Horseman, I'll die a Horseman."

"I was born to be unquestioningly obedient. I won't die that way."

Marsden twisted and gripped the back of the settee, either side of Drew's head, their bodies inches apart. Drew's hot, quick breath tickled his face, his chest rising and falling rapidly, his t-shirt thumping with his heart. Marsden leaned forwards, their lips millimetres apart. Drew's fingertips touched his cheek, but he couldn't feel the burn. His body ached. Drew snaked one arm around Marsden's waist and pulled him close. Flames erupted between them. Marsden ran to the bathroom and jumped in the bath, turning the shower to cold. His skin sizzled as icy water hit his burning flesh. Drew leapt into the bath, smoke rising like souls fleeing the mortal realm. Marsden lowered the shower head and blasted Drew.

"Shit that's cold. That's a passion killer," Drew remarked.

Marsden closed his eyes to block out the way Drew's wet clothes clung to him, the water slithering down his chest. "You've never looked more beautiful."

"I'm covered in scorched flesh and smoke." He shivered. "And I smell like burnt toast. Thank god I don't have a smoke alarm."

Marsden pushed Drew against the wall. They stared at each other as the icy shower rained on them. Marsden's body ached with longing as he bit his lip.

"Just. One. Kiss," Drew murmured, their lips almost brushing. He stroked Marsden's cheek with the back of his fingers then held the back of his head, fire erupting beneath his fingers.

"I should go."

"You're soaking. And smouldering." Drew blew smoke off his fingertips.

Marsden's heart pounded as he leaned closer. Drew's lips parted, water streaking his face like tears. *The water turned to blood, Drew's lips crumbling to ashes beneath his kiss.*

"Stay with me tonight."

"I can't." Marsden caressed Drew's side then stepped out of the bath.

"What would happen if we kissed?"

"We'll die."

CHAPTER 21

Demi straightened her beetroot skull print dress, flicked her hair and opened the door to Wash 'n' Go, the laundrette in *Celebrity Dirty Washing*. She quickly found the cameras then marched to the counter, where a former Page 3 model lurked. Demi couldn't tell if her blouse hid breasts or bowling balls. She was tempted to line up empty beer bottles and roll her down an alley. Smiling, she placed her bag down and tapped her nails on the counter.

"Be about an hour, love."

Demi did a double take. "Oh my god! Sorry, I thought you were a statue. You frightened me!" She clutched her chest, laughing nervously.

"Excuse me?"

"You're the exact shade of bronze as those human statues on Gallows Street. I nearly slotted money in your cleavage. I'm glad you spoke – that could've been embarrassing."

The woman, whose name badge said CHARLENE glared. "Come back for your washing in an hour."

"I'll wait. I've got time to kill between modelling shoots."

Demi sat on a slatted bench while Charlene took her bag to a machine and bent over to load it.

"Jesus! I don't know you well enough to experience the views at Vag County." Demi covered her eyes. Charlene turned around. "I know your glory days died with the dinosaurs, so you're desperate to recapture the adulation you received when your face wasn't frozen by

162

Botox, and society's brainwashed you into thinking women's sole purpose is to be sex objects for men. But do you *really* want everyone knowing the product doesn't match the picture on the tin?" Demi touched her hair then pointed down.

"Who the hell do you think you are?"

"Demi Ceres, a *proper* model."

"Never heard of you."

"That's because photographers want shots of *me*, not my genetically modified melons. My modelling world is a classier world than yours. You're a disappointing Friday night kebab looking at caviar."

"You bitch!"

"It's fantastic you realised the only thing your face could adorn was plastic surgery brochures, so had the sense to flash for cash. Obviously, your boobs weren't impressive enough, but I admire your business aptitude in buying boobs to create a career. Speculate to accumulate and all that jazz."

"I'd keep your mouth shut, babes. You're flatter than a pancake."

"A woman's worth isn't measured by her cup size, Bronze Age. Whoever told you that should reimburse you for the boob job. They conned you. Your boobs look like babies' heads sticking out of your top. I'm tempted to get photos of me kissing them to kick start my career in politics."

Charlene flicked her hair back and pushed her chest out. "I get showered with attention."

Demi rolled her eyes. "Of *course* you do – cheap products attract customers."

Charlene lunged at her. Demi leapt up and headbutted her. Charlene shrieked then scuttled out the back, crying and covering her bleeding nose.

"You haven't done my washing! I can't do it, I've just had a manicure!" Demi rubbed her forehead, hoping she wouldn't bruise.

A man emerged from the back and approached Demi. His face had more creases than an un-ironed shirt and his nose resembled a collapsing speed bump. His bulky physique hinted at a body that was a powerful muscle machine in its youth but was now beaten by age and too many beers.

"Can I help you?" His name badge said GRANT.

"The Oompa-Loompa ran off without doing my washing. That attitude's not suited to a customer-based establishment. And it's *totally* unhygienic to allow staff to work without wearing underwear. This is a laundrette, not a peep show. If I want to see a trimmed bush, I'll visit the garden centre."

"Is this your bag?" He picked it up.

"Yes, thank you." She smiled. "These programmes are great for the community. It proves you're not all layabouts and scumbags, that some of you *want* to repay your debt to the society you crapped over. Though don't mind if I check my bag afterwards. Those clothes are expensive and I know prisoners don't earn much inside."

"I don't follow."

She covered her mouth, hoping her expression was sprinkled with a flavouring of shame. "I'm so *sorry*! I thought you were from a prisoner rehabilitation programme, like that restaurant where prisoners serve the public. Not that I'd eat there – they'd spit in my food."

"What?"

"You look like an ex-gang member. I could imagine you shanking someone after a nightclub brawl, thinking some punk ogled your bitch."

"I'm a boxer." He folded his arms.

"Why are you working in a laundrette? Lose too many fights against opponents and the middle-age spread, did you? This must be such a come-down. One day you're getting your face pounded in the ring, signing autographs, your posters adorning young boys' walls, the next you're washing people's crusty pants on a reality show. Who took the bigger k.o.? You or your career?"

"If waltzing in here and insulting people is your way of getting your five minutes of fame, it's disgraceful."

"If this is *your* way of regaining your five minutes of fame, it's demeaning."

"Charlene's crying her eyes out."

"Her tears would be like water breaking through a concrete dam – her makeup's so thick I can't make out her original features. If she blinks, the wind current will wipe out China."

A member of the production team escorted Charlene out, who clutched a bloodied cloth to her face.

"You broke my nose you fucking bitch."

"Sorry, I can't understand you. You're all nasally."

"I'll fucking kill you."

"I didn't want to mention this – I was raised to be polite – but your nose ruins your face. I've done you a favour. You can have a fake one to match your boobs. I'd get your lips sorted too – any more collagen and midgets could use them as a settee. Soon, you'll be able to pick every feature out of a catalogue. You should change your name to Mrs Potato Head. Like an ugly building with poor foundations – rather than decorating it, it's better to demolish the eyesore and start again."

Charlene sobbed as the woman ushered her out.

"That was horrible," Grant said.

"She loves it! It gave her great air time. She'll be in the papers tomorrow and can use the proceeds to buy a new nose and get her boobs re-done. They're lopsided."

Grant thrust Demi's bag into her arms. "Get out. You're–" The phone rang. Grant returned to the counter and answered it with the fake sincerity of a teleshopping actor. "Wash 'n' Go, where you'll be served by someone you know!" He listened with the expression of someone eating a Christmas pudding but instead of finding five pence, discovered they were chewing a tooth. He hung up, strode to the machines and snatched Demi's bag. "You're welcome to wait."

She smiled, sat on the bench and pulled out her mobile. "I'm in the laundrette…maybe I'll hang *you* on the rack with the dry cleaning...you kiss Archangel Gay-briel with that mouth?" She hung up and pulled a fashion magazine out of her bag. "Nude leggings? I suppose they're hot if you find the wrinkled knee look sexy."

Thirty minutes later, Charlene returned and stormed up to the counter. "What is she doing here?"

Demi winced. "You look like a plague doctor. Shame Halloween's passed. You'd terrify kids."

"Fuck off!" Charlene pointed at the door.

"I'm waiting for my washing. Which you're kindly doing free of charge, due to your rudeness."

"Fetch it later."

"So you can shred my designer clothes in revenge? I don't think so, Booberella. Look on the bright side. It's Christmas! You can paint your cup red, pretend you're Rudolf and cameo in pantomimes with the other has-beens." The door opened and Marsden entered. Demi jumped up and flung her arms around him, kissing him. "Play along. We're on camera." She dragged him to the counter. "This is my boyfriend, Marsden. He's a rock star. As an apology, he's going to perform a song for you."

"What have you done?" he asked.

"There was a big misunderstanding, hurtful comments were made by both parties and I gave her a fetching nose cone. Play her something...sexy."

Shaking his head, he plucked the strings to 'Poisonous Passion'. Charlene strutted to the bench and climbed on it. She swung her hips, fumbling with her blouse buttons. After fighting to free her arms, she tossed the blouse aside and leaned over, squeezing her breasts like customers checking the ripeness of tomatoes.

"I hope one doesn't pop out like a jack in the box," Demi whispered to Marsden. "At this distance it might kill us."

Charlene turned and bent over, dancing as she unzipped her skirt. She stepped out of it, caught her stiletto and fell off the bench, looking less like a glamour model and more like a mangled mannequin. Demi covered her mouth, her shoulders shaking. Charlene untangled her feet from the skirt and stroked her hot pink thong, licking her lips and looking as sexy as a cabbage in a corset. She crawled towards Marsden then rose, using him as a post to dance around. Demi folded her arms, glowering as Charlene thrust her arse against Marsden's crotch, running her hands up her legs as she straightened. Marsden stepped back. Charlene sashayed to the counter and tried hitching herself up. After four tries, she succeeded and leaned backwards, nearly toppling off. She struggled up, rolled over and rose onto all fours before spanking herself with a rolled up copy of *Sexcess in the City*.

"That's the *50 Tips to Turn Him On* issue. I don't recall self-spanking featuring," Demi said.

Charlene returned to the bench and crawled along it. Her knee slipped and she banged her chin. She strolled to the washing machine and danced with the door before leaning in to the drum, thrusting her hips.

Demi nudged Marsden. "Any chance of a string breaking? The machine turning on would be a ratings winner."

The song died.

Charlene backed out of the machine, looking bewildered.

"That was *marvellous!*" Demi applauded. "Forget glamour modelling, with that act you'll be on the Las Vegas strip in no time. The self-spanking will feature in every porno! Making love to the washing machine door was so sexy even *I* want to plunge my face into your twin tubs."

Charlene grabbed her clothes and scurried out the back.

"I *will* come back for my washing. I need a lie down and a cigarette." Demi grabbed Marsden's hand and propelled him out the door.

They ducked down an alley beside a board game café, Game of Scones. Demi laughed so hard she nearly choked on her brilliance.

"I could do a better striptease," Marsden said.

"If this doesn't make the news, nothing will. I hope it doesn't overshadow my performance. I want *my* name in the headlines, not hers."

"You broke her nose. By tomorrow, everyone will know your name."

"Then I can take over the world."

CHAPTER 22

Marsden stopped outside Thanatos police station and pulled petrol bombs and a brand out of his bike seat compartment. He lit the brand and a rag then hurled the bottle through a window.

Screams echoed as the blaze tore through the station, hunting for sacrificial victims. Marsden moved around the back of the building and threw another petrol bomb into the canteen. Startled shouts greeted his ears, followed by running footsteps and an agonised cry. Fire alarms blared. Smoke fled through the broken windows like souls leaving their bodies to burn. He flung another bottle through an upstairs window as the fires razed everything in their way.

Walking along the line of police cars, he elbowed the drivers' windows until they surrendered then popped open the petrol doors and stuffed rags into every tank. He touched the brand to each rag. Flames consumed them, slinking into the tanks.

One by one, the cars exploded, their burning bodies breaking and scattering.

Marsden attached the brand to his bike and absconded into the night. Sirens shrieked in the distance; the new soundtrack to the city.

He parked below the shadows of a broken streetlight. The surrounding houses were dark, as though they'd closed their eyes to the night's horrors. Marsden stalked towards the church, the brand accompanying him. He tried the door.

"The world is dying and you lock your doors?"

He kicked it open. It smashed into the wall then bounced back, hanging like a broken wing. The brand created monstrous shadows that danced to the rhythm of Lemures's dying breath.

He strode down the aisle and stopped at the altar, staring up at Jesus on the cross. "If I nailed someone to a cross then hung a statue of his brutal demise, I'd be labelled a monster."

He tore down the curtain from the confessional and bundled it below the cross before lowering the brand to it. Flames crawled over the curtain, licking Christ's feet. Marsden retreated from the church's sanctuary as the fire consumed Jesus.

The flame on the last petrol bomb danced as it readied itself for destruction. Marsden lobbed it through a window, shattering the stained glass saint. The fire roared into life, giving the church a beautiful demonic glow as though Hell had risen to claim it.

***

"Five officers died in the blaze." Aeron slapped five smiley face stickers underneath Marsden's name on Travel Inn's wall. Morgan leaned against the desk, her cat o' nine tails dangling by her leg. "Police are raiding every rioter's home in the hope of finding the arsonist. Good work. And well done on the church."

"There was no-one inside. No-one will cry over some scorched bibles." Demi folded her arms as she sat on the settee, as far away from Mac as possible. She'd created a cushion wall between them so Aeron could only see Mac from the knees down. "He might as well have painted a cross on a cardboard box and burned that."

"He's created a war between civilians and the police. Torching the church will create a war between civilians and the church. You can't have a battle without soldiers. And what's the cause of most wars? Religion. This phase is

Operation Bible Class. Our focus is creating martyrs so we can slaughter them. Were you not paying attention?"

"Religion is as outdated as Walkmans and crimped hair. The only conflict it will create is between him and Saint Spank-Me-Not." She smirked at Marsden, who lay on the bed, his guitar beside him. "I'd love to be a fly on the wall when he finds out what you've done. He'll never speak to you again. Just as well. You can't have boy scouts tarnishing your image. It'd be like Hitler adopting kittens."

"They can fight to the death," Morgan said. "We can attach giant controllers to them, pretend we're playing Golden Axe for real."

Marsden sat up, glowering at Demi. "How many lives have *you* taken?"

"People can't starve to death overnight. You have by *far* the easiest job. Even Snotbag's take ages to expire."

"We're on a tight schedule, Dems," Aeron said. "This game's about the number of coffins in the cemetery. Your father wiped out millions and created conflict over food rationing which led to cannibalism. You've force-fed a man his McFry's meal."

"And killed a girl in the playground with the fireman's pole. Now I'm becoming famous, I'll collect smiley stickers. People will respect my views because they'll be printed in *Sassy!* I could become the newest diet goddess. Marsden's like the Pied bloody Piper. He whips out his guitar and they follow him to their deaths."

Marsden clicked his fingers. "That reminds me. What was the death toll on the college shooting in America?"

"Fifty, including the shooter." Morgan stuck a black 50 sticker decorated with balloons and streamers on the wall.

"What shooting?" Demi asked.

"After hearing Mars's songs on YouTube, a college kid stole his daddy's gun and massacred his fellow students in the name of God. He reckoned they were sinners and he was saving their souls. The incident has again raised gun law debates in America. Pro-gun lobbyists are taking to the streets with their assault rifles in defiance. It's only a matter of time before bullets rain down on everyone."

"This is what I'm talking about! He has a distinct advantage over me and Warthog. He can kill *fifty* people in the time it takes me to give a rousing speech on the no-food diet."

Aeron tutted. "Diets won't end the world. All you'll do is bankrupt Cadbury's."

"You could've killed McPervert with one kiss," Marsden said. "You *chose* to prolong his suffering. It'd take you a minute to kill someone, so stop bitching and give them the kiss of death."

"You just want to see my waistline expand like a pop-up tent."

"You don't want to wear the cockroach suit," Morgan said.

Aeron nodded. "You'd hate for that image to break the internet."

"Some things can't be deleted."

"Fine, I'll make you some corpses." Demi stood, flicking her hair. "I don't see you hassling Prince of Plagues."

"My drug kills at least two clubbers every weekend," Mac defended himself. "I've infected prostitutes and rent boys within three towns. Think how many wives, girlfriends, boyfriends, other prostitutes their customers will infect. Not to mention my one night stands. I could cripple the country with STIs within a *month*."

"We don't want the image of you having sex in our heads. Some of us hate horror films. I'm going to get a McFry's shut down. You watch people starve when they're forced to cook for themselves. I'll just sit back and watch their laziness kill them."

***

Demi waited until a worker opened McFry's then slipped inside. While the girl prepared the restaurant area, Demi snuck into the kitchen and emptied a bottle of laxative-laced water into each vat. It would save the customers hundreds in colonic irrigation treatments. She emptied a bottle into the vegetable oil, before pouring some into the ice cream.

She crept to the door. The worker was preparing the drive-thru area. Demi grabbed another bottle from her bag and contaminated the drinks.

"I'm a *genius*. I hope they enjoy their chicken McSquits."

***

Demi returned at lunchtime and ordered a salad. Smirking, she toyed with it as customers took food to the crowded tables. One man ran to the toilets. Thirty seconds later, another man followed. Behind her, a woman groaned then scuttled to the toilets.

"They're finally exercising."

The first man emerged, paler than a mushroom. He sat then jumped back up and dashed to the toilet. Within half an hour, people formed queues, clutching their stomachs. Sweat glistened on their faces. Gurgling stomachs and the occasional fart replaced inane chatter. Demi grimaced. Whispering workers exchanged alarmed glances. Mac wasn't the only one who could decimate a population through disease.

Demi carried her salad to the counter, making a show of dumping it in the bin. "I don't know what you've done to my food, but I feel horrendously sick. Judging by the fact the toilets are more popular than a stripper's g-string, I'd say your customers feel the same. The smell is *rank*. I thought this was a restaurant, not a sewage plant. A rat just fainted. I bet your customers didn't order the trots as their McFry's Surprise. I want to speak to your manager."

The boy yelled for the manager.

A young man in a suit appeared. "Can I help you?"

"Are you the manager's son?"

"I'm the manager."

She laughed. "Work experience is it? Your food is *vile*. If I ran a squeegee down these people's faces, I'd collect enough grease to repair the ozone layer. You've poisoned everyone. If I smell one more waft from those toilets, I'll be sick. I'd like a refund and an apology. You should change your stock phrase to 'would you like diarrhoea with that?'"

People queued behind her as the manager refunded her. Someone barged her as they demanded to speak to him.

"Don't touch me, Shitler. I hope you've washed your hands!"

She fought her way out, trying not to touch anyone. When the door closed, she burst out laughing. She'd need a Hazmat suit to walk past this place.

"Serves you right, grease frightnings." She pulled out her phone. "Is that *The Lemures Chronicle*?...There's a food poisoning outbreak at McFry's on Nyx Street. It's chaos. People are queuing at the toilets, which are blocked. The smell is *horrendous*." She hung up then rang Mac. "Operation McSwill is complete. Get your pimply arse down here and infect them while their immune systems are lower than a whore's knickers...I'll delay them."

She pivoted and discreetly chained the door shut with her balances.

"Wait 'til you meet my colleague. You won't want his soup of the day."

CHAPTER 23

Ghostly hymns haunted the cold church. Disjointed voices recited long-forgotten lyrics and sucked contaminated air into the worshippers' lungs. Their fingers touched the hymn book's soiled covers and tainted pages. To them, the paper was a fading cream. To Mac, it was bedecked in colours, like someone spilled glitter over every page. He sneezed, flu germs sprinkling the man beside him. He moved to another pew, touching every person he passed, covering their clothes in purple dots ringed by brown, white and orange. Some received the blue strings of Ebola.

By tonight, the entire congregation would be infected with flu, Ebola and boils. Tomorrow, they would rush to the confessional and purge themselves of their sins in the hope God would save them.

By the end of the week, they would learn God couldn't save the world.

***

Mac returned to each church the next day, flanked by Morgan and Aeron. Sobbing replaced singing as parishioners hid boils and sores beneath clothing, makeup or scarves. Their gazes strayed to fellow parishioners, seeking comfort, redemption or hope, but finding faces identical to theirs.

Mac sat at the back, his hood concealing his face. Finally, he wasn't the most repulsive person in the room.

175

Morgan and Aeron smiled as parishioners enviously studied their unblemished faces.

"You don't have to be here," Mac murmured. "They're not ready to expire."

"And miss an opportunity for a road trip across America with you?" Morgan whispered back.

"You don't even like me. You're here to check I haven't wussed out."

"Nonsense. Just because we won't touch you, doesn't mean we don't like you. You're not *entirely* without charm."

"God has spoken!" The preacher's voice boomed through the church. "He sent a plague of boils!" Some parishioners gasped. Others wept or pleaded for forgiveness. "Deuteronomy 28:27 'The Lord will strike you with the boils of Egypt, with tumours, with the scab, and with the itch, from which you cannot be healed'."

"The itch is never fun," Aeron said. "And you can't scratch it in public."

"We were *warned*! We did not take heed! Now we'll suffer his terrible wrath."

"*I* sent the plague of boils," Mac muttered. "Why's God getting the credit?"

"Those who work behind the scenes never get recognition," Aeron said. "You're the writer. God's the star."

The preacher continued. "So it says in Samuel 5:9: 'But after they had brought it around, the hand of the Lord was against the city, causing a very great panic, and he afflicted the men of the city, both young and old, so that tumours broke out on them'. God is angry! John 1:9 'If we confess our sins, he is faithful and just to forgive us our sins, and to cleanse us from all unrighteousness'."

"Going to the confessional won't save you – I infected that too," Mac muttered.

"Good job." Morgan smiled, sitting a foot away from Mac. Aeron sat on her other side. "It's like attending your family reunion."

"Without the cake," Aeron added.

"And commenting how big you've grown."

"Look at them panicking, thinking the end of the world is upon them. Who'd have thought it'd be so...ugly."

"The Apocalypse, sponsored by Spot-Less. I'm looking forwards to Mars's offering."

"Every good Apocalypse needs a slaughter scene."

"Or people will leave the cinema disappointed and demanding their money back."

"Why do I bother?" Mac sighed, rubbing a gangrene nail on his jeans. Green pus seeped out. "You only care about him."

"Nonsense," Aeron answered. "His are more entertaining. Something you can watch with popcorn."

"Or crisps," Morgan said.

"Eating while watching yours will result in vomiting."

"And his allows for audience participation."

"I could sneeze on your hands so you could spread germs," Mac said.

Morgan's face contorted. "Do you use that line with all the ladies?" She slid another inch away. "Great idea to visit America's Bible belt."

"Mars said the UK lacked the religious fervour required to link boils to God. He saw this preacher on TV and figured he'd be perfect."

Morgan and Aeron whispered furiously, gesticulating wildly. Mac was glad he wouldn't be on the receiving end. Their actions made the inquisitor's chair seem like a comfortable place to sit.

"Can we go? I've sat through so many services I know the hymns off by heart. I'm sick of them patting my arm and telling me God will forgive me. At least they pick up new bacteria with their patronising gesture."

"According to the noticeboard, there's a wedding next," Morgan said. "You should give everyone a gift to remember the special day."

"I could infect hundreds. They'll pass it on to their families."

"It'll be the first wedding we've attended without taking a guest. It's nice to have time off."

"We could have cake," Aeron said.

"You should sabotage the cake, so they leave with Salmonella in their party bags," Morgan told Mac. "Attend the evening do and give out STIs like wedding favours. People *always* hook up at weddings. Try a bridesmaid."

Mac smiled, his blistered lips cracking, blood escaping his cold sore. "This will definitely be a day they'll never forget."

Aeron and Morgan burst into song. "Here comes the bride, with boils on her hide, the wedding guests were angry when they got STIs."

Aeron cupped his hand to his ear. "Can you hear that?"

"The sound of the wedding march morphing into the funeral march?" Morgan also cupped her ear.

"The sweet sound of the fifth seal breaking."

***

Demi entered the commune and flounced to the hall where everyone gathered. The heels of her blueberry knee high boots chimed off the floor. Her apple coloured skirt flowed out behind her. The leader hurried over and grasped her hands. She tried not to recoil, her inner slimeball alarm bleating. He was so nondescript she would have forgotten what he looked like if he wasn't standing in front of her.

"I'm so glad you could make it! My flock are losing faith."

"Worry not, Brother Beard."

"It's Bird."

"Oh, I thought it was a nickname on account of your illustrious beard. You look like Mr Twit." She beamed. "Take me to your people."

He led her onto the stage. The hardest part of her speech would be not insulting the fashionably challenged cultists sitting on the floor like Raggy Doll rejects.

"I'm Demi and I've been touched by God." She fought back laughter. "He touched me in a very special place." She waited for them to smirk. They didn't. They clearly had the sense of humour of a mashed muffin. "My heart." She placed her hand over her heart then scanned their faces, checking to see if she was overdoing it. Apparently not. Maybe she needed to be *more* theatrical. Add glow sticks. "I started my quest several years ago and now I've reached the stage of enlightenment. God speaks with me daily. The only way to truly open your heart to him is through fasting. Jesus fasted when he was tempted by Satan. Through those forty days and nights of loneliness, wild beasts and satanic attacks, 'he ate nothing'. Luke 4:2."

The cultists murmured.

"The end is nigh and when God descends to collect the righteous, will he pick people who live a life of luxury and gluttony over those who choose abstinence? No. He'll choose people who followed his son's example, and I don't mean getting yourselves crucified and kissing traitors."

"What about headaches and stomach cramps?" a woman asked. "Without food and water, we'll die."

"Brother Beard said there were doubters. Those too scared and weak to follow God's teachings." Everyone looked around, trying to spot them. "Headaches are God's way of clearing your minds so you can hear his voice. Stomach cramps are sin leaving your body. That's when it will be hardest to resist. Did Jesus give in and snack on a porkpie? No! Because he persevered, he resisted Satan. He couldn't have done that with his belly weighed down by Yorkshire puddings and tiramisu."

A man raised his hand. "How long do we fast for?"

"Forty days and forty nights. It's a small time period compared to an eternity in paradise. Jesus didn't nip to Tesco's when times got tough. Look at what's happening in the world – riots, boils, violence. Why? Because we've been consumed by *greed*. In McFry's in Lemures, hundreds of people suffered food poisoning. Was it due to poor hygiene? No. God's teaching us a *lesson*. *Food* is our devil. Fasting is our way of saying to the devil 'I'm stronger than you. You can't have my soul!'"

Everyone burst into rapturous applause. Demi smothered her smile. For the first time, she wasn't booed when doing public speaking. Now she knew why her witty social observations were never appreciated: she didn't back them up with Bible quotes.

People knelt up, praying. She bowed her head and left the stage. The only other time she'd brought someone to their knees was when she kicked them for dropping ketchup on her skirt.

"Thank you." Brother Bird gripped her hands, his slimy palms making her question whether he was a frog in disguise. She was tempted to sit him by a pond and feed him flies.

"I like helping the lost." She pulled away.

"Do you really hear God's voice?"

"Of course! Don't you? You're the leader. If he's not speaking to you, you must have angered him. Try washing."

"You say you're a model. That's a world filled with sin."

"I didn't choose to be God's spokesperson. When I fasted for an important shoot, I heard his voice. I asked if I should quit, join a nunnery. He said," she adopted a deep voice. "'No Demi! I have enough nuns! Nobody listens to their pious ways. I need someone to spread my message to those who don't hear it in church. Someone who possesses great beauty, for the common people worship the beautiful. You will become a star and guide your followers to me through your teachings'. The more I fasted, the louder he spoke. Who am I to refuse God's will?"

Brother Bird moved to kiss her cheek. She dodged it and fled. She needed bacterial hand wash. Forget chocolate. Victory had never tasted so sweet.

CHAPTER 24

Sacred City glowed beneath Drew's headlight as he cruised into Misery. He pulled up and killed his bike engine. The light died, darkness claiming the graveyard once more. He looked around before dismounting and pushing open the black gate. It squeaked, betraying his entrance. He wheeled his bike in, hiding it in the bushes that reached out through the railings, like the damned desperate to break free from Hell's eternal suffering.

He crept among the graves; stone gargoyles on sentry duty, waiting for the perfect time to strike and tear his beating heart from his chest. This was the one place where he could believe legendary monsters were real.

Rustling.

He turned, his heart hammering on his chest. A tree danced under the wind's command. He shook his head. Spooked by a tree. If a bat swooped down, he'd probably die from fright. A large tomb lurked at the back of the graveyard. Even from this distance, he could feel evil pulsing within it. He shuddered, his choker glowing in response. His zipped up his hoody. The last thing he needed was his halo betraying him like an angelic bat signal.

"Who goes there?" A four foot high skeleton emerged from a rickety hut, raising his lantern. Shadows prowled in his eye sockets, as though the skeleton's nightmares were crawling free from his tortured mind.

Drew stumbled backwards. "What the hell are you?"

"Ankou. I guard the dead."

"They're not going anywhere."

"I make sure they stay that way."

Drew glanced at the graves, expecting a rotting hand to burst through the earth. Now he wished he'd come armed. If zombies were real, he was in the worst place.

Ankou moved his lantern closer to Drew. "Who are you?"

"Drew. I'm an angel."

Ankou folded his bony arms. "Prove it."

Drew's eyes shone and he unzipped his hoody. The skeleton shielded his eye sockets.

"I had to be sure. If I believed everyone, then I've had three vampires and a werewolf lurking here this week alone." He lowered his lantern. "I've never met an angel."

Drew concealed his halo again. "We're an endangered species on Earth."

"What is your business here?"

"I'm meeting someone."

"That's what they all say. I'll be watching you, angel."

"Please, don't tell anyone I was here."

"If you're going to cause trouble, you can leave. Who's going to come looking for you?"

"No-one. Just…if anyone asks."

"Don't disturb the dead." He returned to his hut.

Bright light drowned the cemetery. A gust of wind battered Drew. He stepped back, shielding his face. That was a more impressive entrance than the Horsemen made. Silence and darkness swiftly descended.

"Were you followed?"

Drew blinked. "No."

A dark haired angel stood before him, clutching a sword. "Hey Drew. I've missed you. Heaven's quiet without you. I have no-one to make mischief with."

"Eden." Drew hugged him, his skin growing hot and stinging slightly. "I've missed you too."

"Are you lonely?"

"I got used to being a pariah."

"What's it like having free will?"

"Terrifying. Incredible. I'm not sure how I'll cope if Father lets me back. Heaven will seem so restrictive."

Eden looked around. "Earth looks different down here. Like being inside a map. It's cold too. And it smells odd." He shivered. "Why is my skin prickling?"

"Earth's tainted with sin. It's like a poison. You get used to it."

"This isn't where I would've chosen to meet."

"The Horsemen would notice you coming to the pub. Angels aren't exactly subtle. The Horsemen don't venture into this city much. If they happened to visit tonight, this is the last place they'd look."

"Why?"

Drew pointed to the tomb. "That's the gateway to Hell."

Eden drew his sword and dropped it. "We're not safe!" He hopped, clutching his foot.

"It's locked. At least, until the fifth trumpet sounds. Then Misery is doomed." Drew handed him the sword. "Should you be carrying that? You'll take out someone's eye."

"I'm on a dangerous mission. Dangerous missions require soldiers to be armed."

"How did you get out? I thought they'd imprisoned you."

"I served my sentence. Michael's visiting, so I snuck out when everyone was busy welcoming him home."

Drew glowered. "He's a hypocrite."

Eden's eyes widened. "Ssh! Someone will hear."

"Will someone see you talking to me? I don't want to get you into trouble."

"I switched off the camera covering you."

"Thanks." Drew smiled. "I don't deserve you."

"You don't deserve *this*. Exile."

"I broke the most important rule."

"But you were right. Nobody will admit it – they're too afraid they'll join you. I was imprisoned because Father wanted to keep us apart. Otherwise, I'd be in exile with you, Mark, John and Jael. And Joshua. That and I…chopped off Grace's hand." He grimaced.

"Why?"

"It was an accident! I don't make a habit of dismembering the family. I was practising with my sword, in case I'm called on to fight, and I didn't know she was behind me. Frightened the life out of me. I'm afraid I was overzealous in my self-defence. She told Father and that gave him a legitimate reason to imprison me. I hoped it would…grow back before anyone noticed." He shrugged. "She's ostracised me. I should remind her about forgiveness. Now the other angels think I'm some kind of angel-mutilating monster."

Drew laughed. "I'm sorry I missed it. I asked Michael if you could come down. He forbade it. I don't know how he expects me to stop the Horsemen with three angels."

"It's like the Spartans all over again."

"They died."

"Whoops. Sorry. Wrong comparison." Eden smiled sheepishly "Is that why you asked me to bring the…" he looked furtively around then whispered in Drew's ear, "package?"

"Yes. Did you bring it?"

Eden pulled a package from his inside jacket pocket. "Don't get caught with it. They'll make an example out of us. It won't end well. Examples always receive the worst punishments. We'll probably be made to sit on Christmas trees. Or turned to stone for water features. I don't want to spend eternity pissing into ponds."

"They'll probably send us to a family reunion with Lucifer."

Eden's eyes widened. "In…there?" He pointed to the tomb.

"I'll tell them I forced you. I can't thank you enough. I put your life in danger asking for this."

"It was thrilling. I felt like a spy. I was convinced I'd be beheaded and de-winged. The most daring thing I've ever done was skinny dipping in the Garden's pool with you."

"Did anyone see you take it?"

"No. They're too busy worrying about what the Horsemen are planning. And because of that hand incident, the others now avoid me. I pretty much have free rein. Maybe I should chop off more angel parts." He laughed then covered his mouth and closed his eyes, ducking. He opened one eye, peeking up at the sky.

"You switched the camera off, remember?"

He straightened. "Right, yes. That was forward thinking of me."

Eden relinquished the package. Drew unravelled it, revealing an iridescent glass dagger. The gold and silver haft was made from the same material as their halos.

Drew stroked the blade. "It's beautiful."

"And deadly."

"It has to be. It's the only weapon that can stop the Apocalypse."

***

Shops' graffitied shutters were closed, like the city had lowered its eyelids to avoid the nightmares the dark would bring. People abandoned one pub or club for another, or swapped the streets for a taxi, or a taxi for a stranger's bed.

Marsden stood cloaked in the caged shadow of the world statue. Christmas lights hung above the street, their twinkling beauty a stark contrast to the litter and vomit below. Like putting makeup on a corpse. Even the statue and the trees flanking it were wrapped in Christmas lights. Marsden ducked out of the lights coiled around his body, wrapped one end of his lights around the lowest tree branch and left the other end by the statue, like a snake poised to strike. He tied another string of lights to the other tree and switched them on.

Now to hunt his prey.

"Sins of the flesh will damn you to Hell!" The pavement preacher thrust leaflets at clubbers. "Repent! Abstain! When Judgement Day comes, only the pure, the holy will rise in the Rapture while the sinners will suffer eternal torment in Hell's fiery pits!"

Some people laughed and mimicked him. Others ignored him or crossed the road to avoid him.

"God's angels walk among us! They wear human faces, but I have seen one. God took my sight because nothing on Earth compares to the angel's beauty. There is only one reason angels are here – to save the righteous!"

"You won't convert them," Marsden said. The preacher's blind eyes stared through him. Healed burns scarred the preacher's eye sockets.

"Don't they know what awaits them? Torture, pain, misery for eternity. Their sins will plague them in Hell."

"Satan has better PR than God. He sells nightmares disguised as dreams."

"Darkness resides in your soul. You will be punished."

"You can't punish something that will never die. I've seen the angel too. God didn't take *my* sight."

"You haven't seen his true form, only the human package that hides it."

Marsden played a chord. The pavement preacher gasped then touched his face. Scarlet tears trickled down his cheeks.

"You're…the devil!" He backed away. "But…I saw you with the angel. Are you one of the fallen?"

"I'm War."

Horror tainted the man's features. "The Apocalypse has begun!"

"Just what you've always wanted. You'll play a part in it, not just a cameo. This could be your big break, get you noticed by the man upstairs."

The preacher tripped over a homeless man and fell against a shop. "What are you talking about?"

"The fifth seal is breaking."

"The martyrs," he whispered.

Marsden smiled. "Welcome to your destiny."

He dragged the preacher down Gallows Street. The preacher shouted for help but his cries were smothered by revellers' laughter.

A woman ran over. "What are you doing? Leave him alone."

Marsden drew his knife from his belt and thrust it into her stomach. Her eyes widened in disbelief. He sheathed the knife as he stepped over her defeated body.

He pulled a noose made from guitar strings out of his pocket and slid it around the preacher's throat. Slinging him over his shoulder, he climbed the statue, tied the noose to the bars then kicked the preacher off. The preacher struggled as he twirled, scratching his throat, rivers of blood seeping down his skin.

Marsden climbed down the statue and perched on the hand. He hooked up the lights with his guitar and wrapped them around the preacher's wrists, spreading his arms. The preacher gagged, stuttered prayers escaping his lips.

"There's no point praying – God's not listening."

Marsden forced the preacher's mouth open and cut out his tongue. Blood gushed from his mouth as he thrashed on his makeshift gallows. Marsden ripped open the preacher's top and carved a horseshoe with a sword through it into his torso. Dipping his finger into the spilled blood, he scrawled *Come and See* on the preacher's dying body. The leaflets scattered over the ground, stained by the preacher's blood as he died on the old execution site, praying for the salvation that never came.

CHAPTER 25

The door slammed. Candle flames died, expelling smoke like exorcised spirits torn from the bodies of the possessed. Silence swept down, suffocating the atmosphere. A cough echoed through Our Lady of Sorrows church.

Priests and bishops turned, mistrust and unease crinkling their faces.

"Welcome," a priest said. "Have you come to pray?"

"Prayers won't save you." Marsden swung his guitar round from his back, his black chainmail chinking. "There's no-one left to listen."

Fear tainted the atmosphere. The raw music of 'Saints and Sinners' floated down the aisle like a ghostly bride about to utter the fateful words 'til death us do part'.

"This is a private meeting. If you haven't come to pray, you must leave. The city is at war."

"I know. I started it. But you're about to play an important role."

"Which is?"

"Breaking the fifth seal."

Unease infiltrated the church.

"You walk in off the street and expect us to believe your insane ramblings about the Apocalypse?" a bishop laughed. "We get reports of Apocalypses every week with the lottery numbers."

"Come and see."

The music died. Marsden gripped the guitar's head and pulled. The black snake detached from the skull body, revealing a sword. The snake coiled around the haft and guard, the silver strings wrapping around the blade to form barbed wire. The scarlet blade glinted, stained by thousands of years of human blood.

An archbishop gasped. "You're...War."

Marsden smiled, his eyes crimson orbs. "And the world's about to drown in blood."

He sliced the archbishop's head off. It dropped and rolled before the body realised there was nothing to keep it alive. The bible he held landed in the blood of the slain.

The men ran for the doors.

Morgan emerged from the shadows and blocked them. "Aren't you prepared to die for your faith? That's not very martyr-like. You've spent your lives warning people about the Apocalypse; the huge party to end the world. Now it's here, you're not R.S.V.P.ing? Isn't this what you've always wanted? Judgement? Redemption? Damnation?"

They turned towards the back.

Aeron materialised. "This is your destiny. It says so in the Bible. You'll finally meet your god so why are you scared? Will your sins see you shaking hands with the devil?"

Morgan kicked a bishop into a priest. They crashed into a small bookcase. Bibles showered them, the pages fluttering like angels' wings. Morgan produced two globes and drew a cross on one with her black nail. An ugly gash travelled down the bishop's body, followed by a horizontal slice. He shrieked as she pinched the four parts of the globe and pulled. His body split into four, his organs splattering the floor like a twisted sacrificial offering.

One of the priests grabbed the door. Marsden severed his wrist. The priest screamed, his hand still gripping the door handle. Marsden rammed his sword through his cheek, straight into another priest's stomach. He struck the first priest with the spiked gauntlet on his forearm. The spikes sunk into the priest's face as Marsden freed his sword.

The second priest dropped to his knees, trying to stem the flow of blood seeping through his cassock. Fear tainted his eyes as he murmured a prayer. Marsden rammed his sword into the priest's mouth, impaling him.

Another priest tried to dodge past Aeron. Smiling, he produced a globe from behind his back, rolling it along the back of his hand.

"Who are you?"

"Your worst nightmare. As much as you bleat to your flock about Heaven's rewards, they're meaningless words to vaporise your fears of me."

"I don't know who you are."

Aeron sighed. "That's the problem when you modernise something. People are too attached to the old stereotype to accept it. But Hollywood reboots classics all the time. Look how many different outfits superheroes have, yet people still recognise them." Aeron raised the hood on his ankle length PVC coat. "Ooh wait I forgot something. You'll get it this time." He reached into his pocket, freeing his scythe. He flicked it to its full length then pressed a button and the blade shot from the top. He thumped it down, glowering, his eyes glowing like the devil's infernal fires.

The priest gasped. "Death!"

"Bingo! You've won the star prize – a one-way trip to Hell. Dad said we wouldn't get respect because no-one would recognise us. It pisses me off you've proved him right." He folded the scythe and lowered his hood. "The scythe's for show. We upgraded to more...practical weapons. Do you know how embarrassing it is trying to sever someone's mortal coil, only to snag a telephone wire? Or get the scythe stuck in a tree?"

Aeron smiled and squeezed the globe. The priest wheezed, clutching his chest. Aeron ran his fingers down the glass. The priest scrammed his bleeding eyes; crimson prison bars staining his face. Aeron jabbed the globe, holes appearing in the priest's body with every poke. He slumped to the floor, his mouth open in a scream no-one heard.

Marsden climbed onto the back of a pew and ran along it. He jumped, grabbing the gold Jesus on the cross suspended above the altar. The cross swayed as he cut the wires. It swung through the air before plummeting as swift as a guillotine blade. Aeron and Morgan hauled a priest over to it, holding him still while Marsden tied him to the cross with guitar strings. He yanked the barbed wire strings off his sword and flung them at the priest. They coiled around his head, biting his flesh. He sobbed, ruby droplets snaking down his face. Marsden thrust his sword into the priest's chest as he begged for mercy.

Marsden plunged his hand into the priest's chest and ripped out his heart. The priest's eyes widened as Marsden dropped it into a collection plate. Crouching, he placed the plate beneath the priest's feet and sprinkled silver coins over the heart. He rose as a bishop snuck up on him, brandishing a gold candlestick.

"Ooh the bishop in the church with the candlestick," Aeron said. "Cluedo's come to life."

Marsden beheaded the bishop and kicked his body away. He wiped the blood from his eyes and faced the last two men.

"Please. Have mercy."

"I don't know what that means." Marsden looked at Morgan. "Any ideas?"

"I could Google it."

"You've dedicated your lives to God. You can't back out now. Your dog collars don't come with receipts."

He stabbed one priest through the heart. Freeing his sword, he carved his sign on the priest's dying body.

"This was a team effort, Mars," Aeron said.

Marsden added two scythes to the carving. The other priest fled down the aisle. Marsden hurled his sword. It spun end over end down the aisle and lodged between the priest's shoulder blades. He hit the floor, gurgling.

Morgan burst into applause. "Fantastic shot! I filmed it. We have to watch it in slow motion. We'll make a night of it – popcorn, cocktails and the massacre of martyrs. Mars, take a photo of us for the scrapbook. This will make a great postcard for Dad."

Marsden scowled as she handed over her phone. He took a photo as the twins flanked the crucified priest, mimicking his death pose. Blood trickled down his face and body, dripping into the collection bowl below and tainting the silver coins.

As they left the church, Marsden freed his sword from the fallen priest's back and slotted it into the guitar body. The neck reformed, life flowing through his veins at the martyr's brutal deaths.

The Horsemen mounted their bikes and travelled towards an abandoned prisoner of war camp twenty miles away in Keres.

Morgan killed her engine. "Newsflash, Bloody Fingers. They have to be martyrs."

"It's a suicide cult. We're going to help them."

"Assisted suicide, I like it," Aeron said. "Juries don't convict people for that."

They sped through the dusty, neglected grounds until they reached a large hall. Morgan flung out her hand and the door burst open. They rode in as people scurried out of the way. They stopped their bikes beside an altar of a golden eagle with a book on its back.

Marsden pulled off his helmet then addressed the cult members. "God tells me you've been waiting for Judgement Day so you can rise to take your seats in Heaven." He drew his sword. "I hope you've booked your table."

He dismounted and grabbed the leader, pinning him to the eagle altar. The leader wriggled, shouting for help. Morgan and Aeron hopped off their bike and held the leader's arms. Marsden decapitated him. His body slithered to the floor, leaving a scarlet trail across the book's gilded pages. Marsden placed the head on the book.

"Let there be blood!" Morgan mounted her bike.

A group huddling near the doors screamed and dived for safety as Morgan rode through them. Aeron juggled three globes before squeezing them. Three people fell, their eyes and ears bleeding. He drew his nail across one globe and a man's throat parted, blood gushing like the red sea. He poked his finger into another globe then yanked it out. A woman screamed as her heart tore through her chest and dropped into her hands, thrashing like a caged beast before dying. He threw the third globe at Marsden, who sliced it with his sword. An invisible blade cut through a man's body, the two halves falling separately.

People scrambled onto tables to get away. Marsden rode his bike onto a table, landing on a man, the bike's hot tyres tearing his flesh and pulverising his organs. Plates and glasses smashed beneath the tyres, the bike leaving a trail of blood.

"You were going to kill yourselves." He stabbed a woman. "This way you're more likely to get to Heaven. Or didn't your leader mention suicide's a sin?"

His bike hit the floor, fishtailing.

"This is so much fun! We should come out with you more often, Mars." Morgan crushed a globe in her hand. A woman's body shattered, flesh and blood raining down on the body by her feet. "I thought hanging out with Angel Delight was turning you softer than a teddy bear's tushy."

Crying and screaming poisoned the air. Marsden turned his bike sharply. It slipped in a puddle of blood and fell, trapping his leg. He and his bike hurtled across the floor, crashing through chairs and tables. He swung his sword, cutting through someone's legs. The bike collided with the stage. A man leapt over him, seizing his chance to escape. Marsden thrust his sword into the man's stomach.

The man's gaping mouth dripped blood onto Marsden's face. He tossed him aside then lay back, breathing heavily and smiling. Flapping wings broke the spell of silence.

"You might need to make several trips," Morgan told the raven. "Don't want you cricking your neck."

"Corpse!"

The raven took off, his pouch full of marbles. He passed over Marsden, casting a brief shadow before leaving them alone with the dead.

Aeron and Morgan lifted the bike and helped Marsden up. He parted his shredded PVC trouser leg, grimacing at the torn flesh.

"Stick a plaster on it, you'll be fine." Aeron knelt and kissed the wound. It healed beneath his lips, leaving a scar.

Morgan placed a large globe on the eagle's back. Through the black glass, wisps of white swirled. One passed the glass, its terrified face locked in a silent scream.

"The martyrs?" Marsden asked.

"Would you like the honours?" Morgan said.

Aeron pouted. "You said I could do this one."

Morgan squeezed his cheeks. "You can do the next one."

Marsden raised his sword above his head. The trapped souls swam faster. The sword plunged into the globe. The glass shattered, accompanied by a thousand tortured screams of the damned.

CHAPTER 26

Scarlet footprints betrayed Drew as he slipped through the gloom, past the blood splattered pews and clotting puddles on the floor. The stench of death and metallic tang of blood coated his throat, as though he was swallowing their souls. He stopped by the bodies of the fallen; living people reduced to brutal horror film props. Their twisted expressions portrayed a world that would die in agony.

Drew approached the crucified priest and crouched to touch the crimson coins. Coldness kissed his skin, like a final goodbye from a dying lover. The priest's heart sat in the centre of the plate, its sacrifice accepted. Tears burned Drew's eyes as he retreated.

"Thought I'd find you here." Marsden stepped out of the confessional and headed up the aisle. His footsteps seemed disrespectfully loud, mocking the dead who would no longer walk this earth.

Drew's heart fluttered. He clenched his jaw. "Were you waiting for me?"

"It was either that or watch daytime TV with Mac."

"My failure is more entertaining."

"I'm sorry."

"'Sorry' is what you say when you crash my bike. You've massacred a church full of men. There's not a Hallmark card that covers this!" He flung his arm out.

"I sense a gap in the market. It's in the Bible, Drew. They *wanted* this to happen."

"They didn't want *this*." Drew gestured to the headless corpses, the crucified priest, the rivers of blood that had flowed over the floor. A place of worship had become a shrine to the dead. "Do you at least feel remorseful?"

"No." Marsden glanced at the corpses. "This is what I was born to do. This is who I am. They were the fifth seal. So I broke them."

Drew fought the tears prickling his eyes. "For all your faults, at least you're not a liar."

"Will it make you feel better if I said the ones which look like 3D jigsaws are the Death Squad's handiwork?"

Drew glanced at the decapitated bishop by the cross. "You didn't exactly kill them with kindness."

"The martyrs had to be *slaughtered*."

"You didn't have to take it literally!"

"You're supposed to follow the Bible in black and white. Kill gay men, force rape victims to marry their rapists, banish women on their period, sacrifice your firstborn. Slaughter the martyrs to break the fifth seal. This is *your* religion. Not mine. Are you saying it's wrong?"

"Of course it's *wrong!*" Drew's choker tightened. He coughed. "Nothing in this world is black and white. A religion can't survive on teachings written two thousand years ago. The world was different then. The King James version has hundreds of differences to the original text, which leads me to question whether today's Bible is the word of God, or the word of the translator." His throat closed, his breath sealed in its ribcage prison. "David and Jonathan were clearly in a homosexual relationship – Jonathan's father accepted David as a son-in-law, but aspects were deleted. David said Jonathan's love for him was more wonderful than that of women. In the original Hebrew text, they kissed until David 'became large'."

Marsden laughed. "The Bible says David had a hard-on? The version I read, they shake hands. The original's more *50 Shades of Pray*."

Purple rain danced in Drew's sight. Marsden's voice became fainter. "The original Hebrew translation says Ashpenaz showed mercy and engaged in physical love with Daniel. Though they were eunuchs."

"Maybe they had toys."

"Left-handed people are more vilified in the Bible than homosexuals. So if God no longer condemns them, he can't condemn me for loving you."

"How can you love me after this?" Marsden glanced at the bodies. "*No-one* can forgive this."

"We're taught everything can be forgiven."

"Bullshit. Hell was created to punish those who disobey, or refuse to ask for forgiveness. Fuck sake, Drew, God cast *you* out because you *questioned* him. That's not forgiving. He cast Lucifer out because he defended man. Yet he's the one seen as the epitome of evil."

"Angels aren't supposed to question Him."

"Because he's a dictator who wants mindless puppets."

Drew studied the slain men. "In Heaven, among the angels and the beauty, it's easy to believe in God and his goodness."

"Clearly not, seeing as you started a one-angel rebellion while you were there."

"I guess I lost my rose-tinted glasses. Now I'm here, with the cruelty, the suffering, the ugliness of some people's souls, Heaven seems like a fairytale and God…is he any better than the devil? At least the devil grants people free will and doesn't punish them for using it."

Drew's choker strangled him. He collapsed, gasping and gouging his burning throat. Smoke rose from the band, escaping to the heavens. Marsden grabbed the choker, hissing as it scorched his fingers. Blood slithered down Drew's neck.

Drew was hoisted into the air, kicking as he dangled on his invisible noose. His wings burst through his skin, blood drops raining on Marsden like spilled rubies from a broken rosary. Drew's heart thundered as blinding light flooded the church. A deafening shriek echoed. Marsden screwed his eyes shut and clamped his hands over his ears. Loud flapping of wings accompanied a blast of air that knocked Marsden off his feet. He skidded into the font, banging his head.

God's eyes bored into Drew's as searing agony tore through his heart. Darkness dragged him into its depths. Unbearable heat consumed him, his wings scorching and turning to ash. His body felt like it was torn into a thousand pieces. Tortured screams haunted his mind as he plunged beneath a lake with a fiery shroud.

Drew smacked onto the blood stained floor, gagging. Crimson tears bled from his eyes, a scarlet veil distorting his vision. His wings burdened his back. Marsden wrenched Drew's choker down, cursing as his ruined skin was scalded again. Drew wheezed and spluttered, the cold tiles relieving his pain. He shakily sat up and fingered his neck, feeling a noose branded into his flesh. His throat burned as though he had swallowed the lake's blazing water.

Marsden ran his fingers through Drew's wings, tiny flames skimming the feathers. Blood speckled his face. "Your eyes turned black. What did you see?"

"My future." His voice was hoarse.

"I guess it didn't have a white picket fence, loyal wife and two children. No wait, I'm confusing it with Hell."

Drew rose unsteadily. Marsden held his arm. They hissed at the burn. Drew wrenched his arm away and pulled himself up on a pew. He turned Marsden's hands palm up. His skin bubbled off his fingertips.

Drew kissed them then frowned. "They're not healing. I'm so sorry."

"What for?"

"I spoke out of turn. Now we've suffered."

"You get punished for having an opinion? This isn't a religion, it's an abusive relationship."

"For fuck's sake, I'm in His house. Where He can hear me loudest. It's shit like this that got me kicked out. I never fucking *learn*!" He yanked his choker. "It's not a halo, it's a fucking choke chain and I've been told to 'heel'."

"Spoken like an abuse victim – blaming yourself for getting a slap." Marsden tore his gaze from Drew's throat. "I'm more toxic than Mac. I've brought nothing but trouble into your life."

"I don't regret a single second of it."

"You don't regret *this*?" Marsden gestured around the church. "You haven't seen the POW camp."

"Yes you hurt me. But you also heal me."

"That's like taking arsenic to cure a cold." Marsden fetched his guitar. "I should do the honourable thing and stay away from you. Let you regain your place in Heaven." He raised his hand to touch Drew's face. "There's no place for honour on the battlefield." He curled his fingers and slipped past Drew.

"If you truly believed that, why haven't you kissed me?"

Marsden turned around. "You take the enemy *then* you take your prize."

Frustration shackled Drew's heart in barbed wire. He wanted Marsden to run back and steal a kiss that would make the fireflies in his stomach dance and leave him breathless.

The door closed.

Drew yanked his choker, but it refused to yield its grip. He kicked over the bookcase and flung the bibles across the church.

"Why did you let him come here?" Tears scalded his face. "Why did you let me love him?" He picked up a dropped candlestick and hurled it down the aisle. "Is this my punishment? You give me the capacity to love him so I can watch him *slaughter* everyone? You inflict human emotions upon me so I suffer their *pain*? This is what I get for *questioning* you? *Murderers* get kinder punishments."

Drew kicked the collection plate. Bloodied coins scattered amongst the bodies, leaving trails like exposed veins through the church's cold corpse. The heart rolled to a stop. He flapped his wings. Silver light flooded the church. Pews shot backwards, crashing into the wall. Windows smashed, the saints desecrated on the pavement. Outside, car and house alarms sang a chorus of misery. The church shook. The wooden chandelier plummeted along with chunks of the ceiling. The spilled candles ignited. Fresh blood seeped from the priests and bishops' eyes.

"You want to damn me to Hell, fine! But you'll have to cut my wings off or I'll return to Heaven with Lucifer."

Drew fell to his knees, shaking, his wings closing. The light faded, leaving the church darker than before. He cast his gaze over the bodies, the gold Jesus and the blood soaked bible lying at the feet of another soul he was too late to save.

CHAPTER 27

"You know what will help my cause?" Demi asked the Horsemen, lying face down on the bed beside Marsden, like a steamrollered octopus.

Morgan leaned against Travel Inn's bathroom doorframe. "A crop dusting plane? There may be vouchers for a weekend course."

"A team of locusts," Aeron said, draped over the settee arm. "Wearing matching outfits as they chomp their way through the Apocalypse."

"Brainwash drugs?" Mac suggested, playing with sugar packets as he slouched in the chair beside the desk.

"Your own doll, Anorexic Annabelle," Marsden said, "complete with diet book, diet pills and weighing scales. With optional accessories, such as Annabelle's Cosmetic Surgery Clinic with miniature working liposuction machine. No! Your death! Celebrities always become loved after they die, no matter how much the media hated them when they were alive. They'll create a slimming drug in your name. 'Demilax'. 'Crap out your fat'."

"No. Though the doll's a brilliant idea. What will help is visiting Africa."

"It's sweet you want to save the tiger, but you wouldn't provide them with a hearty meal. You're more of a snack."

She kicked his thigh. "Fuck off. How do celebs raise their profile? Going to Africa and posing for photos with starving kids."

"There's more to it than photobombing underfed orphans," Morgan said.

"You want to tell starving people they have figures most women envy?" Aeron asked.

"You're not having much luck convincing people here to starve so you're targeting people who have no choice, so it's less work," Marsden said.

Demi rolled her eyes. "Like sticking your sword in people is *work*. It's your equivalent to sex, without the awkward decision to accept their friendship request."

"It's totally different."

"Like bollocks it is. I've seen serial killer documentaries. Knife maniacs substitute one form of penetration for another. You love using your sword because you can't stick your little sword into Fairy Godlover."

"I've used a variety of weapons. The sword's traditional. I don't care how I kill them, as long as they die."

"As much as we'd all love to fantasise about Mars penetrating Drew, let's get back on topic," Morgan said.

Marsden thumped his face onto the bed. "I hope you all fall into piranha tanks."

"Harsh. You know we can't die that way."

"Exactly."

"Going to Africa is a great idea, Dems. Mac can take his drug trade international."

"I'm not having Germoline cramping my style and stealing my photo opportunities! Photographers will take one look at his pus-coated face and bam! He's the cover star for *Diseases Monthly*."

"It's nice to feel wanted," Mac muttered.

"Save your sob story – you're not trying to win over voters."

"Think how charitable you'll look escorting a leper," Aeron said. Mac hung his head. "You can wipe out a huge chunk of the population. Mac, you can spread rare diseases

– make them think they've been cursed, like you did with Congo."

Mac spread a map of Africa on the table and stuck green capsule-shaped stickers in Congo. "I'll increase the spread of AIDS."

"AIDS kills them slowly," Marsden said. "You need something fatal and fast."

"Like our lovemaking could be." Demi leaned towards him for a kiss.

Marsden grabbed her face and pushed her away. "How many times do I have to tell you I'm not a necrophiliac?"

"What the *fuck* is wrong with your fingers? Have you been fondling Gangrene's petri dish?"

"Let me see." Morgan approached him.

"They're fine." Marsden folded his arms.

"I wasn't asking permission." She yanked his wrists towards her. Angry blisters, ugly welts and purple scabs covered his fingers.

Aeron leaned over from the settee. "They look holy."

"They're from when I climbed that Jesus statue in the church."

"We touched that statue. We didn't burn," Morgan said.

"You're neither good nor evil – holy objects don't affect you."

"Maybe he jerked off Jesus of Suburbia," Demi said. "What else could they have been doing in his flat when he should've been starting the riots?"

"Traitorous bitch!" Marsden kicked her off the bed.

She rose and flung her shoe at him. It bounced off his arm. "I can't have my photo taken with starving kids if I'm covered in bruises. I'm not championing domestic abuse victims."

"What were you doing?" Morgan demanded.

"Banging his organ." Demi grinned. "When he was shouting 'Oh God!' was it for God or you?"

Marsden yanked his hands away. "I'll impale you and leave you for the crows." He stood.

"Not with those fingers." Aeron pushed him down. "Demi, Mac, go prepare for your African Adventure."

"I hope you get eaten by a cannibalistic tribe." Marsden flung Demi's shoe at her. "They can use your skin and bones to furnish their tents."

"I hope Virgin Fairy strums your guitar so your penis burns and shrivels. You might *be* less of a dick if you had less of one," Demi retorted, following Mac out.

Morgan gripped Marsden's fingers. "What have you been up to? Lie to us and these little piggies will go to market." She bent his pinky finger back.

"If you can't play or hold your sword, you're useless to us," Aeron said.

Marsden prised Morgan's hands away. "I've slaughtered hundreds and you're threatening me because I've burned my fingers?"

"Burns are something you get when you touch the cooker," Morgan said.

Aeron picked up Marsden's guitar. "Maybe we'll send you back to Purgatory so you can watch the Apocalypse on the big screen."

"I touched Drew's halo."

"I hope that's not a euphemism," Morgan said.

"I hope it is." Aeron winked.

Marsden glared. "He blasphemed in the church and his halo became a noose. He would've hanged. I guess his father doesn't appreciate me saving his life."

"Maybe his father doesn't appreciate you lusting after his prodigal son. Nobody wants a bloodthirsty murderer for a son-in-law. It makes dinner parties tense."

"He said the Bible contradicted his personal beliefs. And God's no better than the devil."

"Ooh a rebel." Morgan fanned herself. "I wouldn't mind him taking me in the confessional while I confess my deadly sins. Commit more with him while we're in there."

Marsden's jaw clenched. "You even *think* about seducing him and I'll use your scythe to tear you in half."

"You're not licensed to use the scythe. You haven't completed the necessary training. Back to business. Angels don't have personal beliefs."

"Why d'you think he got kicked out of the family fold?"

Aeron smiled. "You've added sexual confusion and lust into the mix. A deadly combination. Good work, grasshopper."

"Not long ago, you were threatening to castrate me."

"That was when he was all pious and 'thou shalt not kill'. Everyone hates those killjoys. Now he's getting hanged by his halo for badmouthing God. Hit him while he's vulnerable. Serenade him at his window wearing nothing but a smile." Aeron strummed the guitar.

"What?"

"A soldier of God teaming up with the Horsemen! What could be better?"

"You want me to *recruit* him?"

"We want you to *corrupt* him."

"He'll fall!"

"He's *already* falling. For you." Aeron smiled. "We like Drew; he's a hot bundle of contradictions. We were against you two because he works for the opposing team, and was a bad influence. You were spending more time on Earth integrating yourself with the flesh puppets. We were worried you'd empathise with them and jeopardise our glorious Apocalypse. But it seems *you* were the bad influence on *him*. Your snake has tempted his garden of Eden. Now let him eat your apple."

"No." Marsden snatched his guitar.

"You want him. It's so obvious NASA noted it in their space logs. All you have to do is kiss him. Like in the fairytales."

"The princesses were dead or comatose. You said a kiss would kill him."

"Kill/condemn, we can't be expected to remember *every* minute detail of the Apocalypse. Fighting your desire every day must be horrendous. Surrender."

"I will *not* be responsible for damning him!"

"You already are," Morgan said. "He never experienced lust until you rode in on your red charger, starting wars and stealing his heart like a sexy Hollywood hero. We want you to be with him. Forever and ever until the world explodes, the sun melts and the sky is filled with the sweet sounds of angels' screams."

"He's a pawn to you. Something you can wave in God's face as a victory."

"You make that sound like a bad thing."

"He could die!"

"Better enter his pearly gates quick. He could ride your stairway to Heaven." Morgan imitated being a jockey.

"I'll get you an angel. But not him."

"When the world ends, don't you want him on *your* side? He's on a sinking ship," Aeron said. "Clinging to the sides in the vain hope it'll save him. The only thing that will, is you."

"By tossing him into the sea?"

"That's where the lifeboats are. I can't believe we have to force you to have sex with that hot crumpet. Hell if you won't spread his wings, I will."

"I insist," Morgan said. "I don't want Mars suffering from that pesky human emotion, guilt. I'll happily have Drew's tainted soul on my conscience for one night of passion."

"I bagsied him!"

"I didn't hear you bagsy."

Marsden stood. "Don't fucking touch him."

"You don't want him but don't want anyone else to have him," Aeron said. "I see how it is. You're like those psychos who kill their ex-girlfriends to stop other guys dating her."

"If you touch him, the only songs played on this guitar, will be yours."

Morgan stole it and played a few chords. Marsden dropped to the bed, clawing his head. The music stopped. He rolled onto his back, gasping, and touched his ears. Blood glistened on his fingers.

Morgan tossed his guitar onto his torso, followed by a song sheet. "That's Drew's song. When he falls, make sure he lands on the right side."

CHAPTER 28

Aeron tapped the pile of newspapers beside him on the table in Grease Lightning. They would add excitement to the scrapbook. So far, it mainly consisted of postcards, photos of every cocktail he and Morgan had sampled and the fifth seal. And their glorious tree.

"We're single-handedly saving the papers. People are longing to experience the misery heaped on the church, after reading their star signs and learning which celebrity has cellulite. Right wing papers are blaming immigrants, or violent video games." He flipped a paper to face Morgan and Marsden. "Ooh look, the bare breasts of page 3's Stacey, 19, from Newcastle can cheer readers up while they read about the brutal slayings."

"Sex and death – marriage made in Heaven," Morgan said.

"Priests are welcoming strays back to the flock," Marsden said. "I wonder how they'd feel if they knew the influx has nothing to do with God, but the desire to see where the martyrs were slaughtered. By next Sunday, the pews will be empty again."

"Hymns echoing in a forgotten church. Is there anything spookier?"

Lunchtime news entertained the diners.

"Police discover the butchered bodies of priests and bishops in Our Lady of Sorrows church. Violence continues in Syria after a suicide bomber killed ninety two people. And Charlene washed her last load in Celebrity Dirty Washing.

"Our Lady of Sorrows church was a scene of violence inside and out. Residents nearby were inexplicably struck blind. Some say they saw a silver light and heard a high-pitched noise shortly before losing their sight and are attributing it to a UFO. Doctors are baffled. But it was the bloody scene inside the church that will haunt the police."

"How did Altar Boy react when he realised you went all Quentin Tarantino on the martyrs?" Aeron asked. "Did he make you pray for your immortal soul?" The waiter brought fries over in a model Cadillac. A steering wheel contained bowls of dips and salad. Aeron took a photo and posted it on Pictogram.

"Take you to confession and spank your sins from you?" Morgan contributed.

"Force you to your knees and make you drink from his font of forgiveness?"

"He wasn't exactly pleased," Marsden replied. "Why are you photographing your food?"

"It's what mortals do. I think it's to taunt the starving – 'look what you can't have'. Years ago, they used to say prayers before meals. Now they take photos." Aeron dipped fries into ketchup. "Have you planned the Big Night?"

"Light candles, play soft music, scatter rose petals over the bed," Morgan suggested. "Leave him romantic clues to follow then he finds you on the bed, naked with a rose in your mouth and your gun loaded with the safety cocked back."

"That's so clichéd it's making me sick." Marsden leaned back on the bench seat. "I don't want thorns in my tongue."

"You should record the momentous occasion." Aeron licked ketchup off a fry while staring seductively at Marsden. "It can go in the scrapbook on the 'fun and frolics' page. It's not every day War seduces an angel. Some of us want to share in the glorious moment."

"Your switch from 'touch him and we'll rip your gonads off' to 'get upstairs and hoist his mainsail' is disconcerting. Do we have to talk about it here?"

"They serve sex-themed cocktails, I doubt they mind us discussing pleasures of the flesh." Morgan ruffled his hair and stole some of Aeron's fries.

"He's ignoring my texts."

"So you *do* know how to use your phone?"

"Only when it's someone I want to talk to." Marsden reached for Aeron's fries. Aeron slapped his knuckles with a fork. "You let her have some!"

"As my twin, she's entitled to whatever I have, including fries, clothing and my organs. And my penguin ornament collection."

"Likewise," Morgan mumbled, her mouth full.

Marsden folded his arms. "Shouldn't we concentrate on breaking the sixth seal?"

"We're basking in the brilliance of the fifth. We must savour the sweet taste of spilled blood and shattered lives. Nice touch with the pavement preacher and the Christmas lights, by the way. You made a brutal death festive. Like our tree."

"The bastard had it coming. Every time I busk he tells me I'm going to Hell. I was tempted to hang him with his intestines, but I'm out of practice."

Morgan sipped her Dracula's Kiss cocktail. "It would've been fiddly tying them through the sculpture. I'm disappointed you discarded the advent calendar idea. I was looking forwards to peeking behind each door for my Christmassy surprise." She mimed opening a door. "Ooh, day twenty, a piece of liver."

"Too many witnesses. Why aren't you in Africa with Plague Pit and Twiglet?"

"Mac never made it to Africa," Aeron said.

"Did they lose him off the baggage carousel?"

"Demi insisted they fly first class. We could've teleported them but apparently it's pointless doing charity

211

work unless people *see* you doing it. She's in Africa posing for photos with starving children and pretending to build a school."

"Where's Mac?"

"Airport quarantine."

Marsden laughed.

"It's not funny," Morgan said. "They'll run tests on him and find he's collected more diseases than other people have collected stamps. They took one look at him and refused to let him on the plane. Demi was mortified. Mac's very upset."

He roared with laughter. "Demi's face would've been a picture! I bet she's furious he upstaged her."

"She's convinced he did it to ruin her glittering career. You have to break him out before they kill him with antibiotics."

"Leave him there and have Demi stranded in Africa. We'll destroy this world quicker without them."

"Do *you* want to be the one to tell Conquest you let his son die? He'll use your blood to paint a mural of him killing you. Besides, the contract states we each take a quarter of the world," Aeron reminded him. "We will *not* be the first Horsemen to breach our contract. Unless you *want* to throw away what we've spent our entire lives training for."

"*You* won't be seen by CCTV, I will."

"We're busy." Aeron slurped his Hello Kitty cocktail.

"So am I. I have trouble brewing in the Ukraine." Marsden sighed. "If I do this, will you stop harassing me about Drew?"

Morgan pouted. "I thought you wanted us to be supportive."

"Giving me the *Kama Sutra* and recommending positions isn't supportive, it's embarrassing. Like being given advice from your parents."

"Isn't your daddy the rape and pillage type?"

212

Aeron frowned. "I don't think Drew would go from halo to horny if you burst in, trashed his place then took him at knife point. Not when he's expecting candles and soft music."

"Enough with the fucking candles and soft music!" Marsden slapped the table. People turned around. He facepalmed.

"The book was on sale," Morgan continued. "You've resisted him for so long, I figured you needed advice, flavoured condoms. Ribbed for his pleasure. I thought you'd enjoy Driving the Peg." He glared at her. "Maybe you'd prefer The Lotus."

"I'm going to rescue Mac before you start drawing pictures." Marsden left.

"Someone's more sensitive than a kicked scrotum," Aeron remarked.

"Were the Kama Sutra dice over the top? I thought they'd help if they were shy about picking a position."

"He's probably consumed with sexual frustration but is caught up on saving Drew's soul or something ridiculous. Plus he has to deal with the fact he has another emotion besides murderous rage. It's probably pissing him off."

"We should give Kinky Angel the book. Get him hot under the halo."

"The next time they see each other it will be so explosive, the earth will move and angels will fall."

***

Marsden weaved through the airport crowds, plucking his guitar strings. A fight broke out near the check-in line.

He approached a security guard. "Which way to quarantine?"

The guard pointed. Marsden glanced through each door he passed. Through the fourth door, he saw Mac huddled in the corner of a sterile room in a white paper suit, looking more like a dejected caterpillar than the first Horseman of the Apocalypse.

Marsden kicked open the door. "Quick, before they power hose your cavities with bleach."

"Mars! Thought I was going to rot in there." Mac's pimply face looked worse framed by the tight hood.

"Where are your clothes?"

"They probably incinerated them."

Marsden plucked a fast tune while they hunted for Mac's clothes. They found them bagged in the lab with petri dishes, test tubes and microscopes. Workers stood transfixed, while Mac dressed then bundled the petri dishes into the paper suit. He drank the test tubes. Marsden retched.

Mac frowned, studying a label. "They called me Patient Zero."

Marsden laughed. "Patient Zero is the first person to be infected with the zombie virus and brings about the zombie apocalypse. Which reminds me, I want to make a biological weapon with the plague."

"Why the plague? You're obsessed with me spreading it and now you want to make a weapon from it."

"Because of its horrific historical connotations. It wiped out millions within *months*. People are still terrified of it."

"It's treatable."

"Only if they know they've got it. First symptoms are similar to the flu. People don't believe it still exists, so by the time they realise, it'll be too late."

Mac hugged his suit of diseases. "You'll be free of your glass prisons soon, my pretties."

"Release some now. Revenge for treating you like a chemical spill."

"Revenge is your thing."

"Do you *want* to wear the fucking cockroach suit? Demi's dying to spray you in the face with pesticide."

Mac placed the suit down and spread out the samples. His ulcerated tongue protruded from his bleeding lips. "They all deserve a chance of glory."

"Something airborne. It's the easiest way to spread it through an expansive site and they won't know until it's too late."

"Measles?"

"You're infecting an airport, not a nursery."

"Swine Flu?"

"Didn't work so well last time."

"Pulmonary Tuberculosis?"

"Excellent choice. Hospitals will be unprepared so people will die before they get antibiotics. Hurry up. My fingers are splitting."

Blood drops spattered Marsden's feet, his fingers streaked with ruby rivers. Mac pocketed the petri dish and gathered the others. They ran to a balcony overlooking the airport.

"Release the TB!" Marsden said.

Mac opened the petri dish and unleashed the Mycobacterium tuberculosis bacteria to the people below. "It's beautiful. Like a thousand fairies with blue lights."

"I can't see a damn thing."

"That's the problem with you slice and dice types – no romance."

"I don't find the idea of coughing my lungs up as romantic as you do."

They ran down the escalator. Marsden shoved people aside. One woman hit the steps and rolled to the bottom. Marsden leapt over her.

"You didn't have to push her," Mac scolded when they got outside. "You could've hurt her."

"Says the guy who's given her TB. I've always wanted to push someone down an escalator. The opportunity's never arisen."

They dodged cars and people as they ran to Marsden's bike. Mac placed his suit of diseases in the seating compartment. Marsden passed Mac his helmet and climbed on.

"Won't you have to fumigate it?"

"If you fall off, I'm not explaining to the Terror Twins why your face resembles a smashed egg. They'll think I did it deliberately."

Marsden gunned the engine, weaving through traffic jams and running red lights. He parked in a field close to a private airport and killed the engine.

"That's the Israeli prime minister's plane." Marsden pointed up. "This country is allies with Israel so nobody will expect this. You know who else is an ally of Israel? America. If you want to start a war, piss off America."

Marsden pressed his ruined fingers to his guitar strings and played 'Annihilation'.

The plane banked sharply then straightened. It plunged into a dive before being pulled back up. It tilted and turned like it was controlled by a malevolent manipulator. Mac covered his eyes then risked a peek. The plane exploded. People rushed out from the hangar. Fiery rain fell to earth, torching those it touched.

"Couldn't you have dropped me off first?" Mac asked.

"Conquest should've desensitised you. I'm compensating for his failure."

The plane broke, flattening the hangar. Its blistered flesh burst from its skeleton, scattering across the airstrip and becoming its own funeral pyre. Severed limbs and charred bodies lay amongst the debris.

Marsden used a burning wing to draw a horseshoe with a sword in flames. He restrung the snapped A string then sped away from the scene of devastation, leaving it to burn.

CHAPTER 29

Blood globules spattered the hospital floor. A man wiped his mouth with the back of his hand, crimson trails smearing his skin. He coughed again, blood droplets sprinkling the woman next to him. She inched away but the wheezing woman beside her was as comforting as Freddy Krueger reading bedtime stories.

Infected people lined the corridors. The waiting room became a mosh pit, without the loud music and over enthusiastic dancer. The bitter stench of desperate desolation, vomit and bleach was overpowering. One man shivered like a wooden marionette caught in a storm. Another wiped sweat from his face with his sleeve. Weary nurses called patients into treatment rooms and gave sick bowls to others. Harassed doctors hurried between wards, offering comfort where they couldn't offer cures. Stretchers burdened by moaning patients blocked corridors as they waited for a cubicle to grant them privacy in their final moments.

Morgan leaned against a doorframe, enjoying a stolen bag of Skittles from the concourse. She'd attended funerals less depressing than this place. She was impressed how swiftly Mac's airport gift had worked. It was better than a bottle of cheap whisky from duty free.

"You think you've got problems? Try ending the world with a human pimple, a Funny Bones reject and a psycho on the verge of a coup."

Next of kin shouted at nurses when there were no beds available, or their relative had gone an hour without being seen. Nurses spent so long calming them they were late to their next patient.

Morgan wrinkled her nose at the latest Vomit Fresh fragrance. One child didn't bother wiping the dribble of bile from his chin. A nurse passed Morgan then unlocked a drugs cabinet in the small room. Morgan blew on the back of her neck. She looked around. Morgan removed a globe from her pocket and spun it on her fingertip, the ash swirling.

The spinning globe distorted people's faces as it passed over them. Each face captured resembled rotting dolls until the globe moved and they came back to life; puppets given the cue to dance.

"You."

She squeezed the globe. The man responsible for the blood trail coughed violently, clutching his chest. Fear tainted his eyes as he clawed the woman beside him. She shrank away, hitting his hand off and shouting for help. A nurse ran to him, hollering for her colleagues and forgetting to pull up her mask. He thrashed, striking her as he fought for breath. Blood sprayed the nurse's uniform. He collapsed, blood trickling from his mouth.

Morgan rifled through his pockets and retrieved his globe. She shook it, the headstone pushing through the blackened ground as the ashes caressed it. The raven landed on a plastic chair, his talons clicking as he shuffled. Morgan dropped the marble into his pouch then sat in a wheelchair, allowing her a front row seat to the man's final performance.

Patients screamed and scrambled away, terrified death was contagious. Nurses comforted the patients and moved some to a corridor without a corpse ruining the view. The man's mouth was fixed open, his eyes wide.

A doctor helped the nurses load him onto a stretcher then they wheeled him to resuscitation. Morgan stalked them. The doctor tore open the man's shirt and grabbed the defibrillator, desperately trying to revive a broken shell.

The body juddered as electricity coursed through it, like Frankenstein trying to bring his monster to life.

Shrieking, crying and swearing drowned out the bleeping machines, the whine of the defibrillator recharging and some people's muttered prayers.

The doctor consulted his watch. "Time of death: twenty fourteen."

A porter pushed the stretcher to the morgue. Morgan waved him off and finished her Skittles.

"You *can* taste the rainbow."

A cleaner arrived to wash away the blood. Another man took the empty seat and groaned; a sickly shade of terminal white.

Morgan raised her hood and slipped down the corridor, the raven flying in her shadow. Her coat billowed behind her, her PVC trousers swishing with each stride. She entered a cubicle and watched a nurse taking blood and skin samples from the six year old girl on the stretcher.

"Has she been ill recently?" the nurse asked.

"She's had chickenpox," the mother answered.

"I'll get the doctor."

"I got this one," Morgan said. "I'll free up cubicle space for you."

Morgan slipped a globe from her coat and shook it. The girl coughed uncontrollably, spasmed then flopped. Her mother frantically shook her, screaming for the nurse, the doctor, anyone. Morgan plucked the globe from the girl's Frozen purse around her neck.

"Children make better headlines."

She left the cubicle and the mother's wretched tears.

She pulled her phone out below the 'no mobile phones' sign. "Dita Von Disease, get down here. TB isn't as deadly as it used to be. I've helped two along, but most are fighting it. They have the drugs on site. The only crisis here is where to put the living. Let's change it so they don't know where to put the dead."

***

Aeron strolled through the Israeli embassy gates, flashing his ID at the security guards. Sirens screamed as they raced towards the tragedy.

"I'm here for my eight o'clock Salsa lesson with the deputy prime minister."

Their gazes didn't shift from the gates.

"I'll go straight up. I'll have a coffee, black, one sugar, and a Custard Cream…make it two – you only live once."

Aeron stepped over the ruined wall into the embassy. Dust and cement rained onto him. He stopped at the burning van and took a photo of the back doors. Marsden's sign was painted on the back in ashes. Aeron Pictogrammed the photo using the hashtags #HorsemenoftheApocalypse #Apocalypse and #VanDamned. He opened what remained of the glove pocket. Plucking a globe from the papers, he shook it in the dead driver's face. Ash settled on a fresh grave like a tossed bouquet. The raven landed on the van's roof and hopped onto the bonnet.

"Corpse!"

Aeron dropped the marble into his pouch. "Stay close. This place may be rigged."

The raven cocked his head then hopped onto Aeron's shoulder. Glass crunched beneath Aeron's black biker boots. A woman sat against metal detectors, sobbing. Her face bore the brunt of flying glass, making her resemble a voodoo doll.

"Not severe enough," Aeron told her. "There has to be at least five deaths or it'll get bumped down to page six after a double spread despairing at twelve year olds sexting each other, how yoghurts give you cancer, and which celebrity ate testicles on last night's TV."

He approached a man lying in the middle of the floor, his skin tainted with a shroud of smog and grime.

"I don't usually get intimate on a first meeting, but for you I'll make an exception."

He raised the man's top, studying the ugly bruises covering his chest like armour. He glanced over his shoulder at the van.

"Stopped it with your chest, huh?"

"Who are you?"

Aeron pulled his hood up. "The last person you'll ever see. Good job I'm pretty."

He freed a globe from the man's pocket. The man gave a final gasp as paramedics crouched beside him. Aeron rose, patted a paramedic's shoulder then added the marble to the raven's pouch.

Broken glass, crumbling bricks, dying embers and injured people littered the entrance. Smoke, dust and sulphur formed a toxic perfume that lingered like a ghost. The fire crew rushed in to extinguish the van.

Aeron clicked his fingers.

The ceiling collapsed. The paramedics abandoned their patient to help the fire crew dig their colleagues out. Aeron retrieved globes from the firemen's uniforms and shook them like maracas. He rose, twirled and passed them to the raven.

"Was that too unbelievable for a natural occurrence?" The raven pecked his shoulder. "Even if they can't figure out how the ceiling collapsed, they'll never blame me. They'll label it 'freak accident'." He opened every door he passed. "If I was the deputy prime minister, where would I hide?"

Aeron formed his fingers into a gun and darted around a corner. He peered around then scuttled to a pillar. Risking a glance, he pivoted from its shadow, running at a crouch. The raven took flight as Aeron did a forward roll towards the stairs. The raven strutted up the bannister as Aeron ran up the stairs then slid down the other banister, before vanishing down a corridor.

"There's bound to be a secret bunker."

The raven landed on his shoulder. Aeron followed a man in a suit through corridors then down a flight of stairs.

"Hope he's not taking me to the basement for photocopying supplies."

The man stopped at a door at the far end and placed his hand against a scanner.

"Jackpot! Not even the prime minister keeps his photocopying supplies behind a palm print entry system."

Aeron snuck through the door before it closed. He surveyed the room, noting the security team, advisors and the deputy's family.

"The man of the hour. We have a date."

He drew a gun from his inside pocket and aimed it at the deputy prime minister. The deputy's wife screamed.

"You're not supposed to see me! You'll give the game away!" He shot her. "Now you can see me."

Everyone turned at hearing the gunshot. The deputy rose as two people rushed to the wounded woman. Aeron shot three of the security team, two advisors and another member of the deputy's family. Security fired blindly, the bullets passing through Aeron's phantom frame.

"I'm sorry I've revoked your invites for the end of the world party, but the guest list is too long."

Aeron shot the deputy. He collapsed into his chair, his forehead tainted by a bloodied third eye. Aeron pointed his gun at the remaining security men whilst he collected the globes, pretending he was robbing the corpses. He deposited the marbles into the raven's pouch, blew imaginary smoke off the barrel of his gun then strode out of the secure room, leaving behind the bodies of a fallen government.

CHAPTER 30

Rain hammered on Grease Lightning's windows like a lone survivor begging to be rescued from a horde of hungry vampires. People rushed in, droplets staining the floor. Christmas decorations swayed each time the door opened. Four of the Horsemen had claimed the furthest booth.

"We need to hang out somewhere classy," Demi said. "You don't see top models slumming it in a diner. If I hear one more satisfied burp, I'll ram a napkin down someone's throat."

"You've been back five minutes and you're whinging," Aeron replied. "Did you get your photo ops?"

"Yes. Where's Morgan? She'll want to see these."

"Manning the hospitals."

Demi flicked through her phone. "This is me telling Francois about obesity. Here I am helping Francois dig a hole. This is me giving Francois and his sisters clothes. This is me teaching Francois how to write my name."

"They weren't *all* called Francois," Marsden said.

"I wasn't paying attention to their names. I was there to build my profile, not make penpals. So I called them all Francois. They didn't mind."

"I thought you were there to build a school."

"Do you honestly believe celebrities do anything useful when they're out there? No. They pretend for their cameras then bugger off back to their luxury hotels."

"They're not your clothes you're giving them are they?"

She snorted. "I'm not gonna waste designer clothes on people who work in *fields*. I did a drive by before I left, taking bags people left out for charities."

"You *stole* from charities?"

"To give to the poor kids in Africa. The clothes were going there anyway, I just delivered them personally. Like a sexy Santa." She frowned. "Damn it! I should've worn a sexy Santa outfit! I'd definitely make the papers."

"No-one wants to see your baubles."

"Want me to lick your candy cane?" She winked.

"It's inappropriate to dress sexily for children," Mac mumbled.

"This isn't about the *children*, Barfbag, this is about me getting into magazines."

"By helping children."

"They were props in my photos. Like the spade."

"I never thought I'd say this." Marsden gestured to a photo of Demi with a group of kids wearing *We Love Demi Ceres* t-shirts, "you make them look fat."

"You think so too? When I told my driver they didn't look starving because their bellies stick out, he thought I was an idiot. I'm glad you agree."

He shook his head. "Did you catch Malaria?"

"I can't catch diseases."

"I was hoping you'd fall down a well."

"I wasn't digging a well. I sent these photos to magazines and newspapers. Soon I'll be invited to those glitzy charity balls that cost more to host than the amount they raise. I should buy new dresses."

"You could send the money to Africa," Mac suggested.

"What would they spend it on? The latest iPhone?"

"They could buy food."

"I didn't see *one* supermarket the whole time I was there. No wonder they're starving to death. The place I stayed in didn't even have internet! I couldn't check if I was trending on Chatter."

"You weren't," Marsden said.

"I deserve a treat after Chicken Pusarole humiliated me by getting dragged off to quarantine. Seeing him stripped naked and hosed down is an image that will haunt me 'til my dying day."

"It'll haunt me too," Mac mumbled, scratching a scab on his arm.

"No-one cares about you, you're ugly. I didn't know whether to cry or vomit at the sight of your pimply buttocks getting sandblasted."

"They sandblast cars, not people," Marsden said.

"I swear that turned me gay. His arse looks like the surface of the moon. I half-expected to see Armstrong's flag planted in his butt crack."

Mac pouted. "As a last resort, I told them who I was."

"Bet that went well."

"They brought someone down for a psych evaluation." His shoulders slumped.

"As touching as this reunion is, we have work to do," Aeron said, rising and switching on the news.

"A bomb exploded at the Israeli embassy during this morning's rush hour," the newsreader announced. *"The Israeli prime minister was killed on Wednesday in what is believed to be a terrorist attack whilst visiting the UK. Secret Service has tightened security at private airfields. They don't believe the killings are related."*

"They were done by the same freakin' person," Marsden said. "I leave a calling card so I get recognition for my hard work, but nobody's paying attention."

"Elizabeth Bloodbathary hits the headlines again," Demi muttered. "I bet I don't even get a mention."

"Local hospitals have closed their doors to non-emergency patients following an outbreak of Pulmonary TB. Many people were admitted showing symptoms of the disease and hospitals had to issue immediate quarantine zones. Public Health is trying to locate where the outbreak occurred. Anyone showing symptoms should go to the

hospital immediately. A Government leaflet on spotting the symptoms will be delivered to every home in Lemures."

"Why are you idiots stealing the headlines?" Demi fumed. "I went to Africa!"

"I killed the Israeli government and Mac's making TB popular again," Marsden told her. "Lots of celebrities go to Africa. You have to do something unique to make the evening news."

"I got covered in mud for *nothing?*"

"If you'd destroyed crops whilst you were there, it wouldn't have been a wasted trip."

"I didn't go on holiday to do farming."

"I'll spread TB in hospitals outside Lemures," Mac said. "Flu too. Their bodies can't fight both."

"We have an update on the bombing of the Israeli embassy," the newsreader interrupted the weather report. *"Let's go to our reporter live at the scene."*

The image cut to a man standing near the Israeli embassy as it burned in the background. Sirens wailed like a film trailer soundtrack.

"A delivery van was driven through the front of the embassy and the bomb detonated whilst the van was inside. Israel's deputy prime minister was visiting following the death of the prime minister. We don't know if he was the intended target." The camera zoomed in on the wreckage as dazed people stumbled out. *"We're awaiting news of casualties. A symbol of a sword through a horseshoe was found on the van and it's been discovered this symbol has appeared at other, seemingly unconnected tragedies. So far, no militant group has claimed responsibility."*

"Stop stealing my headlines!" Each of Demi's words was delivered with a sharp blow to Marsden's back.

He laughed, fending her off. "Stop harassing starving kids and start decimating the food supply."

"I'm going to help Morg at the hospital," Aeron said. He vanished.

A waiter switched the channel to a celebrity version of a game show.

"Should I go on a game show?" Demi mused.

"Is there one where you get covered in gunk and poisonous spiders?" Marsden asked, writing down chords for a new song.

"I'd pay to watch that," Mac said.

"We should start a Chatter campaign."

"Like you losers have followers." Demi folded her arms. She spotted a woman entering and waited for her to walk past, an evil smile twisting her lips. "Oh when's the baby due? Do you want my seat?"

The woman glared. "I'm not pregnant."

"In that case, you should take a seat in the gym across the road. You've clearly had enough food for today."

The woman sat at a table at the far end, hiding her face behind a menu.

"You're nastier than the Pear." Marsden played his new chords then scribbled down changes.

"Like most art forms, it's unappreciated by the uneducated. Let's ditch this shithole. We never have fun anymore, just the two of us."

"I'm still here," Mac said.

"Thanks for that thrilling status update."

Marsden laughed. "You're such a bitch."

"Come on, Mars. Pretty please?"

"We have different ideas on what constitutes fun."

"I'm happy to use your sword to make human kebabs. The rate this country's sliding into obesity it'll take 'em years to starve themselves to death. I have to compete with fast food restaurants and increasing portion sizes."

"And being hindered by your incompetency."

"Excuse me, are you Demi Ceres?" a voice asked.

"Like anyone else would be this beautiful." She smiled at the teenage boy.

"Could I have your autograph?"

"I'd be delighted! Mars, give me some paper." She stole his song sheet and ripped off a corner.

"I'm writing on that!"

She took his pen. "Stop being a baby. I'm giving this lovely boy my autograph. What's your name, honey?"

"Luke."

She scrawled Luke a message, signed it and handed it over. "Want a picture too?"

"Oh wow! Yeah!"

She nudged Marsden. "Take his phone."

He picked up Luke's phone and took a photo. Demi kissed Luke's cheek as the flash blinked. He turned chilli red, took his phone back and scuttled off, thanking her.

"He'll upload that to every social networking site and everyone can see what a friendly, attractive person I am."

"Then they'll meet you and see you're more toxic than SARS," Mac said.

"Are you still here? Don't you have boils to lance?"

"What did you write?" Marsden asked. "'Live thin, die young'? 'Food tastes better in reverse'? 'Air has no calories'? 'Burger and fries go straight to the thighs'?"

"I could make bumper stickers and distribute them at my slimming club." Her phone bleeped. "I've been tagged. Mars! Why did you get the diner sign in the photo?"

"I thought it'd be nice to let your fans know where you hang out."

"How the hell am I supposed to be a diet diva when I'm photographed in a fucking *diner*?" She thumped his arm.

"I could edit a different background in. A toilet cubicle. No, a Halloween background. Oh but then no-one will tell you apart from the skeletons."

"I can't believe how petty you are. You'll regret this."

He blew her a kiss. Mac laughed.

Demi raised her eyebrows. "You think this is funny, Pus in Boots? You won't be laughing when I drop kick you into a vat of Penicillin."

"Aeron and Morgan said the Apocalypse requires all of us," Mac said.

"No, it requires *four* Horsemen. Consider yourself on Death Row. And there won't be a last minute pardon."

CHAPTER 31

"I want to kiss a girl and I need you to make it happen."

Marsden glanced up from amending his strategy folder to see Demi standing at the foot of Travel Inn's bed, wearing blood clot coloured lingerie and a look of determination.

"You're not gay and I'm not a dating website. You want a girlfriend, go and get one like everyone else."

"I don't want a girlfriend, I want to be famous."

"What are you doing here? You're supposed to be squatting in the Bohemian with the other cockroaches. How do you keep getting in here? Did you crawl up through the plughole?"

Mac, who sat at the desk, mixing Red Mist, laughed.

"Eyes to the wall, Weeping Beauty." She gestured with her finger. "Mars, I've studied the media. You keep banging on about changing strategies when the current one doesn't work, so that's what I'm doing. Modelling isn't getting me noticed. What happens when two straight celebrities kiss on stage? Overnight fame."

"They have fame to begin with, otherwise nobody would care. People kiss all the time. It's hardly front page material. Mostly it's stomach churning."

"They become top news stories on websites, the video spreads quicker than Fleabag's STIs and it becomes the new water cooler topic. Guys find it hot—"

"Oh *god*. You're one of those pathetic types who'll fake bisexuality to get a guy's attention. Desperation's as attractive as the Prime Minister in a bunny girl outfit. Have some self-respect."

"Self-respect won't end the world. Tonight, at your gig, you'll play a sexy song that will seduce a famous girl into kissing me. She's got to be hot though. Demi Ceres would never go gay with a minger."

He burst out laughing. "I'm getting that printed on a t-shirt. Do you ever listen to yourself and think 'I sound like a complete twat bandit'?"

"No."

"You sound like a complete twat bandit." He crossed out Demi's predicted body count and lowered the number by twenty thousand. It was a shame bitchiness couldn't decimate populations the way it destroyed self-esteem. He tapped his dagger pen against a map of the world. "If you destroy crops in war-torn areas of the Middle East and parts of Africa where they're already starving, you'll get back on target. Those who couldn't flee their cities when the rebels moved in are your prime targets. Rations are scarce so this should be easy. Sabotage any aid that other counties are flying in."

"I want an A-list celebrity. Not some reality star."

"You're. Not. Gay."

"Everyone has someone they'd go gay with to save the world."

Marsden raised his head. "You're doing it for fame! They'd call you an attention-seeking whore. And we're supposed to *end* the world, not save it. Speaking of which, Mac, add poison to your drugs. People aren't dying fast enough. You should've annihilated Lemures by now."

"Sorry," Mac mumbled. "Modern medicine is fighting my diseases."

"It can't fight strychnine."

"That's a horrible way to die."

"It's quicker than TB and they'll die smiling."

"It's a grimace of pain, caused by their muscles spasming and freezing in place at time of death."

"It looks the same. If modern medicine is fighting your diseases then create something new they *can't* fight. Or bring back Polio."

Demi eyed Mac. "Mac, who would you go gay with to save the world?"

"You used my name? I was beginning to think you didn't know it."

"I can exclude you from this conversation, Grotbags. Quite frankly, your phlemy voice makes me wish your diseases would eat through your vocal chords."

"Mars."

Demi rolled her eyes. "*God* would go gay with Mars."

Marsden scowled. "Thanks for making me uncomfortable."

"You're not uncomfortable. I saw your bedtime reading. The Kama Sutra? You're not that flexible. Or experienced." She leaned forwards. "Which position do you want me in?"

"Is there one called The Dismembered Skeleton?"

"Hang on," Mac said. "You want to kiss a girl at his gig? Even though you're supposed to be a hot couple?"

"Shut it, Scarlet Pimpleswell."

Marsden smirked. "Cheating on me gives me an excuse to dump you. Sympathies will be on my side." He gathered his papers and stood, pushing his guitar round his back.

"It's not cheating if it's with a girl! Where are you going?"

"To write such a steamy song, the woman will turn you. I'll be free of your harassment." He left.

Her shoe hit the door. "I'll get you for this, war zero".

Marsden cackled all the way to the Razor and the Rosary. He ran upstairs and entered Drew's flat. Drew sat on the settee, playing his PS3, wearing charcoal jeans and a black t-shirt with a motif of a winged vampire girl bursting into flames.

"Die you bastard!" Drew's teeth clamped his tongue as he hammered the buttons, a frown slicing between his eyebrows.

"Whatcha playing?" Marsden dropped beside him.

"*Uncharted Territory.*"

"Thought you would've chosen something...biblical – getting points for converting sinners. Or one where you're on a quest for a sainthood."

"That shit's boring. And you'd die. You don't get a sainthood when you're alive."

"What use is that?"

"You can access Heaven's VIP areas. And get a lap dance from a sexy nun."

Marsden laughed. "Are you serious?"

"Prove me wrong." He poked his tongue out then swore when Drake was shot. "That was your fault. To what do I owe this pleasure?"

"Demi's this close to going in a meat grinder and I can't operate machinery." He raised his hand. "And I have to write a sexy song."

"Shit! They're not healed?" Drew reached for Marsden's fingers, stopped and picked up his controller.

"Small price for saving your life. The Terror Twins could've healed them, but they're teaching me a lesson. I like the burns. I never get to play the hero. Next time I'll wear a cape."

"Want me to leave you alone?"

"I need inspiration."

Drew's embarrassed smile made Marsden's chest tighten. He spread his papers on the coffee table then removed his jacket.

"Why a sexy song?"

"Demi's latest get-famous-quick scheme. I wish we'd brought her father and left her in a field frightening crows."

"Your bosses bought me a present." Drew tossed the Kama Sutra dice on the table. They suggested Driving the Peg in the living room. He resumed his game.

"I got those. And the book. They flanked me and went through it like a catalogue. It was the most embarrassing moment in my life. And I've been seen in public with Demi."

"Why are they approving now? No, approving's the wrong word. *Insistent.*"

"It's part of their master plan. They want you on our side like a mascot but without posing with kids in a furry suit for photos. I have something for you."

"Your naked body, covered in ice cream?"

Marsden could almost feel Drew's warm tongue gliding over his skin. "The shop was out of neopolitan." He pulled a scroll from his inside jacket pocket and handed it over.

Drew paused the game and pulled the black ribbon sealing the scroll. He unrolled it. "'Damnation'."

"It's your song."

"Wow, does this mean we're a proper couple now? Should I tell my other lovers I'm going steady with you?" He laughed when Marsden hit him with a cushion. "Play it for me."

"I can only play it once. We all have a song that could finish us."

"You said you'd kill the others if you could. Why not play their songs?"

"I don't have them." Marsden scowled. "Only the Death Squad can play them. They're the only ones without a playlist. Death can never die."

Drew lifted the sheet, his skin paling. "So this..."

"If I play it, you'll fall."

"Why are you giving it to me?"

"I don't want it and I sure as hell don't want the Terror Twins having it. If Demi found it, she'd take up guitar lessons. She wears spite like cheap perfume."

"What if you destroy it?"

"I wouldn't take the risk in case it kills you."

Drew thrust it at Marsden. "Keep it."

Marsden pushed it away. "I hold the life of humanity in my hands and I kill someone every time."

"I don't trust you with humanity's life. I trust you with mine." He rolled the scroll and tied the ribbon. "Take it or I burn it."

Marsden reluctantly pocketed it. "You're making a mistake."

"What if I fall, then you play it?"

Marsden shrugged. "Maybe it would bind you to me."

"We can think up creative ways to spend our time."

Marsden laughed. "You're no angel."

Drew smiled. "I didn't buy my halo and wings off eBay."

"Your wings are beautiful. I've only got these." Marsden pulled off his t-shirt and twisted away, showing Drew the tattoo on his back of black demon wings flanking a sword. He dressed and turned around to see Drew had removed his t-shirt. His breath caught in his throat.

"Don't get excited, I'm showing you mine." A tattoo of white wings decorated his back, with FALLEN across the centre.

Marsden traced the word, tiny flames consuming the ink. Drew jumped and swore. "You haven't fallen."

"It's a reminder not to."

"Does it hurt when your wings emerge?"

"It never used to, but the longer I'm in this form, the more connected to it I become. It's like it's moulded itself to me." He yanked his t-shirt on.

"Way to spoil the view. I thought Leviticus forbade tattoos."

"You know the Bible better than I do. We must've been swapped at birth. I should be galloping around the world, leaving a trail of bodies like Hansel's breadcrumbs while you open a soup kitchen and go carolling."

"First rule of warfare – know your enemy."

CHAPTER 32

"You stole my headlines, you headline-stealing whore!" Demi charged into Travel Inn like an aggressive bout of rabies and beat Marsden with a rolled up magazine.

"What the fuck?"

Mac chuckled as he marked off schools on the map he'd spread over desk. It felt nice not to be the recipient of her venom. He wished there was an injection to vaccinate him from her spite.

"Headline. Stealing. *Whore!*" Demi whacked Marsden's back, shoulders and arse.

"I'm not awake enough to deal with your shit. And lower your voice. You'll get us thrown out." He rubbed his eyes then sat back on his heels. "Did the bombing in Israel overshadow you being snapped in Cheap and Cheerful?"

"You usurped me in my favourite magazine!" She flung it at him.

"*Build Your Own Skeleton?* I'm so sorry!" He caught *Sassy!* magazine against his bare chest then scanned the cover. "Three celebrities have bags under their eyes! Some plasticised singer reveals her favourite flavour of tea!" He gasped. "Sweet murderous mayhem, a reality TV star was photographed wearing odd socks. Send him to the stocks! Dems, I don't know how you function with this in-depth knowledge of current affairs buzzing around the empty space in your head like furious bees."

"Shut your cake hole and turn to page six."

"But page four tells me what knickers style makes my bum look big. And page twelve warns me of style sins I shalt not commit. How could I leave Travel Inn without knowing whether my handbag secretly says I'm a slut?"

"Page. Six. Cock Jockey."

"You'd better not be tricking me into looking at naked pictures of you. There's nothing in my stomach to puke up." He flicked to page six. "That woman who's famous for being famous walked her dog without wearing *makeup*? Good job they zoomed in on her pimple, or I'd have missed it. I can't take any more of this drama. Give me conflict in the Middle East any day."

"*There.*" She jabbed a picture then smacked him across the head.

"My fake girlfriend's snogging a woman. I'm so humiliated. You're dumped. I have to find a remote cabin to recover from my broken heart and write a best-selling album – 'Skeleton in my Closet'." He read out the passage. "'Ultra skinny model Demi Ceres is spotted putting something in her mouth when she enjoys a tongue sandwich with actress Grace Monroe at her boyfriend's gig'. This deserves the Nobel prize for journalism."

"Look at the next picture."

"'Up and coming sexy rock god, Marsden Slaughter, doesn't appear too devastated as he cosies up to bar owner, Drew Angelo. The hunky pair spent all evening exchanging flirty smiles and smouldering looks. No wonder Demi was forced to seek affection elsewhere'. Fuck's sake."

"You've *humiliated* me!" She slapped him.

"*You're* the one tonguing some actress. I'm just sitting at the bar."

"Giving him your 'fuck me' eyes. *Look* at the size of your photo compared to mine!"

"Should we whack them on the table and measure them?"

Demi dropped the magazine over Mac's map. He jumped. "What do you think?"

Mac studied the photo of Marsden at the bar whilst Drew leaned on it, their arms almost touching. "That's the image they'd use on romance books. I should know – I spread herpes on their pages." He'd also taken to sneaking into sex shops and spreading STIs on sex toys and edible underwear. No-one would expect to get gonorrhoea from a candy thong.

Demi pulled out her phone, her hands shaking with fury. "The Great Unwashed reckon you look more in love with him than you ever did with me and I'm trying to get your attention. Everyone's praising you for being the latest celeb to come out."

"I wasn't aware I was a celebrity or that I had to declare my sexuality. Straight people don't. I should hold a press conference, or make a moving speech at some ceremony. Isn't that how celebs do it? Wow, my Skeleton in my Closet album now has a deeper meaning to it. This could win me awards."

"I hate you!"

"If I'd known getting my photo in your magazine would cure your rampaging lust, I'd have done it sooner."

"I'll still play with your plectrum."

"You've been caught cheating. Betrayal can't be forgiven."

Demi flung her phone onto the bed. It hit Morgan.

"What in Purgatory's going on?" Morgan sat up, looking like she'd been dragged through brambles and attacked by crows. Her Jack Skellington vest was twisted and had ridden up her stomach.

"Rainbow Spite humiliated me in front of the world! Now everyone's calling me an attention-seeking whore." She snatched the magazine and passed it to Morgan.

Mac swore as it cut his finger. Green pus trickled down his skin. He sucked it.

"I *warned* you." Marsden smirked.

"You can feel the chemistry," Morgan said. "It's turning me on just looking at it."

"I'm good at faking it." Demi flicked her hair. "So good, that actress invited me back to hers. Said there was somewhere else she wanted me to put my tongue. She's not even gay."

"Not you. Guitar Hero." She nudged Aeron who lay with his face pressed into the pillow. "Our team is in a trashy magazine."

He rolled over and sat up, looking like he'd been electrocuted. "Dems, you look like you'd rather be eating barbed wire. But Mars! Hot, hot, hot!" He peered over the magazine at him. "Did you two have sex?"

Marsden dressed and grabbed his guitar. "I have a bombing of the British embassy in Israel to check out."

"Don't bother. Only one life."

"Please say it was the ambassador."

"Nope. A soldier."

"Shit. I have to enrage Jordan or Egypt."

"Target Syria. They're always up for a scrap. Or Gaza. We need America involved. Increase the terrorist attacks in America. The president is itching to bomb countries and he'll have the public's support."

"I'll send my saboteurs in to start coups."

"Uh, *hello*? We've got bigger issues to deal with," Demi cut in. "Like his constant usurping of me. If I don't become famous, how the hell will I lead the world into famine?"

"Create drought in Africa, floods over here, or introduce a fast-spreading crop disease and make it impossible for farmers to cultivate anything. No crops, no food. No food, famine. It'd be *much* quicker than making people starve themselves because you've insulted them."

"But I *like* insulting people." She pouted. "Crops won't cry over my razor sharp putdowns."

Marsden gasped and dropped to his knees, screwing his eyes shut and gripping his head. Mac focused on his map, wincing.

"You don't learn quickly," Morgan remarked. "*You* are not in charge. *You* don't give orders. For death's sake Mars, it's too early to deal with your insubordination. Go sit on the naughty step 'til I've woken and warmed up my spanking paddle." She put the globe away. Marsden lay on the floor, his face buried in his arms. Mac leaned down and patted his shoulder. "Mars has a point, Dems." Morgan got out of bed, adjusting her pyjama bottoms which were covered in Jack Skellington faces. "Your quest for fame has overshadowed your quarter of the Apocalypse. We've been lenient and let you have fun, but today you'll wipe out harvests."

"I have a photo shoot later. I need a manicure, pedicure, Brazilian, maybe a vajazzle."

"A what?"

"You stick jewels on your lady garden."

"Why?"

"To make it pretty."

"It's a body part, not a feature wall. Your photoshoot isn't until this afternoon. Mac, mix up wheat leaf rust. Dems, you'll kill crops of wheat, rye and barley. Start in Kenya, work your way through Africa then Asia. The effects will be devastating."

"I'll never get another photo shoot!"

"Who the hell will see you in *Kenya*?" Marsden sat up, his face rash-red. "Especially if you're wearing a bee keeper suit. Boy will your bum look big." He put his phone to his mouth and made a static noise. "Crop control to Major Bum. You're blocking the sun. Over."

Aeron roared with laughter.

Demi glowered like a Gorgon. "Don't you have a reputation to salvage? Rock gods can't be gay. People expect it from pop stars with their girly voices and choreographed dance moves. Your career will nosedive spectacularly."

"It'll have yours to keep it company." He walked out.

Demi released a strangled scream and stamped her foot. "He's *ruining* my plans!"

"If you want to steal headlines, kill crops," Aeron said, changing out of his colourful dinosaur print pyjamas.

"Nobody will know it's *me*."

"Nobody knows the wars are Mars's doing but he's still topping the bill. The only way to starve people is to destroy their food. Flood food warehouses and ruin Christmas. You have two smiley faces below your name. That changes *today*. Or we'll send you back to Purgatory in the cockroach costume."

Demi scowled and flounced out. Aeron stalked her.

"Just you and me." Morgan smiled at Mac. Nerves gnawed his stomach at her shark smile. "Should we go shopping? Feed the ducks? Help Scouts deliver the Christmas post?"

"I'm going to spread E. coli and measles around schools. Infect children before the Christmas holidays."

"Go, spread your germs like pestilential Santa Claus. I'll collect TB sufferers from the hospital and await your gifts."

"I'll create a new drug, Herbal T, delivering the gift of epidemic typhus. Its mortality rate is ten to sixty percent, providing they don't receive treatment. And I'm going to start creating rare strains of diseases that will attack the antibiotics administered and turn vaccines deadly." He sounded a lot more confident than he felt. This might not even work.

"Ok. But don't get distracted from your first mission. Think of the children."

"Children fall easily. They carry more germs than me."

"Technically it'll be children who end the world. That's one in the eye for those who equate the childless with unnatural monsters."

"I'll spread germs in toy shops so they'll get two presents for the price of one."

"Forget Santa, *you* should be the face of Christmas."

"You'll never see my face on the back of a Coke lorry." He sighed.

Morgan dressed then vanished. Mac fetched a box of spray bottles and coughed green capsule-shaped bacteria into them. Slotting the bottles into a rucksack, he trudged out of Travel Inn.

He stored the bag under his bike seat and mounted, flicking up the arrow kickstand. School traffic conspired against him. Morgan had taught him how to filter through traffic, but it looked dangerous. Why did they need ridiculously big cars for tiny passengers? Going food shopping in Freger's didn't require an SUV. It wasn't hunting in Borneo.

He slipped into a school when parents escorted their kids in. A quick scout led him to the kitchen. He sprayed every piece of food, even contaminating plates and cutlery before randomly spraying toys, bikes and the occasional child.

"What's that?" a little boy asked after Mac sprayed him in the face.

Mac put his finger to his lips. "I'm delivering sleeping dust, so everyone stays asleep on Christmas Eve. If you tell, the magic won't work and Santa won't come."

He left via the back entrance then consulted his map before riding to the next school. He sprayed passing children then snuck into the school and contaminated the food, cups and tables.

He was surprised he wasn't stopped. His wasn't a face people wanted around children. A boogeyman's e-fit would cause less nightmares. By the end of the day, hospitals would again be inundated with the sick and the dying.

This year there wouldn't be any kissing under the mistletoe.

CHAPTER 33

"Operation Rock the World. Can anybody tell me what that is?" Aeron stood at the easel with the A1 pad and a red marker pen. Morgan stood to the side, armed with her whip. Marsden and Demi sat on the bed. Mac slumped on the settee, like a deflated plague mascot. Marsden resignedly raised his hand. "Anyone who isn't Mars."

"What's the point me being here when you won't let me participate?"

"You can participate in the ideas."

"Can't I text them in?"

"No."

"Is it the sixth seal?" Mac said.

Morgan applauded. "Give the man a gold star."

"We're out of gold stars," Aeron replied. "Budget cuts."

"Are you going to kiss me?" Mac asked.

"No. Cold sores are contagious. What's the sixth seal? Again, anyone who isn't Mars."

"We'll get this over quicker if you let me answer," Marsden said. "If it isn't in *Sassy!* Demi won't know."

Demi kicked him.

"How will anyone learn if they're not allowed to think for themselves?"

"Look what happened when you let Demi think for herself – she decides becoming famous is more beneficial than destroying crops."

"You think shagging Kinky Angel is more beneficial than starting wars." She poked her tongue out. "Make war, not love."

"We've discussed pros of Mars shagging Drew." Aeron rubbed his brow. Training seals would be easier than working with this lot. Revelations made it sound easy. "Tomorrow, we'll practise positions from the Kama Sutra. Dry humping only – it's a lesson, not an orgy. I've done my stretches; I'm ready to be mounted." He faced the easel and twerked.

"I'm busy tomorrow," Marsden said.

Aeron spun back around. "Not anymore."

"The sixth seal is the earthquake that will pollute the air so the sun goes dark and the moon turns red."

"Would you like to take the class?" Aeron pointed his pen at him.

"Gladly." He stood.

"Sit down! You're not authorised to take a class."

He sat and sighed. "How do we start the earthquake?"

"I'm getting to that." Aeron glared. Excluding Marsden from meetings might be a good idea. He didn't need the constant reminder Marsden's military DNA was more qualified to lead Project Apocalypse. Though his temperament wasn't suitable for a leadership role. Grumpy leaders led to bad morale and mutinies. He wouldn't create a fun competition with smiley face stickers – he'd carve them into everyone's flesh. Morgan slapped Marsden's hand with her whip. "Thank you, Morg. We're targeting Mauna Loa volcano on Hawaii's Big Island. It's the biggest volcano in the world and the lava pile measures 56,000 feet. Why's it so significant?" He scanned the room. "Mars?"

"You pick me on me when I *don't* know the answer."

Morgan moved to the front. "It's one of the most active volcanoes and has erupted 33 times between 1843 and 1984."

"So it's been dormant for years."

"Research shows it could awaken in the future. That future has come."

"It's like a celebrity who shot to fame in the eighties and is now appearing on *Celebrity Dirty Washing* to recapture their glory days. Like Demi in twenty years."

Demi punched him in the nipple. Marsden dead legged her. She screeched, clutching her leg.

Aeron smiled. "The world's largest super volcano lurks below Yellowstone National Park in Wyoming, USA. It's erupted three times in 2.1 million years and hasn't erupted for 600,000 years. When it does, it'll deposit a ten foot deep layer of plant killing ash up to one thousand miles away."

"What idiot thought it would be a good idea to build a park on a volcano?" Demi snorted. "It's asking for trouble."

Marsden facepalmed. "Why do I have to work with you idiots? I'm requesting you get replaced by monkeys."

Morgan whipped his leg. "Two thirds of America could become uninhabitable due to toxic air. We'll strike both volcanoes, almost simultaneously."

"Mac." Aeron pointed the pen at him. "After the volcanoes erupt, you'll infect those made homeless with Typhus, which thrives in unsanitary conditions."

"I'll pretend to be a doctor and claim I'm vaccinating them, when I'm really giving them Typhus."

"Genius!" Morgan said. "I'd kiss you if you weren't so repulsive."

"Make him wear a plague mask," Demi said.

Marsden shuddered. "They're freaky."

"Freakier than a face full of pus?"

Mac folded his arms. "Only some have pus. The others are lesions and sores."

"Well *excuse* me for not being a professor of pimples. Wear a gimp suit. Then we won't have to see any of you."

"I can't help the way I look."

"That's a defeatist attitude. Have you tried a face transplant?"

Aeron laughed. "Demi, ruin or poison survivors' food stocks."

"I could pretend to help the victims! My profile needs good publicity after Mars's stunt."

Marsden placed his hand on his heart. "I'm sorry me sitting at the bar ruined your dastardly plan to become famous by tonguing a woman."

Morgan lashed their hands. "Save it for after class."

Marsden glared. "I'll stab that through your heart in a minute."

Morgan flogged him.

"Mars, we have a special role for you," Aeron said.

"I'm *not* wearing the cockroach suit."

"You're erupting the volcanoes," Morgan said.

"Are you throwing me in?"

"Tempting, but we need you for the seventh seal. Aer and I will take you to the top of each volcano and you'll serenade them."

"I want to make them erupt, not get them into bed."

Demi winked. "That's what she said."

Morgan struck Demi's hand. "Your music will enter the volcanoes' hearts and cause an explosion."

"And give me a face full of lava and toxic ash."

"Don't be so negative," Aeron said. "Morg and I will teleport you away." He frowned. "This is the biggest moment of your life. You don't seem enthusiastic."

"Getting pelted in the face by lava isn't my idea of fun. I'll look like Mac."

"Thanks," Mac muttered. "Why is it pick on Mac day?"

"You're ugly, smelly and filled with pus," Demi said. "You don't have a *single* redeemable feature."

"I'm a nice guy."

"No-one cares. I like how *Mars* gets the headline acts while Lice Boy and I are support artists. This is a *joint* venture."

"Telling a volcano its dress makes it look pregnant *won't* cause the Apocalypse." Marsden smirked. He turned to Aeron. "Isn't seal six earthquakes?"

"Yes."

"Volcanic eruptions *can* cause earthquakes, but usually it's the other way around."

Aeron stared at him for an uncomfortably long time.

"Earthquakes happen when tectonic plates rub against each other," Marsden said. "Not because of volcanic eruption."

"How 'bout we rub against each other and make the earth move?" Demi nudged him.

"How 'bout I gut you and wear you as a scarf?"

Aeron snatched up a red folder marked *Project Apocalypse* and flicked through it. "Shit. Wrong plan. This is for Operation Fanfare. Apologies people, we'll be back after the interval." He hummed and flipped the pages until he found one with a painting of the four Horsemen. He'd added a second Death on the green horse but the marker pen stick figure didn't quite match the oil painted ones.

Demi groaned and flopped back on the bed like an unconscious praying mantis while Aeron and Morgan had a hushed, heated discussion. Aeron flipped the sheet over and grabbed another file.

Marsden shook his head. "Why am I saddled with you amateurs? It's insulting."

Aeron wrote on the pad then snapped the file shut. "The sixth seal is cosmic disturbances caused by nuclear war or a global earthquake. This is in the Bible so don't let the plot holes ruin a good story. The earthquake will cause volcanic debris to pollute the earth, turning the sun black, the moon red and causing meteor showers."

"I fail to see how an earthquake will cause this," Demi said. "Doesn't the ground just shake like a belly in a breeze?"

"I appreciate you finally contributing, but shut up. Never mind earthquakes that cause roads to split in half, we're talking major quake. Worldwide."

"So there *is* a volcano," Marsden said.

Aeron flicked through the file then fetched the file for Operation Fanfare. "Fuck's sake!" He flung them across the room. They hit Mac in the face, bursting a boil. Pus and blood erupted, streaking his face. "We've double booked the fucking volcanoes." He rubbed his forehead. It was bad enough Marsden showed them up with his knowledge and strategies, but double booking the volcanoes made them look incompetent. At this rate they couldn't organise an explosion in a fireworks factory, let alone an Apocalypse.

"This is what happens when you spend the Apocalypse drinking cocktails."

Morgan smacked his leg and put her finger to her lips, shooting him a warning look.

"Can't you erupt Mauna Loa for the sixth seal then Yellowstone Park for Operation Fanfare?" Mac rubbed his face and retrieved the files. Papers spilled out. Aeron growled. Mac sat, holding tissue to his cheek.

Aeron threw up his hands. "The impact will be lost."

"Scrap the earthquake and go with nuclear war," Marsden said. "My people are pissing off North Korea. Any day now they'll hit the red button. I'll ramp it up, insult the supreme leader's hairstyle."

"*We're* ending the world, not North Korea," Morgan said.

"Have the earthquake for the sixth seal and erupt volcanoes for the seventh."

"The seals will be too close together. The world won't have time to catch its breath before we make it scream again."

"This is a fucking *disaster*!" Aeron kicked the easel over then flung the pen. It bounced off the desk and landed in the bin with a ping.

Five minutes of excruciating silence dragged by, each second more painful than the last. Aeron glared at the easel, hoping it would burst into flames.

"Go with volcanoes for Operation Rock the World and we'll plan something else for Operation Fanfare," Marsden spoke.

"We can't *wing* this! How professional will we look when we tell our employer 'we double booked the volcanoes, we don't have a Plan B'–"

"You *don't* have a Plan B?"

"'–but you'll still get your Apocalypse'. You think they'll say 'No problem, send in the ninjas. Or the zombies. Everyone's looking forwards to them'. No they fucking *won't*!" He stamped his foot.

"How fucking professional do we look with smiley face progress charts and a cockroach suit?"

Aeron's eyes glowed like burning brimstone. He flicked out his scythe, the blade kissing Marsden's chin. His low voice filled with venom. "One more criticism and you can watch the Apocalypse from Purgatory. Morgan will take up your sword."

Marsden pushed the scythe away and eyed Morgan. "You'll have to prise it from my cold, dead hand."

She smiled. "With pleasure."

"Is Operation Fanfare a parade?" Demi asked. "I can organise that for Mardi Gras. The fancy dress shop has a sale on beaded necklaces. All the popular celebs are down with the gays."

"Except you," Marsden said. "Oh. Wait. You're not popular."

"I've sold my story to *Sassy!* about how I helped you accept your sexuality and the distress your attraction to men caused you. I'll look like girlfriend of the year."

"Or like someone so desperate for fame she'll hang on to a gay guy to bask in his glory. The media love degrading women. Do you want to give them ammunition?"

Morgan smacked their hands again. "This is the Apocalypse, not Disneyworld! There is no parade. Operation Fanfare is the seventh and final seal. There are seven stages, known as the seven trumpets that angels play."

"*Angels* cause the Apocalypse?" Demi nudged Marsden. "You can tell Halo 3 to blow your trumpet."

Aeron laughed. Marsden glowered.

Morgan lashed Demi's knee. "The first trumpet causes fire and brimstone."

"What *is* brimstone?" Demi asked.

"Sulphur. It burns like liquid fire and emits noxious gases. It's yellow but burns blue and drips like candle wax. Inhaling it destroys your respiratory system and can cause death. When volcanoes erupt, brimstone is released with lava."

"So the Bible has volcanoes twice."

Aeron and Morgan looked at each other.

"Thin Lizzie's right," Morgan said. "Brimstone comes from volcanoes, and if fire and brimstone is the first stage of Operation Fanfare, we need the volcanoes. But Operation Rock the World *also* requires volcanoes. We *have* to use them twice. Revelations says so."

"This is a fucking *joke*. Clearly they ran out of ideas and have left us with *shit*." Aeron ran his hand through his hair. "Fine we'll go with Marsden's idea of erupting Mauna Loa for Operation Rock the World and Yellowstone Park for Operation Fanfare."

"That was *my* idea," Mac grumbled.

"Oh. Well done Mac."

Mac sighed, his shoulders slumping.

"Or we say 'fuck Revelations' and stage our own Apocalypse," Marsden said. "Revelations mentions nothing about War playing the guitar, Pestilence drug dealing and Famine being a fame-hungry bitch. Actually it doesn't mention Pestilence at all."

"Even the Bible pretends I don't exist," Mac said glumly.

"I've planned several methods, all a damn sight more creative than a natural disaster film." He reached under the bed and retrieved a black file. "If we want this to be the most memorable Apocalypse ever, we have to decimate tradition. The Apocalypse has been in print for centuries. Let's give them a twist ending they won't see coming."

Aeron snatched it then he and Morgan flicked through the papers and maps, their faces stony. They shared a glance then Aeron ripped them up and tossed them in the bin. He lit a match and dropped it on top of them.

"What the fuck?" Marsden leapt up. Morgan prodded him in the stomach with her whip.

"They're completely unworkable." Aeron clapped. "Class dismissed! Enjoy this funfair we call Earth. Soon the rides will close forever."

CHAPTER 34

Drew sat at a table in the Razor and the Rosary, chewing his finger and flicking his beer bottle as he watched the door. A single candle in the centre of the table banished the gloom, its crimson wax dripping onto the table like humanity's bloody tears. Every engine that passed jump-started his heart. He felt like a spy about to betray his country and face the noose if he was caught.

The door opened and two men and a woman entered. They glanced around then approached Drew's table. He rose and locked the door, peeking out the window at the deserted car park. The lone working lamp fizzed then died.

"Can't you put a light on?" John asked. "I feel like I've walked into a medieval dungeon."

"If the Horsemen pass and see a light on at this time of night, they'll get suspicious." Drew returned to his seat. The candle reflected in their silver chokers, creating fiery nooses around their necks. "Do you want them making angel rings out of us, like they did to Joshua? I won't become a trophy on Death's finger." He drank some beer. "Progress reports?"

"I need more money," Mark said. "Pestilence's drug is expensive. The plan isn't working. People are still dying."

"More would die if you didn't buy it. I'll ask Michael for money. It's the least he can do."

"Why isn't *he* here?"

"It clashed with a function at the golf club. Have you managed to find a cure?"

"Only with my own blood but that's not always effective and it's not a long term solution."

"How are things with the prostitutes?"

"Most of them have been treated at clinics. But they've probably already passed the diseases on."

Drew nodded. "Jael, how did it go in Israel?"

"I managed to alert everyone. The bomb still exploded and a soldier died, but he was the only casualty. So far there's been no backlash from militant groups."

"I stopped the cults from starving themselves. They took some convincing. Famine's quite the show-woman when she's not insulting people."

"Is there a point to this?" John leaned back in his chair, folding his arms. "Father cleansed the Earth and started again with Noah. What if this is His will?"

"You think Father is responsible?"

"Sin is celebrated. Murderers are the new celebrities. They get book deals, not prison sentences. The Ten Commandments mean nothing. People can't even remember them. Adultery is accepted as part of a relationship. People marry for a few days then divorce; they have countless children out of wedlock. They're even allowing homosexuals to marry! Talk about mocking the sanctity of marriage."

Drew's heart raced, his tongue sticking to the roof of his mouth. He picked the label off his beer bottle, watching distorted shadows writhe up the walls. "Adultery makes more of a mockery of marriage than gay people. And the Bible allows bigamy, polygamy, concubines. Tell me how that protects the sanctity of marriage?"

"Mankind is a cancer on this earth. It's time Father started again. It needs it more now than it did in Noah's day."

"Who would He start afresh with? Is anyone so free from sin they should be the ones chosen to be saved?"

"Clearly not, judging by the number of people you've blinded."

Drew glared. "How many times is He going to kill the world and start over because mankind isn't behaving how He intended? He gave man free will. He can't murder them for embracing that. Father created sin, otherwise Adam and Eve wouldn't have fallen from grace. If you find a family so pure they're worth saving above everyone else, how will they reproduce without committing incest?"

"Are you saying Noah's family committed incest to repopulate the earth?" Jael's eyes widened.

"Unless Father had spare mankind moulds left over. The Bible doesn't go into details."

"That's blasphemy!"

"Blasphemy is the least of my problems."

"Don't start sprouting your twisted ideas again," John said. "We listened to you in Heaven and it got us exiled. We listen to you here and there's only one place left to go. I won't be damned for you."

"The world is worth saving. Yes parts of it are rotten, but parts of it are beautiful. The bad makes the good worth fighting for."

The angels exchanged glances. A bike engine purred outside. Drew tensed, waiting for it to die and Marsden's footsteps to approach the pub. After a few beats, the bike roared away. Relief coursed through Drew.

Drew stood. "The fifth seal has broken. The sixth seal is imminent. If you think this war is pointless, return to Heaven and await the death of mankind. When the sixth seal breaks, the world will soon die and we might die with it. But I'd rather die on my feet than live on my knees."

"That's exactly why you're here and not basking in Father's love," John muttered.

"I've seen the good in the world," Jael said. "I'm fighting with you, Drew."

Drew looked at Mark and John.

"I'll stay," Mark said.

"Fine, I'll stay," John said. "But I still think the world needs cleansing."

Drew smiled and raised his beer bottle. "To the end."

***

"How do we create an earthquake?" Demi shivered as December's frigid air caressed her. "Jump up and down the same time as China? Roll people down Mount Everest?"

The five Horsemen gathered on Gallows Street around the silver hand sculpture. Aeron sat on the world while Morgan perched on the thumb. The city centre was besieged with last minute Christmas shoppers.

"You couldn't snap a stick, let alone collide tectonic plates," Marsden replied. "Let's get the horses and gallop across the world."

"That was Plan A but we couldn't get clearance from health and safety," Morgan replied.

"They ruin all our fun," Aeron grumbled.

"Like the time we wanted to resurrect dinosaurs and start the dinopocalypse."

"Or when we thought it'd be funny to dress people as reapers for street art. They thought that would cause mass heart attacks."

"We're Death, they should accept our plans result in people dying. That's our trademark."

Aeron and Morgan produced globes from their pockets. Instead of graveyards, the globes contained rocks. They banged them together three times.

"Well that was fun as a funeral," Demi said. "Can I go? I've got a fashion show to prepare for."

A rumble emanated from beneath them. Lemures rattled like a skeleton hanging from a gallows. Marsden, Mac and Demi fought to keep their footing. Aeron and Morgan smiled and jumped off the sculpture. Cars shifted in the desolate street. Alarms blared, warning of the end of the world.

Bricks tumbled from buildings to die on the road. Windows shattered, raining onto people running for safety. The world sculpture rolled off the hand and escaped down Gallows Street, mowing down shoppers. People dashed out of buildings only to fall into the cracked road, their screams severed as they disappeared into the Earth's bowels.

A streetlight died as its falling body obliterated a parked car. Night's sepulchral cloak smothered them, the ground becoming more violent as its taste for human blood intensified. A shop's sign plummeted, smashing through the window and silencing a shriek. Blood dripped over the ruined window. A bench near the town centre toppled as the ground fractured like a broken heart. The darkness was filled with the sounds of chaos, destruction and people's terrified screams.

Christmas lights detached from their overhead wires, one demolishing an inflatable Santa. His suit burned, the lights sparking SOS signals no-one saw.

Morgan smiled at Marsden. "Are you ready to break the sixth seal?"

"And begin the end of humanity?" Aeron asked.

"And the world as we know it?"

Marsden shrugged. "I have nothing else planned."

They each laid a hand on Marsden's shoulder then Morgan smashed a globe and they disappeared.

"I'm not staying here to be swallowed by the road." Demi folded her arms. "It's not a fitting end to a rising star."

"Lemures Council will set up rescue centres in schools and halls," Mac said.

"Thanks for that juicy community gossip."

"I'll make them sick and you sabotage their food."

Demi smiled. "Let's cancel Christmas."

***

Marsden lost his balance and grabbed the twins. Amps and wiring strangled the volcano.

"The view's stunning." Aeron smiled.

"Shame it'll be drowning in lava," Morgan said.

"Better than a shopping mall."

"Or another cookie cutter housing estate."

"Can't you bang a globe to start this?" Marsden asked.

"Would you want to see globes banging throughout an Apocalypse film?" Aeron nudged him. "Don't you want excitement in your life?"

"I don't want a face full of lava and brimstone and have my skin slip off my face like dripping wax."

"Just play the song, hot stuff." Morgan slapped his arse.

"Stop molesting me."

"It's one of the few things health and safety *do* approve of."

Marsden swung his guitar round and freed his black and red plectrum. He plugged the guitar into the amp. 'Broken Minds' blasted around the volcano, the ground shuddering. Marsden eyed it uneasily, his fingers bleeding as they plucked the chords to end the world.

Aeron removed a crimson globe from his pocket and rolled it up his arm, across his shoulder and down into his other hand, the small volcano inside quivering. He held his arm out, smiled then opened his hand. The globe tumbled into the heart of the volcano as Marsden hit the final, raw chorus. Every string surrendered to his touch. The volcano shook, the globe shooting back up in a blast of ash. Aeron caught it then the volcano inside erupted, the globe exploding. The twins grabbed Marsden and vanished.

They watched from a distance as the volcano spewed suffocating ash from its toxic heart. Fiery tears seeped down its trembling sides. Darkness spilled across the sky, the iridescent moon turning crimson, stained with humanity's blood.

CHAPTER 35

Lemures lay battered, bruised and broken. Morgan, Aeron and Marsden reappeared in Gallows Street. The hand sculpture's life line was almost severed. Glass littered the cracked pavements. Shops' signs hung like condemned men. Some lay shattered on the floor. Streetlights crushed cars or fell into buildings. A telephone pole lay tangled in its wires, like an escaped asylum patient still wearing a straitjacket.

Darkness swallowed the city. The scarlet moon hid its face beneath the night's veil. Meteor showers reigned the sky. Ash swirled silently; embers of a cremated world.

"How far are we from Hawaii?" Marsden asked.

"Seven thousand miles," Aeron replied. "We're safe from the volcano."

They brushed ash from their clothes and patrolled the ruined street, jumping holes in the road and dancing out of the way of cascading bricks. The city fell to its knees around them; a desperate worshipper begging for salvation.

"Isn't it beautiful?" Morgan leapt onto a parked car, shielding her eyes as she scanned the devastation. "To think, most people in one day only manage to do their laundry, watch TV and update Friendzone about their dull routine."

"I've Chattered: 'broken 6th seal & caused major quake #shakeitupbaby #ApocalypseNow'." Aeron pocketed his phone. "The Chatter account was a good idea. We can update people about the Apocalypse in an upbeat, witty manner. Alleviate the seriousness of everyone perishing. And we can alert them there actually *is* an Apocalypse happening, if people haven't noticed."

Marsden growled, rueing the day someone decided a glorified Halloween prop should be in charge. "The whole world would've noticed my Apocalypse without needing to be told via Chatter."

Aeron rolled his eyes. "Are you going to be bitter throughout the entire thing? You're spoiling the party atmosphere we've tried to create." He placed a globe in Marsden's hand. "This is the grudge you've been holding. It's like a grenade. If you don't get rid of it, you'll be the one raining down on people like a 3D jigsaw." He took the globe, pretended to pull the pin out in his teeth and threw it down the street. The road exploded.

Stress lines snaked up the corner of a shop. Items in the Wiccan shop, the Cup and Sorcerer, lay in shards on the floor. Morgan somersaulted off the car as it moved with another tremor.

Aeron stopped at a split in the road; an open grave awaiting its eternal resident. "I thought we'd be able to see Hell. Hello down there filthy sinners!"

"What can you see?" Marsden joined him.

"Sewers. That's disappointing. And rank."

"Maybe Hell is a network of sewers overseen by the Teenage Mutant Ninja Turtles, with Splinter as the devil."

"Makes sense."

Aeron backed up then sprinted towards the split and sprang over it, his coat flapping like Dracula's wings. Marsden and Morgan followed.

Marsden looked around. "Where is everybody?"

"Buried beneath their homes?" Aeron crossed his fingers.

"Let's hunt out unlucky buggers who got hit by trees, power lines and flying hubcaps," Morgan suggested. "I love those hilarious deaths. Then we'll check on Dems and Mac. They're spreading joy in schools like happy little elves. Demi's arranged for the press to come, so we could usurp her in the papers.".

"We'll see you later." Aeron slapped Marsden's shoulder. "Keep survivors entertained in their darkest hour. Live Chatter pictures, using the hashtag ApocalypseNow. Let's get this party trending!"

Marsden saluted and jogged to his bike's hiding place. It was the only thing untouched in the debris-strewn alley. He fired it up and sped through the shaking streets, ducking as a sandwich shop sign hurtled overhead. He swerved around parked cars, drew his sword and decapitated a man fleeing across the road. Finally it matched the Apocalypse in his plans.

"Shit!" Marsden braked sharply, his bike skidding sideways. It stopped at the edge of a sink hole stretching across the road like a fatal wound in the world's body.

He looked down. Injured, dazed people hunted for an escape.

"Help us!" a woman shouted.

Marsden swivelled his guitar around and played a few verses of 'Cyanide Society'. A man spied the woman climbing out of the hole and yanked her down.

"She's trying to escape! She'll leave us here to die!"

Her shrieks were muffled by punches and kicks.

Marsden texted Morgan the survivors' location. Abandoning his bike, he hunted for a board then gathered bricks, positioning them at the edge of the hole. He retreated, mounted his bike then sped towards the ramp. It collapsed as his bike launched into the air. On landing, the bike pitched him over the handlebars. He swore as he crashed through a car's windscreen, onto the driver. Blood streaked the man's face, glass twinkling in his skin, shards protruding like icebergs. He gripped the steering wheel, a pole spearing his chest. Marsden crawled out, knocking glass off his jacket. He gritted his teeth as he hauled the bike up, cursing at the scratched paintwork.

"And health and safety banned horses."

He raced away from Gallows Street to the Razor and the Rosary. A sink hole had swallowed a car. The pub door flattened a bush. The only working lamp had been severed like a cut throat and fallen though Drew's bedroom window. Marsden stepped through the battered threshold. The world sculpture sat against the bar. The surface was scratched, scarred and stained with blood. A pair of legs protruded beneath it. Chairs and tables lay on their backs. Window glass littered the floor. He leaned over the bar to see smashed bottles and spilled drink.

"Drew!"

He ran upstairs and kicked open the door. Shattered photo frames, the toppled TV, and DVDs littered the living room. The Kama Sutra dice on the table told him to perform the Flower in Bloom in the closet. He dashed into the bedroom. The chest of drawers lay on its side and the Victorian lamp was half through the window like a trapped burglar.

Swearing, he ran downstairs to the kitchen. Pots and glasses lay in pieces on the floor.

"If you've wasted your life saving ungrateful mortals..."

He hurried down the cellar steps.

"Drew!"

He flung himself at Drew, squeezing him so hard flames erupted between them.

"Ow! Shit! Shit! Mars! What the fuck?" Drew pulled away, slapping the flames.

He fought the urge to hug him again and cover him in kisses. The flames died, the burning dulling before vanishing. He couldn't stop smiling.

"Are you ok? I've never seen you so…alive."

Marsden hesitated. How could he explain that destroying the world was the most exhilarating thing he'd ever done? "I'm just glad you're alive."

"Morgan rang and ordered I get my 'Heavenly arse' down to the cellar or she'd wrap my halo so tightly around my 'angel wand' I could sing in a boys' choir. She even texted me detailed instructional pictures. I have no idea how she got my number."

"Death always finds you."

"She said if I destroyed the greatest love story by saving 'ungrateful mortals', she'd make punishment from my father seem like a tickle fight. She backed it up with what she'd do to you."

"Medieval torturers could learn a lot from the Terror Twins. I taught them everything they know."

"What's it like up there?"

"The Apocalypse."

Drew squeezed past him and ran upstairs. He manoeuvred around the world sculpture. "I hope nobody comes looking for that. Being arrested for stealing from the town would result in a feature in the Bad Angels section of the *Angel Times*. If Heaven had a newspaper."

"Don't go outside!" Marsden chased him into his flat. "There's nothing left for you to save."

Drew righted his TV and switched it on, flicking through news channels showing splintered roads, demolished houses, flooded streets, fallen trees, and people being winched to safety. Each report contained a death toll competing for the highest number of fatalities. Missing person hotlines crawled along the screen.

"The death toll continues to rise after Mauna Loa erupted last night," the newsreader spoke with sombre glee. *"One hundred and eighty people have been killed but emergency services fear that total will grow. Many people are still unaccounted for. Seismologists said they've monitored Mauna Loa since its last eruption in 1984 and it has shown no signs of becoming active. The president of the United States described the scenes as 'harrowing'."*

It cut to shaky scenes of lava flowing down the volcano then shots of it destroying towns. People's agonised screams were captured as they were scalded alive.

"Jesus," Drew whispered. "Did the earthquake cause this?"

"We did."

"'And I beheld when he had opened the sixth seal, and lo, there was a great earthquake; and the sun became black as sackcloth of hair, and the moon became as blood'."

"It's hardly prize-winning literature."

Drew rushed to the window. "What are you covered in?"

"Ash."

"You might as well be drenched in their blood."

Marsden stared at Drew's back, dread and fear writhing in his stomach. Even Drew couldn't forgive this.

"People have predicted the end of the world since the Bible was written. How many 'raptures' have we lived through? The panic over the Mayan calendar running out, the zombie apocalypse everyone was excited about. The Apocalypse is the most anticipated event since the *Singing Sensation* final."

"The world can be saved. *People* can be saved!"

"I haven't met anyone I want to save. Except you."

"Who hired you?"

"I don't know. God?"

"Why would God destroy something He created?"

"God didn't create Earth, the universe, *any* of it. Mankind wasn't formed from clay like Golems. How many gods have ruled over the centuries? You can't seriously believe your god is the only one? He inherited the crown."

"I've read Heaven's history books. You think I didn't notice the discrepancy between the dates of when God created the Earth and how old the Earth actually is?"

"You didn't just question God, you confronted him with evidence? No wonder you were evicted."

Drew stared out the window. "Is this it? Perpetual darkness until we die?"

Marsden stepped closer to Drew and reached out to touch his back. He stopped himself. "You're scared." The realisation sucked the breath from his body.

Drew glanced over his shoulder. "I've been terrified of this my whole life. I knew it was coming. It's not like *Game of Thrones* where I'm watching the show before reading the books."

"I've longed for this moment my entire life."

"Is it how you imagined?"

"No." Marsden lowered his gaze. "When I'm out there, I feel alive. But I know how much you hate this."

"I don't enjoy the destruction of mankind."

"I *do*. I don't want you to be scared. I want you to ride with me." His throat felt like brimstone had lodged in it. "Go back to Heaven. You can't stop this."

Drew gripped the windowsill. "I'm not some weak do-gooder who'll stand by while you trample the Earth. Who do you think curbed Pestilence and Famine's tallies?"

"I know."

Drew spun around. "What?"

"I know about your four angel army and your clandestine meetings. It's my job to gather intelligence on the enemy. I know you've been buying Mac's drugs, setting up self-esteem courses for Demi's victims, flying grain and antibiotics to Africa. I don't know how you swayed that cult."

"I told them she was the devil and showed them pictures of the devil as a beautiful woman. Then I flashed them. Blinded the entire fucking cult. Clearly there's no-one left with pure souls. Michael's arranging my disciplinary hearing. I've blinded sixty people in the past month. I won't be allowed back in Heaven now. I don't know if I want to go back. All this time I thought I was winning battles when I was deluding myself into thinking I can stop this."

"No. You *were* winning."

"Because you let me."

"You were fighting Mac and Demi, not me."

"Jael saved the embassy in Israel."

Marsden's jaw clenched. "I *warned* my bomber to watch for angels."

"Why haven't you warned Pestilence and Famine?"

"The Terror Twins keep reminding me I'm not in charge. Plus I want Demi to wear the cockroach suit."

"Cockroach suit?"

"The Terror Twins have a death tally and the loser has to wear a cockroach suit."

Drew laughed. "Why are they in charge?"

Marsden snorted. "Privilege of breeding."

"What would you have done if you were in charge?"

"Slaughtered your angels and made the others watch, as a warning."

"Would you have made me watch too? Tortured me? Killed me?"

Marsden's eyes prickled. His chest ached. The tears sparkling in Drew's eyes made his throat burn.

"Maybe it's best I don't know. When the Apocalypse is over, we—"

Marsden closed his eyes. Nausea flooded him. "Don't say it."

"Not saying it won't stop it happening. It's not like a spell, which only works if you chant the incantation."

"Knowing it and hearing it…"

"I want to save the world. You want it decimated. Divorce lawyers call it 'irreconcilable differences'."

Marsden stepped closer to Drew so they were almost touching. "There is something we both want."

"What will that matter when I'm dead?"

"Join us and I'll keep you alive."

"You're asking me to betray everyone on Earth and in Heaven so I can have the guy I want?"

"So you can live."

"I want to be with you, Mars. More than I've ever wanted anything. But I can't let them die so I can have you."

"God damned Lucifer for siding with mankind. What the fuck do you think he'll do to you? Join us and we'll protect you."

"Doing the right thing makes me who I am, no matter how much it hurts me." Drew wiped his eyes with the heels of his hands.

"God wouldn't suffer for you. Don't suffer for him."

"I'm not fighting for God. Would you give up the Apocalypse if I asked?"

Marsden bit his lip until he drew blood. He shook his head.

"What comes next?"

Marsden stepped back and focused on the ash falling victoriously from the sky. "We'll awaken the volcano below Yellowstone Park."

"The death toll will be astronomical."

"It's the end of the world, not a New Year's Eve party. The only fireworks will be the volcano spewing ash and lava. There'll be no point making resolutions because there'll be no-one alive to keep them."

"So when the clock strikes midnight—"

"America will die."

CHAPTER 36

Cars joined in crash matrimony, bumpers kissing on the cracked road outside Tempest Road Primary School. A splintered tree crushed the climbing frame, its poles reaching for the sable sky. The seesaw's seats lay in the dirt, the severed beam scraping the ground. The roundabout spun as though pushed by children's ghosts, bathed in the light of the bloody moon. The hopscotch vanished into the yard's yawning mouth. A torn red cardigan writhed on the fence.

"Playtime's over, shitbiscuits." Demi opened the gate. "Time to learn a valuable lesson – don't take stuff from strangers."

They trudged up the long driveway and entered the school, Mac keeping his head lowered and his hands in the pocket of his yellow hoody. He wished he could have stayed behind in Purgatory and infected people from there. They only needed four Horsemen. They didn't need him. They were going to get caught and arrested. Nobody would believe he was a qualified doctor. Or that Demi was a nurse. Nurses were supposed to be nice.

"Did you have to wear that?" Demi indicated to his hoody.

"It's cheerful."

"You should be blending in, not glowing like neon pus. You look like a druggie, not a doctor."

"I don't criticise *your* clothes."

"*I* have good taste."

"You wear what magazines tell you to wear. You have no taste of your own." Mac averted his gaze from Demi's hard stare. Why did bravery feel so uncomfortable?

"You poor things!" a woman grabbed their arms, dragging them in before Demi could unleash her venom on him. "You look half-starved." She patted Demi's hand.

Demi muttered under her breath. "You look like an advert for pantomime fashion fails."

The woman turned to Mac. "Are you alright, love? You don't look well."

Demi grimaced. "He always looks like that. Birth defect."

"I'm terribly sorry!" Her cheeks pinked.

"Don't worry." Mac smiled, his cold sore splitting and weeping. "I'm Doctor Macies, this is Nurse Ceres."

The woman led them to the school hall, where people sat on the floor in small groups. Mac was surprised she hadn't asked for ID. Maybe security risks weren't important now the world was ending.

Children's Christmas decorations were strewn around the room, some hanging from the ceiling. The Christmas tree in the corner collapsed against the wall like a drunken Santa, crushing the empty boxes masquerading as presents and revealing their deceit.

Mac climbed on the stage. "Excuse me." A muted din filled the hall. "I'm a doctor and–" he cleared catarrh from his throat, feeling more useless than a spoon in the zombie Apocalypse. "I want–"

"For the love of kidney beans!" Demi hopped onto the stage. "Oi! You can post your survivor selfies later. Doctor Macies wants a word."

A hush descended. Someone coughed.

"Following the quake there's been a Typhus outbreak," Mac announced. People chatted. Demi shushed them. "Typhus thrives in unsanitary conditions, hence its nickname, Jail Fever. Symptoms include severe headache, fever, a rash which starts on the chest five days after the fever, cough, muscle pains, falling blood pressure, stupor, sensitivity to light and delirium. It has a mortality rate of ten to sixty percent if untreated. I'm here to vaccinate you."

"Clear your throat," Demi whispered. "You sound like you're gargling pus."

Mac's shoulder's drooped, his gaze travelling to the floor.

"What are the side effects of the vaccination?" someone asked.

Mac stuttered, conscious of his phlegmy voice. "Local reaction, fever. A small price for three years' protection against a killer disease."

"Do we need it?" a woman asked.

"Do you *want* your children contracting Typhus?" Demi asked. "I suppose it'll save the heartbreak of telling them you couldn't get them Barbie's Fuckingham Palace for Christmas."

People tapped their phones.

"What are you doing?"

"Googling it," a man replied.

"You deserve to die. Take comfort from saving money – your family's funeral will cost less than their presents."

She left the stage. Mac tripped as he stepped down. He erected a table at the far end of the hall, his tongue prodding his cold sore in concentration as he lined up phials of Typhus like soldiers ready to wage war against the innocent. Blue bowling pin-shaped bacteria floated in the phials. If people could see the beauty of diseases, maybe they wouldn't hate him as much. He placed a box of clean needles beside him that he had stolen from a shelter then strapped on a surgeon's mask. Nobody would trust a doctor with as many skin conditions as he had.

A man sat in the chair opposite Mac. "I have the symptoms you mentioned."

Mac prepared the needle then injected him with Typhus. "You'll need another injection in four weeks."

Demi removed her coat, revealing a short, tight black nurse's outfit. Mac sighed. Teaming up with her was a bad idea. She didn't steal the spotlight; she smashed everyone else's spotlights so they remained in the shadows.

"What are you doing?" Mac whispered.

"Your crater face isn't a crowd-puller. The only people who'll come to you are astronauts." She put her hands on her hips. "Who wants a vaccine?"

Men surged towards Mac's table like an unstoppable wave of the zombie virus.

"Go and ruin their food," Mac said through gritted teeth.

"I'll get them so worked up you can spread STIs while you're here. Seeing as we don't have stickers to give them."

"I'm not spreading STIs when there're children around."

Demi mimicked him in a whiny voice. "Tell people it's Sex Ed but more interactive than worksheets and watching disgusting birthing videos."

"You hate the idea of me…fornicating."

"I'm not going to watch, you perv! I had to witness your pizza cheeks getting hosed, I certainly won't watch them thrusting above the PTA."

"Hey sweetheart, I'm coming down with something," a man said. "Want to sit on my lap and see if you can feel it?"

"Not even the heroine in *The Princess and the Pea* could feel anything under your beer gut. You look nine months pregnant. Are you giving birth to a baby or a lifetime supply of cheeseburgers?"

Mac injected him. He swore then stomped off.

"I should've been a nurse," Demi mused. "My bedside manner is brilliant."

"Oi, nurse," another man called. "You look hot. Want me to stick my thermometer in you?" His friends laughed.

"Stick it in a pencil sharpener. It's small enough to fit."

"If you didn't dress like that, you wouldn't get comments," Mac said.

"*Typical* man's response – blame the woman for the fact he's a lecherous slimeball. I suppose you think I'm asking to be raped."

"Nobody deserves to be raped."

"If a guy spoke dirty to their daughters, they'd kill him. They're so hypocritical they make me sick. Watch." She beckoned to the teenage daughter of the second jerk. "Hey honey, fancy raising my blood pressure?"

"What did you say?" the man demanded.

"*You* can make lecherous comments, but if someone says it to *your* girl, they're out of line?"

"Fucking whore."

"Sorry sweetheart, my outfit doesn't make me a whore, like your football shirt doesn't make you a footballer. Dr Macies has shagged more people than I have. Are you going to call him a whore? Or does your opinion change depending on genitalia?" Demi kneed him in the groin. "Whoops. I've broken your thermometer." She smiled at the girl. "Your daddy's a creep who thinks women are sex objects. Keep away from him or you'll grow up believing that's an acceptable way for men to behave."

"We're here to spread disease, not break up families," Mac said. "Now you know how Mars feels when you sexually harass him."

"I don't harass him! He wants me, he just doesn't know it yet."

"He wants that angel."

"Oh please. Mars is incapable of loving anyone. It's not the angel that turns him on, it's the thought of taking what belongs to God and corrupting something pure. The way Daddy War took Mummy War to spite her father." Demi snatched up phials and needles. "Let's see who can infect the most people. Loser wears the cockroach suit."

"That's not fair! Everyone will flock to you."

"You should wear a sexy nurse's outfit then." She grimaced. "On second thoughts, this is *Contagion*, not *Nightmare Before Christmas*."

She strutted away and set up her own table. Mac slumped in his seat when everyone queued at Demi's table. Now she was stealing the only thing he was good at.

After half an hour of sitting alone, he moved everything over to her.

Demi smiled. "Thanks, I've run out."

"You're stealing my tallies! How would you like it if I starved people?"

"I'd love it! We should switch jobs. Yours is far easier. I can insult and infect them at the same time. There're kids over there you can start on."

"You pick on kids too?"

"I'm an equal opportunities ambassador." A pregnant woman walked past, her bump escaping her top. "Ugh! You're fertile, congratulations. If I wanted to see protruding belly buttons, I'd go to a museum of the macabre."

"Ex*cuse* me?" The woman raised her eyebrows. "Childbirth is beautiful."

"Some screaming, bloodied creature ripping its way out of your vagina isn't beautiful. Don't let your partner watch the birth or the next time he goes down on you, he'll envision a head watching him from inside your love cave." She smiled. "Vaccine?"

The woman stormed off.

"You cost me a death," Mac grumbled.

"I've infected half this hall. How many have you done, Phlegmington Spa? Three? You're a disgrace to diseases. They'll revoke your licence to kill."

"If the angels fight back, I hope you die first." He folded his arms.

"Did they stop us coming here? Stop us slaughtering the martyrs? Stop us breaking the sixth seal? No. They twitched their wings, polished their halos and mourned the loss of mankind. We have an angel who knows everything and he's too busy sharing 'fuck me' glances with our Vlad the Impaler to stop us. This world's ours for the taking. Now shut up and infect children. Those snotty little germ bags will spread your diseases quicker than we could."

"Typhus isn't passed from person to person."

"Give them something that is. God, *I* should be in charge of the Apocalypse. Not only would I wipe everyone out, I'd get an Oscar for doing it."

Mac gathered supplies and slunk over to children, injecting them when their parents weren't looking. After an hour, he ducked into the toilets to make more. He clicked the last lid on when the door opened. He swept his phials into his bag and scuttled back to the hall.

Demi smiled smugly. "I opened the tinned food and binned it, sprayed the rest with E. coli then threw perishable food out the windows for the rats."

"We should move schools."

"You go. My date with fame has arrived." She smiled at the news crew and unzipped her dress two inches. "Starvation just turned sexy."

CHAPTER 37

Drew rode through ruined streets, avoiding potholes and weaving around cars. One car united with railings in a bruising kiss. In a side street, the coroner loaded a body into his van, while another sprawled in the gutter. A church's stained glass windows lay like confetti around it. Boarded up shops and windowless houses flanked the road, watching the parade of the damned.

Drew parked in the alley behind Salvation and slipped through the back door. He burst in to Michael's office to find Harriett bent over her desk, her white skirt around her ankles, her white lace knickers concealing a pink arse. Michael spanked her. She flinched then moaned.

"How many typos were in that document?" Michael demanded.

"Fifty."

"You're being spanked for each one."

Harriett gasped. "Yes, Mr Archer."

Drew rubbed his face. "I'm pretty sure that's *not* a disciplinary method taught on management courses."

Michael whirled around. "Haven't you learned the act of knocking?"

"I'm sorry my bad manners exposed you indulging in one of the seven deadly sins. Greed in there, lust out here...five more and you finish your sticker album."

Michael dragged Drew into his office and slammed the door. He pushed Drew into the small chair. "Watch your tongue or I'll cut it out." His eyes glowed gold.

"You just collected the wrath sticker, well done. The Horsemen are destroying the world and you're roleplaying erotic novels! What's wrong with you?"

"Are you *judging* me? You – who accused Father of lying about how He created the world."

Drew gritted his teeth. "I didn't say that, I asked why dinosaurs weren't mentioned in the Bible. You can't judge me when instead of saving mortals' souls, you've done a brilliant job copying the stereotypical successful businessman: big office, golf clubs, Jaguar, shagging your secretary..."

"How can I inspire people to better themselves without demonstrating the rewards?" Michael took his seat behind the desk.

"Material possessions and casual sex? We should *influence* people, not join in with their debauchery."

"What do you want?"

"What do you *think* I want? Sexual harassment advice? I need your help."

"Shag whatever mortal girl's caught your eye then ask for forgiveness. Do you think I hired Harriett for her secretarial skills?"

"Anyone who makes fifty typos in one document doesn't have secretarial skills."

"I forgot. You like them with horns, not halos. How the *hell* did that happen? Jesus Drew, I knew you were a rebel, but..." He shook his head. "You're in a *lot* of trouble. I don't blame you. Warquest is beautiful. For a violent, murdering scumbag. Of all the people in the world, you fall for *him*?"

Drew's mouth went dry. His heart raced. "I haven't fallen for him."

"Heaven watches everything."

"How does it feel, knowing Father's watching you and Harriett? Must be like starring in your own porn film."

"One of the perks of being boss is I can switch off Heaven's CCTV. But Harriett's naughtier when she knows

278

we're being filmed." Drew grimaced. "Don't give me that look. That moment you and Warquest shared in the shower was so steamy, Harriett had to relieve me."

Drew covered his eyes. "Fuck."

"It doesn't matter what fucked up feelings you have for that psychotic parasite. Father wants you home."

"There's an Apocalypse outside. Or have you had your head too buried in Harriett's breasts to notice?"

Michael gripped his gold pen. "Your shithole pub has been destroyed and your charity cases are dead. You've served your sentence. Father's forgiven you. You can go home. Unless you *like* being strung up by your halo. Did you enjoy your view of Hell? That was my idea, by the way."

"You fucking–" Drew leapt up.

"I can send you downstairs for an extended holiday if you like. I have exclusive access to the Fallen Angels suite."

Drew slumped in his chair. "The world's ending, Michael and *nobody's* stopping it!"

Michael clasped his hands in front of him, a gold watch burdening his wrist. "Interfering now would be like standing in the path of a runaway train and hoping your body acts as a brake. We need to save our energy for fighting Hell when the fifth trumpet sounds. We have to pick our battles. If we try to fight every skirmish, we'll die."

"If you'd helped when I asked, the fifth and sixth seals wouldn't have broken and we wouldn't *need* to fight Hell. I *warned* you they would decimate mankind. You're the defender of Heaven. You could stop this Apocalypse alone. Or did you find your sword in a Kinder Surprise?"

"Curb your tongue. We're not blocking the building of a new supermarket. The Horsemen can *kill* us."

"You could've stopped them coming here!"

"I'm defender of Heaven, not Purgatory."

"So you *do* remember your role?"

"Do you?"

Drew bit his lip. "So there's nothing we can do?"

"You could kill them."

"They're immortal."

"*Nobody* is immortal. Pestilence can be cured by a healer or antibiotics. Famine will die if you feed her. Smash the Deaths' globes of life. Unfortunately, it means they'll return to Purgatory and their father will take their place. Death will never die. You have to use Warquest's weapon against him and play his song, 'Peace'. The Deaths introduced him to the first line. It wasn't pretty." Michael smirked.

"They tortured him?" Sickness churned Drew's stomach.

"They were trying to make him shag you. I admire his self-control. And yours. The saving grace is you can't touch each other." He laughed. "That must be frustrating!" Drew glared. "If you can't play his guitar, which will burn your fingers off, use the weapon inside it."

"His sword."

"One stab to the heart. Or cut off his head. Not even Horsemen can rise from that."

"I can't touch his guitar. What makes you think I can touch his sword?"

"If you kill him, you save the world. Are you not willing to suffer to save mankind? Surely their lives are worth a few blistered fingers. That's the problem with society – nobody is willing to make sacrifices for what they want. They think it should be given to them." He stroked the crucifix resting on his desk. "This world needs a new martyr. Father would be proud of you. For once in your life."

"This from someone who'd rather spank his secretary than help save the world?"

Michael glowered. "I *am* helping, you ungrateful pariah."

"If nobody's immortal, are you saying Father can be killed?"

"You think I'm telling the only angel to stand against him since Lucifer fell?"

"I'm *nothing* like Lucifer!"

"Keep telling yourself that if it helps you sleep at night."

Drew's jaw clenched. "There are four other Horsemen. What will killing War achieve?"

"Famine's an idiot. She could've crippled half the world, but she's too obsessed with chasing fame. Pestilence is doing well with his drugs, STIs and now his Typhus outbreak, but his lack of confidence hinders him. War's causing the most problems. Riots, conflict in the Middle East, the crumbling of society. *He* slaughtered the martyrs and broke the fifth seal. *He* erupted the volcano and broke the sixth seal. Death doesn't *need* the others. They're here because the contract declares they must destroy a quarter of the world each. War could obliterate the planet single-handedly and believe me, he wants to. Without him, the Apocalypse is fucked. *You* have to stop him. Feel free to kill the others too."

"Why me?"

"He's so infatuated with you, he'd probably let you kill him if you asked." Michael laughed. Drew gripped his thighs to stop himself strangling Michael. "You should've killed him the second he walked into your pub. You knew who he was, yet you let him fetch the others. How does it feel having the death of the world on your conscience because its murderer gives you a boner?"

"I was *told* to let him gig at my pub."

"You weren't told to fall in love with him. You went off script and fucked up the play for everyone."

Drew looked out the window, fighting the urge to beat Michael to death with his golf clubs. He'd never hated anyone as much as he hated Michael right now. Angels were incapable of hatred. Maybe he was no longer an angel. "Pestilence isn't in the Bible. So why is he here?"

"Cabinet reshuffle. Death found the workload of reaping and spreading diseases too much so donated his pestilence DNA to create that god awful creature. I would've drowned that wretch at birth. Conquest and War amalgamated and combined their DNA."

"Marsden has *two* fathers? Were they lovers?"

"Sorry to spoil your Brokeback Horseman fantasy but only a mummy and a daddy can create a baby. Warquest has the blood of *two* Horsemen. That's why he's so powerful and burns you more than the others." Michael pressed a button on his phone. "Harriett, bring me a coffee."

Drew sat back, playing with his hands. Harriett entered with a tray. She poured milk and coffee into the cup then stirred sugar in while Michael slipped his hand up her skirt. She squirmed.

Drew scowled and folded his arms. "You've been here longer than I have. Don't you want to save people?"

"I don't trouble myself with humans' trivial lives. They live for ninety years, if they're lucky. We live for infinity. They're ants in an ant farm. Though less intelligent." He pulled Harriett onto his lap.

"If we work together..."

"We don't fight. We certainly don't wage war against the Horsemen. That's suicide." He sighed. "Why can't you accept things? Do you realise how much your behaviour upsets Father?"

"*My* behaviour? I'm not the one plundering Harriett's Garden of Eden."

Michael unbuttoned Harriett's jacket and stroked her white lacy bra. "I'll lend her to you for an hour."

"She's not a possession you can loan out. Show her some respect."

"It'll be my pleasure." She smiled, her fingers straying to her breast.

"Don't you have a document to rewrite? Try using spellchecker." Harriett sashayed out, buttoning her jacket. Drew rubbed his forehead. "Mars– War says the Horsemen are independent contractors."

"Father created them but we didn't have the budget to keep them on the payroll. They're freelance mercenaries. They kill for money. Except War – he kills for pleasure." He chuckled. "You have terrible taste in men."

"Don't fucking judge me when you traded your purity ring for a cock ring. Who hired them?"

"That's confidential."

"We could petition them to stop it. Everyone has their price."

"The planet is like a mortal with terminal cancer. Pump drugs into it but in the end, you have to pull the plug. In two thousand years, there'll be another Apocalypse. You could stop that one." Michael smiled. "I'm curious. Is it War's beauty that arouses you? Or the thought of being touched by hands drenched in humanity's blood?"

Drew jumped up and punched Michael in the face. He shook his fist, glancing at the ceiling. "Forgive me, Father. The sanctimonious prick deserved it."

Michael's gold and white wings spread as he sprang over the desk and flung Drew against the wall, pressing his golden sword against Drew's throat. Drew gasped and struggled, his wings breaking free.

"Strike me again and you'll never find your way back to Heaven. You can die with your precious mortals." Drew wheezed, black rain dancing in his vision. Michael pulled a DVD from his pocket and slapped it against Drew's chest. "This should help you. If you *really* want to save the world, kill the Horsemen."

CHAPTER 38

"We row, row, row our boat, through the lava stream. When it burns your face right off, you won't have time to scream," Aeron and Morgan sang as they used their scythes to paddle leisurely through the lava around the base of Mauna Loa. Aeron wore a purple lei, Morgan a red one. They decided against wearing grass skirts and coconut bras. It would ruin their sombre, professional image. Plus, Aeron mused, his cleavage wasn't impressive enough. He'd have to stuff.

"It's like being in a Halloween fun house." Morgan prodded a body as they sailed past.

"Or the lake at home."

"Minus the leviathan."

"We should've brought them with us. They'd love a holiday. Pity it isn't summer, or they could've made beach trips fun for everyone."

Aeron photographed them in the boat. They'd reinforced the bottom with globes so it wouldn't melt. Losing their feet to lava would sour the relaxing mood. And make dancing difficult.

"I'd kill for a cocktail," Aeron said.

Morgan squeezed a globe and vanished. She reappeared moments later holding two blue cocktails topped with blue flames. "Two Flaming Volcanoes. Seems appropriate. I went to that cocktail bar we visited in Hawaii. I almost didn't get served – they had 'more important' things to worry about. I showed them more important things to worry about and they gave me the drinks on the house. I didn't tip them. Rudeness mustn't be rewarded."

They clinked glasses and sat back to drink them as the boat floated downstream. Burning ash fell around them like dying fairies falling from the sky. The crimson moon provided a haunting atmosphere.

Aeron glanced at another corpse face down in the lava. "It amazes me why people live by volcanoes. Did they learn nothing from Pompeii?"

"Mortals live in denial – death, natural disasters, being bitchslapped by Sharktopus – they never think it'll happen to them."

"Help!" A man waved at them from a rooftop. Morgan waved back. "Help me!"

"Help's on its way!" Aeron produced a globe. "I bet I can hit him from here."

"Ooh I'll take that bet."

"Hold my glass."

Aeron stood and drew back his arm, raising his knee like a professional bowler. The man waved frantically. Aeron flung the globe. It hit the man in the face, knocking him into the lava.

Aeron threw his arms up, catching the man's soul globe the lava rejected. Lava dripped from his hand, as though he held the man's still beating heart, his burning blood streaking his skin. "And the crowd go wild! They've never seen a throw so accurate."

Morgan roared with laughter. "Hit him right in the wickets! I filmed it. We can take a snapshot for the scrapbook."

"Let's find more survivors."

They picked up their scythes and scoured the ruined village.

"There." Aeron pointed.

They paddled to where a family huddled on a roof.

"They look like tourists," Morgan said. "What a fun holiday they must be having. I wonder if they'll sue their travel company. I'll save them the paperwork."

She stood, windmilled her arm then released the globe. It crashed through the posts holding the roof. The family screamed as the roof collapsed and they slid towards the lava. The mother grabbed the youngest child and the roof while her husband and two other children plunged to their scorching deaths. Morgan narrowed her eyes and pelted the woman's fingers with globes until she surrendered her grip. She flailed as she and the child slithered down the roof and vanished beneath the lava.

"I give her a one for the execution of that dive," Morgan said. "Not a single extremity was pointed. Did you see the splash she made? No medals for you, Little Miss Butt Flop."

Five globes bubbled to the surface. Morgan scooped them up. They rowed in silence, enjoying the view. It was nice to take time out for a river cruise. Their dad had wonderful memories of sightseeing on Earth, but they'd been too busy working.

"I hate to admit it, but I'm nervous about the seventh seal," Aeron said. "What if it doesn't go according to plan?"

"It will. Everything's in place. We have to be patient."

"We have no Plan B."

"Plans Bs are for people who have no confidence in their Plan A. There are plenty of ways to break the seal. Ours is the best."

A man stood beside the lava flow, waving his arms. Morgan saluted him with her cocktail.

"Aloha!" she called, taking a sip.

"We need help!"

"I'd say you're beyond help," Aeron replied, rowing slowly past. "There's no room in the boat. The next one should be along…never."

"My wife is sick."

"Why didn't you say?" Morgan asked. "Sick people are our speciality. You won't find our cure in shops. Aer, row to shore."

"Aye, aye captain." Aeron rowed to shore and they jumped out. "Lead the way, puny mortal."

The man led them to a crumbling house. "The lava struck before we could leave. No-one was expecting it."

"I'd say living by a volcano would guarantee you'd be expecting eruption at some point," Morgan said. "You became complacent."

They followed him up what remained of the stairs to a bedroom. A woman lay in bed, moaning.

"She's too sick to evacuate. I'm not leaving her." He knelt beside the bed and took her hand.

Aeron clapped him on the arm. "Don't worry, we've got this." He pulled a death globe from his pocket.

"What's that?"

"Magic."

"Will it take away her pain?"

"Yes." Aeron put the globe on the floor, demonstrating fancy footballing skills before flicking it up and kicking it into the wall. The woman thrashed then lay still. He rescued her soul globe and shook it, watching the new headstone rise from the ashes.

"You killed her!" The man hugged his wife, sobbing.

"She was holding you back." Morgan waved her hand dismissively. "Now you can evacuate, start a new life somewhere safer."

"I didn't want her to *die*! I wanted to take her with me."

"I want a My Little Pony ride-on horsey but you don't see me whining like a kid who didn't get the last Jammy Dodger."

She and Aeron left, shaking their heads at the man's ingratitude. They'd kindly stopped their lava cruise to assist him and he didn't even say thank you. No wonder the lava targeted his house.

"Hey!" Aeron spied people climbing into their boat and gave chase. "That's ours!"

The people scrambled in and rowed away. Aeron and Morgan stopped, looked at each other, threw five globes into the lava then linked arms and skipped around.

"Row, row, row our boat, through the fiery stream, wait 'til it begins to sink then we'll hear you scream." They did fake screams.

The boat lurched, rocking as the group clung to the sides or each other. Aeron and Morgan waved as the boat plunged beneath the lava, the people's screams silencing as the lava claimed them. The boat popped to the surface, five scalded people slumped in the seats. Aeron materialised in the boat and steered it back to Morgan, standing up like he was punting in Venice.

"See what happens when you steal people's things? That wasn't nice."

He and Morgan rummaged in their skeletons for their globes and played catch with them before shrinking them.

"Corpse!" the raven landed in the boat so they filled his pouch with the marbles.

He flew away as they dumped the corpses in the lava. This would be one of the many towns where there would be no-one left to bury the dead. The boat disintegrated, so Morgan made a raft of globes and they resumed their journey, the mood subdued now they'd been victims of a robbery. It wasn't something Death should face. They reached a couple shouting for their attention. Simultaneously, they hooked their scythes around them and yanked them into the lava. They high-fived each other as the shrieking people vanished below the fiery river.

"Marriage vows say 'til death do you part'," Aeron said, plucking their globes from the lava. "We made sure they kept them."

"I like we get a mention in wedding vows. Makes me feel like we're part of the happy day."

"We're part of everyone's day in the end."

They blew kisses to distraught survivors as they rowed past.

"We row, row, row our boat past your wretched screams, today is the Apocalypse, we'll see you in your dreams!"

CHAPTER 39

Marsden burst into the pub and rushed towards the stairs.

Sasha dashed out from behind the bar, blocking him. "He doesn't want to be disturbed."

"Is he watching porn?" He smiled. "Emailing them saying the missionary position *doesn't* bring them closer to God? And that's *not* what nuns wear under their habits?"

"He'd visited his brother–"

"Drew doesn't have a brother."

"Michael owns Salvation."

Marsden backed out of the pub and circled it to where the streetlamp had fallen through Drew's bedroom window. He shinned up it, swinging around when he reached the top. He sprang through the window and entered the living room. The PS3 protruded from the TV. A beer bottle spilled its contents into the carpet like a dying heart pumping out its last drops of blood.

"Drew?" He checked the kitchen then pushed open the bathroom door. "You'd better not be on the toilet. I'd like to keep that part of you a mystery." Drew was curled up on the floor. His eyes mirrored the glassy gaze of a doll, whose only human appearance was its plastic shell. Marsden's heart constricted seeing him look so broken. He knelt and touched Drew's tear-stained face. His fingers blistered. Drew didn't flinch. "You ok?" Relief surged inside him when Drew blinked. "Are you *drunk?*"

Marsden grabbed his arm and pulled him up.

"Don't fucking touch me!" Drew struck Marsden in the mouth, knocking him down.

"What the fuck?" He touched his lip, ruby droplets glistening on his fingertips.

Drew seized Marsden's jacket and dragged him into the living room. "Get the fuck out of my flat!"

Marsden struggled to break free, his jacket sizzling and melting. "You're ruining my favourite jacket!" He prised Drew's hands away, rising.

"Get. The fuck. *Out*!" Drew's palms slammed into Marsden's chest.

Marsden grimaced. Hand prints burned into his t-shirt. "What's wrong with you?"

Tears trickled down Drew's face.

"Does this have something to do with the brother you hid from me?"

"Michael's a dick, but he's not a bloodthirsty psychopath like you."

"I'm not a psychopath! I have emotions. Maybe not quite like other people's..."

Drew marched to the PS3, ejected a disc and flung it at Marsden.

Marsden caught it, read the title and closed his eyes. "Fuck. I'm sorry."

"You're not *sorry*! You don't even *care*!"

"I'm not sorry I killed them, I'm sorry I've upset you."

"I watched you *massacre* innocent people! I'm more than *upset*!"

"The martyrs *had* to be slaughtered. Those were my orders. We signed a contract."

"It's probably just as well we're allergic to each other. Your touch would be stained with their blood." Marsden studied his clean palms. "I don't want you near me."

Marsden blinked, his eyes burning. The pain etched on Drew's face would be the image he saw as he closed his eyes. He curled his hands into fists, hating the strange, horrible feeling consuming him, hating hearing those poisonous words from those lips.

"You *knew* I killed them! You told me you loved me as we stood amongst their corpses! It's not like I've spent the last few months pretending to be a musician then you've discovered I'm responsible for the death of mankind."

"It's different…watching them die. Every time I close my eyes, I hear their screams."

"Where did you get this? Michael?"

"It doesn't matter."

"Why did he film it instead of stopping us? Why give it to you? He's turning you against me."

"You've done that yourself. I never want to see you again."

"No." Marsden gripped Drew's arms. Drew hit him off. "You're the *only* person I don't want to kill in the worst kind of way. This can't end because–"

"You're a soulless murderer who gets more pleasure from killing people than anything."

"I've never denied that, but that's *not* how *you* see me."

"Tell me you hated every single second of that. Tell me you'd give it up."

"I've never hidden anything I've done from you – the Winter Wonderland, the riot, slaughtering the martyrs. You know it all. You've seen the aftermath. Why does seeing me in action change anything?"

"I convinced myself you were doing your job. But you *enjoy* it."

"Some people are lucky enough to do a job they love. Killing silences my demons."

"Every night in my head when I make love to you, I'm making love to a monster."

A lone tear slipped down Marsden's face. "My father only loves the torment and misery I inflict. You love something else in me. Something I didn't know existed. Please don't take it away."

Drew wiped his eyes. "If I stop the Apocalypse, I'll betray you. If I help you, I betray my family."

"We're on opposite sides. You're not betraying me by stopping the Apocalypse. It's your mission." Marsden grabbed Drew's face and rested his forehead against Drew's, needing the physical pain to banish the agony of his breaking heart. "I love you. A life without you is worse than death."

Drew sobbed, hugging Marsden. Pain burst through Marsden then Drew shoved him away and dropped into a chair, doubling over.

"If I could cut out the part of me you hate and destroy it, I would."

"I hate that you're a Horseman."

Marsden reached behind and yanked the sword free. The snake coiled around the haft, its eyes glowing red at the promise of blood.

"I can't *stop* the Apocalypse, I don't want to. I'm War. I live for bloodshed."

"You can rebel!" Drew stood.

"I haven't spent my whole life training for this, only to throw it away." He offered the sword to Drew. "I'm *this* close to achieving the only thing I've dreamed of. If you're going to stop the Apocalypse, you have to stop *me*."

"I can't!"

"As long as I'm alive, I'll hurt you. How will you bear these bloodstained hands touching you? Why would you make love to a monster?" His gaze penetrated Drew's. "You hate that I'm a Horseman. There's only one way I will stop being a Horseman."

Marsden plunged the sword into his heart.

"No!"

Marsden dropped to his knees. Blood trickled down his chin. He collapsed, his hand shaking as he fought to stop himself pulling out the blade. He'd seen hundreds of people die. It looked easy. Yet death wasn't coming for him. The one time he wanted to see the twins and they weren't there. If they were getting drunk on those bloody cocktails...

Drew pulled the sword out, hissing as its imprint branded his flesh. He dropped it. Marsden staggered up as the wound sealed.

Marsden picked up the sword and thrust it against Drew's stomach. Drew's t-shirt ignited. "Kill me!" Drew shook his head, his tears falling faster as he killed the flames. "Clearly I can't kill myself."

Drew cast the sword aside. It struck the wall, clattering to the floor by the TV. Marsden pulled his guitar over his head, freed a song sheet from inside it and held them out. 'Peace' was written at the top of the sheet. "One song."

"You said the twins had your sheet."

"With them in charge, there was always a chance of me dying. Second rule of warfare – always have a Plan B."

"I can't play this thing. I can't even touch it." Drew ran his fingers over it, wincing. "I feel their torment, trapped inside. It's a dungeon of damned souls."

"Think of all those souls I'll destroy."

"Stop it."

"I can't. But you can. One soul to save billions."

"It's not 'one' soul. It's *your* soul."

"If you want to save the world, you have to make a sacrifice."

"Michael said the same thing. Funny I'm the only one who has to make that sacrifice."

"You're the only one who wants to save the world." Marsden shoved the guitar against him. "Play it!"

"No!" He pushed Marsden against the wall, the guitar trapped between their burning bodies.

Marsden's heart raced. Drew was close enough to kiss. "*Kill me*! Or I will kill them all."

Drew kissed him. Their scorching lips created pleasure and pain so intense, Marsden didn't want it to end. He ripped Drew's t-shirt from him. His lips and tongue were on fire, but he pulled Drew closer, the kiss burning through his body. The guitar burst into flames. Drew was the sweetest poison he'd ever tasted. Their skin crackled and blackened. Drew's wings burst through his back, ruby droplets streaking the feathers. Marsden ran his fingers through them before wrapping his arms around Drew. His heart thrashed. Drew's purity scorched through his blood, turning his veins silver. Every nerve was aflame. Intense pain robbed his lungs of air.

They pulled apart. The burning guitar dropped to their feet. Smoke spiralled from their bodies.

"You'll be damned for eternity."

Drew stroked Marsden's hair, his glowing eyes reflecting Marsden's red ones. Marsden's heart stopped momentarily. This was Drew's true form. Beauty had never looked so dangerous. Black veins crawled under his skin. "I'll still love you in Hell."

Marsden held the back of Drew's head, kissing him deeply. Now he'd tasted him, he needed more. Their bodies ignited, embracing them in a fiery shroud. Blood seeped through their cracked lips, the stench of their blistering skin smothering Drew's fruity scent. Drew's hands melted to Marsden's face. Ringing echoed through his ears and shadows danced behind his eyelids as pleasure flooded him, drowning the pain. His heart slowed, his life slipping away.

Searing light poisoned the night. A high pitched squeal was accompanied by flapping wings. Drew's hands ripped away from Marsden's face. Marsden covered his ears, the sound piercing his brain. Drew fell to his knees, gagging and clawing his choker. Scarlet tears wept down his neck. Marsden dropped beside him and tugged his choker. Drew screamed like the tortured damned.

A flash of gold tore his wings from his back.

The room darkened. Silence killed Drew's screams.

White feathers floated down, resting in Drew's blood.

"No!" Marsden held him tightly.

"Play…it." Drew wheezed.

"Then there's no way back for you!"

"It's already too late."

Marsden swiped the tears streaking his face and rescued his fallen guitar without extinguishing it. He slotted the sword into it then pressed his ruined fingers against the scalding strings. Drew's eyes closed. Marsden played 'Damnation', his treacherous fingers knowing the chords.

Drew gasped as the choker slipped from his neck and rolled into the wall, a blackened, twisted halo. His tattoo bled, the white wings turning black as the blood dried.

Marsden dropped to his knees. Numbness consumed him. He stroked Drew's back. His skin didn't blister.

It felt like something had died.

"Congratulations." Morgan applauded as she and Aeron materialised, wearing leis. "What a kiss! It was so hot I nearly orgasmed."

"Jizzballs. I think I did," Aeron said, pocketing his phone. "I got it all on film."

Aeron held a large globe containing an angel chained to a tombstone by barbed wire. Scarlet droplets glistened on the angel's wings. The globe shook then shattered with a shriek.

"What the hell is that?" Marsden asked.

"We lied about Operation Fanfare," Morgan said. "There's only one thing that will make the angels sound their trumpets – mourning the loss of a fallen one. Drew's damnation was the seventh seal. You've just broken it."

CHAPTER 40

"Good job Romeo! You broke the seal in such a sexy style!" Aeron slapped Marsden's back. "We should hold a countdown and reveal the nation's favourite seal break before the world ends. This will be number one. Pity your serpent didn't taste his apple – that would've been Apocagasmic. You could've taken his virginity and the world in a single thrust." He did an over exaggerated pelvic thrust.

Marsden hit his hand away. "*That's* why you forced that fucking book on me?"

"Don't be crude. It's a pleasure book. Life's too short to not chase your dreams. Or so those Friendzone memes say."

Marsden stood and punched him. Morgan punched Marsden in retaliation. She should discipline him for attacking his bosses. He swung for her, but she ducked and kneed him in the stomach.

She grinned. "Times like these I'm glad I kept up my Krav Maga class."

"Why the hell did you torture me to keep us apart? You made me think I'd kill him!"

"Forbidden love is the hardest to resist. It made you want each other more. If we'd given our blessing from the start, you wouldn't have had the delicious anticipation. Plus the seals would've broken in the wrong order. Even chaos has order. We used your fear of being labelled a traitor to make sure you resisted True Love's Kiss until the end."

"You set me up!" He snatched up the beer bottle and hurled it at her. She ducked and it smashed against the wall.

"Why are you complaining? You've got everything you've wanted – the man you love and the glory of breaking the final seal."

"*Look* at him!" He pointed at an unconscious Drew. A ruby necklace and fingernail gouges tainted his throat. "You think he'll want me now?"

"Have you read erotica? It's not about liking the person, it's about being unable to resist their sexy charms."

"He will hate me for the rest of his life. They took his fucking wings because you made him an accomplice to the thing he was trying to *stop*."

"You make us sound like geniuses."

Marsden swung his guitar, obliterating a lamp and the remains of the TV. He brought his guitar down on the treacherous disc that decimated Drew's feelings for him. He stamped on it, grinding it into the carpet.

Morgan smiled. A Horseman having a tantrum like a hormonal teenager wasn't an everyday occurrence. She wished she'd brought snacks. "Listen." She cupped her ear. "What do you hear?"

Marsden lowered the guitar. "Nothing."

"Exactly. You've stolen one of God's angels and he hasn't fried you with a lightning bolt. Your insides should be mush. Heaven is silent."

"Out of respect for the dead," Aeron said. "Should we have a coloured ribbon for this event? An international day on the calendar?"

"There won't be another calendar. And nobody to wear the ribbons."

"We'll wear them."

"Let's go for black."

"Red would signify the blood that's been shed but that's been taken."

"Black's taken too. Mostly by death awareness groups or mourning a massacre."

"Perfect!" Aeron smiled.

"We'll put a sword on it. No, let's have a rainbow one. According to the Bible, God created a rainbow after flooding the earth. To cheer up the people he didn't consign to a watery grave. We can wear one after destroying the earth. Plus it'd show support for Mars and Drew."

A low trumpet note rumbled through the sky. The pub shook and they hit the floor. Cracks crawled across the angel wings burned into the ceiling. Crimson tears seeped through the spiderweb of destruction, stalking the fracture lines before dripping onto the floor. Fire writhed over the lines, consuming the blood and reaching out to lick their skin.

"Everyone out!" Aeron commanded.

Marsden slung his guitar onto his back, picked Drew up and ran downstairs. Morgan and Aeron smashed a globe, reappearing in the crumbling car park. They stumbled, catching each other. Ominous clouds formed in the sky like a troop of deadly warriors merging on the battlefield to wage war against mankind.

Another note echoed across the sky, lamenting the loss of an angel. The clouds' stomachs tore open, spilling their blood upon the world.

Morgan and Aeron twirled, arms spread. "It's raining blood, hallelujah." Aeron spun under Morgan's arm then twirled out.

At the playing of another note, a hail storm of fire rained onto the skeletal trees surrounding the car park, setting them ablaze. The trees turned black under the fire's ravaging tongue, the branches curling like fists. Flames dropped from the branches, devouring the grass with gluttonous delight.

"What is this?" Drew held out his hand. Blood and fire dropped into his palm. Marsden lowered him.

"The end of the world," Morgan said. She cocked her head, trying to see if he looked different now he was no longer one of God's slaves. A noose branded his bare neck. Crimson rain slid down his torso. "You really are a Heavenly delight. I could lick you like a lollipop. Though I prefer you unconscious. You're less judgey."

"Isn't it beautiful?" Aeron tilted his head back, the rain splashing his face. "It belongs in gothic photography."

"Or a graphic novel."

"We should see how Operation Fanfare's faring in the States." Aeron pulled out his phone. "Does anyone have popcorn?"

"I've got Skittles."

"They'll match our ribbons. We can taste the rainbow as well as wearing it."

On the screen, Yellowstone Park trembled as its volcanic heart awoke from its 600,000 year repose to wreak revenge. A fountain of ash, rocks and lava exploded through the ground.

Aeron took a selfie of him and Morgan posing in the bloody rain. He pointed the camera at Marsden and Drew. Marsden raised his middle finger. Drew looked downright miserable. Morgan shook her head. Some people were terrible at parties. Aeron uploaded the photos to Chatter, adding *7th seal broken & angels are blowing their trumpets. The Apocalypse just got sexy #ApocalypseNow* to the photo of the fatal kiss. Drew's bleeding wings added something special to the photo.

More notes spread dread with their haunting sound. People rushed into the street, to be drenched in the clouds' bloody fiery tears.

Drew touched his neck then his back.

"You two should kiss and make up," Morgan said. "Hollywood loves rain-drenched kisses. The fire and blood will make it unique."

Aeron raised his phone to capture it. Drew caught Marsden's eye then looked away.

"*How* long have you waited for your first kiss? You could look a *little* happier. Or after all that build up, did it fail to light your fires?"

"I know what this moment is missing." Aeron crushed a globe and disappeared. He materialised holding two cocktails. "Drew, a toast. Which would you rather?" He raised one glass. "Kill Me Now or," he raised the other. "Fall From Grace?"

Drew glared. Aeron shrugged and posed with them as Morgan took a photo. He passed one to her. They clinked glasses and sipped through the awkward silence.

Motorbike purrs could barely be heard above the torrential din. Demi and Mac ran over, sheltering under Demi's large transparent umbrella. Mac wore a surgical mask and gloves, his hoody pulled over his face so only his eyes peeked out.

"Come on you two, I need a photo." Aeron motioned for them to face him. "Mac, I can't see you. Say 'Apocalypse'."

"I wasn't allowed to share her umbrella if she could see my face," Mac mumbled.

"He's *not* being in my photo," Demi said. "I'm done posing with props to improve my image."

"We're a team, Dems," Aeron reminded her.

"There's no 'Demi' in team." She glanced up. "Is this blood? My clothes will be ruined!"

"What's that sound?" Mac covered his ears.

"The first trumpet," Drew whispered. "A third of trees will burn."

"With any luck it'll decimate Christmas trees," Aeron said. "Ruin Christmas for everyone."

"Nothing like a burnt tree and toasted presents to spoil a festive day," Morgan said.

"They could use it to cook their turkeys."

"And roast their chestnuts."

"That must be done on an open fire. It says so in the song."

"Stop!" Marsden said. "My brain can't cope with stereo right now."

Drew folded his arms, shivering. "*I* did this?"

Marsden removed his jacket and draped it over Drew's shoulders. Drew moved to push it off then slipped his arms in and zipped it up.

"*Him*?" Demi scoffed. "He can't even say 'oh god' without begging for forgiveness and spanking himself with rosary beads."

"It was a team effort," Morgan said.

"Michael's committed all of the seven deadly sins and he's an arsehole," Drew said. "I've done *everything* Father wanted, but I share *one* kiss with Marsden and it ends the world?"

"Must've been some kiss," Demi muttered.

"Michael's a big cheese," Morgan said. "One of daddy's favourites. He sins, he asks for forgiveness, he gets it. Plus he sins with angels. You tongued the enemy – twice – and you're unrepentant. You were kicked out of Heaven for questioning your father. That's the worst sin an angel can commit. Look what happened to Lucifer. Got his own kingdom and everything."

"Michael's right. I'm as bad as him. I should be sent to the burning lake."

Marsden's eyes blazed. "For questioning a dictator?"

"For falling in love with the destroyer of mankind."

Demi snorted. "Uh, hello? It was a team effort."

"You're not exactly a five star match on Cupid.com," Aeron said. "You had your earth-shattering kiss the audience was waiting for, the seventh seal is broken and we can sit back and watch the world fall around us. So Mars, what's it like kissing an angel? Did the earth move? Did his lips fertilise your heavenly garden until the wood grew?"

"At least you'll always remember your first kiss," Morgan said. "Something to tell the grandkids."

"I Chattered the video. It's already trending under the hashtag HottestKissOfAllTime."

Marsden glowered. Covered in blood, he looked like he'd just stepped off the set of *Saw*. Morgan stepped back. She didn't fancy being 'bloody rain babe'.

"The second one has a lot to live up to. Don't expect Apocalypses every time. We don't have the budget," Aeron said. "We'll stand guard if you want to pluck his harp."

"Blow his trumpet."

"Open his pearly gates."

"Stop!" Marsden raised his hand. "Or I'll play the Apocalypse Song on your vocal chords."

"If you time it right, you could hit his right notes as the second trumpet sounds."

"You upstaged me *again*!" Demi kicked Marsden's ankle. "I was being the Vaccine Vixen then the photographer buggers off to photograph bloody rain!" She opened her coat, revealing her nurse's outfit. "Forty quid this cost!"

Aeron snorted. "Forty? I've seen it on eBay for twenty five."

"I bent over so many times I've pulled a back muscle, it's sodding freezing and they won't use my photos because *you* snogged Paradise Lost!" She punched Marsden's arm.

Marsden grabbed her coat. "Hit me again and I'll tear you like wrapping paper." He pushed her away.

"After everything I've done to save mankind, I kill them with a kiss," Drew mumbled, looking sick.

"You're a reverse Prince Charming," Morgan said.

"*He* was the seventh seal?" Demi raised her eyebrows. "If I'd shagged him, I would've broken the seal like a glutton breaking lent?" She stamped her foot. "This could've been my moment!"

"He wouldn't have fallen if you'd done it. God forgives lust. That's why Michael gets away with treating his secretary like a blow up doll. But they're only allowed to love him."

"*I'm* fucking lovable!"

"So are piranhas," Marsden said.

The trumpet blared through the streets. Blood streaked the houses. Sparks fluttered like fireflies before smouldering on any surface they touched. A woman screamed as burning hail ignited her hair. The haunting tolling of church bells echoed through Lemures.

Drew ran his hands over his head then stared at his crimson palms. "How can we fix it?"

Morgan patted his face. "This isn't something you can fix with superglue and sticky tape."

"Whose blood is this?"

"Humanity's?"

"I'm hoping for angels." Aeron crossed his fingers.

"The seventh seal depended on me falling?" Drew asked. "Regardless of what happened to the martyrs and the volcano? If I hadn't fallen, they would've been in vain?"

"Not in *vain*," Morgan said. "Fun's never wasted. We would've found another way to break it."

"Do you have a glass box that says 'break glass for seventh seal emergency'?"

"That's a great idea! Why didn't we think of that?"

"I have four alternative endings," Marsden said.

"You're. Not. In. *FUCKING CHARGE*!" Morgan beat him with her whip.

"I should be."

People hurried into the pub, shrieking as fiery hail showered them, then fleeing when they realised there was no salvation. Ruby rivers trickled down their faces. Flames smashed through the windows upstairs. Streets swam with blood as the trumpet's fanfare faded.

"Why do you think you were sent here, Drew?" Aeron asked. "The world doesn't need another super-hot bartender."

"Punishment for disobeying Father. I was given a tally of souls to save or I'd never be allowed back into Heaven." He glanced at Marsden. "You made that damn near impossible. I didn't volunteer at shelters and drug centres because I *enjoyed* it."

"Not so saintly after all." Demi smirked.

"I was sent here to save them."

Morgan made a buzzing sound. "Wrong answer. You tell yourself you're the saviour of the broken if it helps you sleep at night."

"You were sent here because you're the key," Aeron told him. "For the seventh seal to break, an angel had to fall."

"Your daddy chose *you*."

"The rebel in the ranks."

"Do you think it's Fate you and Mars ended up in the same city?" Morgan asked. "The world's a big place, Angel Delight. Do you believe in Fate? Destiny? Or is everything part of your daddy's divine plan?"

"You're lying!" He lunged for Morgan. Marsden held him back. Drew fought him off.

"Why would we lie?" Aeron asked. "We've got what we wanted. Why should we care about ruining your relationship with your father? He's fond of forgiving heinous crimes if you beg. Wear an 'I ♥ God' t-shirt at Christmas."

"Don't beat yourself up." Morgan rubbed Drew's arm. "If you'd obeyed Michael and killed Mars, the seal would've broken and this blood would be Marsden's. Michael tricked you."

"Michael told you to kill me?" Marsden demanded. "I'll fucking kill that hypocritical son of a bitch!"

"*You* told me to kill you," Drew said.

"I was trying to be noble."

"You tried to *kill* yourself?" Morgan whipped him. "We've worked hard on creating the *best* Apocalypse the world has ever seen and you nearly ruin it because you want to be *noble*? You don't even know what it means! And Michael was wrong, by the way. Peace doesn't kill War. Love does. So it's probably just as well you didn't do the dirty deed, or Mars would've died. That would've been anticlimactic." She laughed.

"You *told* me to seduce him," Marsden said. "Even though I would die?"

"We needed the seal broken. And technically, we only need *four* Horsemen…"

Marsden dived for her. Aeron delivered an uppercut to his stomach.

"Why are you so upset? It turned out alright in the end."

"I swear on my sword, when this Apocalypse is over, I'm mounting your heads on spikes outside my bedroom door," Marsden spat.

"We'd rather be inside," Aeron said. "Then we can watch you enter Heaven." He winked at Drew. "Keep our minds off being on spikes."

"Why would Father send me here to fall if it meant breaking the seventh seal and ending the world?" Drew interrupted.

Morgan smiled. "Who do you think hired us?"

CHAPTER 41

Drew glared. "You're lying."

"For someone who won't cheat at Suddoku, you're quick to doubt others' honesty," Aeron said. "Our contract asked us to end the world and your daddy signed on the dotted line." He pulled his tablet out, tapped the screen then turned a document towards Drew, his finger tapping the golden signature at the bottom. Drew pushed it away. "The email accidentally went in the 'junk' folder with the other dodgy-sounding emails, like Russian babes needing a husband and the Nigerian prince with cash problems. Luckily I downloaded it before it got deleted. Lucifer was pissed. He'd planned it for summer, when everyone would be distracted by bikini babes. He didn't want to destroy mankind though, just religion, and figured starting again would wipe it out, create people who had no concept of religion. God coughed up the cash first. Christmas celebrates Jesus's birth, now it will celebrate the world's death. No peace on Earth and goodbye to all men. And like zombie Jesus, the world will rise from its grave."

"Why would He want to end the world?"

"People realised enjoying this life is more beneficial than supposed rewards in Heaven. Religion's regime is crumbling. It happened to every god before him."

"Like celebrities on reality shows," Morgan. "They're on the verge of being evicted so they use shock tactics to grab the public's attention. Shame he doesn't have fake boobs to jiggle." She shimmied her shoulders.

"Rather than being rejected by the world, he's destroying it. Restarting with obedient puppets who won't use the free will he gave them to surrender to the sins he created."

Drew shook his head. "God is loving, forgiving."

"He kicked you out for disobeying him, sent you here to break the seventh seal and rewarded you by taking your wings. Buy him a nice tie for Father's Day."

"And Homer Simpson socks," Morgan added. "You can't be surprised – he has form. In Noah's time, he drowned the filthy sinners. That was a great Apocalypse but all everyone talks about is one man building a boat. Hardly 'bums in seats' viewing. And he totally plagiarised that from Deucalion when Zeus flooded the world. Someone needs to sue Noah for copyright infringement."

"Who's going to stop it?" Drew asked.

"Nobody. So wrap up warm and enjoy the fireworks. Don't forget to steal a kiss from Mars when the clock strikes midnight. Even if you hadn't fallen, there would be nothing you could do because it's *your* side who wants the world to end. People have rendered God impotent so he's having a major tantrum, stamping his feet, throwing his hail around and everyone you know will die. With ultimate power comes the ultimate price. Humanity's about to pay the debt."

***

Marsden kicked open the office door. Harriett was bent over Michael's chair, wearing a French maid's outfit and licking cream off Michael's lap.

"I hope you've learned your lesson about spilling things on me."

Marsden slammed the door. "What will you do to me when I spill her blood on you?"

Michael groaned then fastened his trousers. "Leave us, Harriett. Bring more cream in later."

"Don't bother, Harriett. The kiss of death can't be sweetened with dessert." Marsden shut the door after her then sat in the small chair and played with the golden scales of justice on the desk. He winced and sucked his fingers. "Glad the death of the world hasn't killed your sex life."

"Apparently it turned Drew on too." Michael smirked. "This had better be important, Horseman."

"I'd say your death is pretty fucking important." Marsden drew his sword.

"Killing me isn't in your contract – I drew it up. Father will smite you."

"Not killing you isn't in there either. I read things before I sign them. If I die, the Apocalypse dies with me."

"Hate to dent your hero ego, but you're not the only Horseman in town."

"They couldn't finish a child's jigsaw."

"Drew should've killed you."

"The seal would've still broken."

"Yes, but you'd be dead. He clearly preferred to have humanity's blood on his hands than yours. He must have a fetish for murderous psychopaths. He's a disgrace to the family. At least he'll be remembered. Lucifer was responsible for angels falling, Drew's responsible for mankind falling."

"Lucifer stood up for mankind against God. Like Drew."

"And he'll be punished the same."

"God's banished him?"

"Why do you think I took his wings? An angel without wings can't return to Heaven. It's like having your VIP pass confiscated. You have to watch everyone enjoying the hospitality behind the ropes."

"*You* grounded him?" Marsden lunged across desk and grabbed Michael's shirt, ignoring his burning hands.

"Father's orders." Michael hit his hands away. "Once the world ends, Drew will be cast into the burning lake to spend eternity with Lucifer and his motley crew. He'll be hailed a hero. Once he's been punished for a thousand years. Father plans to send him straight to Hell but I feel he should suffer the consequences of his treachery and be forced to watch the world die, knowing he was the one who killed it."

"I own his soul."

"That song lasts as long as Earth does; a tiny clause I included. You missed the small print."

"Fucking bastard!" Marsden smashed Michael's face against the desk.

Michael shoved him away and wiped his bloody lip. "Congratulations on achieving the Apocalypse you've always wanted. Is reality as satisfying as fantasy?"

"I have something for you."

"You have nothing I want."

"Come and see." Marsden beckoned and led the way out onto the dance floor. Three crucifixes protruded from the floor, each burdened by an angel.

"Cut them down!"

Marsden held his sword to Mark's throat. Mark hissed as smoke engulfed him.

"Give Drew back his wings."

"Drew chose you over his family. Their deaths will burn his conscience."

"Their deaths are on you. Drew's wings and they live."

"You won't kill them. He'll never forgive you."

Marsden slit Mark's throat.

Michael rushed forwards as blood gushed down Mark's chest. Blinding light and an agonising scream filled Salvation. Scorched wings stained the colourful windows.

"Michael, please," Jael begged. "Drew was trying to stop this. *You're* the one who betrayed humanity."

Marsden smiled at Michael. "Once I've killed these angels, I'll invade Heaven and kill every angel there. No point having a Defender of Heaven if there's no Heaven left to defend."

"You'll never find your way to Heaven."

"God sacrificed Drew. Give him back his wings."

"I'm not a traitor."

Marsden stabbed Jael through the heart. She gurgled, blood dribbling down her chin. Another flash of light and tortured scream punished the former church. Blackened wings shadowed the floor.

"Last chance to save an angel." Marsden strolled over to John and ran his bloodied sword down his face.

"The Apocalypse is God's will."

"Yet Drew's being damned for it."

"There were many ways to break the seventh seal and make the angels mourn. Only one involved betraying Heaven. You can kill every angel, but you'll never force me to go against God."

"Then I'll return these puppets to their master." Marsden beheaded John. He shielded his eyes as John returned to Heaven. Wings burned into the roof. Marsden pointed his sword at Michael. "On your knees and pray for the mercy I won't show you."

Michael ducked as Marsden swung his sword at his neck. He ran into his office and locked the door. Marsden stalked him and kicked the door open. Michael dived behind his desk, emerging with his sword. Large white wings flecked with gold sprouted from his back.

"I'm the Archangel of battle and defender of Heaven. You won't survive this."

"I'm the Horseman of war. If I go to my grave, I'm burying you beside me." Marsden cast off his jacket, revealing his black chainmail. His eyes turned scarlet.

Their swords clashed, each strike chiming like bells of doom announcing the death of mankind. Marsden tackled Michael onto the desk, but Michael blocked his sword and kicked him. Michael sat up and sliced at Marsden, who deflected it and counter attacked. Michael spun away, leaving feathers behind.

Marsden pocketed them. "I'll make myself a quill to sign your death warrant."

Michael touched his sword, a fiery shroud crawling over it. Flames abandoned the sword every time it touched Marsden's. He sliced Marsden's arm. Marsden twisted in against him and threw him over his shoulder into the wall. Fractures crawled through the plaster.

Harriett burst in. "Michael!" Her wings fluttered out.

Marsden grabbed her, putting his sword to her throat. She squealed as she sizzled. His hand burned where he held her.

"Change Drew's fate or she dies."

Michael shook his head, rising. "Traitors must burn in Hell."

"Then kiss Lust goodbye." Marsden slit her throat. Harriett's blood spurted over Michael as she crumpled to the floor. Her feathers drank the blood, turning crimson. Blinding light flashed through the office. Wings turned the windows black, casting disjointed shadows on the floor.

Michael cursed and threw a lightning bolt. Marsden shielded himself with his guitar. The bolt ricocheted, catapulting him into a bookshelf. The glass shelves smashed. He leapt up. Their swords collided with a fierce kiss. Michael stabbed at him, so Marsden knocked Michael's sword aside and spun in, elbowing his jaw. He swept Michael's legs from under him and stabbed his sword down. Michael rolled, the sword piercing his wing. He gasped and plunged his sword into Marsden's foot. Marsden swore and yanked it out.

Michael hit it out of his hand and staggered to his feet. "You'll never defeat me. I have God on my side."

"I don't see him. Taking a toilet break is he?"

Michael flicked his hand. Hail bulleted Marsden, drawing blood. Thunder rumbled in the bowels of discontented clouds. A lightning bolt struck Marsden's chest. He flew through the doorway and hit the floor, electricity crawling over his chainmail, scorching his skin. He groaned as he forced himself to his feet in a shower of hail and lightning. The lightning exploded on his chest, flinging him to the far end of the dance floor.

"Surrender or die." Michael stalked him, brandishing his scales of justice. Hail rained down on them both.

Marsden rose and slammed his sword into the floor. Red lightning crackled across the floor, splitting it. The church shook. A furious whinny and galloping hooves echoed in the distance. A red horse climbed through the hole. Marsden mounted it and they charged towards Michael.

Michael flew towards them, flinging lightning, his sword glowing. Marsden lay back on his horse as Michael's sword swept over him. He turned the horse around and sliced Michael's wing.

Michael dropped to the ground. Marsden rode towards him.

"Let Drew return to Heaven."

Michael tried to rise. "He's shamed Father, broken the seventh seal and sided with a filthy Horseman. He will *never* be welcome in Heaven."

Marsden raised his sword. "Then you'll meet him in Hell."

"Mars! No!" Drew froze in the doorway.

Michael leapt up, opened his scales of justice and stabbed Marsden's thigh. Marsden fell from his horse, pain ripping through his leg. A gold dagger protruded like a victory flag. Smoke seeped from the searing wound. He struggled to stand. The horse tossed his head and kicked Michael in the stomach, catapulting him into the wall.

"Go on Horseman, kill me. Show Drew the monster inside you."

"Mars, don't. He's my brother."

"You're right, Drew. I'm a soulless murderer who enjoys killing people. I'll enjoy his death more than anyone's."

He thrust his sword into Michael's heart. Michael screamed, falling to his knees, staring in horror as blood pumped over his hands. His wings flapped as a beam of light penetrated the club.

Marsden kicked him down and planted one foot on his back. He raised his sword. "May the Lord have mercy upon your soul."

Michael screamed, his wings igniting beside him, his back saturated in blood.

Drew's eyes widened. "What have you *done*?"

"He took your wings. Doesn't the Bible say 'an eye for an eye'?"

Marsden pulled the dagger from his thigh and threw it. It bounced, dripping blood onto the floor. He collapsed, holding his wound. Blood seeped through his fingers.

"It doesn't change anything," Drew said. "I'm stuck here until I'm cast down to meet my long-lost brother. That's a reunion I'm dreading. I hope there'll be cake."

Marsden gritted his teeth, fighting the blackness threatening to devour him. Distant hooves galloped towards him. "I won't let that happen."

"The seals can't be closed with superglue and sticky tape, Morgan said so."

"I'm going to stop the Apocalypse."

CHAPTER 42

Salvation trembled, the blood-streaked windows shaking.

Marsden staggered up. "Shit."

The cry of the second trumpet resonated through Lemures; a siren warning of impending suffering and darkness.

Marsden growled. This was why his father warned him to banish emotions from the battlefield. This wasn't in his strategies. He looked at Michael's bloody body then at his scarlet hand.

"Shit."

A sinking feeling poisoned his stomach. So this was how it felt to make a mistake. He looked at Drew, whose stunned gaze rested on Michael's body. Marsden's legs buckled and he grabbed his horse's stirrup, his blood betraying his fall. His quivering hands parted his torn trousers. His wound glowed. The toxin slipped through his veins, golden fire flowing in its wake. The hooves grew louder, the noise of Lemures fainter. Colours faded to grey.

"No!" He willed the holiness from his body. He couldn't leave the battlefield in the middle of a war.

"Nice one," Aeron said, materialising with Morgan. Their skulls grinned beneath their hoods. "Bit quick–"

"That's what she said." Morgan said. Aeron high-fived her.

"Overexcitement can lead to early...release."

"You'll control it with experience."

"Don't be nervous, enjoy it."

"Poor mortals are still coming to terms with the first one. Let them get their breaths back before plunging them into destructive hedonism. At least you got us presents. I had to get mine from Harriett's cleavage. Seemed slightly disrespectful rooting around in her fun bags." Morgan shook the globe, the angel inside igniting before exploding into ash. A silver ring formed, rolling around inside the globe. Morgan smashed it, retrieving the ring from the shards and slipping it onto her left middle finger. Silver angel wings rested on the band. "Complements my outfit don't you think? I have a matching set." She waggled the fingers on both hands, showing off the ring from Joshua.

"I can't believe you turn dead angels into jewellery," Drew muttered.

"Relax, buttercup, she's in Heaven. It's her essence I've turned into jewellery. Shows other angels how badass we are. Turning people's ashes into jewellery is the newest trend. At least I didn't manufacture her into a diamond to stick on my tooth. That would be tacky and insensitive. In video games, you always get good things when you loot the enemies you kill."

"*I* killed them." Marsden squeezed his thigh. He shivered, death's frigid finger stroking his body. "I deserve the rings."

"We're a *team*, Mars. There's no room for glory hunting in a team."

"There are three there you can have." Drew flung his arm in the direction of the crosses. "Killing the martyrs not enough for you? You have to murder the only angels who helped me?"

"I was trying to get your wings back." Marsden grimaced. Hell's fires surged through his body.

"Dead angels aren't a currency Heaven accepts."

"My, you have been busy. Don't worry, you'll get your notches." Morgan clicked her fingers.

Marsden dropped to the floor, yelling as invisible claws ripped his skin.

Aeron raised Marsden's chainmail and PVC top. "Ooh. They look raw." He took a photo with his phone then thrust it in Marsden's face. Five inch long gouges carved his back below his demon wing tattoo. Silver and gold halos now hung around the haft of the sword. Every vein was gold. "It's your scoreboard. I'm Chattering this." Aeron kissed the gouges then stood.

Marsden collapsed. Thundering hooves stopped beside him. His heartbeat slowed. He stared into the grey horse's red eyes. Crimson eyes glowed under the rider's hood.

"It's time to go home," the rider spoke.

"The war isn't over."

"It's not your war anymore."

"I will…never…" he could barely hear his own words "…surrender."

"Don't worry, Dad, we've got this." Morgan's voice sounded far away.

"What?" Drew knelt beside Marsden and took his hand.

"If I don't administer the kiss of life to our favourite Horseman in the next thirty seconds, he'll die. It's his severe allergy to holy objects. Thank god Michael interrupted your kiss. You were giving him the kiss of death. Bet that was embarrassing – your brother catching you snogging a Horseman." Morgan kissed Marsden.

Marsden gasped, Morgan's lips icy against his. The hooves became quieter, the grey monotones brightening to vivid colour. Lemures's noise blared into his hearing. Coldness slipped through him. His wounds sealed, leaving scarlet scars. His horse vanished. Drew dropped his hand and turned to Morgan.

"If you can save people with a kiss, why are you letting them die?"

"If I go round kissing everyone, I'll get a naughty reputation." She poked Marsden. "Kinda disappointed I didn't catch fire, Mars. Your kiss with Drew promised blazing passion. My butterflies merely gave a death twitch." Morgan helped him up. "I can't believe we didn't bring our armour."

"I can't believe I'm the only one who did. We came to end the world, not sunbathe by the pool." He felt hollow, as though his soul had abandoned him.

"Just as well – I didn't bring my bathers either."

Aeron took Michael's globe from his pocket. His angelic form burned before forging a gold wing belt buckle. "Not sure it'll go with my outfit, but you can't refuse trophies." Aeron pocketed it. "Why kill God's right hand man, Mars? Antagonising the boss won't get you Fridays off. Or is this one of your alternative endings to keep the audience guessing?"

"Michael amputated Drew's wings." Each trumpet blast cut fresh wounds inside him and counted down Drew's remaining days. "So I made sure Michael couldn't return to Heaven either."

"God wouldn't bloody his hands for one angel. Even the angel who ended the world."

"Will you stop saying that?" Drew snapped. "I know what I did."

"Someone's a Grumposaurus. Nap time, is it?"

Marsden sighed. "When the world ends, Drew goes to Hell."

Saying it made it real, stealing his breath and tormenting his mind. Knowing they would soon be parted forever sliced a scar into his heart that would never heal. Every scream he heard he would imagine it was Drew's. The sounds that helped him sleep would now keep him awake.

"To think you bollocked *us* for not sticking to your strategies." Morgan admired her rings. "The worst *we* ever did was drink cocktails. *You've* murdered Heaven's henchman. This is exactly why you're not in charge – you don't practise what you preach. You let revenge rule your head."

Another trumpet blast punctured the heavy silence.

Aeron winced. "Accelerating the Apocalypse was a bit of a blooper, Mars. Or have you broken up? What better way to get revenge on the lover who's spurned you than damning them for eternity? Beats keying his car."

"Let's see if we've made the news." Morgan led the way into Michael's office.

Aeron switched on the TV and clicked on the news. "It doesn't feel right watching this without cocktails and fries. We have nothing to toast."

Morgan vanished and returned with four cocktails. "Angel's Delight for Drew, Death in the Afternoon for Mars." She handed two out. "Apocalypse Now for me and Happily Ever After for Aer."

"Scenes of panic are rife as the earth was hit by bloody rain and fiery hail," the newsreader announced.

"That's old news," Morgan said, clinking glasses with Aeron.

"Meteorologists are baffled by this unexpected event. Wildfires have devastated Australia, America and parts of Europe. Firefighters tackling the blazes haven't ruled out arson." Scenes cut to burning forests worldwide. *"In America, the world's largest dormant volcano under Yellowstone Park has erupted, drowning the park in lava and toxic smoke. Hospitals have been inundated with burns victims and those suffering from smoke inhalation. The death toll stands at two hundred and continues to climb. Scientists warn the toxic air could render a third of America uninhabitable."*

Morgan smiled. "It's nice when your successes make headlines."

"The earthquake that has literally shaken the world caused a mountain to fall into the sea. Beachgoers phoned the coastguard when the sea appeared to be filled with blood. We'll bring you more on this story in our bulletin at ten."

Grainy phone footage showed red sea lapping sand, wind whipping the microphone as the second trumpet lamented the world's demise.

"This happened in India," Drew said. "They thought it was the Apocalypse. Turned out to be algae. Chemicals turned the water red."

"People are always quick to blame the Apocalypse." Aeron tutted. "When it *is* the Apocalypse, no-one suspects it!" He switched the TV off.

Drew paced. "The world is *dying*! And I'm standing here, doing sod all."

"I wouldn't say sod all. You broke the seventh seal. That's something you can put in your Records of Achievement. Are you going to drink your cocktail or…?"

Drew glowered at him. "The second trumpet's sounded, so a mountain has fallen into the sea, a third of the seas will turn to blood, a third of ships will be destroyed and a third of sea life will die."

"Gold star!" Aeron clapped. "You should've attended our Apocalypse classes. Demi and Mac were *useless*. I'd snog you but Mars looks like he'd turn me inside out and hang me on a washing line to flap in the breeze."

"With pleasure," Marsden growled.

"You have to stop this!" Drew pleaded.

"That's your father decision," Morgan said. "Horsemen have never broken a contract. We *won't* be the first ones who fail. Not when we've worked so hard and ordered all that celebratory Apocalypse merchandise."

"We can't let him burn in Hell," Marsden said.

"Mars, this is a once in a lifetime event. How many times have you heard our fathers, our grandfathers, talk about when they ended the world? Do you want to recount the time we *failed*?"

"All the years we've trained for this," Aeron said, drinking Drew's cocktail. "Mmm, this *is* a delight. All the times we played Apocalypse as kids and bragged about how we'd give the world the best damn Apocalypse it's ever seen. Well Mac was always too sick to join in and Demi just wanted to play Kiss Chase with you."

"Even then I knew you twatapusses would bugger it up."

"Do you want to throw it away when we're *this* close to returning home heroes?"

"The burning desire to end the world hasn't died." He looked at Drew, who studied the blood puddle where Harriett had lain. "But I'm not letting him get damned. So if there's a way to save him *and* end the world, I'd like to hear it."

"Your devotion's sweet, even when your relationship died with Demi's modelling career. You never got to taste his forbidden fruit."

Drew's eyes met Marsden's. Drew looked away.

"Knowing his feelings are as cold as Michael's ashes won't unleash as much torture on my soul as knowing he's suffering in Hell will."

"Michael's ashes are still warm." Aeron tapped his belt buckle.

Drew rubbed his forehead. "I don't know what I feel. You killed my brother in front of me."

"You said he was a dick."

"I didn't want him dead!"

"There's no point reasoning with him," Morgan said. "He was raised on revenge and bloodshed. Forgiveness is a dirty word in his household. If you don't smite at least ten of your lover's enemies, it's not true love. His parents celebrate Valentine's by killing one of each other's enemies and giving them their heart."

"St Valentine was beaten and beheaded. It's a more fitting way to honour him than heart shaped chocolates," Marsden said. "Drew, Michael sentenced you to Hell. If that's what he does to his brother, I'd hate to see how he treats his enemies."

Tears slipped down Drew's cheeks. "In the past twenty four hours, I've seen the man I love slaughter innocent people, I've become one of the despised fallen, my brother hacked my wings off, my father ordered the Apocalypse and sent me here to break the final seal and you murdered five members of my family. The last thing on my mind is changing my relationship status on Friendzone."

"I killed Michael for you."

"I begged you not to!"

"Fuck's sake Drew, I tried to kill myself so you could save the world and I'm stopping the Apocalypse to save your soul. That's more of a declaration of love than a fucking diamond ring."

"Mars, you know what we do to traitors," Aeron said. "It doesn't involve a trip to the theme park."

"Though there will be screaming," Morgan said.

Marsden faced them. "I can't do this alone."

"Not content with destroying the best Apocalypse ever, you want to muddy our names too?" Aeron folded his arms.

"We'll be the most legendary Horsemen in history."

"The Horsemen who failed. That's a trophy we'll hoist to the crowd's cheers."

"They don't throw parades for failures," Morgan added. "I was looking forwards to riding on a flowered float and blowing kisses to people."

"What people? They'll all be dead. You want to ride a parade past their corpses?" Marsden said. "We'll be the Horsemen who rebelled. The Horsemen who fought Heaven. The Horsemen who defeated God."

"*What?*" Drew demanded. "Are you going to kill *all* my family? Thank god we're not getting married – there'll be no-one on my side of the church."

"I'm throwing away the *only* thing I've ever wanted. I'm betraying my legacy, my father, my team. You said the one thing you'd want me to give up, was being a Horseman. I'm becoming what I despise more than anything: a traitor. For *you*. A thank you would be nice."

Marsden threw his sword down and knelt before Morgan and Aeron. "Help me. Or execute me for treason."

CHAPTER 43

"Can anybody tell me what Operation Beard is?" Aeron underlined the words with his purple pen. Morgan stood the other side of the easel with her whip.

"A creepy Santa convention to wheedle out paedo Santas?" Demi asked, flicking through *Catwalk* magazine whilst sandwiched between Drew and Marsden on the bed in Travel Inn.

"Is it the third trumpet?" Mac asked. He sat on the settee, making a list of Yellowstone Park refuges to infect.

"Do we dress Mars as Jesus and convince people to help us? They'd sin quicker than a monk in a strip joint."

"Monks take a vow of chastity," Drew said.

"That'd crumble like a soggy digestive the minute a stripper shakes her bonbons in his face and tweaks his bell pull."

"That's actually a good idea, Dems." Aeron wrote it on the board.

"I'm *not* wearing sandals and a robe. Or growing my hair," Marsden objected.

"I won't be part of this." Drew stood. "I can't believe the Horsemen hold Apocalypse meetings in Travel Inn."

"I told you they're a joke."

Morgan whipped Marsden's knee. "Grease Lightning lacks privacy. And there's nowhere for the easel."

"Why is an angel here?" Demi asked. "Did he get trapped and can't find his way out? All I hear is this constant judging buzzing noise. Someone open the window, I'll roll up a magazine."

"He's helping us."

"When he says something helpful he can stay."

"Same applies to you, Twiglet," Marsden said.

"Operation Beard is top secret." Aeron tapped the pad. "If any of you Chatters this..." He pointed his pen at them.

Demi rolled her eyes. "Oh yeah I'm going to blab about it during my lingerie shoot. I don't want to be famous for being a nut job."

"You'll never do a lingerie shoot," Marsden retorted. "You lack the entry requirement – boobs."

Demi smacked him with her rolled up magazine. "Models are photoshopped."

Morgan lashed them both then re-joined Aeron by the pad.

"Operation Beard is fraught with danger and could result in death," Aeron explained.

"Isn't that the point?" Mac asked.

"*Our* deaths."

"No friggin' way," Demi cut in. "We're here to kill mankind, not ourselves."

"Mars killed five angels – John, Mark, Jael, Harriett and Archangel Michael," Morgan tapped the silver and gold smiley face stickers on the wall. She and Aeron flashed their rings then bashed them together saying 'kerching!' "When the Apocalypse is complete, Drew's got a one-way ticket to Hell. Mars is upset and wants to stop the Apocalypse."

"Not after everything we've worked for," Demi said.

"You've killed *two* people," Marsden said. "Ten year olds have higher murder counts."

"We're not destroying our greatest achievement so you can hump Drew's halo."

"This isn't about sex!" Marsden thumped her thigh then rubbed his hand after he hit bone. "This is about justice and vengeance."

"Switch Drew for a different damned angel, then tell me it's not about sex."

Morgan smacked their knuckles. "Mars plans to kill God. We're going to help him."

"Shouldn't we vote on this?" Mac asked.

"I'm sorry, were you under the impression this is a democracy?"

"If we're risking our lives on a crusade because Mars doesn't want to lose his boyfriend, we deserve a say," Demi said. "He wouldn't do it for us."

"She's right," Mac mumbled. "If we wanted to stop the Apocalypse for one person, Mars would kill us and tell us there's no room for sentiment on the battlefield. Why should we do it for him?"

"I don't *want* to stop the Apocalypse," Marsden said. "If there was another way, I'd take it. I don't even *want* you there. You're so incompetent you'll be a hazard."

"You make it sound easy," Demi said. "'Going to kill God' like you're picking up tampons from Freger's. *Nobody* attacks God. It'd be like covering yourself in jam and sugar then kicking a beehive. Getting what you want comes with a sacrifice. But *you're* not the one making it. You claim you're stopping the Apocalypse for Wingman but *you're* not the one who will end up dying because Drew has daddy issues. He should go on chat shows like everyone else."

"You wouldn't be at risk of dying if you were proper Horsemen. If you die, it'll be your own fault."

"Can't we…continue the Apocalypse then when it's over, rescue Drew from Hell?" Mac suggested.

"That's a great idea."

"In the meantime, I'll sit on the Inquisitor's Chair while you destroy the world," Drew muttered.

"If we defeat God, everyone will remember our names," Aeron said. "We break into Hell, we may never leave."

Demi pouted. "I don't want to be famous after I *die*! I want paparazzi chasing me now, while I'm young and fabulous and flashing my knickers isn't disgusting."

"I'm killing God, with or without your help." Marsden poked her.

"*With* our help," Aeron corrected.

"They're right though. I'd kill their lover so the Apocalypse could continue."

Demi fetched her balances and thrust them against Drew's chest. "Give me one good reason why *I* shouldn't kill *your* lover so the Apocalypse can continue."

"Because I'll kill you too." Marsden drew his sword.

"I'm going to die anyway. Might as well take a souvenir with me and fuck up your plans." She lifted Drew's chin. "You aren't worth dying for, pretty boy." She lowered her balances and whispered in his ear. "His kiss set you on fire. Mine will suck the life from you."

Drew pulled a chocolate bar from his pocket and tapped her under the chin. "Suck this."

"Dems, sit down. This is a team event. Like bobsleighing. We're all getting in the damn sled," Aeron said. For once he'd like a meeting to go smoothly, especially now they had a special guest. "Drew, you know Heaven's layout, how many angels guard God, what he eats for breakfast, what he's allergic to, where he spends his afternoons."

"I won't help you kill my father."

Morgan patted Drew's face. "We're doing this for you. The least you can do is help. Unless you *like* the idea of your insides being eaten for eternity."

"How would you like it if I enlisted your help in killing your fathers?"

"Demi lives for the day Famine chokes to death on a chocolate éclair," Marsden said.

"At least I don't threaten to kill him every week," she replied.

"That's how they say 'I love you' in the War household. We cannot talk about it outside this room," Aeron continued. "This room is God-proof. But not Santa-proof, so you're all on his naughty list."

"I thought this was an action plan meeting," Drew said. "All that's gone on is bickering, hand slapping and name-calling."

"Welcome to Horsemen HQ," Mac mumbled.

"Yet you're the ones they've entrusted the Apocalypse to?"

"I can't believe it either," Marsden said. "If I'd been in charge, I would've ended the world in a week."

"We only get to end the world once," Morgan said. "Some of us wanted the fun to last."

"Drew, if you'd been rallying the troops with Heaven's blueprints and secret info, instead of sulking in the corner like a moody teenager who got the wrong make of smartphone, this meeting would've been more productive," Aeron said.

"I tried, but my best friend, Eden, was imprisoned in Heaven and Michael only spared me three angels."

"There're only five of us, yet we still managed to end the world. Now's your chance for revenge. Get up here and start helping."

Drew joined Aeron at the pad. "Fine, give me the pen."

"You do not have control of the pen."

"I'll use my own pen."

"You do not have control of the pad."

"How am I supposed to draw blueprints?"

"Don't get smart with me, sunshine. I'll draw the blueprints. Take off your top."

"Why?"

"I can see why God kicked you out. Just do it." Drew yanked off his slate t-shirt which had a burning guitar motif. Aeron smiled. "Talk us through these blueprints."

"Why do I have to be topless?"

"We've altered our plans to save you, we deserve a nice view while we plot to murder your father." Aeron jabbed his pec. "Just be thankful you're not naked."

"Aer, let him dress," Marsden said.

"You of all people should want to see Drew topless. I thought you were cool."

"We're all risking our necks, we should all enjoy the reward," Morgan said.

"For the love of rice crackers!" Demi stood, thrusting her finger at Marsden. "Captain Queerbeard has a husband's bulge and can't concentrate."

"You're such a fucking bitch!" He kicked her in the back of the thigh.

"Ow!" She backhanded him with the magazine. "Are you always nasty when you're horny? Go into the bathroom and jerk out your rage. Take Mac's pots in case you don't survive this momentous meeting of the parents, so the War line doesn't die with you."

"Don't be shy Mars, show the class," Aeron said.

Marsden scowled. "Get on with this before someone gets a black eye."

Demi smirked. "Don't flatter yourself, it's not that big."

Morgan laughed then lashed them both and slapped Drew's arse. He jumped.

"I didn't do anything!"

"You're the cause of Marsden's disruptive behaviour."

He sighed. "St Peter guards the gate."

"Is he armed?"

"He has the keys to Heaven."

"How does he expect to defend Heaven with *keys*?" Aeron asked. "Magical, are they?"

"Michael was the defender of Heaven, but Marsden killed him."

"Good work, Mars! You rid us of a threat." He drew a gravestone on the pad with 'RIP Michael' on it.

"How many angels are there?" Morgan asked.

"I've never been bored enough to count. There are three spheres of angels. The first sphere is the Counsellors. Seraphim are the caretakers of God's throne. They have six wings – two cover their face, two cover their body and two cover their feet. Four of them guard the throne and they burn constantly."

Aeron scrawled *Seraphim – hosepipe treatment.*

"Cherubim have four faces: man, ox, lion and eagle and four conjoined wings covered in eyes. They guard God's throne and the Garden of Eden."

Aeron shook his head. "We won't have time for sightseeing. Is the Garden of Eden as beautiful as rumours say? Or are the brochures misleading?"

"It's stunning. Also in that sphere are the Thrones. They're a wheel within a wheel and their rims are covered in eyes."

Thrones – pepper spray.

"I'm avoiding them," Demi said. "Circus freak shows died when knickers were invented."

"The second sphere is the Governors. Dominions regulate duties of the lower angels. Orbs of light are attached to their swords' pommels. Virtues keep the cosmos in order. Powers are Heaven's warriors, bearers of conscience and keepers of history. They distribute power amongst mankind. No Power has ever fallen. The third sphere is Messengers and Soldiers. Principalities collaborate with Powers. They're armed with sceptres and wear crowns. There are seven Archangels. Um, six. They're concerned with politics, military matters, commerce and trade. Then you have Angels, the lowest order."

"Are you a lowly angel?" Demi asked. "We're attacking Heaven with the help of the angelic equivalent to a *cleaner*?"

"This is madness!" Drew slapped his legs. "You can't ram-raid Heaven and slaughter my family!"

"We sadly don't have clearance for a ram-raid," Morgan said.

"They don't care about family," Marsden said. "Look how they treat those who disobey!"

"What will your family do? Send you to your room? Confiscate your bike keys?"

"They won't cast me onto a burning lake to suffer for eternity!"

"War will do his 'thou hast disappointed me' face," Aeron said. "All sad puppy eyes and pouting lips. It breaks your heart."

"He'll lock me in the dungeon for a month."

"Doesn't Conquest get a say?" Drew asked.

"Why would he?"

"Michael said War and Conquest combined their DNA to produce you."

"You're lying."

"Angels can't lie."

"Newsflash, Fall Out Boy, *you're* no longer an angel." Demi poked her tongue out.

Drew glared at her. "Conquest isn't Mac's father – Death is. Death donated his pestilence DNA to create Mac in a cabinet reshuffle."

"Did you know about this?" Marsden glared at Morgan and Aeron.

"No." Morgan looked shocked. "Typhoid Mary's our half-brother?"

They looked at each other then at Mac.

"I'm not seeing the resemblance," Aeron whispered, a bit too loudly.

Mac pouted. "I wondered why I didn't look like Conquest. Great. I'm a test tube baby."

"You were probably created in a petri dish," Demi said. "Like other diseases."

"Conquest *and* War? That explains your temper," Aeron said to Marsden.

"I don't have a temper!" He threw the remote at him. "I wondered why Conquest helped with my training. I thought Mac's incompetence and unwillingness to learn battle techniques disappointed him."

Mac folded his arms. "He always preferred you."

"Do you blame him? You can't conquer a cold, let alone a country."

Demi stood. "At least your father isn't Jabba the Gut, so leave your teenage identity angst outside. We have more important matters to deal with. Like how the hell we get into Heaven, what weapon is powerful enough to kill God, and will there be a film crew?"

CHAPTER 44

Morgan produced a globe. Ash covered the graves in smoky kisses. She ran her black nail along the glass, a smile teasing her violet lips before she hurled the globe. It shattered, taking everybody with it.

***

Blank, misshapen headstones jutted out of the uneven midnight ground, as though the occupants were buried where they fell. Black skeletal trees guarded some graves, each tree standing alone beneath the tombstone grey sky. Dread crept through Drew's veins; an unwelcome intruder plucking notes of doom on his nerves.

Ash shrouded everything.

Marsden ran his thumb over Drew's forehead. "Sorry, I smeared it."

Drew's skin tingled, anticipating the burn. Part of him missed it. It was simpler before – they couldn't be together because it would have devastating consequences. Now it was Marsden's actions that kept them apart. God forgave sinners if they repented. But Marsden was unrepentant and Drew wasn't God. Maybe Marsden could stop the Apocalypse, but it wouldn't bring the angels back to life. If he'd decided to stop it sooner, they would never have died.

A raven landed on a Celtic cross headstone. "Corpse!"

Morgan tickled him under his beak. He flew onto her shoulder.

"I'd forgotten how much I hate this place." Demi wrapped her strawberry trench coat around her. "It's like Halloween died here. If Jack Skellington pops up, I'll punch him right in the pumpkins."

Execution drums banged the funeral march to welcome them home.

"Are we in Hell?" Sweat pricked Drew's underarms.

"Hell's too hot and cold at the same time," Aeron said. "Nice for a holiday but stay too long and you get heat exhaustion and hypothermia. The weird temperature drives many to insanity. The constant screaming grates your nerves. Torture sounds so…samey."

"Heaven's too bland," Morgan added. "It's peaceful and spiritual with everyone as sickly sweet as a sprinkled cupcake. Plus all that gold is tacky. It's like a relaxing spa break then after a couple of days you want to throw your cocktail over the angel serving you. This is Purgatory."

"Where's the purifying fire?"

"There's been extensive remodelling." Morgan kicked the ground, churning the ash. "Here are the embers."

"Where are the lost souls?"

"They were so goddamn whiney they spoiled the ambience." She beckoned. "Word of warning: don't skinny dip in the lake. The leviathan will gobble you like Smarties."

A crypt lurked in the darkest corner of the graveyard. Black arrow railings surrounded it, waiting to snag flesh. They passed under an arch of two scythes and climbed black obsidian steps leading to the crypt. Swords created pillars supporting the covered entrance. Large balances sat on the roof. Black and silver skulls formed the walls. Some skulls had fangs. Silver hinges stretched across metal coffin doors.

Morgan and Aeron each placed a small globe imprisoning a black key against the doors. The globes melted and they slotted the keys into the headstone locks. The doors scraped open, unleashing an anguished moan. The twins lit skull lanterns and carried them through the corridors. Footprints in the dust betrayed their passage. The lanterns cast eerie, twisted shadows that crept along the walls. Black ivy crawled over the stones, its tendrils hanging like serpents poised to strike.

Drew tried ignoring siren songs whispering in his ears as they descended steps into darkness. Aeron and Morgan stopped at black skull gates. Thousands of trapped souls swam around the gate, begging for release, even if it meant being cast into Hell.

Drew shuddered. "Can't you send them on?"

"This isn't a bus terminal," Aeron replied.

"They're supposed to experience temporary suffering from fire to be purified so they can enter Heaven."

"Or Hell. Where did your father get his wacky idea that the only way to purify your soul is through physical punishment? Whip a murderer a hundred times and he'll still be a murderer."

The souls reached for Drew, their mournful moans penetrating his mind.

"Aw they think you're here to save them."

"Sometimes we pretend to unlock the gate," Morgan said. "You should see their little faces when they realise we're teasing them."

She and Aeron laughed and high-fived each other.

Marsden led the way out, joining Demi and Mac. Aeron and Morgan extinguished their lanterns and hung them up before locking the door.

"I can't believe this is your home," Drew said to Marsden. "It's...soulless."

"Heaven ain't exactly party central." Aeron blew a raspberry. "This place is beautiful. It has character. Heaven's all clouds and pearls and people in bad clothes and Jesus sandals."

"You've never been to Heaven, have you?"

"Guess our invites got lost in the post."

Silvery light bathed the gravestones with an ethereal glow. Drew shivered, but wasn't cold. There was no temperature. Purgatory was sinisterly still, as though it was trapped in its globe.

"Where's the light coming from?"

Mac pointed to a dead tree on top of a blackened hill. Silver halos hung from the branches.

Drew touched his bare neck. "Whose are they?"

"The fallen and defeated," Marsden said.

"We got bored of playing ring toss with them." Morgan weaved between graves, the raven stalking her.

Drew jogged after her. "Where are we going?"

"There's only one way to get to Heaven. Unfortunately, the number 666 bus is out of service."

Morgan opened the door of a large black barn. Stables lined both sides. Dusty cobwebs hung from beams and ash covered the floor. A white nose appeared over the first door. Drew stroked it, the horse's breath warm on his fingers.

"That's Conquest's horse, Hastings," Morgan explained. "Named after the great battle. Seemed unfair to change it to Bubonic Plague."

Hastings studied him with blood red eyes then pulled his upper lip up into a smile.

The stable opposite held a big black horse.

"Famine's," Drew said. "Isn't he supposed to be skinny?"

"He's bulked up in retirement," Aeron explained. "Though Famine hasn't slimmed down."

"My father's an embarrassing abomination," Demi said.

"What's the horse called?" Drew stroked his silky neck.

"Pavlova. It's Famine's favourite dessert."

"Maybe your hatred for overweight people stems from hatred of your father."

"Don't psychoanalyse me, Judas."

"I'm *nothing* like him! Judas's treachery caused Jesus's death."

"Your traitor's kiss caused the death of the world. You're right; you're worse than Judas. You weren't even paid."

"You're worse than being trapped in an Iron Maiden and rolled down a hill," Marsden said.

The stable beside Hastings housed a pale grey horse with a charcoal mane and tail and eyes the colour of fresh blood.

"This is Erebus." Morgan stood under his neck and worked his lower lip, adopting a deep voice. "Pleased to meet you, going to eat you. I'm partial to rump steak and your rump is fiiiiine."

Drew patted him. "I'd taste of disappointment."

Banging echoed through the barn, followed by an indignant whinny.

"War's horse," Aeron said. "Only two people are mad enough to ride him."

"He's bitten every stable boy," Demi said. "One has a hole where his butt cheek should be."

Drew warily approached the last stable. The tall chestnut horse nuzzled the door latch then gripped it in his teeth, working it free. When he realised the bottom latch was secure, he kicked the door and snapped at Demi, his ears pinned back. Drew recognised him from Salvation.

"Twigs have more nutrients." Marsden stroked his nose. "This is Camelot."

Camelot stretched his neck and bit Mac. Mac swore and leapt away, green pus dripping down his arm. Camelot trotted around his stable, his tail flowing like a flag. He picked up his empty bucket and tossed it out of the stable. It clattered by Demi's feet.

"Cam, meet Drew," Marsden said. "Be extra nice to him."

Camelot stuck his head over the door. His snorting nose inched towards Drew. His soft rubbery lips explored Drew's face then he licked him.

"He likes you." Marsden smiled, kissing Camelot's neck.

Demi glowered. "Let's see you win War over that easily. I guarantee he won't lick your face."

"I'm meeting your father?" Drew asked Marsden.

"I'm meeting yours."

"To kill him."

"I'll speak to him first."

"How would you like it if I chatted to your father then murdered him?"

Marsden shrugged. "Depends on your motives."

"Enough jibber-jabbering," Aeron said. "We have an invasion to plan."

They left the stables and headed for a black hill. A winding path led to an imposing black castle. Each wall was flanked by hexagonal turrets topped by crenulations.

"It's so dreary," Demi moaned. "I can't come back here after sampling the Bohemian's luxury."

"If we don't stop the Apocalypse, there won't *be* a Bohemian," Marsden said.

Demi poked her tongue out at him as they reached the wooden doors. Aeron lifted the stone step and retrieved a large pewter key.

"That's not a great place to hide your spare key," Drew said.

"Nobody wants to break in."

The doors creaked open, revealing a grey passage. Morgan took a brand by the door and walked down the corridor, lighting skeletal hand sconces.

"What are those slits in the walls and floor?" Drew asked.

"War booby-trapped the castle," Mac said.

"To keep out burglars?"

"To train Mars in the art of surviving," Aeron explained. "Or 'avoiding getting killed by daddy's crazy ideas'. He calls that passage the Blade Runner."

Morgan slotted the brand into the ribcage stand and pressed a button on the wall. Spikes shot up through the floor. Axes, swords, flails, spikes and daggers swung out from the walls. Guillotine blades dropped from the ceiling.

"He designed it for my thirteenth birthday," Marsden said. "Best present ever."

"Not a fan of games consoles?" Drew asked.

"They'd sold out."

They followed Morgan into a room that was one hundred feet long. A giant gargoyle fireplace occupied most of the back wall. Bones filled the fireplace, so it looked like the gargoyle squatted on them. In the far corner, a spiral stone staircase escaped the room.

"My babies! You've come home!"

A skeleton in a black robe rushed over, bony feet clicking on the flagstone floor. He enveloped Morgan and Aeron in a bear hug, nuzzling them.

"How was Earth? I got your postcards. Very thoughtful. I'm so excited you're back! We weren't expecting you 'til after the seventh trumpet." He bounced. "I've cleaned your rooms and oh! I made you furniture with the antique bones I've collected over the years. They're simply *darling*! Demi, you look like you've suffered a tragic steam roller accident. Mac! How you doing my little pusbag?" He playfully punched Mac's arm. "Where's the hero of the hour?" He picked Marsden up and shook him like a ragdoll. "Who's this?" Crimson eyes peered at Drew from under the hood.

Drew stepped back. Now he knew why humans feared him.

"This is Drew. A fallen angel," Morgan explained. "He cut the ribbon to open the Apocalypse."

"How *marvellous*! We've never been visited by an angel. I'll tell cook to set an extra place. I hope you don't think our halo tree is insensitive. They're so pretty twinkling in the branches." He beamed at Aeron and Morgan. "I heard you two got special jewellery." They flashed their rings. He sniffled and wiped his eye sockets. "My babies. All grown up. Conquest! Famine! Our wayward foals have returned to the stable."

The door opened and a human beach ball with legs waddled in. Demi's shoulders slumped as he kissed her.

"Ugh, you taste of grease. Did you lick an oil spill?" Her nose wrinkled.

"There are no calories in kisses. You're looking thin, dear."

"I wish I could say the same about you, Father. Your head looks like a pimple on an arse cheek."

"Someone has to eat your share."

"You don't have to eat Africa's too."

"If you wore green, people would think you're a stick insect and put you in a display tank. I could floss my teeth with you."

"You'd be too busy licking food off the floss. We should take you to Earth to plug the volcano."

Conquest entered the hall. His shaggy black hair and beard were a stark contrast to his silver armour. Marsden's eyes watched Drew from Conquest's ruggedly handsome face. Drew glanced at Mac. There was no resemblance.

Conquest hugged Mac. "Well done on the pandemics, son. You're quite an entrepreneur with your drugs trade." He eyed Marsden, smiling. "I hear you broke the seals."

"I didn't have much competition. Where's War?"

"With the vampires."

"Vampires?" Drew asked.

"They have no souls. Where d'you think they go when they die?" Marsden asked.

"I didn't think they existed."

"Vampires are great for training – they can't die here so it's like fighting tough opponents."

340

"Do they feel pain?"

"Yes, but they heal, so no harm done."

The door banged open, shaking the walls. War marched in, encased in black armour. A sword swung by his side, leaving a crimson trail alongside scarlet footprints. He removed his helmet. At six five, he towered above everyone. Drew eyed War's sharp cheekbones, cropped black hair, emerald eyes and stubble. He appeared to be mid-thirties and looked more suited to modelling than slaughtering. He was definitely Marsden's father.

War flung the helmet at Marsden, who caught it. "Of all the *billions* of people on Earth, you fall in love with a fucking *angel?*"

"Demons are in short supply."

War slapped him across the face with his gauntlet, leaving a bloodied lip. "What the fuck were you thinking? Killing *Michael?* You broke *every* rule I taught you. I should leave you rot in the dungeon. He nearly killed you!" He slapped him again.

"War, leave the boy alone," Conquest said. "His slaughter of the martyrs was magnificent." He smiled at Marsden.

"Don't protect him, Conquest. He fucked up."

"You think I don't know that? I let my desire for vengeance overshadow reason. I won't make that mistake again."

"Why didn't you tell me you fancied men? All these wasted years spent capturing females and locking them in your room only to have you kill every gift. I thought there was something *wrong* with you!"

"They weren't there to kill?"

"No!" He hit Mars across the head with his sword, leaving a bloodied smear.

"Leave him alone!" Drew said.

War inflicted his glower on Drew. "Who are you to tell me how I treat my son?" He prodded the red noose around Drew's neck. "*You're* the one who stole my boy's heart?" War scooped Drew into a suffocating embrace. "Welcome to the family!"

CHAPTER 45

"You're *not* going to cut off his gonads and mount them on a welcome plaque?" Demi asked. "Turn his knob into a knocker?"

"Don't give him ideas!" Marsden thumped her arm.

"Having your knob on the door means I'd get to bang it." She winked.

"Don't hit my daughter!" Famine mumbled, eating a cherry bakewell tart. The cherry dropped, a bulge in his stomach catching it. "Demeter, you're too good for him. You don't want someone who comes home every night covered in blood. I don't want to hear any more talk of his knob."

War smiled. "I thought I'd raised a psycho. Discovering I delivered the wrong sex is a huge relief."

Demi folded her arms. "Instead of explaining he was gay and releasing them, he butchered them. That's *exactly* what a psycho would do."

"I didn't know I was gay," Marsden said. "I thought War was testing me."

"I was, but to see if you were a psychopath. I didn't want to give up my lineage to someone who starts wars purely to murder people. I was worried you'd abandon strategy and political gains for wanton bloodshed. I'm relieved I was wrong. Not only is Fallen Angel gorgeous, your union broke the seventh seal. Fucking hell, your mother's never kissed me like that."

Marsden raised his eyebrows. "You're not mad?"

"I couldn't be happier! I thought you were as soulless as Purgatory. Or that you were asexual."

"So did I."

"I'm honoured you brought him home to meet me."

"I didn't. There's a change of plan."

War pointed his sword at Marsden's chest. "*Don't* tell me you've fucked up. This is the greatest Apocalypse we've ever seen, though it pains me to admit that. *We* slaughtered the trumpeters after each one sounded." He turned to Drew. "I keep their trumpets in my cabinet. You can see them if you like. They're a bit rusty. Blood does that."

"I made a funky necklace out of the angels." Death pulled it out of his robe. Ten tiny angels imprisoned in jars hung off a chain. "They're my chain gang."

"I made my wife a beautiful cloak from their feathers," Conquest said.

"I bet you ate your victims." Demi prodded Famine's belly. It jiggled.

"I left them to starve in gibbet cages. It's more than you've done. The only thing you're hungry for is fame."

Drew folded his arms. "Do you greet all your guests by regaling tales of how you murdered their family?"

"We don't have guests," Death said.

"Wonder why."

"Let's see your trophies." War turned Marsden around, moved his guitar and yanked up his chainmail. "Nice! Though you might want to think about how you and Fallen Angel engage in the battle of the flesh. He won't to want to stare at those when he's plunging his sword into you."

"Fuck's sake, Dad." Marsden fought him off. "When the world ends Drew will go to Hell."

War chuckled. "There's a kick in the kidneys. Have you infiltrated his defences and seized his crown?"

"No!"

"Get upstairs and mount that beauty before the final trumpet sounds! Jesus, what's the matter with you? I claimed your mother the night I stole her from her father's castle." He marched them to the spiral stairs.

"I'm stopping the Apocalypse!"

Deathly hush fell over the castle like a cascading cobweb. Mac coughed. Death tented his fingers. Conquest reached for his bow. Famine paused, a Battenburg half in his mouth. Crumbs tumbled out.

"The fuck you are." War flung him against the wall and punched him in the face. "I didn't raise a fucking traitor!"

"We need to plan strategies."

War sighed. "Kiss, undress, talk dirty, have a fondle then thrust your sword through his drawbridge, conquer his castle, plant your flag and boom. This is *embarrassing*. If you want tips on pleasuring a man, ask your mother. Her tongue raises my flagpole every time."

"Dad!" Marsden punched his shoulder. War whacked him across the head.

"I love romance!" Death bounced on the spot. "I can get rose petals. I've grown beautiful blood red roses in my garden. They smell like decomposition. You need music! Now Drew's no longer an angel, your guitar will work on him. You have to feel comfortable with each other. Don't be nervous."

Aeron smiled. "We said to use rose petals and music."

"You're romantics, like your daddy." Death hugged them.

"I find eating off each other sexy," Famine contributed.

"Ugh, nobody wants to picture you feeling amorous." Demi's lip curled. "I'm surprised you can find your sausage under all those rolls."

"Fling him down and claim him," Conquest suggested. "You won him in the battle, take what's yours."

War frowned at Marsden. "If you never touched those girls…are you a *virgin*?"

"Why is everyone so interested in my sex life?" Marsden tried wriggling free.

"Because you don't have one," Demi said. "When a hot person doesn't have a sex life, there's clearly something wrong with them. I *told* you your sword was a substitution for your lack of sex."

"You'll find out when I stick it in your heart."

War shoved Marsden and Drew up a few steps. "I can't believe I have to force you to enjoy the pleasures of the flesh. This is getting more fucking humiliating by the second. Sling him over your shoulder and make him scream his father's name. This guy fell from Heaven for you. He wouldn't have done that if you didn't give him a boner."

Demi sniggered.

"I'm going to kill God!"

War dragged him down the stairs. Their bodies collided. "*Excuse* me?"

"I'm killing God so Drew doesn't go to Hell."

"Why didn't you fucking tell me? I thought I'd raised a soldier. Wars before whores, Mars. You *know* that. You take the enemy *then* you take your prize!"

War marched him out into the corridor and through a portcullis into the battle room, the others trailing. A land filled with tiny figures burdened a large table supported by a statue of Atlas. Marsden picked up a Yeti action figure squeezed onto a throne.

"I replicated Heaven to scale," War said. "You're here somewhere, Drew, as a Power Ranger."

"This is blasphemy!" Drew exclaimed "You can't use Bigfoot to represent God!"

War rolled his eyes. "It was the only model Death could grab from the shop. God models aren't exactly the top toy for Christmas. Making models relaxes me."

"What models do you make?"

"Battle scenes, executions...you should see my working torture chamber!"

"It's brilliant," Marsden said. "It's got tiny thumbscrews."

"Not in to model planes?" Drew asked.

"Why would anyone make a plane?" War asked. "Nobody would die."

"Why do you have a model of Heaven?"

"I was going to kill your father." War laughed heartily at their shocked faces. "Lucifer hired me. He was pissed off about being cast into Hell. Unfortunately, God could no longer afford us and I lost my opportunity." He hugged Marsden. "You don't know how happy I am you want to achieve the one thing I never could! Although, had I succeeded, you and Fallen Angel would never have met as he'd be a crucified skeleton."

"Will we die?" Demi asked.

"You and Mac will die. You couldn't fight a bowl of jelly."

"I *told* you." Demi folded her arms. "I'm dying for his lover when he wouldn't die for mine."

"No offence, breadstick, but you're as lovable as nits."

"Don't speak to my daughter like that," Famine said.

"You have a tongue in your mouth? I thought it only contained food. Drew, we've been out of Heaven a while so I don't know how well trained God's army is." War raised his eyebrows at Drew expectantly.

"The Archangels have military training and the Powers are warriors. I was never told plans."

"What was Michael doing on Earth?"

"Shagging his secretary," Marsden said.

"I can't believe he got more action than you. How the hell did you resist each other? You clearly don't have my sex drive."

"One more word and I'll feed you to the leviathan."

"Hell, even Pustard Tart has more notches on his bedpost. And he's disgusting."

"Don't insult my son," Conquest said.

"You're jealous I raised the only competent foal." War grabbed a chestnut horse model and galloped it towards Heaven, neighing and stamping his feet. "Your first task is to eliminate St Peter." He waved a miniature sword and attacked Darth Vader, emitting a high-pitched squeal as St Peter died. Marsden facepalmed.

"He looks nothing like St Peter," Drew said.

"You're lucky Death stole a nativity scene from a primary school otherwise Jesus would've been a Thundercat. Who's disabling St Peter?"

"Can't we knock him out and steal his keys?"

War growled. "This man asked to be crucified upside down because he 'wasn't worthy' to die the same way as Jesus. Does that sound like someone who will stand by while you duct tape him and storm Heaven? There are always four guards around God's throne. Either take them at switch over, or eliminate them in fours."

"If we take them at switch over, we'll kill eight simultaneously," Marsden said. "Limit the angels who come for us, though it's riskier."

"Good point. Drew, do they leave the throne at switch over?"

"No. They swap at the throne."

"He's very paranoid for someone who's never had a threat to his kingdom. Perfectly doable, there are six of you. Though you'd lose the element of surprise."

"Mac can kill one with an arrow, leaving us with seven," Marsden said.

"It's one thing spreading disease, but I can't kill angels," Mac said.

"You've already killed one."

"I still have nightmares about it."

"I'm not participating," Drew said.

"Then you're not fit to love my boy." War rubbed his face. "You call yourselves Horsemen!"

"I'm not a Horseman."

"If you marry my boy you will be."

"There isn't a space for another Horseman," Demi said. "We've already got one extra because Death cocked up the numbers and refused to fix it."

Death glared at her. "I love my baby foals."

"He could be the new Conquest," War continued. "I know we amalgamated that position but we could reverse it."

"I should inherit that position," Mac argued.

"You have no claim to Conquest's throne, only Death's. And I don't rate your chances against the Terror Twins. No offence, Chicken Pox, but you can't lead a Conga line, let alone an army into a bloodbath. Drew can be the Horseman of natural disasters. While you lot are killing the Seraphim, Mars, you're tackling God. You don't know how proud and terrified that makes me."

"You're not scared of anything," Marsden said.

"You could die and be cast down to Hell. That scares the shit out of me. It'd break my heart turning up my stereo to drown out your screams."

"You could break me out."

"I would eventually, but time downstairs would allow you to reflect on how you fucked up."

"Why do you have to kill God? Can't you negotiate a peace deal?" Drew asked.

"No. Do you honestly think a god who ordered the *annihilation* of mankind, would even *consider* negotiating a peace deal?"

Drew walked out. Marsden watched him, torn between following and hearing his father's plans.

"Go. I'll fill you in later. I'll have to simplify this for these twatwursts, break out the puppet theatre. Every day I rage the War line isn't in charge. You think it's bad working for the Terror Twins? At least they never made you do touristy stuff."

"Well excuse me for wanting to sightsee before we destroyed Earth." Death folded his arms.

"An evening cruise along the river Seine in Paris was embarrassing and awkward. *Everyone* thought we were a couple."

"The twins have a scrapbook," Marsden said.

War scowled. Death clapped.

Marsden ran outside and skidded to a stop. Ash and stones swirled like spirits around his feet. Drew had vanished. Cursing, he searched the graveyard. Dead brambles crunched under his feet. Some smothered gravestones in a prickly embrace. Blood dripped from gravestones where the thorns punctured the stone.

Marsden stalked towards the figure silhouetted under the halo tree. Drew touched the lowest halos. They tinkled as they bashed together.

"Does this upset you?"

Drew lowered his hand. "My family's halos being used as fancy lighting? No, that doesn't upset me at all."

"Remind me to never show you my father's trophy room. Or let you see my back again."

"I never expected him to be accepting."

"Not everyone's a judgemental, domineering dictator."

"If he gives you a gauntlet for your birthday, what does he do when he's pissed at you?"

"Locks me in with the lost souls."

"Is it horrible?"

"Do you know how it feels to have hundreds of desperate fingers groping you, their woeful cries echoing down your ears? Eventually, they're irritating more than pitiful then you stop caring."

Marsden's heart raced. Before it was Drew's damnation preventing him from kissing him. Now it was doubt. To be rejected by the only person he'd ever wanted would cause a wound that might never heal. This was a fear he'd never experienced. Why was it easier to kill a man than to love one?

He climbed the tree.

"What are you doing?" Drew called. "You'll fall."

"I can't die here."

Marsden reached the top and edged along a thin branch. Unsheathing his sword, he hooked a halo then slung it over his arm and jumped. He landed in front of Drew and held out the halo.

"This is yours."

"They're identical."

"I'd know yours from a thousand halos; I spent enough time glaring at the damn thing. Besides, it was at the top and has my skin stuck to it." He tilted the ring, touching charred bits clinging to it.

"I'm not an angel anymore."

"Your father stole this from you. It's only fair you steal it back. I wish I could return your wings." He opened it and put it around Drew's neck. "I could make you wings out of Conquest's wife's cloak. They'd be useless for flying though. You'll just have to wear them in the bedroom."

"My neck's felt bare." Drew touched the choker. "Now your tree has an empty branch."

Marsden shrugged. "I'll make one out of foil."

Drew laughed. Marsden kissed him before his courage deserted him. He pushed him against the tree, surprised he missed the burn. He nibbled Drew's lower lip then sucked it.

Drew gently pushed him away. "I don't think I'm ready for this."

"Sorry it's not a fiery kiss like last time."

"I don't expect third degree burns every time."

"I know you can't forgive me."

"I'm supposed to, but you killed my family. I don't know if I can ever forgive that, even if your motives were born from love. Well, your idea of love. But the

Apocalypse means everything to you. And you gave it up. You did the one thing I asked of you." He pulled Marsden closer and kissed him. Marsden's hands quivered as pleasure flooded his veins.

Marsden gently kissed his neck, tasting Drew's fruity scent. Drew squirmed and laughed when Marsden's lips explored under his chin. He kissed along Drew's jaw then flicked his tongue over Drew's lips. Drew's fingers scraped the neck of the guitar, twanging the strings. Marsden ran his hands down Drew's sides and squeezed his arse.

Drew smiled. "Am I really the only person you've ever been attracted to?"

"Yeah. I thought I was incapable of being attracted to anyone."

"I knew it was the wings and halo that tempted you."

Marsden lifted Drew, their kisses becoming urgent as Drew's legs encircled his waist. Marsden's body ached and he thrust against Drew, their bodies not feeling close enough.

Drew groaned, his breathing heavy as he ran his hands down Marsden's chest. "They're in there, plotting to kill my father and we're out here..."

"Kissing under halo light like soppy romantics. Ugh. You're right. We should go to the crypt." He stepped back and lowered Drew.

Drew grabbed his hand. "I don't want to go to the crypt."

"There's plenty of the castle to explore. Wait 'til you see the dungeon!"

"I want to go to *your* room." His lips brushed Marsden's ear. "It's a shame to waste those books Morgan and Aeron bought."

"Are you sure?"

"I fell for you. Don't let me fall in vain."

CHAPTER 46

Writhing brands lit the castle's passages, like Hell's fires had been captured and fought to escape their binds. Marsden led Drew up spiral stairs. Nerves and excitement battled in Drew's stomach. He could barely breathe. He'd fantasised about this moment for months. Now it didn't seem real.

"Mars!" War's voice boomed off the walls. Marsden's shoulders slumped. "You're staying until you know the strategies by heart. Hesitation takes your head. I won't bear the shame of you failing because your mind's in the bedroom, not the battle. It was bad enough Michael nearly ended you because pretty boy distracted you. I refuse to infiltrate Hell to say I told you so. Lucifer and I aren't speaking."

Marsden's eyes narrowed as he stepped down to join Drew, his body shaking. His jaw tightened, his free fist clenching.

"Drew and I have things to discuss."

"Hard to discuss things with his tongue in your mouth. Sex will be more passionate *after* you've claimed the victory and taken him as your prize. The memory will be sweeter when it's crowned with killing his father."

"For me. He doesn't think patricide's a romantic gesture."

"Nonsense! He'll be so impressed with your battle skills and overcome with relief you're alive, he'll undress the second you trudge back, drenched in his father's blood."

"That's hardly an aphrodisiac," Drew said.

"Bollocks! You should've seen the passion between Mars's mother and me the night I slaughtered her rescue party. Nothing says 'I love you' like a severed head with a rose in its teeth."

"I thought romance was dead," Marsden replied.

War pointed to the doorway.

Marsden's lips brushed Drew's ear, sending shivers through him. "I won't cry if you kill my father."

"You *can* rescue me from Hell?"

"Easier than sacrificing virgins." War eyed them with a sly smile.

Marsden looked at Drew. "Either the world dies, or God does."

"I want to save the world. But I don't want you to kill Him."

"You *can't* save the world. It was rotten before you arrived. But you can stop it drowning in humanity's blood."

"By drowning it in God's?"

"There must always be a sacrifice."

"I'm the only one who has to make it."

"No you're not. I can't be a Horseman of the Apocalypse if there's no apocalypse. If you really want to play the dutiful martyr and go to Hell when the world ends, fine, I'll rescue you. But I'm still killing God."

Marsden trooped into the battle room. Drew followed.

War blocked him. "Not you, Heaven Deadly Sins. I can't risk you betraying Mars to regain your wings."

"I'd never betray him."

"You thought you'd never betray God, yet you're near our plans, preparing to bed your father's killer. If Mars wasn't in love with you, I'd kill you and make your head into a flowerpot for Death. I can't believe he'd risk the entire operation by bringing you here. I thought I raised him better than that. In fact, to be safe..." He bound

Drew's hands behind his back and slung him over his shoulder. "Come see our guest room."

"I won't say anything!"

"It's this or I kill you, and I won't let my son love a corpse. He's already emotionally stunted."

"I blame the parents."

War strode down a corridor, dodging the gauntlet of axes, guillotines and spikes. Drew ducked as a blade almost beheaded him.

"The gauntlet's random so no-one can learn it."

"Who would break into your castle?"

"It's so no-one can break *out*."

War opened a metal door and descended narrow stone steps, pausing on each one as spikes shot up through the others.

"Isn't this is a bit extreme?" Drew asked.

"No."

War carried him through a winding passage before opening a barbed wire gate. He crossed a flagstone floor carpeted with crimson straw then lowered Drew and unbound his hands. He shackled Drew's wrists to the wall and his ankles to iron rings in the floor.

Brands in the corners thrashed like possessed demons. Whips, paddles and torture implements were displayed artistically on one wall.

"That's my feature wall." War beamed.

"Most people have a bright colour or exposed brickwork."

"It's exposed stone."

"With torture equipment."

"It's more interesting than patterned wallpaper and baby photos. Don't sit against the wall."

Drew shuffled forwards. Spikes shot out from the wall. One kissed his back, snagging his t-shirt. His heart thundered. "Is everything lethal?"

"Only the fun parts. Mars spent hours here growing up. I'm glad I could share it with you."

"The pleasure's all mine."

"If you escape, I'll kill you. Nothing personal, I'm a concerned parent protecting his son."

"A concerned parent wouldn't encourage his son to lead a suicide mission."

War laughed. "You're a gem." He backed out, rolling the barbed wire gate closed.

***

War entered the battle room.

"Where's Drew?" Marsden picked up one of the Teenage Mutant Ninja Turtles representing Seraphims.

"In our guest room."

"Did you sit him away from the wall?" He made Michelangelo stab the Yeti God.

"Of course." War smiled.

"He stays an hour then you're moving him to my room. If you want to shackle him there, fine."

War laughed. "You've never had foreplay, you're not experienced enough for bondage."

Marsden glowered. "So he can't escape. Any longer than an hour, he'll die. Then I'll ride through Heaven with your head on a stick instead of a flag."

"A night in the dungeon will toughen him up."

"Or scar him for life."

"It didn't do you any harm."

***

Rustling. Drew tensed, the chains clanking. Despair seeped from the walls. The torture instruments glinted under the halo tree's glow. Dark patches betrayed their former use. A skeleton sat opposite him, its eternal smile belying its discomfort.

A spike thrust through the skeleton's ribcage then retreated. A large flail swung from the ceiling, hit the neck shackles on the back wall then returned to its hiding place.

Drew's body temperature soared, his underarms prickling. For a guest room, it wasn't very welcoming.

His beating heart marked the passing of time.

A glass box above the end shackles opened, hot tar gushing over the floor.

"Shit!" Drew scurried until his shackles tautened then glanced up, breathing hard. Glass boxes suspended above each shackle contained different delights: bubbling lava, a guillotine blade, a heavy ball, lye and above him, a grid of blades.

He hung his head, trying to still his thrashing heart. Wretched sobbing echoed through the wall behind him.

"Hello?"

Silence swelled with each second until it became suffocating.

A ring chandelier dropped, spikes protruding from the outer edges. It spun sickeningly fast as it swung. Drew ducked and it soared over his head. It collided with the skeleton, before swinging towards Drew again, lower. The skeleton slumped in defeated repose. Drew dived on his back. It passed above him, his t-shirt rippling. His heart hammered, desperate to be released from its bony dungeon. He closed his eyes, praying for a quick death. The chandelier plummeted and spun towards him, scattering the straw.

"Don't move!"

Marsden unlocked the barbed wire door then ran in, ducking a swinging wrecking ball. He hurdled a row of spikes then yanked up a lever. The chandelier rose to the ceiling.

"War's not used to guests. He got overexcited and wanted to show off his favourite room."

"What happens to people he hates?"

"They visit the room next door. Or get chucked into the oubliette."

"Who does he torture?"

"The soulless and the ones that can't go to Hell. God's orders."

"I heard someone crying in there."

"Newbies always cry. They soon learn it's futile." Marsden unlocked Drew's shackles. "If he offers to show you his photo albums, refuse."

"What if I want to see your baby photos?"

"The ones in the album are his favourite tortures. They're artistically done, but I doubt you'll find a quartered corpse artistic, no matter how well displayed the organs are. Are you hurt?"

"I nearly died, I'm traumatised, but I'm not hurt."

He pulled Drew up. "Careful where you stand."

"Who's that?" Drew pointed to the skeleton.

"Jones. He's there to terrify guests. He was War's first victim, so he has sentimental value."

"War doesn't strike me as sentimental."

"He is, just not in the conventional way."

Several flagstones plummeted, vanishing into darkness.

"What the fuck? What happens if we're on them when they fall?"

"We fall with them."

"Where?"

"I've never found out. But it's not Disneyland."

They jumped onto the next stone then the other stones rose. Marsden skipped across a couple then more stones dropped. Drew just made it onto Marsden's stone. His heart pounded.

"Isn't this more exciting than *Uncharted Territory?*" Marsden smiled.

"Exciting isn't the word I'd use."

"It's more exhilarating when real lives are at risk."

The stones rose so they crossed again. Marsden shoved Drew onto the bottom step as his stone fell. Marsden leapt for the step. Drew caught his hand, his legs dangling in the darkness.

Drew trembled, pulling him up. "What happens if a stone below the shackles falls?"

"You hang until it returns. If you grab the neck shackle, you live."

"War said you spent a lot of time here."

"Playing torturer and victim with the twins. Purgatory doesn't have play parks. We learned all about medieval tortures from Death's stories about people he collected."

They raced through the winding passage and up the spiral stairs, avoiding spikes, bursts of fire and swinging weapons.

"Your father's insane. Why do the others let him do this?"

"This is our wing. Death's wing is full of artefacts he's collected from Earth. His garden is stunning."

"His roses smell like dead people."

"He's not great at cultivating life. His rockery is filled with skulls. Conquest is a talented artist and has battle murals everywhere. Famine has a bed in the kitchen."

"How the hell are you as sane as you are?"

"I have a wonderful mother."

"Who gives your father hearts for Valentine's?"

"He's hard to buy for." Marsden stopped at the top of a hexagonal tower and unlocked the door. "Welcome to my humble abode."

Drew peered in. "Is it booby trapped?"

"I've disarmed them."

Marsden's dungeon bedroom had a grey flagstone floor and shackles on the walls. Arched alcoves were carved into the walls. One housed a claw foot bath, one had a bookcase, one had a black metal four poster bed and another held a chest of drawers. At the far end, a skeleton sat in an electric chair, which was decorated with skull lights.

"That's my first victim. I stabbed him in the heart. I was merciful when I was a kid."

"Does he have a name?"

"He did once."

A well dominated one corner and in the middle of the floor was a foot high square wall, topped with a black grate. Mournful sobbing echoed through the chasm.

"Is someone down there?" Drew leaned over. Marsden ran his hand over his arse, making pleasure shoot to his groin.

"Surprised they're still alive. It's a hell of a drop." Marsden leaned over it. "Don't make me come down there and gag you with your intestines!" The sobbing died.

Marsden grabbed Drew's jeans pockets and pulled him towards him. Drew kissed him softly, his nerves sparking, his hands slipping under Marsden's top and stroking his back. He stopped when his fingers found the five notches. Marsden pushed him onto the bed and straddled him. He pulled Drew's top off and threw it on the floor. Drew's skin tingled as Marsden's rough fingertips explored his chest. They kissed passionately as Drew slid Marsden's chainmail up his body, parting only long enough to cast it aside. His hands skimmed up Marsden's arms then down his chest, caressing his scars. His pulsing heart drowned out the whimpering from the oubliette.

Marsden's fingers danced down Drew's sides. "It feels weird without the searing agony."

"Getting scorched wasn't exactly erotic."

Marsden pinned Drew's hands by his head. Drew's neck tickled beneath Marsden's warm lips. He kissed Marsden's shoulder, his skin tasting metallic from his discarded chainmail. Drew's body throbbed with lust, excitement and a tinge of fear as Marsden kissed down his chest and stomach then undid his jeans, slipping his hand inside. Drew's fear intensified with the pleasure.

Marsden smiled and squeezed Drew's erection. Drew gasped, his fear gone, pleasure his only sensation. He kissed Marsden hard as he undid his trousers, easing his hand inside. Marsden groaned and bit Drew's lip.

"Mars! Get your arse downstairs." War stood in the doorway.

Marsden sat up, red veins snaking through his irises. "Get out of my room."

Drew moved his hand to Marsden's thigh.

"We have an assassination to plan."

"Ten minutes longer won't jeopardise it."

"You don't take his angelhood then insult him with ten minutes! Your seduction must last all night." War marched in. "You're a temptress." He pointed at Drew. "You're ruining my boy's concentration."

Marsden fastened his trousers. "You have thirty seconds to leave before I turn your organs into modern art."

War unhooked a bucket from the well then threw it over both of them.

"Fuck!" Marsden snatched the bucket and hurled it at War's head. It bounced to the floor. War gripped the back of Marsden's neck and marched him out. "I'll dunk you in the lake with the leviathan."

"I preferred you when you were asexual. Your focus was unparalleled."

"One day I *will* kill you."

"I'll rip you apart like a Christmas cracker and wear your intestines as a festive hat."

The door slammed.

Drew zipped up his jeans and touched his lip, a ruby droplet clinging to his finger. He sat up and looked out the barred window, his hands shaking with unspent lust. The halo tree bathed the graves in an eerie shroud.

Drew moved to another window. Black mountains dominated the land, their treacherous sides jagged and deadly. Grey paths snaked through them, disappearing from sight. A lonely place to die.

He walked to another window, stopping to study a weapons wall. Outside this window, silver flames rose from a lake's blackened surface, dancing to the music of screams that escaped its depths. Leviathan's monstrous shadows rippled beneath it. Drowning beneath the flames, were the trapped souls of Purgatory.

CHAPTER 47

Inside the globe, Lemures drowned in ash. Morgan smashed it, everyone protecting their faces from flying shards.

Drew stumbled as they appeared on Gallows Street. Ash sprinkled from the scarlet sky, like cremated souls cast down from Heaven.

Broken buildings had been driven to their knees above shattered roads, streetlights bowing their heads to worship the tumultuous skies. A man lay in the gutter, a bottle smashed beside his bloodied face, his empty wallet lying on his chest. A woman died trapped beneath a car, and a teenage girl hung out of a flat's window, the pane wedged in her back. Her arms and hair dangled, blood spattering the ground.

Across a boarded up shop, red graffiti pleaded 'Lord have mercy on our souls'.

"There's no mercy here," Drew murmured, feeling sick. "And no souls left to save."

The third trumpet's woeful wail disturbed the silence.

"Shit." Marsden looked around. "Has our return sounded that?"

Demi smirked. "Shame War kept you after class. You could've blown Drew's trumpet and the apocalyptic one simultaneously."

"One more word and you're going in a sausage grinder."

The sky darkened, the ground shaking once again. Fear's tendrils uncoiled in Drew's stomach, spreading its poison through his body.

"Is anyone else bored of earthquakes?" Demi sighed. "This third trumpet better be good. I need something to grab the headlines."

"Newsflash, we're stopping the Apocalypse. Your campaign of terror is over."

"Thank god! It was interfering with my celebrity lifestyle."

Unnatural luminosity drowned the city.

"What's happening?" Mac shielded his eyes with his hoody.

"Wormwood," Aeron replied.

"It's a star that falls to Earth and poisons a third of the world's water," Morgan explained. "Don't you remember our play, when we dropped that vampire from the castle into the lake? She wore a large cardboard star with 'wormwood' written on it. Well, she did until the leviathan ate her and spat out the star. Just as well really. It took me ages to make that."

"Oh. I thought you were just being mean to her."

Morgan gaped. "*Mean?* That was *art.*"

"You should've poisoned the water," Demi told Mac. "All you'd have to do is bathe in rivers and reservoirs."

"How do we stop it?" Drew asked.

"You suck the fun out of everything. You could hang a safety net then catapult Wormwood back up, but you'll probably take out the sun."

"And that would ruin the fourth trumpet's fun," Morgan said.

Blinding light tore through Earth. They covered their eyes, shockwaves rippling through the city. Windows that survived the earthquakes dropped from their frames to die on the ground. Car alarms were resurrected with deafening whines. Darkness swooped and silence reigned again.

"That was anti-climactic," Demi remarked.

"That's what she said." Morgan winked.

"Don't drink the water," Aeron warned.

He and Morgan headed to where Erebus pawed the dead man in the gutter. They climbed onto a broken bench and jumped onto Erebus's double saddle. Demi collected Pavlova from a health shop. He followed her out, munching nuts as she lectured him on the dangers of overeating. Hastings walked up behind Mac and nudged his back. Camelot cantered down the street, whinnying in outrage, a man hanging onto his mane. Camelot skidded to a stop by the missing chunk of road, shaking his head and depositing the man into the hole. The man's screams died before he did. Camelot reared in victory then trotted to Marsden.

Marsden sprang onto him then helped Drew up.

"I'd feel safer on Hastings," Drew commented.

Camelot reached back and nipped Drew's toes.

"Go ahead. If you want a face full of pus."

"Isn't it easier to reach Heaven from Purgatory?"

"You can't get to Heaven from Purgatory," Aeron told him. "There's no bridge."

"Lost souls get there after being purified by fire."

"No soul has ever left Purgatory. Sorry handsome, your daddy lied to you. Again."

Demi and Mac mounted their horses.

"Great, we've become clichés," Demi muttered. "If I become fat from riding this thing, I'll make you suffer."

"Each time you breathe, we suffer," Marsden replied.

"Aren't people supposed to be nicer when they're in love? Love clearly doesn't bond well with your DNA."

"Anthrax will bond wonderfully with yours."

Erebus stamped his hoof, flicked his tail then led the other horses away from Gallows Street.

Chaos ruled in the city. Marsden strummed his guitar. A fight erupted as two people lay claim to a broken lamp. Marsden played 'Lacerated Wrists', showing them their scars in their twisted reflections.

A man threw himself off a shop roof, his body breaking on a burnt car. Erebus rummaged in his pockets. Morgan leaned down and plucked a globe from the man's coat. She slipped it into Erebus's mouth. He shook his head then spat the marble into her hand. She relinquished it to the raven perched on a fallen streetlight.

"Corpse!"

"Why are you still tormenting them?" Drew asked.

"I like playing the guitar," Marsden replied. "I can't help it if it controls them."

"Buy a guitar that isn't powered by your sword."

"That'd take the fun out of it."

The horses avoided ruined cars and potholes.

"I need some things from the pub."

"Don't even *think* about mounting Mars's stallion," Morgan warned. "We don't have time for your love story to reach a Hollywood ending. Meet us at Travel Inn. Will we need a room for the horses?"

"I expect so," Aeron said. "They don't have stables."

"Shame we didn't book in advance. It would've been cheaper."

"Threatening to kill the receptionist might waiver our fee."

"Maybe they'll toss in a breakfast bag."

"And complimentary cake."

Camelot trotted towards The Razor and the Rosary, his tail high. When they reached the pub, Drew slid off.

"It's still standing at least."

"Do you want me to come in?"

"Staying outside won't make the inside any prettier."

"It'll make the outsider prettier." Marsden dismounted and led Camelot into the pub. He removed his bridle. "Don't wreck anything."

"Can't you tie him up outside? My insurance won't cover Apocalyptic horses. This is what they call 'an act of God'."

Camelot leaned over the bar to steal snacks.

"Not only does he use you as a catalyst for the Apocalypse, he screws over your insurance claim. I don't have Cam's rope to tie him up and I can't use his reins. He might hurt himself."

"How can you be caring for an animal but heartless about people?"

"People are arseholes. If it wasn't for you, I'd accelerate the Apocalypse. Maybe after I've killed God, I'll restart it. The rot needs to be cut from this world." He followed Drew upstairs. Chunks of ceiling covered the living room floor like comatose drunks.

Drew rescued his PS3 and blew dust off it. "Reckon this still works?"

He put it on an armchair buried under plaster then gathered his games. He entered his bedroom. A large portion of ceiling crushed the bed. The chest of drawers was a pile of splinters and stakes.

"You seem pissed," Marsden said.

"What if you don't survive?"

"I wouldn't do this if I thought I'd lose."

"God's omnipotent. He'll destroy you."

"Nobody is too powerful to die."

"That's what scares me."

Drew stuffed debris-covered clothes and still-edible food into his kitbag. He slotted his PS3 and games and the *Kama Sutra* in and zipped it up. They headed downstairs and found Camelot rubbing his neck against the world statue. Marsden buckled the bridle on him and led him out. They mounted then Camelot trotted down the devastated streets, occasionally bucking.

"Sorry," Marsden said. "He's excited."

Camelot ploughed into a woman crossing the street. Marsden laughed and patted Camelot's neck.

"Why didn't you stop him?" Drew asked.

"How many people can say they got run down by one of the Apocalyptic horses? She'll dine on this for years."

They reached Travel Inn and Marsden led Camelot inside. He untacked him and let him loose in the room with Erebus. All the furniture had been removed. As soon as he stepped into their room, Drew yanked him into the toilet.

"I have something for you."

"In here? I thought you were classier than that."

Drew reached into his bag and removed a dagger. The gold and silver haft was carved with religious symbols, the blade was iridescent glass, like a rainbow trapped in an icicle. "The haft's crafted from the same source as our halos."

Marsden took it. "Shit!" He dropped it and examined the angry imprint brand on his palm. "I can't hold it."

"You'll have to. It's the only blade capable of killing my father."

CHAPTER 48

The horses' hooves rang off the road like church bells announcing a funeral.

"I can't believe Angel of Harlem gave you that God-Be-Gone weapon, because you stroked his golden staff," Demi remarked. "If you'd shagged him, he might kill God for us then we wouldn't have to risk our lives. How did he get it? He hasn't visited Heaven and had no plans to kill God before he left. Yet he magically hands over a weapon he claims will kill him."

"Where's this portal?" Marsden asked Aeron and Morgan.

Aeron imitated zipping his mouth shut. "Prying ears and all that jazz."

"How *did* Drew get it?" Morgan asked. "I doubt they hand them out with the halos."

"He still has a friend in Heaven."

"How does he know that will kill God? It hasn't been tested."

"He didn't say."

"You didn't tie him to a chair and wire his gonads to a car battery? You've changed."

"Holy objects kill *us*," Demi said, "not the man who made them. He's hardly likely to create something that can kill him then leave it lying around like an old pizza box."

They passed a moss-stained sign. The name MISERY was smeared with blood. Demi rolled her eyes. This place was more depressing than an Emo therapy group.

The horses walked along Cemetery Drive. Railings surrounding the graveyard were partially concealed by bushes. Dying ivy strangled tall black gates, revealing rust beneath the gates' peeling skin. *Sacred City* was formed with black barbed wire across the top of the gates.

"I'm *not* lurking in a cemetery at night, dressed like this." Demi gestured to her silver gloss PVC trousers and top. A shield badge of balancing scales protected her heart. "The press will think I'm into cosplay. *Nerds* like cosplay."

"The press have forgotten you," Marsden replied. "Can you move in that?"

"Female superheroes wear skin-tight, impractical outfits. I would've chosen something sexier but it's fucking freezing and I don't want scars."

"My outfit's practical, protective and stylish," Morgan said. "There's no danger of my boobs popping out during an energetic bout of spin kicking." She wore a corset with armoured fibres woven amongst the fabric while Aeron wore a moulded chest plate. They both wore badges of crossed scythes in a horseshoe, black PVC trousers and their long coats.

Morgan dismounted, unlocked the gates with her globe and pulled them. They protested with a pained groan before surrendering. Morgan mounted behind Aeron and they entered the cemetery.

Graves crumbled, toppled headstones bowing at the feet of a broken stone angel. A rickety hut guarded the far corner.

"What's that for?" Demi pointed.

"The Ankou," Morgan replied.

The horses picked their way across the uneven ground of forgotten graves. Some graves had collapsed, exposing shattered coffins.

"Shouldn't we be in a church?" Mac asked, holding his helmet on. He wore Conquest's armour, which was two sizes too big. His badge had a bow with a syringe instead of an arrow.

"Too obvious," Morgan replied.

"And they're full," Aeron said.

"God will be pleased."

"They go for the free wine."

Wind kissed their faces, running its fingers through their hair and slipping beneath their armour. The sky was dark, as though as a bottle of ink had spilled over the clouds after Fate had written humanity's misery memoirs.

They stopped outside a stone crypt. Crimson ivy smothered the walls, snaking down the doors and escaping along the floor.

Aeron and Morgan consulted a pirate map, talking in furtive whispers. Aeron jabbed the map then pointed to another crypt. Demi sighed. Why hadn't someone invented a rocket to fly to Heaven? They managed to get to Jupiter.

"Is there a problem?" Marsden asked.

"No." Aeron smiled. "Making sure we have the right crypt."

"What's in the other one?"

"Gateway to Hell."

Marsden's eyes narrowed. "You don't know which one it is."

"Nonsense. The gateway to Hell has a pentagram." Aeron rolled up the map and slotted it under Erebus's saddle. "Open it."

Marsden slashed the ivy with his sword. The doors parted, gouging the earth.

Crack!

The sky darkened further as the fourth trumpet grieved for mankind's damnation.

Marsden kicked the crypt. "Everything we do accelerates the fucking trumpets!"

Demi smirked. After all Marsden's bitching about them ruining his Apocalypse, it was satisfying watching him fail to stop it. She doubted any of his precious strategies included an escape button.

"What's the fourth one?" Mac asked.

"Complete darkness for a third of the day," Aeron said. "The sun, stars and moon get struck and lose part of their light."

"Maybe God's saving on his energy bills," Morgan suggested.

"Didn't one of the others turn the sky dark permanently?" Demi asked. "Revelations is like a film franchise – the same plot packaged as sequels."

Aeron and Morgan lit their skull lanterns and led the way inside. Alcoves filled with bones flanked the path. The horses' hooves echoed through the passageways, leaving tracks in the dust. Fading trumpet notes stalked them. Cobwebs dangled from the ceiling, fine silk nooses to hang the unwary. Some brushed their faces; ghostly fingers reaching through the darkness to tease them with a lover's caress. The lanterns cast eerie faces on the wall.

Demi tapped Mac's armour. "This is a flattering light for you."

"It's pitch black."

"Exactly."

The path forked like a serpent's tongue. Smoke spiralled from the left corridor, beckoning them into the darkness. The right passage pulsed with painful light and heat.

Aeron pull an origami paper decider from his pocket and moved back and forth between the paths, opening and closing the decider.

"You don't *know?*" Demi asked. "If we end up in Hell, I will *personally* pull out your entrails."

"You can't hold sausages, you'll never master entrails." Marsden poked her.

"I'll do yours first."

"I'll force feed you."

Demi looked at the twins. "Do you know the correct path or not?"

"Of course." Morgan smiled. "But the look on your face was priceless, Dems. War kept us up 'til we could recite the plan in our sleep. Well, we didn't *have* to stay all night, but a half-naked, soaking Marsden is a sight not to be missed. Especially when he's smouldering with rage and unquenched lust."

"It's the right path."

They turned around. Drew approached, wearing Conquest's spare silver chest plate.

Demi glared. It wasn't fair the hottest men she'd ever seen only had eyes for each other. They deserved to die for being so selfish. "He's lying. He doesn't want daddy dearest butchered like a Jack the Ripper victim."

"Or it's a double bluff," Mac said.

"Drew's right," Marsden said. "But take the left path if you don't trust him. Hell needs a talking skeleton to terrify newcomers."

Demi flipped him off. "If you're hoping to stop us, Kinky Angel, bugger off. Thanks to the sodding Apocalypse, my modelling career's over."

"So why are you against stopping it?"

"Because I trust you as much as I trust a 'fat-free' product. And it's not fair I'll die because you can't take a bit of spanking."

"If you'd participated in the Apocalypse, you wouldn't be in danger of dying."

"If you've come to preach, I'll shove your bible so far up your arse, you can turn the pages with your tongue."

"I did everything Father asked and he's banishing me to Hell for eternity. I'm coming with you."

She smirked. "Mars unleashes his Midas touch on you and you change sides? That must've been one *hell* of a hand job."

Marsden slapped Demi upside the head then offered his arm to Drew. Drew glanced at the black spiked gauntlet and accepted his hand.

Demi backhanded Marsden. "Hit me again and I'll demonstrate my kiss of death you've been nagging me to use."

"You can't kill me."

"Who said anything about killing *you*?" She flicked her gaze to Drew.

Erebus led the way down the passage. They shielded their eyes against the light. Ivy crawled over the tunnel roof and dangled, poised to strike.

"Stop!" Aeron reined Erebus to a halt. "There's a pit, eight feet wide. We'll have to jump it."

Morgan held her lamp over the pit. Anguished screams rose to meet the light.

"Where does it lead?" Mac asked.

"Hell."

"Why's there a pit to Hell on the path to Heaven?"

"Only the worthy reach Heaven," Drew said. "There are several pits. One leads to Purgatory."

"Have you been here before?" Morgan asked.

"I didn't fly from Heaven. That would've alerted the world I was here."

"That would've been a glorious sight," Demi remarked. "A naked angel swooping down like a giant bird of prey, your trouser snake dangling like tinsel caught in a breeze."

"I wasn't naked."

"You're a flesh suit of disappointments."

"You'd better ride in front," Morgan said.

"Good thinking." Demi smiled. "He can be sacrificed if he fucks up. How did you cross it?"

"I flew."

"Try flying without your wings, Traitor's Gate. Can't we take the stairs? My arse is getting chubby from sitting in this saddle."

"There isn't a stairway to Heaven."

Marsden dismounted. "Cam can't carry us both."

Drew slid into the saddle. "How will you cross?"

"Magic. Jump, Cam."

Camelot galloped towards the pit. Drew gripped the reins and Camelot's long mane. Camelot leapt, landing on the other side with a triumphant whinny. He reared, kicking his front legs.

"Shit!" Drew leaned forwards, hanging on.

"Don't throw him into it!" Marsden shouted.

Camelot trotted on, his tail like a flag. Morgan slithered off Erebus and waited by Marsden while Erebus sailed to safety. Aeron turned Erebus around, both of them bowing. Mac yelled and grabbed Hasting's mane as he charged over the pit.

Demi nudged Pavlova. "If you dump me in there, you can forget the sugar lump I brought you." Pavlova's ears pricked up. He landed on the other side then nuzzled Demi's leg. She fed him a sugar lump from her pocket.

"Did you bring treats for the rest of us?" Aeron asked.

"Cyanide capsules."

"I'll pass. I find them sour."

Morgan extended her scythe then sprinted for the pit. Aeron closed his eyes as she planted the scythe on the edge and vaulted across, her coat billowing. She landed and twirled to bow, smacking Mac across the head with the scythe. Aeron jumped off Erebus and hugged her, spinning. Their coats swirled around them.

Marsden ran towards the pit.

"Is he insane?" Demi asked.

"Not according to medical experts," Aeron replied. "But War paid for a clean diagnosis."

Marsden sprang off the wall and grabbed the ivy above. He swung across, averting his eyes from the enticing darkness. He stretched his toe towards the edge. The ivy snapped. He plummeted, his curse echoing around the passage.

"That fucks up our mission," Demi said. "I hope someone has a Plan B."

"Marsden does," Morgan said. "He also has the dagger."

Demi leaned towards the pit. "Thanks for ruining everything, Wankenstein!"

A tortured scream answered her.

Drew glowered at her. "One more word and I'll toss you down there to fetch him."

"You can't even stamp on chocolate."

"I'm going down." Drew dismounted.

Morgan grabbed him. "You think Lucifer will let you leave? We're on a mission to save you from Hell and you want to dive in there like it's a giant ball pit?"

"We can't leave him!"

"We'll collect him afterwards."

"Like lost luggage," Acron said.

"He's in Hell, not the airport," Drew retorted.

Morgan waved her hand dismissively. "He'll be *fine*. It's Lucifer I feel sorry for. He'll bear the brunt of Marsden's failure." She patted Drew's cheek. "Anyone who's been escaping his father's dungeon since he was ten can easily escape Hell."

"But he has the dagger."

"We only have your word it'll kill God. He's so old, our arrival may induce a heart attack. Pensioners don't cope with home invasions."

Drew mounted Camelot and they turned away from the pit.

"Your luggage has been reclaimed." Marsden stood on the edge of the pit.

"That wasn't you screaming?" Disappointment raged in Demi's gut like hunger pangs. Just *once* she'd like golden boy to fail at something.

"No. My guitar snagged on a rock. Nearly strangled me. A demon climbed the walls like a lizard and rescued me."

"Why would a *demon* rescue you?"

"Apparently, we have the same goal."

"Killing God?"

He looked at Drew. "He said to tell you his name's Urban Storm."

Demi snorted. "Clearly fake. I'm glad you had time to chat while we were stuck up here."

Drew looked towards the pit, his brow furrowed.

"Does that name mean something to you?" Marsden asked.

"I've seen it in Heaven's history books. Never trust demons."

Morgan smiled. "Now the gang's reunited, we have a kingdom to steal."

CHAPTER 49

Ivy on the wall morphed into black and crimson serpents, darting at them, whispering tantalising promises. Morgan tickled one as they passed.

"Don't listen to them," Drew warned. "They're tempting you into Hell."

"Anyone who falls for a talking snake *deserves* eternal torture," Demi scoffed. "Is a platypus going to give us fashion tips?"

"People hear what they want to."

"You're a goody two shoes who'll fall at his daddy's feet, beg for forgiveness and betray us the second God turns his beardy face to you."

Drew glowered.

"Didn't wanna hear that, did you Saint Celibate?"

"What childhood trauma made you so bitter and toxic? Did your father starve you then eat in front of you?"

"I was born fabulous."

Footsteps marched towards them, armour clanking and weapons dragging along the ground. Distorted silhouettes created monsters in the tunnel then their fathers stopped before them. Morgan frowned. How did they beat them here?

"We're taking you home," Famine spoke. "This mission's too dangerous. Demeter, you'd snap like a stale breadstick. God won't surrender because you've insulted his dress sense."

"What would you know about danger? The most dangerous thing you've done is order a double cheeseburger without a napkin."

"You're no warrior," Conquest told Mac. "You're not fit to bear the title 'Horseman'."

"I don't want my baby foals hurt," Death said. "I'd be so upset."

"I want the pleasure of killing God," War said. "You don't create the greatest assassination plot the world has ever known then give the glory to your substandard son."

"This must be a test, to prove how much you want to get to Heaven," Drew said. "You have to kill them."

"Just because we're going to kill *your* father, doesn't mean you can make us kill ours," Aeron snapped.

Demi jumped off Pavlova and rammed the base of her scales into Famine's stomach. "Now you're one of your beloved kebabs."

Famine collapsed, coughing blood as Demi twisted the scales before wrenching them out.

"Don't bleed on my boots, they're handmade. I'm surprised you're not leaking barbecue sauce." She mounted Pavlova as the others stared at her. Blood pooled where Famine fell. Demi flicked her hair. "If I'd known killing God meant killing my father, I wouldn't have boycotted the idea. You should've told me the perks."

"I wish you'd shown this enthusiasm on Earth, instead of wasting your time chasing fame," Morgan said, smashing Famine's globe and rescuing the tiny balances inside.

Conquest charged at Mac. He scrambled off Hastings, dropping his bow and syringe. Famous battle dates were carved with silver into the bow's black wood. His helmet fell off and rolled along the ground.

"Fuck's sake," Marsden muttered.

Mac grabbed the bow and fired a syringe. "I'm sorry, Dad." It bounced off Conquest's armour.

"You're no son of mine!" Conquest declared. "My son should relish bloodshed, send armies marching to their deaths on the battlefield and rejoice in the music of men's dying screams. Not skulk around dark alleys, coughing on people and looking away when the bodies fall. Marsden's my true son. But I got stuck raising the centre of diseases because someone fancied an upgrade." He raised his bow and fired. The arrow lodged in Mac's shoulder, between the armour joints.

Mac grabbed it. "I can't believe he shot me!"

"I can't believe he missed," Marsden remarked. "He can shoot out a man's eye from a hundred feet away with both eyes closed. Unless he's deliberately missing, to cause maximum pain."

Conquest struck Mac across the face with his bow. Mac cried out, stumbling backwards. He steadied himself against the wall, ducking when a serpent snapped at him. Conquest fired an arrow into Mac's leg, below the knee plate. Mac fell, clutching it. Conquest advanced, aiming for Mac's head.

Conquest crumpled to his knees, his bow and arrow tumbling from his grip, his head bouncing to a rest against the wall. Mac scrambled away, frantically rubbing his face as Conquest's body toppled. His globe sailed through the air. Aeron caught it, shattering it in his fist and picking the miniature bow and arrow from the shards.

"You killed my father!" Green tears trickled down Mac's face, burning his sores.

Marsden wiped blood from his eyes. "I saved your life."

Mac's eyes closed as he slipped into unconsciousness.

"Thank god I killed Famine first," Demi said. "I'd never have forgiven you for denying me that pleasure."

Death held two globes. Aeron slid off Erebus, exchanging uneasy glances with Morgan.

"Please don't make me do this," Death begged. "It's your duty to create the Apocalypse. No Horsemen have ever stopped it."

"We'll be the first," Aeron said.

"We're making history," Morgan added.

"Annihilate the world then help me make my garden beautiful. I'm thinking of adding slate to my rockery and coloured lights in the skull border, so it's like a rainbow twinkling out of their eye sockets."

Death moved his hands to bang the globes together. Morgan and Aeron seized an arm each, twirled underneath and flipped Death, catching the globes as he fell.

"I taught my baby foals well." Death jumped up and removed his scythe from his robe. "But this is the only way to keep you safe."

Death swiped at Morgan. She backflipped away. Aeron dropped into a backwards bridge, the scythe passing over him. He flipped up and swept Death's legs away. Death landed on his knees and swung the scythe. Morgan jumped it, snapping a kick into Death's chin. He rose and attacked Aeron. Aeron blocked the scythe then kneed Death in the ribs and delivered an upwards elbow strike to his chin. Morgan grabbed the scythe, planted it down then swung around it, kicking Death with both feet.

As he fell, Aeron caught him and tipped him upside down. A globe rattled through his ribcage. Morgan forced open his jaw and the globe fell out.

"We're sorry," they said, both holding the globe.

They dropped it. It shattered, a tiny scythe falling out as darkness swept down the tunnel, a shroud of silence smothering the earth. Death collapsed into a pile of bones in a robe, the crimson lights in his eye sockets fading to black. Morgan slotted the miniature scythe through her coat's button hole. They hugged each other and Erebus, who nuzzled their hair.

"Just you and me." War approached Marsden.

"The honour of killing God can be yours. I'd rather not have 'you murdered my father!' thrown in my face every time Drew and I argue. There's no comeback for that."

War swung his sword at Marsden, who deflected it with his guitar and sliced War's leg. Marsden somersaulted backwards from War's attack then blocked with his sword. Clashing metal echoed through the tunnel. War spun away and hooked Marsden's legs, kicking him on the way down. Marsden rolled to his feet as War's sword crashed down. Morgan sighed. Once again they were forced to endure entertainment without popcorn.

Marsden charged at War, who flung him into the opposite wall. He slithered down, groaning. Serpents writhed over him, deadly fangs glinting, flickering tongues exploring his face. Drew ran to pick him up. War marched over and shoved Drew. He skidded on his back.

Marsden launched himself off the wall, catching War with a spinning kick. He stumbled, so Marsden slashed his knee between the armour. War hit him in the face with his shield decorated with the sword with a horseshoe. Marsden tossed his guitar aside.

"Fancy living dangerously?" War threw his shield, hitting Mac.

"We'd better rescue Zombieland before they kill him," Morgan told Aeron. Mac regained consciousness as they removed the arrows. The arrows vanished, his wounds healing. They hoisted him onto Hastings. Aeron slapped his helmet on.

Marsden twisted away from a slice and jabbed War, earning a strike across his chest that slipped off the chainmail.

"Hurry up," Demi groaned. "This is boring."

War knocked Marsden's sword out of his hand and kicked him to the floor.

"Traitors must be executed." War raised his sword.

"I'm not a traitor."

Marsden yanked Drew's dagger out of his thigh sheath and stabbed it through War's heart.

War dropped his sword and collapsed. Marsden rolled onto his side. Aeron stamped on War's globe and rescued the small sword. Their fathers vanished.

Marsden leapt up. "Where'd they go?"

"They were an illusion," Drew said.

"You couldn't have mentioned this *before*?" He snatched up his sword then rescued his guitar. He grabbed the dagger, wincing.

"You must prove your worth to enter Heaven. If I'd told you they weren't real, the decision would've been easy."

"Let's toss him in the pit, feed him to the demons," Demi said. "What else isn't he telling us?"

Morgan and Aeron eyed Drew suspiciously. Morgan tapped the tiny scythe. Demi had a point. Maybe they *should* leave Drew for the demons, until they'd killed God. Better safe than slaughtered.

Drew raised his hands. "This whole tunnel is filled with challenges. The pits stay the same, but others are different for each person."

"Throughout this plotting he's been 'I'll never help you kill my father!' Then he shows up all 'you pin him down, I'll stab him in the beard'," Demi said. "Did Mars's touch make you ejaculate your morals?"

Marsden pointed his sword at Demi's throat. "He's with us."

"That's as believable as me bathing in chocolate. He's been desperate to stop the Apocalypse. Guess what? He got his wish. All you've ever wanted is to end the world, until he gave you your first hard-on. He's seduced you into doing what he couldn't and we're all gonna die."

"Demi's right," Mac mumbled. "We were the only two against this. Morgan and Aeron, you always do what Mars wants. What *we* want doesn't matter. Like you keep saying – *he's* not in charge."

"I am now." Marsden mounted Camelot and offered Drew his arm.

"So you *both* get what you want," Demi muttered. "He saves the world, you get the leadership role you've been bitching about since you could talk. What do we get? Headstones with our names engraved."

"You'll be in an unmarked grave. You're pissed it's interfering with your photoshoot for drain rods."

"If you betray us…" Morgan jabbed Drew. "You'll wish we left you to burn in Hell."

"I'm on your side."

"Same rule applies for you, Mars. If he betrays us, you'll suffer with him."

"If he betrays us…" Marsden glanced at Drew. "I'll kill him myself."

They mounted and continued down the tunnel.

Demi scowled. "Thought I was rid of that fat slob."

Morgan shook her head. "Some of us like our father, unlike you heartless cretins."

"Your father's not an acid-tongued blob, a battle-obsessed armour jockey or a bloodthirsty psychopath."

"If you've got daddy issues, go on a chat show," Drew said.

"I've just discovered my father's alive. Some sympathy wouldn't go amiss."

"I'm sorry your father isn't dead."

"So am I!"

The tunnel snaked upwards, the light intensifying. They crossed more pits before stopping at a bridge spanning two lethal cliffs.

Demi sighed. "Why's it so hard to get to Heaven? It's not like it's Utopia. 'Don't do this, can't do that. You must dress like a knob'. They ban everything fun."

Marsden nudged Camelot to the edge. Stones crumbled beneath his hooves, tumbling into the river of lava surging three hundred feet below. Camelot retreated then galloped towards the bridge.

"What are you doing?" Drew asked. "You'll kill us!"

Camelot raced across the bridge. It broke in his wake, cascading into the lava. Camelot leapt as the bridge fell. He landed on the cliff and reared.

"Thanks a lot! How are we supposed to cross?" Demi shouted. "If you thought with your brain instead of your sword, we'd succeed at something!"

"I'll succeed better without you ruining things."

Demi turned to the others. "He's destroyed the bridge so we can't cross and you think they're not traitors?"

Morgan narrowed her eyes. Putting Marsden in charge was a bad idea. He wasn't a team player. Luckily she'd suspected his strategy would involve rushing in and doing what was best for him regardless of everyone else. He may have brilliant strategies for the Apocalypse but he had no idea how to lead a team. She produced a globe from her pocket and smashed it on the floor. The four of them disappeared, reappearing on the other side of the bridge.

"You could've waited, Mars," Aeron said.

"Typical man – jumps in, waves his sword around and fucks it up for everybody." Demi slapped Marsden across the head.

"I didn't know the bridge would collapse, or that they had a globe for it."

"Don't tell me Mr 'Don't Fuck Up My Apocalypse' missed an important part of the plan? I thought reaching Heaven's gates would've been covered."

"The latest information I had was the bridge was sturdy. The twins neglected to mention the globe. That's not my fault."

"Gotta keep the audience guessing," Aeron said.

Morgan smiled. "We had contingency plans for when you fuckwits cocked it up."

"Castaway was the last to cross the bridge." Demi pointed at Drew. "Why didn't he warn us?"

"I flew across it," Drew replied.

"Convenient."

"You keep saying you don't want to die, I did you a favour leaving you on that side," Marsden said.

"The globe is our only Heaven Travel card," Aeron said. "We'll have to hitchhike back."

"Skin Demi and make a bridge from her bones. Or stretch her and use her as a zip wire."

"I hate you." She kicked him.

They nudged their horses towards two gates made from spiked black bars that sizzled with electricity. Barbed wire lined the top and anti-climb spikes decorated the massive walls imprisoning Heaven.

"What happened to the clouds?" Demi asked.

Drew laughed. "It's not Care A Lot."

St Peter stepped in front of the gates. "Who goes there?"

"The Horsemen of the Apocalypse," Aeron announced. "Today's a good day to die."

CHAPTER 50

"You don't have authorised access," St Peter said.

Aeron frowned. "Damn. It's one of these 'if you're not on the list, you're not getting in' places. We dressed up for nothing."

St Peter eyed Drew. "You don't belong here, Lost Brother."

Marsden thrust his sword into Peter's heart. Peter dropped, his eyes wide. Marsden kicked him off the blade and used it to hook the key from Peter's neck. "That was disappointingly easy." He hissed as the key burned his fingers.

Drew offered his hand so Marsden relinquished it.

Drew swore and dropped it. "He's right. I don't belong here anymore."

Morgan jumped off Erebus, scooped up the key and unlocked the gates. "You evil types are such an inconvenience." She wrenched the gates, cursing them when they didn't open. How could they hope to kill God when they couldn't open gates? She paused then tugged the gate sideways.

The gates squeaked then slid into the walls. Aeron pulled Morgan up and led the way in.

From the top of the gates, an angel blasted a golden trumpet, lamenting the loss of Heaven's guardian.

"Shit. The fifth trumpet," Drew said.

"What does that do?" Mac asked.

"A star falls, with the key to a bottomless pit and unleashes hordes of locust-tailed horses that torment those

387

without the sign of God. Some say it's Satan releasing his demons, in the form of locusts."

"*Locusts*?" Demi scoffed. "You'd think God would have something better than bugs. Florence Frightingale could plan a better Apocalypse."

"That's the first compliment you've ever given me," Mac said.

"It'll be the last."

"Mac, shut that fucking angel up," Marsden said.

Mac reluctantly raised the bow and fired a syringe into the angel. He fell, the notes dying with him until another angel replaced him.

"We're running out of time. If anyone fucks up, we die," Aeron warned.

"No pressure." Demi looked around. "Where are the clouds? The harps? People in unflattering white robes that look like sheets with head holes?"

"No wonder there's sin if that's what people think awaits them," Drew said.

"First my father's alive and now Heaven's a lie. What a shit adventure this is."

The gates banged shut, electricity crawling over them.

Drew cried out as his back tore. Black wings unfurled, his choker glowing red.

"He's a demon!" Demi pointed. "Kill him!"

"I'm not a demon. It alerts angels I've fallen." Drew touched the black feathers.

A dark forest awaited them, bare trees offering no protection from whatever lay beyond.

"Lead the way, Fallen Angel." Aeron reached over to pat Drew's arse.

The forest was eerily silent, hiding the horrors within. The deeper they travelled, the warmer it became, the stark forest becoming a jungle. Vines swept down to imprison them in their lair. Serpents' whispers broke the suffocating silence. They lay low on their horses, leaves brushing their faces. Marsden slashed a path with his sword.

Demi turned around. The jungle healed. "What the hell is this place?"

"Heaven," Drew replied.

They fought through strangling vines and thick leaves then broke free of the jungle.

"Welcome to Eden."

Multi-coloured jewels decorated the ground, sparkling as light from angels' halos shone onto them. In the distance, a waterfall plummeted into a clear pool. Trees bordered the garden, their leaves coloured glass. The violet sky matched Morgan's lips.

"You're sacrificing *this* for Purgatory?" Demi asked Drew.

"I'm not sacrificing it; it was taken from me."

"Have you skinny dipped in that pool?" Morgan asked.

"Once. Maybe twice."

She fanned herself. "I'm sensing a gap in the market for angel erotica."

"Stop!"

A Cherub appeared then turned so the human, ox, lion and eagle heads looked at them in turn. The eyes covering its wings blinked.

"Your human face looks like it got crapped out of a constipated troll," Demi said. "You look nothing like the fat monstrosities that piss water into fountains. Is everything associated with Heaven a lie?"

"What is your business?" the Cherub asked.

"It's not the entertainment."

Marsden decapitated the Cherub's human head. The Cherub crumpled to the floor as more Cherubim appeared. Camelot twisted so Marsden could strike another. Hastings galloped into the fray, barging a Cherub aside. Morgan freed her scythe and cut off a Cherub's head. Pavlova knocked Cherubim flying so Marsden and Morgan could behead them.

"Hark us using our scythes for harvesting," Morgan said. "We're proper reapers now."

Aeron hooked his scythe under a Cherub's chin and tossed him over Erebus's neck. Mac fired a syringe into him before he hit the floor.

Fallen Cherubim lay around them. Rubies formed from their spilled blood.

Drew stared at the bodies. "You never said you'd slaughter your way to God."

"If you knew, you'd stop us," Marsden said.

"How soon before they notice?" Aeron asked.

"They'll already know," Drew replied.

Morgan dismounted and gathered the Cherubim's globes into a drawstring pouch. She shook one and broke it, rescuing a white wing brooch. She pinned it to Aeron's coat. "Ooh pretty. We'll smash the rest later. It can be like trick or treating – gather the goodies then enjoy our spoils when we return home. We need a gumball machine."

They passed the waterfall, riding single file beneath an arch of red and white roses and purple tulips, into a hedge maze.

"You've *got* to be kidding," Demi said. "Paranoid much?"

"Clearly you weren't listening at the meeting," Aeron said.

"The hand puppets didn't sell it."

Marsden led them down a dead end and waited. The thorny hedge parted and they moved through before it sealed again. The hedge shrunk to a foot high, revealing a fountain in the centre before climbing to fifteen feet tall. A hedge slid forwards, blocking the path to their right. They turned left. Another hedge blocked them then vanished.

They finally reached the large glass chalice fountain. Tiny silver stars flowed from it, becoming water as they hit the bottom. The Horsemen skirted it and followed Marsden to the next pathway, dodging the moving hedges.

They reached the end and the hedge fell away to reveal twenty foot high black railings topped with spikes.

"How do we get in?" Mac asked.

Drew slid off Camelot, closed his eyes and walked through the railings. "Religion's greatest weapon is belief. There are no railings."

Demi jumped off Pavlova and walked into the railings. "Son of a bitch!" She rubbed her head. "I told you he's a traitor. Now we're trapped."

"Turn sideways and slip through," Marsden said.

"I'll wedge your head through so angels can read you the Bible until your ears bleed, and cut off your wicked trouser snake that tempted Drew into tasting your forbidden fruit."

"Why not remind that angel gluttony is a sin?"

She marched through the railings. "I don't see him."

"See?" Drew said. "Stop calling me a traitor."

"Stop behaving like one."

"How do we get the horses through?" Mac asked.

Demi reached into her pocket and pulled out a sugar lump. Pavlova walked through the railings and lipped up the treat. The other horses followed and crowded Demi. She fed them then she and Drew mounted.

Marsden yelled, nudging Camelot into a gallop. The horses charged through Heaven. Marsden smiled as blood dripped from his sword. This was how the Apocalypse was supposed to feel. Angels swarmed, diving to grab them. Marsden slashed any who got close. Blood rained on him and Drew; a scarlet shower drenching them in the Angels' misery.

Mac shot a syringe into an Angel's throat. The Angel hit the ground, pestilence exploding through its body. Demi pulled out her balances and swung the flails above her head, clouting an Angel in the face. It snagged its cheek, ripping it off.

"Cut flesh off the other one – you have plenty to spare."

Morgan and Aeron extended their scythes and swiped at Angels. Aeron hooked one around the neck and dragged it down. Morgan decapitated it. One by one the Angels fell, their screams echoing through Heaven's silent sanctuary.

"Go!" Mac lined up another syringe. "I'll fight these."

"We can't leave you!" Drew objected.

Mac fired the syringe. Another Angel crumpled, its skin rotting, its body riddled with every disease in Mac's system.

"What happened to your 'I can't kill Angels' speech?" Demi asked. "Did you find your bloodlust in a recent Herpes outbreak?"

"I don't want to die."

Marsden cut down another Angel then turned Camelot away, his back scorching with his Angel kills. Demi chased him, stopping when Powers lined up in front of them. Aeron and Morgan arrived, swinging their pouch. Morgan sported a silver bracelet made from linked angel wings.

"We'll get the rest when we leave," Aeron said. "Like an Easter egg hunt."

A Power offered a sword. "Drew, take up your sword and repent."

"You're a Power?" Marsden twisted to stare at him. "I thought no Power had fallen."

"They hadn't." Drew slid off Camelot, his wings spreading. "I'm sorry, Eden. I can't. The fifth trumpet has sounded. Demons have escaped. Heaven doesn't need you, but humans do. Save them or you'll die here. There are three demons who will help you. Find them."

Eden glanced at the other Powers then ran.

"You're one of the fallen!" Another Power unsheathed his sword and swung at Drew.

Drew blocked with his arm and punched the Power. As he stumbled backwards, Drew swept up his sword and plunged it into the Power's heart. He retreated, sheathing his sword, his eyes glistening. Marsden yanked him up.

Demi smirked. "I hear there's a fight in a playgroup – why don't you join that one? Gain confidence before fighting the big boys."

Marsden stabbed a Power in the throat before he could draw his sword. Camelot bucked, kicking one who'd snuck up behind him. Demi struck one on the head then kicked him in the face.

"If your teeth have scuffed my boot, you're paying for the repair." She examined her silver boot then kicked him again.

Aeron decapitated two Powers simultaneously. A Power swung his sword at Demi and overbalanced.

"You're like all holy men," Demi said. "You don't know how to use your instrument. You can't whip it out and wave it around – you have to penetrate someone or your efforts are wasted." She clubbed him with the flails. "Bugger off you lot, I've got this."

Marsden laughed. "You won't defeat them by mocking their fashion sense and buying them Diet Divas gift cards."

Demi twirled her flails, slammed them into a Power's face and tore it off. "Guess I've spent too long with you." The Power collapsed, shrieking. "Sooner we get back, sooner I can lead the restoration operation on Earth. That's *bound* to get me in the papers. Especially now celebrities have been culled."

Camelot and Erebus fled, leaving Demi's vile threats and blood-curdling battle screams behind. They raced towards a castle, which towered above the land, surrounded by a moat. The white crystal path running alongside the moat was inlaid with gold chunks and semi-precious stones. The castle shimmered as though made from iridescent ice.

"God lives in a *castle*?" Marsden asked.

"Where did you expect him to live?" Drew replied. "If you say on a cloud, I'll punch you."

"It's extravagant for someone who condemns covertness and greed."

"I questioned that before getting banished. Also, how Adam and Eve populated the world with two sons."

Aeron laughed. "I would've loved to have seen God's face when you asked if Abel and Cain shagged their mother."

"I didn't say 'shag'."

"Is the dagger made from the same material as the castle?"

"Yes, forged from God's power. The only thing powerful enough to kill God is God himself."

"Confession time," Morgan said. "Did you take the dagger to kill God?"

Drew looked at the floor. "No. I wanted it for protection."

"From what?"

"You. And Michael. This dagger can kill everyone. Especially Horsemen."

"Mars, guard that dagger with your life."

"Aeron, fetch St Peter's body," Marsden said. "And two pieces of that bridge."

Aeron smashed a globe, vanishing as Morgan moved into the front saddle.

Aeron reappeared, St Peter's body slung over his shoulder like a rolled up carpet. "He's not dead."

"He soon will be."

Marsden arranged the wood into an inverted crucifix then tied St Peter to it with guitar strings. Aeron helped him stake it in the ground. Marsden pulled a lighter from his pocket and ignited St Peter's clothing. St Peter screamed.

"Did your father orchestrate this?" Drew demanded.

"He wanted me to take you at knifepoint and cut you for every minute God delayed lowering the bridge. I don't have faith in your father-son bond." Marsden mounted Camelot. "St Peter is burning! I will burn all your saints and butcher every angel until you let us in!"

The drawbridge lowered and Powers rushed out.

"Ugh! What's that smell?" Demi stopped Pavlova beside them. Blood spattered her silver outfit.

"The smell of victory," Marsden answered.

"It's roasted saint *seasoned* with victory," Morgan said.

"Did you kill all the Powers?" Marsden asked Demi.

"Except the one that ran away. Bets he ran straight to daddy?"

"He's on my side," Drew said.

"There's a big difference between supporting a rebellion and helping to murder your father."

Aeron disappeared, reappearing with the Powers' globes. He broke one and rescued the gold sword pendant inside. Wings flanked the haft. Hastings cantered towards them and they charged through the Powers. They galloped across the drawbridge and through the courtyard, hacking down angels. Frosted glass doors at the end parted, revealing a white marble hall four hundred feet long and two hundred feet high. Gold fig leaves crawled up marble pillars supporting the crystal ceiling. A throne dominated the far end, emitting blinding light. Saints, rulers and Angels of the upper hierarchy filled the hall.

Six Archangels blocked the throne.

"A welcoming party, how lovely," Aeron said. "I thought we'd be turned away at the door."

"I think they're asking us to dance," Morgan said.

"Everyone must dance with the reaper. I hope they know the danse macabre."

The Archangels drew their swords. The Horsemen attacked. Swords collided and screams of pain echoed around the hall. Mac yelled when a sword sliced his thigh. He punched the Archangel in the face, hissing when his fist burned. Two Archangels pulled Demi off Pavlova and beat her.

"If you ruin my face, I'll cut your heads off and give them to Death for his rockery."

Marsden beheaded one Archangel then leapt onto the other one and slit his throat.

"My hero!" Demi kissed him.

"You can thank me by not dying."

"I'd rather shag you."

Morgan slit an Archangel from his groin to his throat. "Ooh I can fix you with a zip and keep my pyjamas in you."

Aeron swung his scythe into an Archangel's skull. Mac shot one in the throat then hit another across the face with his bow. Marsden blocked an attack then swept the Archangel's legs away. As he fell to his knees, Marsden plunged his sword down through his mouth.

"We'll have so much jewellery we can open a shop." Aeron scooped up the Archangels' globes containing gold belt buckles.

Marsden strode towards the throne, a bloodied trail stalking him. Golden ivy coiled around the throne, trapped inside the glass. Seraphim blocked it, their eternal flames keeping him back. A man with white hair and beard sat on the throne. He wore white chainmail and a golden chest plate His white boots were winged, his hands protected beneath gold armoured gloves. His eyes were white with black pupils.

"Horsemen aren't welcome in Heaven." God's voice had a hypnotic quality, seeping through their brains and chilling their blood.

"This isn't a social call."

"What do you want?"

"To stop the Apocalypse."

"The world's riddled with cancer. I'm replacing it with a new mankind. A better mankind."

"How many times are you going to start over? Mankind isn't meant to be perfect."

"You don't care about mankind. You exist to destroy it. You're the upgraded version of pest controllers."

"Let Drew return and I'll restart the Apocalypse."

"The fallen are banished forever."

"Despicable humans can repent, but your sons can't? I bet you've never got a 'World's Greatest Dad' mug for Father's Day. Why did you make him the catalyst?"

"It needed a fallen angel and he showed contempt by questioning me. I trapped him in that shell to tempt one of you. Lucky coincidence the most powerful Horseman fell for him. Though had it been one of the others, the Apocalypse would be continuing."

"You bastard!"

"You can leave with your life intact. Or I can cast you down to Hell."

Marsden ascended the glass steps. Purple fire rippled through each step he stood on. "If I'm going to Hell, I'm taking you with me."

Seraphim ran at him, engulfing him in flames. He threw one Seraphim down the steps, a fiery trail following.

Aeron pierced the Seraphim with his scythe. "Damn! We forgot the hosepipe."

Marsden slashed a Seraphim across the stomach and kicked the third into the fourth.

God flicked his wrist, catapulting Marsden across the hall. The ground fractured where he landed. The floor collapsed, revealing a pit. Hellfire danced beneath him, awaiting their feast. A scythe swept down, catching him. Morgan yanked Marsden up then twirled and gouged the third Seraphim. Demi lashed the fourth while Mac fired a syringe into it. God descended the steps, flinging his hand out. A lightning bolt electrocuted Marsden. He yelled, his body juddering and sparking.

Demi walloped God across the back of his knees with her flails. He stumbled, his armour chinking. "Careful you don't snap a hip, old man. Waiting lists are long."

God zapped her with lightning. She screamed, flying backwards onto the steps. God clapped and thunder snarled through the palace. Burning rain melted their armour and ignited their skin.

"Can't you do Sudoku and rant about young people like other old geezers?" Demi grunted. "Great, you've singed my outfit. You're buying me a new one."

Mac fired, the syringe piercing God's arm. He pulled it out and crushed it. A gust of wind propelled Mac into the wall. Morgan slashed God's legs, Aeron ramming the scythe into his back.

"You dare to enter my Kingdom and attack me?" He picked Morgan and Aeron up then threw them. They landed in a tangled pile. "Mankind is poison. I'll rebuild Earth in Heaven's image and only the pure and righteous will inhabit it. Sinners will be cast down to Hell to burn with the fallen."

"I won't let you destroy them," Drew vowed.

"Repent or your suffering in Hell will make you wish you could die like the mortals you love."

"Annihilating mankind because they've disobeyed you makes you as bad as those genocidal dictators who've blighted history. You gave them free will and created sin. You can't kill them for making their own choices."

"They made the *wrong* choices."

"Lucifer was right. I should've stood with him."

God flung his hand out, electrocuting Drew and smashing him into the wall. God yanked a handful of halos off his belt and threw them. They bound Drew to the wall, scalding him with every movement.

The Horsemen staggered up.

"For too long humanity has trembled under your dictatorship," Marsden said. "It's time the world had a new leader."

He swung at God, who grabbed the sword, sending electricity travelling into Marsden. Marsden hit the floor, blood marking the spot. Mac was thrown amongst the horses. Camelot kicked him.

"Santa has the white beard market cornered," Demi said. "Can't you get your own identity?"

A lightning bolt burned her outfit. She screamed as Morgan smothered her with her coat. Aeron spun, his scythe cutting God's leg. A bolt hit his chest, ricocheting into Morgan. She fell to her knees.

A hailstorm of brimstone whirled through the hall, battering the Horsemen's exposed flesh. Scalding rain fell faster. Thunder shook the castle. More of the floor fell away, opening pits to Hell.

Lightning bolts rebounded off Marsden's guitar as he sliced God. Aeron and Morgan hooked their scythes around God's legs and yanked him off his feet, Mac firing syringes into him. Demi struck God's legs. With each blow they dealt, a halo clattered to the floor.

God raised his hand. Marsden hacked it off. It writhed before fusing back onto his wrist. Morgan and Aeron cut off his other arm and threw it away. God screamed then the arm shot back towards him, reattaching itself.

"He's like a bloody Hydra," Aeron commented.

"But hairier," Morgan said.

"And he only has one head."

"Wonder if that grows back."

Marsden reached for the dagger, touching an empty sheath. "Shit."

God flung lightning bolts. They spasmed as electricity controlled them like electrocuting puppets.

"You'll burn in Hell for your treachery!" God hissed.

"You'll die for yours."

God gasped, touching the dagger in his neck. "You...would kill your father?" He staggered. Golden blood streaked his throat, snaking down his armour.

"You would damn your son for starting the Apocalypse you ordered?" Drew twisted the dagger. "I won't let you destroy mankind. I'm not paying for your sins."

God dropped to his knees, light exploding from his body. They shielded their eyes as an unearthly scream tore across Heaven and turned the world black. Marsden swivelled his guitar around and strummed a fast rock song, 'Bleeding Empire'.

A loud trumpet blast rang out through Heaven.

Drew stared at God's lifeless body, tears trickling down his face.

Morgan gathered the Seraphims' globes, splitting one to reveal a fiery winged armband.

"Shit, we need to seal the gates," Marsden said. "If four Angels escape, they'll command an army of two hundred million mounted troops. The last thing we need is their horses spewing fire, brimstone and plague over the world when we're trying to save it."

Morgan broke a globe and disappeared, returning seconds later. "We're locked in."

Marsden wrenched the dagger out of God's neck then removed his chest plate. Ignoring his burning palm, he sliced God open.

"What are you doing?" Drew wiped his eyes. "Are you going to hang a trophy in your room so I can be reminded I'm a murderer?"

"A trophy would be nice." Marsden parted God's chest and plunged his hand inside.

Demi wrinkled her nose. "It'll be hard for Drew to be aroused by your touch now he's seen you treat his father like a lucky dip."

"Step aside, hotstuff." Aeron barged him aside. He and Morgan rummaged in God's body.

"Please stop!" Drew said.

Morgan retrieved a crimson globe. She cleaned it and held it up, its light bathing everyone in a bloody glow. "Are you ready to save the world?"

"And sound the seventh trumpet?" Aeron added.

"With a glorified paperweight?" Demi scoffed.

"The seventh trumpet proclaims glory to God as the ruler forever." Aeron placed the globe on the floor. "We all have to smash it."

"The seventh trumpet? We really are Horsemen of the Apocalypse," Marsden said.

"Glad our merchandise won't go to waste," Morgan said.

Marsden relinquished the dagger to Drew. Raising their weapons, they struck the globe. Thunder pealed through the castle. Heaven trembled as an earthquake rattled it. The ground split, bloody hail and ashes raining down on them.

Aeron smiled. "God is dead. Long live the Horsemen."

###END###

ABOUT THE AUTHOR

C L Raven are identical twins and mistresses of the macabre from Cardiff. They're horror writers, as 'bringers of nightmares' isn't a recognised job title. They spend their time looking after their animal army and drinking more Red Bull than the recommended government guidelines. They write short stories, novels, comics and articles for *Haunted Magazine* and *Living Paranormal Magazine* and have been published in various anthologies and horror magazines. Several short stories and novels have also been long and shortlisted in various competitions. Last year, they won third prize in the British Fantasy Society Award. They were published in the *Mammoth Book of Jack the Ripper,* which makes their fascination with him seem less creepy. They've been working on indie horror film, *Clownface* and will soon be writing and directing their first short horror film, *The Black Kiss.* Every Friday night, they host The Graveyard Shift on Vitalize Radio. Along with their friend Neen, they prowl the country hunting for ghosts for their YouTube show, Calamityville Horror and can also be found urb exing in places they shouldn't be. They also gracefully fall off poles as they learn PoleFit, and ungracefully faceplant as they learn gymnastics.

Connect with us online:
Blog - www.clraven.wordpress.com
Twitter -@clraven @CalamityHorror
Facebook - C.L.Raven-Fanclub
Calamityville Horror fan page -
www.facebook.com/CatsTalesOfTerror
Instagram - clraven666 calamityvillehorror666

ACKNOWLEDGEMENTS

It wouldn't be an acknowledgements page without us thanking our mum, Lynette, for never forcing us to get a 'proper job' and for looking after our animal army when we're selling our books at horror cons.

Thanks to Dave for yet another brilliant cover.

Thanks to Mark Adams for getting us a job on indie horror film, *Clownface*, and for asking us to contribute a film script for a body horror anthology. It's something we've always wanted to do, so thanks so much for giving us this opportunity.

Thanks to Huw Lloyd for always letting us back on The Undead Wookie podcast, even though we never watch the films we're meant to talk about.

Thanks again to Peter Germany, Wil Maltby, Mykal and Janette Lewis and Laura Pierce Francis for your unwavering support.

Also, thank you to everyone who's bought a book from us at horror cons.

Disenchanted

C L Raven

Once upon a time, in lands far, far away, everyone lived happily ever after. Until now. If you thought you knew the fairytales well, think again. In a modern world without morals, where beauty does not always equal goodness and evil sometimes wins, the heroes of the legends learn the hard way that survival will take more than just a pretty face, and a handsome prince does not mean salvation. Ten broken fairytales that are definitely not for children's bedtime.

Soul Asylum

C L Raven

The blood wanted to prick a conscience that couldn't bleed.
Poe could keep his telltale heart.
I couldn't hear it beating.

Ravens Retreat harbours a sinister secret. Inside its
blackened heart lurk the ghosts of patients and staff who
died when the asylum was burned down in 1904. Over a
hundred years later, the West wing survives and now the
patients want revenge.

Their eternal repose is disturbed by a malevolent
poltergeist and the ghost tours led by the asylum's resident,
Phineas Soul, which attract the attention of journalist
Mason Strider. His attempts to expose Phineas as a fraud
have catastrophic consequences when it is Ravens Retreat's
dark heart that's exposed as it awakens to claim the lives of
those who dare to enter its brutal past.

Some things should never be disturbed.

DEADLY REFLECTIONS

C L RAVEN

Death is only the beginning...

You're born, you live and you die. And sometimes, you come back.

When the veil between life and death is torn down, the darkest souls crawl from the shadows to wander the world that rejected them.

But these are not the restless spirits that haunt the pages of folklore, or the childishly gruesome tales whispered over torchlight. These are the ghosts that dwell in the deepest dungeons of your imagination and prey on you when you think you're alone: bored ghosts trapped in the monotony of office life at the Scare Department; a haunted jail where the prisoners believe in revenge over rehabilitation; a mirror that steals the souls of whoever falls under its spell; and a ghost bride who makes sure the wedding vows are never broken.

Thirteen stories that prove the monsters in your mind might just be real.

The past is no longer a nightmare.

ROMANCE IS DEAD

C L RAVEN

Don't give your lover roses, give them nightmares.

Ten disturbing stories about the dangers of falling in love. Nothing says 'I love you' like giving your lover a heart for Valentine's. Especially when it's ripped from their body before they've drawn their last breath.

"I'd made a terrible mistake. I should have killed him in the shower."

Gone are the expensive chocolates in fancy packaging, the wilting roses from the petrol station forecourt and the heart-print boxer shorts. Valentine's is about to get bloody. And some unfortunate lovers will learn the true meaning of 'til death us do part.'

Real love is worth killing for.

The Malignant Dead

C L Raven

1645. The year Scotland died.

"Ring a ring of roses."

Dirty white rags dangled from windows, like hanging men left on gallows for the city to witness their shame.

The Bubonic Plague is ravaging Edinburgh. Despite the council's best efforts, people are dying. Soon there will be more people buried under Edinburgh than living in it.

"A pocketful of posies."

When the plague doctor dies from the disease after a week, the council hires student doctor Alex McCrae, promising him one hundred pounds to cure the wretched pest. But a man who makes himself a hero, makes himself enemies. And when the council can't afford to pay McCrae, they hope he'll succumb to the disease.

"Ashes, ashes."

But the plague isn't the only way to kill a man. And in the city of the dead, it's not just ghosts who return.

"We. All. Fall. Down."

SILENT DAWN

C L RAVEN

Silent Dawn isn't real.

She's a terrifying computer game character who erodes players' sanities. Just because her legend dates back to the 1600s, doesn't mean she's real. Just because people are vanishing, doesn't mean she's real. Just because she's standing in the corner...

Reality is an illusion.

Drake Skelton, Ben Crewe and Keira Black are seventeen-year-old outcasts. Their obsession with *Silent Dawn: Asylum* seems normal, until game features creep into their town: missing persons' posters, defaced patient records, the mutilated Victorian patient who hanged herself in the woods.

Her madness infects you.

As more people play the game, the veil between her reality and theirs is torn down until they can no longer trust their own minds. But this is real life. Computer game characters don't kidnap teenagers, or poison their minds with a siren song of suicide. Yet there's something...the flash of her red dress from the corners of their eyes. The shadow that creeps across their walls at night. The sinister humming that warns them they're not really alone...

She's coming.

The Devil's Servants

C L Raven

1649. The year Edinburgh burned. Scotland was cursed by witches and in 1649, the witch panic was at its peak. No-one was safe from the executioner's flames.

Below the imposing behemoth of Edinburgh castle, nineteen year old Nessie Macleod is forced to watch her mother, Isabelle, burn to death for witchcraft. Her mother's crime stains her more than the ashes that scatter across the Esplanade. Shunned by Edinburgh's townsfolk, she's also hounded by the witch pricker, John Brodie. Brodie killed her mother and now he's coming for her.

The daughter of a witch is always a witch.

When old Annie Dickson is accused of cursing the flescher's pigs through witchcraft, she suffers for days at Brodie's hands before betraying three women and starting a witch hunt that sees one woman killed and another executed before the baying town.

Nessie is lured to Greyfriars Kirkyard, where she's haunted by the ghosts of the women burned for witchcraft. They want revenge on Brodie and his men. Nessie learns her grandmother was executed during the North Berwick witch trials in 1597 for conspiring to kill King James VI. She left behind everything Nessie needs to stop Brodie and lay the witches' ghosts to rest. But using objects to harm people is witchcraft and there's only one penalty the courts will impose: Death.

"Never wish for the flames."